# STORIES
# LUST, G\_\_\_\_ ~
# DESPERATION!

MW01383312

"PAPERBACK CONFIDENTIAL is an essential reference for anyone interested in the writers who make reading the old paperbacks so much fun. I'd have given an arm and a leg to get hold of a book like this long ago when I first got interested in paperback writers, and having it now is a real treat. Grab this one and set aside some time to get lost in it. I did."
                                                                    Bill Crider

"PAPERBACK CONFIDENTIAL is a must for any fan and collector of crime fiction – but more than that it is an important and essential history about the men and women and their work which made paperback crime, mystery, thrillers and noir such popular pulp masterpieces and classics we cherish today!"
                                                                    Gary Lovisi

"Brian Ritt's PAPERBACK CONFIDENTIAL isn't just an essential reference work for anyone who's a fan of hardboiled and noir fiction. It's also highly entertaining reading in its own right, packed with information and written with passion and flair by an author who loves the genre. Whether you bought great books by these authors fresh off the drugstore spinner racks when they were new, like I did, or have only recently discovered this great era of exciting fiction, don't miss PAPERBACK CONFIDENTIAL."
                                                                    James Reasoner

# PAPERBACK CONFIDENTIAL
## CRIME WRITERS OF THE PAPERBACK ERA

## BY BRIAN RITT
### EDITED BY RICK OLLERMAN

STARK
HOUSE

**Stark House Press • Eureka California**

PAPERBACK CONFIDENTIAL: CRIME WRITERS OF THE PAPERBACK ERA

Published by Stark House Press
1315 H Street
Eureka, CA 95501, USA
griffinskye3@sbcglobal.net
www.starkhousepress.com

ISBN: 1-933586-61-3
ISBN-13: 978-1-933586-61-8

Cover design and text layout by Mark Shepard, SHEPGRAPHICS.COM
Proofreading by Rick Ollerman

*The publisher would like to thank Rick Ollerman and*
*Mark Shepard for all their work with Brian on this project.*

First Stark House Press Edition: September 2013

REPRINT EDITION

# *Table of Contents*

# Paperback Wonder
*by Rick Ollerman*

> *The Gold Medal seal on this book means it*
> *has never been published as a book before.*
> *To select an original book that you have not*
> *read before, look for the Gold Medal seal.*

Book readers from the 1940's to the 1950's, the era of the "paperback
original" novel, recognize the above statement as the somewhat redundant
closing remarks of Fawcett's Gold Medal line of books. Those beautiful, yel-
low-spined paperbacks with lurid and garish covers that promised thrills
and adventures of all kinds, often featuring sultry and alluring women,
square-jawed men and ruffled sheets, and that brought us such wonderful
writers as Peter Rabe, Cornell Woolrich, David Goodis and hundreds of others.

The paperback original was a new take on the "pocket sized" book phe-
nomena that took off at the same time the era of the pulp magazine was
ending. Indeed, Gold Medal's success brought about the end of the pulp era
as it then existed.

The pulps were that great popularizer of literature between the world
wars, the days of Munsey's and the Thrilling Group and Fiction House and
Street & Smith and all the other publishers that put out dozens of titles
each month. Imagine climbing out of your time machine in front of a
bustling New York newsstand, ogling hundreds of brightly painted covers
emblazoned with names like *Captain Future, The Shadow, Doc Savage, The
Phantom Detective, Ten Detective Aces, Weird Tales* and *Black Mask*. Ethereal fog-
bound figures appeared on the covers, and there were masked vigilantes,
fedora-wearing detectives and blazing guns; covers promised women in
peril, men in peril, "yellow" peril, "spicy" stories, aviation tales, westerns....

Some of these titles lasted for decades, some coming out monthly, some
bi-monthly. Others lasted for just a few months, occasionally even just a
single issue. But as an industry of wonder they were there, packing the
newsstands month after month, bringing their form of culture to the
wide-eyed and the adventurous, the reader who wanted nothing more

than to get the most entertainment out of their dimes and their quarters as they possibly could.

Paperback books at that time were simply used as hardcover reprints and publishers didn't differentiate a whole lot in the titles they released. There were works of classic literature and philosophy put out alongside the popular fiction of the day, the only common denominator being the low cost of the books themselves. Thus you had Rudyard Kipling alongside Jane Austen and Sigmund Freud–and Agatha Christie. The quality of the books themselves ranged from volumes that were designed to be portable but somewhat durable, to books that were designed to be mostly disposable (such as the "GI" editions given to soldiers in World War II).

Slick magazines were around too, and these were also named for the kind of paper they were printed on. Instead of the low-grade paper used by pulp magazines and comic books, the slicks were printed on clay-coated paper and appealed to a higher-browed audience than kids or readers seeking more action-oriented adventure stories. They cost more to buy and consequently they paid more for their content, and quite often they serialized longer works that could later be reprinted as novels. It was the goal of many a pulp writer to break into the slick market, and from there into hardcover books. When Dashiell Hammett left the ranks of *Black Mask* he went on to the slicks, though he was quickly replaced in the pulp world by writers like Frederick Nebel and Raoul Whitfield, authors that could give the readers the same kind of hardboiled thrills they'd been used to for so long.

So much content was needed for the pulps there was no way most single authors could keep up with writing a monthly title. House names like "Robert Wallace," "C. K. M. Scanlon" and "Brant House" were created to be the regular bylines of popular monthlies like *The Phantom Detective* and *Secret Agent "X"*. Indeed, determining the real names of all these stories is probably impossible since many records no longer exist, though pulp scholars study many of the books looking for common phrases and other telltales that give clues to the real identities behind the pseudonyms. On the other hand, some writers could more than keep up, sometimes contributing most or occasionally even all the stories in a single issue, all of them appearing under different names.

Everything changed for the publishing industry when Signet brought out the paperback version of the famous, or perhaps even infamous, *I, The Jury* by one Frank Morrison Spillane, better known as Mickey.

When *I, The Jury* was published in hardcover, it enjoyed only modest success, selling around seven thousand copies. But when the mass market paperback edition was released, it became a genuine phenomenon, selling more than two million copies over two years.

Now this got people's attention: why did readers overlook the hardcover version and flock to the paperback one? What made the book catch fire? Was it the price? The cover? The availability in spinner racks across America?

Whatever it was, business began to boom. When Fawcett, already a publisher of pulps and comic books, decided to get out of pulps and take their chances with the revolutionary idea of publishing *original* paperbacks, nobody knew how it would go over. Determined to try something different, the new "Gold Medal" line would offer mysteries, westerns, and yes, mainstream novels, but–and this is important–they wouldn't shy away from sex. The titillating content pales to what we have in the mainstream today, but for its time, the more frank portrayal of relationships between men and women (and later, other combinations) certainly helped catch the attention of the public.

Gold Medal caught the attention of the writing community, as well. Their compensation model was much more author-friendly than anyone else's. Their innovation? They paid when the books were printed, before they were sold, as opposed to paying royalties months down the road based on the number of copies purchased by customers. This meant hefty up front payments for the writer, which was a tremendous improvement over the old system which too often had authors hounding publishers and begging loans from their agents. And since a successful book was often reprinted many times, authors had little to complain about with this upstart new operation.

This success was the death knell of the pulps. Pulp writers flocked to paperbacks, and if they found success there, began to think they belonged in hardcover, where the business was still a lot tougher. But the successor to the pulps was always the paperback; the cheap, brightly colored, widely available book of the masses, conveniently sized to fit in pocket or purse, to be carried on trains, brought home or even left behind for others.

In addition to Mickey Spillane, the success of the paperback format gave us names like John D. MacDonald and Erle Stanley Gardner, both prolific pulpsters, or "fictioneers," who went on to even greater, more widespread careers with paperback originals. The paperback format brought us such enduring legends as David Goodis, Richard Matheson, Wade Miller and dozens of others whose reputations have often grown throughout the years.

Among this group are first rate writers still waiting to be rediscovered by today's readers, people like Dan Cushman and Dan Marlowe, Richard Deming and Richard Wormser, Henry Kane and Frank Kane; long-time book-a-monthers like Peggy Gaddis and James Noble Gifford; writers like Orrie Hitt and Ennis Willie, whose real names sound more like pseudo-

nyms. There are writers who remained successful, or became more successful, in the decades following the paperback boom, guys like Lawrence
Block and Donald E. Westlake.

Fawcett Gold Medal wasn't the only publisher of paperback originals,
merely the first. Dell gave us those interesting "map back" books, so-called
because the back cover of each book had a crude drawing of "the scene of
the crime" while inside was printed a cast list of characters for the reader
to be familiar with before they even started reading.

Pocket, New American Library, Handi-Books, Monarch, Lion, Belmont,
Nightstand and Signet were just some of the many publishers that gave us
everything from private detective novels, mysteries, juvenile delinquent
fiction, stories of "forbidden love," westerns, and yes, even "nurse" novels
(do your own research).

"Sleaze" novels were popular, too, books that were even more explicit
in their sexual depictions, skirting the line between what could safely be
sold in stores and what could bring criminal charges under decency laws.
These books were quite often written under pseudonyms and were frequently huge sellers, providing steady incomes for those fast writers who
could meet the publishers' heavy demands. Lately these books have started
to come out of the dark, with reprints appearing under the real names of
the original authors, especially when those real names belong to now-
famous writers willing to take ownership of their past.

Sadly, traditional mass market paperbacks, like the pulp magazines of
the early part of the last century, are mostly fading away, though they still
appear in some genres. The newer inch-taller, "easier to read" versions
that publishers have been printing (that cost three dollars more than the
inch shorter versions) are out there, but they wouldn't even fit in a traditional spinner rack. Not that there are many of those around anymore,
either.

The penny dreadfuls in England gave rise to the pulp magazines in
America in the early twentieth century. Comic books were another source
of cheap, mass market entertainment and while they still survive, they
are no longer the affordable items they once were. With a single issue having much less content and costing almost four dollars each, and with their
tendency to tell single stories across multiple titles, and with a style that
has gone to less "reading" in an attempt to be more "movie-like," they are
no longer the presence in the lives of young readers they once were.

Like a lot of boys who grew up reading, I haunted the public library
from an early age, discovering and devouring treasures like the Alfred
Hitchcock and the Three Investigators books (at least the ones by creator
Robert Arthur) and moving on to the Hardy Boys series (it didn't seem to
matter a whole lot who "Franklin W. Dixon" really was). I found comic

books on a wall stand at Salk Drugs on the corner of 54th Street and
Lyndale Avenue in Minneapolis where I perused each month's titles under
the watchful eye of the pharmacist behind the counter. If I saw a spinner
rack I was pawing through it, looking at all the titles, even the ones buried
behind others in the slots at the bottom, looking for anything worthy of
the money earned from my morning paper route.

As comic books rose in price and shrunk in page count, I moved more
and more to those beloved paperback books. I discovered science fiction
and later westerns, then mysteries and thrillers and other sorts of crime
fiction. I dabbled in bestsellers. I turned my young nose up at those
strangely objectionable covers of books like Gardner's Perry Mason
series–how could these scantily clad ladies have any relation to the stories
they showed on TV with Raymond Burr? And all those series books, starting with "The Executioner" and going through every violent noun imagi-
nable: The Annihilator, The Demolisher, and on and on.

I can appreciate them now, however. Like that part of me that would
take that time machine back to that busy newsstand in New York, drool-
ing over all the pulp titles I never got to see, it wouldn't be bad to go back
to the Gold Medal days and see stacks and stacks of those bright yellow
spines spinning around in the racks in front of me.

Certainly the closest I'll ever come was the time I was at an antiquari-
an book fair and a vendor was acting as the agent for a family who found
hundreds of pristine, NEVER READ Gold Medal books–they'd been purchased and stored by their recently deceased father as they were released.
I was able to hold and smell and feel first printing, first edition paperback
books by Peter Rabe that, despite their actual age, were really brand new.
They were that well preserved. Unfortunately, instead of the ridiculously
low price on the cover, they were asking upwards of thirty dollars. Apiece.
Oh to be wealthy, or better yet, to make my own attic discovery....

Just who were the writers who pounded out all those millions upon
millions of words that went into these books? What names did they publish under, what specific kinds of books did they write? How did they
effect their peers, the market, the public?

This book is a wonderful source of information about these influential
and trailblazing pioneers. Some of these authors are easily recognized by
even a casual reader, others may be a complete mystery. All of them,
though, have contributed significantly to the popular literature going
from the pulps to the slicks to the wonderful paperback original. Paperback
Confidential tells their stories. It gives you recommendations for other
authors based on the styles or influences of others. There's an index of
real names and pseudonyms at the end of the book, the PseudoDex, that

tries to identify all the various aliases each author has written under. There are lists of titles for suggested "further reading" for each author.

Dip in and enjoy. Read it cover to cover or browse it at random. Pick a page, follow the recommendations from entry to entry. Let it inspire you to pick an old, unread copy of something off your shelf. You may have to reglue the binding and be careful how far you crack the covers, but it all works.

Celebrate the era, the works, the personalities, the times of those decades not quite so long past. Read, and enjoy, the way you did back then. Or the way you would if you had one of those time machine things and could take a spinner rack tour of newsstands and drugstores across America, say maybe sixty or seventy years ago....

*Littleton, NH*
*2013*

# *Introduction*

*by Brian Ritt*

This book chronicles the life and work of authors who wrote hard-boiled crime fiction or were otherwise significant figures in the paperback era from the 1930s-1960s. The earliest authors I explore are those who wrote for the pulp magazines: Dashiell Hammett, Raymond Chandler, Carroll John Daly, Frederick Nebel and Raoul Whitfield, among others. *Black Mask*, which began in 1920, is today considered the pinnacle of pulp fiction magazines, and Hammett, Chandler, Daly, et al., were a few of its most successful practitioners (although at the time, *Black Mask* was intended to be merely lowbrow "popular" entertainment, launched by literary lights H. L. Mencken and George Jean Nathan as a way to finance their sophisticated periodical, *The Smart Set*).

The type of hardboiled crime fiction popularized in *Black Mask* and similar pulps laid the groundwork for the stories which began to be published when the "paperback original" (aka PBO) began to make its mark in 1949. Although the concept of the "paperback"–an inexpensive, portable, disposable form of media–had been around since 1938, beginning with the reprinting of Pearl S. Buck's literary classic, *The Good Earth*, the concept of a paperback novel which had never before been printed in book form came to fruition in 1949, when the Fawcett publishing house began its Gold Medal line of books. As the pulps were dying out during the late 1940s, their most successful writers of crime fiction made the move to paperback originals. Therefore, in terms of the material covered in this book, I chose authors whose hardboiled crime writing appeared in pulps as early as the 1930s, who wrote for radio shows and B-movies (later to be known as film noir) through the 1940s, and who wrote PBOs and television scripts during the 1950s and '60s, until loosening censorship restrictions caused a seismic change in the landscape of crime fiction. This period–the late 1930s through the 1960s–is what I'm terming the "paperback era."

When an author submitted an original novel to a publisher during the paperback era, the publisher retained the right to change the title as needed to increase saleability. Among authors covered in this book, Vin Packer's proposed title, *Why Not Mother?* was changed to the sin-insinuating, *The Evil Friendship*; Bruno Fischer's *The Golden Boy* became the more action-oriented, *Run For Your Life*; Peter Rabe's *The Ticker* was changed to the exclamatory *Stop This Man!*; and it takes no effort to guess why Harry

Whittington's *Never Find Sanctuary* became *Backwoods Tramp*. Not only PBOs, but, when reprinted in paperback, hardcovers also occasionally underwent title changes. In George Axelrod's play *The Seven-Year Itch* (later the famous Marilyn Monroe movie) a great joke is made about this, when the marketing director of a paperback publishing house suggests changing the title of Nathaniel Hawthorne's classic *The Scarlet Letter* to *I Was an Adulteress*.

A number of the authors covered in this book wrote novels which became controversial. Books by Erskine Caldwell, Irving Shulman and Mickey Spillane were attacked by teachers, psychologists, religious leaders, citizens' groups, and even members of congress as being obscene and corrupting moral influences. In 1952, the House Select Committee on Current Pornographic Materials charged a group of paperbacks (which included a book by Caldwell, as well as books by two other writers covered in this book—Hal Ellson and John Faulkner) with "offensive infractions of the moral code" and accused them of "artful appeals to sensuality, immorality, filth, perversion, and degeneracy."

The writers covered in this book were versatile and able to write successfully in a variety of genres; however, they often became known for specializing in one particular area of crime fiction. If you want an idea of what some of the writers specialized in, I've noted some paperback subcategories below:

*Private Detective:* Cleve F. Adams, Marvin Albert, William Ard, Michael Avallone, Robert Leslie Bellem, Carter Brown, Howard Browne, Raymond Chandler, Peter Cheyney, Carroll John Daly, Norbert Davis, Richard Deming, Thomas B. Dewey, G. G. Fickling, William Campbell Gault, Frank Gruber, Brett Halliday, Dashiell Hammett, Frank Kane, Henry Kane, Ed Lacy, Jonathan Latimer, John D. MacDonald, Wade Miller, Frederick Nebel, Earl Norman, Talmage Powell, Richard S. Prather, Mike Roscoe, Bart Spicer, Mickey Spillane, John B. West, Raoul Whitfield

*Noir:* Gil Brewer, James M. Cain, David Goodis, Patricia Highsmith, Day Keene, Dan J. Marlowe, Peter Rabe, Jim Thompson, Harry Whittington, Charles Williams, Cornell Woolrich

*Police procedural and police-related:* Jonathan Craig, Evan Hunter (as Ed McBain), William P. McGivern

*Espionage/secret agent:* Edward S. Aarons, Donald Hamilton

*Juvenile Delinquent:* Hal Ellson, Irving Shulman

*Lesbian-themed:* Ann Bannon, Vin Packer

*Backwoods-themed:* Erskine Caldwell, John Faulkner, Harry Whittington

My hope is that this book will function as a kind of menu. I've provided the names of the dishes, the ingredients, and, through my descriptions, I hope I've managed to capture a bit of each writer's flavor; and that you will be encouraged to go to your local five-star bookstore (whether real or virtual) and feast on these delicacies to your heart's content.

*Burbank, CA*
*March 2013*

# AUTHOR ENTRIES

# Edward S. Aarons

(also wrote as Edward Ronns, Paul Ayres). Born in Philadelphia, Pennsylvania, 1916. Died in New Milford, Connecticut, 1975.

 Edward S. Aarons was the creator of Sam Durell, a paperback adventure hero whose career lasted for more than twenty years and forty novels.

Aarons graduated from New York's Columbia University with degrees in literature and history. During World War II, he served in the United States Coast Guard, 1941—1945. Upon his release, Aarons worked short stints as a salesman, fisherman and newspaper reporter.

His first three novels (written as by Edward Ronns) were for the low-budget publisher, Phoenix Press: *Death in a Lighthouse* (1938, a.k.a. *Cowl of Doom*), *Murder Money* (1938) and *The Corpse Hangs High* (1939).

He found better paying markets and a wider audience when he successfully began publishing short stories in the pulps during the 1940's. Most of his stories (as by Ronns) were published in *Detective Story Magazine*. Aarons' experience writing for the pulps taught him a stripped-down, action-oriented prose style. He continued publishing in the pulps throughout the '40's, and published a few stories in the new digest-oriented markets during the early 1950's. Aarons became successful enough so that by 1945, he could become a full time writer.

Aarons' most successful books were the more than forty paperback novels—starting with *Assignment To Disaster* (1955) and ending with *Assignment—Afghan Dragon* (1976)—featuring CIA espionage agent Sam Durell. According to the website, spyguysandgals.com, Durell "possessed a nice balance that readers wanted in a hero. He was desirable by women but had no overwhelming urge to bed each that he met, though he did enjoy the company of several throughout the series. He was a man of action but was definitely human and subject to normal frailties, as his many scars indicated. He was also a patriot who loved his country but who often had few good words for the bureaucrats who ran it."

Each Durell assignment takes him to an exotic locale somewhere around the globe, although sections of the stories take place in the U.S., especially in the bayous of Louisiana (Durrell is part Cajun). *Assignment—Madeline* (1958) places Durell smack dab in the middle of the Algerian conflict. *Assignment—Cong Hai Kill* (1966) takes him to Thailand. In *Assignment—Black Gold* (1975), he fights to protect a country in Africa.

Aarons created villains for the series who harken back to his pulp background—they always represent a threat to at least a nation, if not the entire world. The *Assignment* villains are either sadistic thugs with bone-crunching strength, or criminal masterminds like Dr. Von Handel in *Assignment—Star Stealers.*

After Aarons' death, the series continued, ghostwritten under the name Will B. Aarons.

**Further Reading:**
*Sam Durell "Assignment" series:*
ASSIGNMENT TO DISASTER (1955)
ASSIGNMENT–SUICIDE (1956)
ASSIGNMENT–BUDAPEST (1957)
ASSIGNMENT–ANGELINA (1958)
ASSIGNMENT–CARLOTTA CORTEZ (1959)
ASSIGNMENT–LILI LAMARES (1959)
ASSIGNMENT–ZORAYA (1960)
ASSIGNMENT–BURMA GIRL (1961)
ASSIGNMENT–KARACHI (1962)
ASSIGNMENT–MANCHURIAN DOLL (1963)
ASSIGNMENT–THE GIRL IN THE GONDOLA (1964)
ASSIGNMENT–CONG HAI KILL (1966)
ASSIGNMENT–SCHOOL FOR SPIES (1966)
ASSIGNMENT–MOON GIRL (1968)
ASSIGNMENT–NUCLEAR NUDE (1968)
ASSIGNMENT–STAR STEALERS (1970)

NIGHTMARE (1948)
COME BACK, MY LOVE (1953)
GIRL ON THE RUN (1954)

**As Edward Ronns**
DEATH IN A LIGHTHOUSE (1938)
THE CORPSE HANGS HIGH (1939)
THE ART STUDIO MURDERS (1950)
THE DECOY (1951)
THE NET (1953)
THEY ALL RAN AWAY (1955)
GANG RUMBLE (1958)

---

**If you like Edward S. Aarons,** you might like: Donald Hamilton, Earl Norman

# Cleve F. Adams

(also wrote as John Spain, Franklin Charles (with Robert Leslie Bellem)). Born in Chicago, Illinois, 1895. Died in Glendale, California, 1949.

Cleve F. Adams' Rex McBride is perhaps the moodiest private detective in crime fiction. According to Francis M. Nevins, "He has the capacity for long, brooding silences, sudden ribald laughter, mad fury, and aloof arrogance." (1001 Midnights: The Aficionado's Guide to Mystery and Detective Fiction, by Bill Pronzini and Marcia Muller)

Before Adams turned to writing, he worked as a copper miner, soda jerk and accountant. In 1933, he began writing stories for the pulps. He published over a hundred stories in magazines such as Black Mask, Dime Detective, Detective Fiction Weekly, Clues, Ten Detective Aces and Double Detective. For Clues magazine, Adams created detective fiction's first female hardboiled private eye, Violet McDade—a 350-lb, former circus fat lady, who'll backhand a man as casually as she'll wipe a spot of mustard off her mouth.

Adams' introduced Rex McBride in Sabotage (1940, published in abridged form as Death Before Breakfast, 1942), in which the private detective battles commercial saboteurs plotting to destroy a dam project in Nevada. Up Jumped the Devil (1943, published as Murder All Over, 1950) takes McBride to San Francisco to track down the theft of his client's $100,000 jewels. Shady Lady (1955), the final McBride novel, was published after Adams' early death from a heart attack; it was completed by Adams' friends and fellow crime writers, Robert Leslie Bellem and W. T. Ballard. (Adams had dedicated various books to Bellem and Ballard, as well as pulp scribe Dwight V. Babcock.) Other McBride books include And Sudden Death (1940) and The Crooking Finger (1944).

Adams wrote two books about private detective John J. Shannon. In The Private Eye (1942), Shannon, searching for a missing heir in Arizona, encounters a corrupt town where two warring mining companies both want to pay for his services. The final Shannon book, No Wings On a Cop (1950, published posthumously), was again completed by Robert Leslie Bellem.

Under the name John Spain, Adams wrote two books about Bill Rye, bodyguard to corrupt politician Big Ed Callahan. Both Rye books, Dig Me a Grave (1942) and Death is Like That (1943) deal with corrupt local politics.

If the storylines for some of these books sounds familiar, there's good reason—Adams admitted borrowing from the plots of Dashiell Hammett's Red Harvest and The Glass Key for a number of his own books.

A resident of Southern California for a number of years, Adams was a member of a local writing group, The Fictioneers, whose members included fellow pulp scribes W. T. Ballard and Raymond Chandler.

Vincent Starrett, a contemporary of Adams and a well known writer of the times, summed up the appeal of Cleve Adams' work: "[Adams] is far and away the best writer of the hardboiled school who has come along in recent memory to delight those of us who, in the safety of our homes, like to be frightened by events which, if we were part of them, would send us scurrying to the nearest sanatorium."

**Further Reading:**
*Rex McBride series:*
AND SUDDEN DEATH (1940)
SABOTAGE (1940; as DEATH BEFORE BREAKFAST, 1942)
DECOY (1941)
UP JUMPED THE DEVIL (1943; as MURDER ALL OVER, 1950)
THE CROOKING FINGER (1944)
SHADY LADY (1955)

*John J. Shannon series (complete):*
THE PRIVATE EYE (1942)
NO WINGS ON A COP (1950, expanded by Robert Leslie Bellem)

THE BLACK DOOR (1941)
WHAT PRICE MURDER (1942)
CONTRABAND (1950)

**As John Spain**
*Bill Rye series (complete):*
DIG ME A GRAVE (1942)
DEATH IS LIKE THAT (1943)

THE EVIL STAR (1944)

**As Franklin Charles**
THE VICE CZAR MURDERS (1941, with Robert Leslie Bellem)

---

**If you like Cleve F. Adams,** you might like: Dan J. Marlowe, Steve Fisher

## *Marvin Albert*

(also wrote as Mike Barone, Al Conroy (with Gil Brewer), Albert Conroy, Ian MacAlister, Nick Quarry, Anthony Rome). Born in Philadelphia, Pennsylvania, 1924. Died in Cote d'Azur, France, 1996.

Marvin Albert was a professional's professional, equally adept at writing mysteries, westerns and men's adventure. His novels contained strong plots, well-developed characters and detailed settings.

Albert served in the Merchant Marines during WWII, as Chief Officer on Liberty Ships. After the war he worked as a copy writer for Philadelphia *Record* and as a researcher for *Look* magazine. The success of Albert's western, *The Law and Jake Wade* (1956), allowed him to work as a full time writer.

Albert, as Anthony Rome, wrote a series of three books about private detective Tony Rome: *Miami Mayhem* (1960, reprinted as *Tony Rome* in 1967, as by Marvin H. Albert), *Lady in Cement* (1962) and *My Kind of Game* (1962). Rome is an ex-cop who quit the force after officials persecuted his policeman father, who was trying to expose department corruption. He is a compulsive gambler who lives on his houseboat, *The Straight Pass*, in Florida (a precursor to John D. MacDonald's Travis McGee); he smokes Luckies, owns a mangy tomcat named Tangerine, and carries.38 Police Special, Lugar, won in a poker game. *Miami Mayhem* was filmed as *Tony Rome* in 1967, starring Frank Sinatra, Jill St. John and Richard Conte. *Lady in Cement* was filmed in 1968, starring Sinatra, Raquel Welch and Conte.

Numerous mystery reviewers and connoisseurs of the hardboiled highly tout Albert's six-book Jake Barrow series (as by Nick Quarry) as containing some of his best writing. Fast-paced action and '50's-style sex-and-violence are hallmarks of the series. In *The Hoods Come Calling* (1958), Barrow must find his estranged, soon-to-be ex-wife's killer while he is being suspected of and hunted for the crime, and is pursued by both the police and his wife's hoodlum connections. *No Chance in Hell* (1960) takes Barrow from New York City to Santa Fe, New Mexico, where he travels to protect a friend's daughter from a ruthless killer. According to reviewer August West, on vinpulp.blogspot.com, high points in the novel include, "an unbelievable escape scene in the NYC sewer system and a wild cat-fight with Barrow letting the girls go at it."

Albert wrote numerous movie novelizations, mostly light comedies, including (as by Marvin H. Albert) *Pillow Talk* (1959, starring Doris Day and Rock Hudson), *Lover Come Back* (1962, starring Day and Hudson), *Move Over, Darling* (1963, starring Day and James Garner), *The Pink Panther* (1964) and *What's New, Pussycat?* (1965, starring Peter O'Toole and Peter Sellers, screenplay by Woody Allen). He also adapted his own novels into screenplays:

*Duel at Diablo* (1966, starring James Garner and Sidney Poitier, based on *Apache Rising*), *Rough Night in Jericho* (1967, starring Dean Martin and George Peppard, based on *The Man in Black*), *The Don is Dead* (1973, starring Anthony Quinn, based on the Nick Quarry novel of the same name).

**Further Reading:**
LIE DOWN WITH THE LIONS (1955)
THE LAW AND JAKE WADE (1956)
APACHE RISING (1957)

**As Albert Conroy**
THE ROAD'S END (1952)
THE CHISELERS (1953)
NICE GUYS FINISH DEAD (1957)
DEVIL IN DUNGAREES (1960)
THE LOOTERS (1961)

**As Nick Quarry**
*Jake Barrow series:*
TRAIL OF A TRAMP (1958)
THE HOODS COME CALLING (1958)
THE GIRL WITH NO PLACE TO HIDE (1959)
NO CHANCE IN HELL (1960)

TILL IT HURTS (1960)
SOME DIE HARD (1961)

**As Anthony Rome**
*Tony Rome series (complete):*
MIAMI MAYHEM (1960; reprinted as TONY ROME, as by Marvin H. Albert, 1967)
THE LADY IN CEMENT (1961)
MY KIND OF GAME (1962)

---

**If you like Marvin Albert,** you might like: Howard Hunt, John D. MacDonald

## *Benjamin Appel*

Born in New York, New York, 1907. Died in Roosevelt, New Jersey, 1977.

Benjamin Appel was raised in the violent, poverty-ridden section of New York known as Hell's Kitchen, and his stories vividly reflect that area's hardscrabble environment. His stories make you look at the women—sweating, wiping away the sweat, sweating more—scrubbing floors to put something besides bread and water on the dinner table. They make you look at the men—sweating, wiping away the sweat, sweating more—breaking their backs while packing and loading boxes onto trucks in the blazing sun. Appel's stories make you listen to the crying babies living in sweltering tenements, smell the vomit of a dope addict puking in a back alley, and feel the syphilitic chancres on a buck-a-throw whore.

Appel published his first novel when he was twenty-seven. *Brain Guy* (1934, aka *The Enforcer*) tells the story of Bill Trent, a cunning, intelligent "rent collector" who loses his job during the depression. Having grown up in Hell's Kitchen, Trent decides to put his brains to work planning heists. Trent doesn't start out tough, nor does he start out at the top. He has to fight his way up the dog-eat-dog chain-of-command, coarsening his character and conscience in the process. With James M. Cain's *The Postman Always Rings Twice* having been published the same year, the reviewer for *The New York World-Telegram* wrote thusly about *Brain Guy*: "Jimmy Cain hasn't even a running chance as dean of tellers of hardboiled stories. He is completely outpointed, outsocked, outslugged, and outcursed by Benjamin Appel."

Appel's other notable novels include *The Power-House* (1939), a story about union corruption; *The Dark Stain* (1943), a story about racial prejudice; *Plunder* (1952), a non-NYC-based story, about two GI's who plan to take control of Manila's post-war black market; *Sweet Money Girl* (1954), about two ex-Army buddies who both fall in love with the same selfish, opportunistic tramp; and *Life and Death of a Tough Guy* (1955, aka *Teen-age Mobster*), the story of a young Jewish kid who kicks and claws his way into an Irish gang. Appel's gritty short stories about life in New York are collected in *Dock Walloper* (1953) and *Hell's Kitchen* (1952).

Writer Nelson Algren said of Appel, "[His] stories have never been prettied up for the parlor. Their forthrightness will do more than leave the reader feeling that he has read an honest story: he will feel as well that he has met an honest man." (*Hardboiled: An Anthology of American Crime Stories*, edited by Bill Pronzini and Jack Adrian)

Further Reading:
BRAIN GUY (1934)
THE POWER HOUSE (1939)
THE DARK STAIN (1943)
HELL'S KITCHEN (1952; short stories)
PLUNDER (1952)
DOCK WALLOPER (1953; short stories)
SWEET MONEY GIRL (1954)
LIFE AND DEATH OF A TOUGH GUY (1955, also published as TEEN-AGE
MOBSTER, 1957)
THE RAW EDGE (1958)

---

If you like Benjamin Appel, you might like: David Goodis, David Karp

# William Ard

(also wrote as Ben Kerr, Mike Moran, Jonas Ward, Thomas Wills). Born in Brooklyn, New York, 1922. Died in Clearwater, Florida, 1960.

William Ard was the creator of Timothy Dane, a New York-based private eye who, during the blood-and-bullets, Spillane-crazed 1950's, was a throwback to the Hammett-Chandler tradition, when private eyes adhered to a moral code, and scenes of sex and violence were written for a dramatically justified reason—not just for purposes of sensationalism.

Ard came from a well-to-do family and graduated from Dartmouth College, where he was a member of Sigma Chi. He also belonged to both the Pelican Golf Club in South Carolina and the Carlouel Yacht Club in Florida. After graduation, Ard worked for six years as a copywriter for the Buchanan Advertising Agency (whose name he would later adopt for the protagonist in his series of Westerns) and for the New York division of Warner Bros.

The acceptance of Ard's first novel, *The Perfect Frame* (1951), allowed him to quit his job and become a full time writer. *The Perfect Frame* introduced PI Timothy Dane, an ex-Marine who held a law degree. Ard's most successful and well known Dane novel is *Hell is a City* (1955). The book's setting is New York, where the city officials from the mayor on down are corrupt and on the local mob's payroll. In this atmosphere, winning elections, not justice, is what counts. In the novel, a young Latino shoots a vice cop who was about to rape the boy's sister. But the political bigwigs portray the case as the cold-blooded murder of a heroic officer. Dane's job is to protect the boy from those who want him silenced. In the vein of Billy Wilder's film noir, *Ace In The Hole*, journalists, politicians and law enforcement officials all exploit the situation for their own opportunistic purposes. Other notable Timothy Dane novels include *The Diary* (1952), *Don't Come Crying to Me* (1954) and *Cry Scandal* (1956).

Ard's most successful books were a Western series for paperback publisher Gold Medal, starting with 1956's *The Name's Buchanan* (as by Jonas Ward; made into the movie, *Buchanan Rides Alone*, in 1958, starring Randolph Scott). Over six feet tall, Buchanan is an easy-going, affable, chuckling drifter, who sheds his "gentle giant" skin and erupts into violence when justice calls for it. Ard wrote three more Buchanan novels— *Buchanan Says No* (1957), *Buchanan Gets Mad* (1958) and *One Man Massacre* (1958). The series became so successful that Gold Medal continued it after Ard's death, using John Jakes, Robert Silverberg and others to ghostwrite.

Ard produced over thirty novels and numerous short stories during a

ten-year period, before his untimely death from cancer at age 37.
**Further Reading:**
*Timothy Dane series (complete):*
THE PERFECT FRAME (1951)
.38 (1952; as YOU CAN'T STOP ME, 1953)
THE DIARY (1952)
A PRIVATE PARTY (1953)
DON'T COME CRYING TO ME (1954)
MR. TROUBLE (1954)
HELL IS A CITY (1955)
CRY SCANDAL (1956)
THE ROOT OF HIS EVIL (1957)

*Lou Largo series:*
ALL I CAN GET (1959)
LIKE ICE SHE WAS (1960)

**As Ben Kerr**
SHAKEDOWN (1952)
DOWN I GO (1955)
DAMNED IF HE DOES (1956)
I FEAR YOU NOT (1956)
CLUB 17 (1957)
THE BLONDE AND JOHNNY MALLOY (1958)

**As Jonas Ward**
*Buchanan series (complete):*
THE NAME'S BUCHANAN (1956)
BUCHANAN SAYS NO (1957)
ONE-MAN MASSACRE (1958)
BUCHANAN GETS MAD (1958)
BUCHANAN'S REVENGE (1960)

**As Thomas Wills**
YOU'LL GET YOURS (1952)
MINE TO AVENGE (1955)

---

**If you like William Ard,** you might like: Thomas B. Dewey, Raymond Chandler

# *Michael Avallone*

(also wrote as Mike Avalione, Mike Avallone, Mark Dane, Steve Michaels, Edwina Noone, Priscilla Dalton, John Patrick, Jeanne-Anne dePre, Dorothea Nile, Sidney Stuart, Nick Carter, Troy Conway, Dora Highland, Stuart Jason, Vance Stanton, Max Walker, Lee Davis Willoughby). Born in New York, New York, 1924. Died in Los Angeles, California, 1999.

Whoever came up with the phrase, "Variety is the spice of life," must have been thinking about Michael Avallone.

Avallone, who dubbed himself "The Fastest Typewriter in the East," wrote everything from private detective novels to "sleaze" books; from Gothics to science fiction stories; from screenplay novelizations to TV tie-in books. He wrote non-fiction articles, reviews and memoirs, as well. He even wrote a driver's ed manual. He wrote more than two hundred novels—during an especially productive year, he completed twenty-seven books. He approached each project with the same degree of enthusiasm, sincerity and professionalism—if he had written *Macbeth*, he would have put no less effort into such books as *The Cunning Linguist* (1970, as by Troy Conway) or his TV novelization, *Love Comes to Keith Partridge* (1973). A complete bibliography of every book he wrote and every pseudonym he used would be a near-impossible undertaking. Here's Avallone's own take on the subject:

> "Ever since I discovered pencils, I have set out to prove the theory that a writer can write anything—or should be able to… Liner notes, music biographies, personality articles, poetry, cover copy, all of these I have done because of a long-standing love affair with the English language." (*Private Eyes: 101 Knights* by Robert A. Baker and Michael T. Nietzel, pg.138)

The most entertaining, outlandish, loony, metaphor-mixing, simile-spouting, pun-prattling character of Avallone's is private detective Ed Noon. Noon was featured in approximately 30 novels, starting with *The Tall Dolores* (1953) and ending with *High Noon at Midnight* (1988). Noon started out in the series as a typical Manhattan-based, tough-talking PI—with the requisite amounts of wisecracks, sex and violence. During Noon's middle period, he got involved with the kind of high-tech gadgets and spy missions associated with James Bond. During the latter part of the series, Noon became a personal troubleshooter for none other than the President of the United States himself.

Noon has an encyclopedic knowledge of baseball and old movies—sometimes these passions serve as mere one-liners in a story, sometimes whole plots are woven out of them. Avallone peppers his Noon novels with colorful supporting characters: a 440-lb female mattress tester, in *The Case of the Bouncing Betty* (1957); a 6-foot 4-inch ex-circus performer billed as "the Shapeliest Amazon in the World," in *The Tall Delores* (1953); a gold-toothed, beret-wearing villain, in *The Case of the Violent Virgin* (1957). Similes and metaphors in the Noon novels are often just as colorful. And they seem to share a common theme:

"Her hips were beautifully arched and her breasts were like proud flags waving triumphantly. She carried them high and mighty." (*The Case of the Violent Virgin*, 1957)

"She was breathing hard, firm breasts rumba-ing in the field of [her] Kelly Green [sweater]." (*The Hot Body*, 1973)

"One of her breasts rolled into view like a cantaloupe rolling off a display in a fruit store." (*The Crazy Mixed-Up Corpse*, 1957)

Avallone constructed a complete, self-contained world for the Noon novels—book reviewers referred to it as the "Nooniverse," and to Noon's sometimes off-center syntax as "Noonisms."

Using the name Troy Conway, Avallone also wrote a series of nearly twenty "sleaze" books about secret agent Rod Damon, aka The Coxeman. The Damon novels started during the late '60's and joined such other soft core James Bond parodies as 0008, The Man from O.R.G.Y. and The Lady from L.U.S.T., among others. The Damon novels are fun and entertaining, and sport punning, double-entendre-laden titles such as *Keep It Up, Rod!* (1968), *The Billion Dollar Snatch* (1968), *It's Getting Harder All the Time* (1969), *I'd Rather Fight Than Swish* (1969) and the aforementioned *The Cunning Linguist* (1970), among others.

Avallone wrote short stories and non-fiction articles in magazines as diverse as *The Saint Detective Magazine*, *Western Action*, *Ten Story Sports*, *The Pulp Collector*, *Ellery Queen's Mystery Magazine* and *Baseball Stories*.

Later in life, Avallone was an enthusiastic volunteer for the Mystery Writers of America—serving on its Board of Directors, editing its newsletter, and working as chairman of its awards, television and motion picture committees.

**Further Reading:**
*Ed Noon series:*
THE TALL DOLORES (1953)
VIOLENCE IN VELVET (1954)
THE CASE OF THE BOUNCING BETTY (1957)
THE CASE OF THE VIOLENT VIRGIN (1957)
THE CRAZY MIXED-UP CORPSE (1957)
THE VOODOO MURDERS (1957)
MEANWHILE BACK AT THE MORGUE (1960)
THE BEDROOM BOLERO (1963)
THERE IS SOMETHING ABOUT A DAME (1963)
LUST IS NO LADY (1964)
THE DOOMSDAY BAG (1969)
SHOOT IT AGAIN, SAM (1972)
THE HOT BODY (1973)

ALL THE WAY (1960)
THE LITTLE BLACK BOOK (1961)
STAG STRIPPER (1961)
LUST AT LEISURE (1963)
SHOCK CORRIDOR (1963, movie novelization)

**As Troy Conway**
*Rod Damon—The Coxeman series:*
COME ONE, COME ALL (1968)
THE BILLION DOLLAR SNATCH (1968)
THE WHAM! BAM! THANK YOU, MA'AM AFFAIR (1968)
IT'S GETTING HARDER ALL THE TIME (1968)
I'D RATHER FIGHT THAN SWISH (1969)
THE CUNNING LINGUIST (1971)
A STIFF PROPOSITION (1971)
KEEP IT UP, ROD (1973)

**If you like Michael Avallone,** you might like: Carter Brown, Henry Kane

# W. T. Ballard

(also wrote as Neil MacNeil, Harrison Hunt, John Shepherd, P. T. Ballard, John Hunter, Parker Bonner, Sam Bowie, Jack Slade, Clay Turner, Walt Bruce). Born in Cleveland, Ohio, 1903. Died in Mt. Dora, Florida, 1980.

Willis Todhunter Ballard was a regularly featured writer of *Black Mask* magazine during that seminal pulp's heyday. His stories featured series character Bill Lennox, a troubleshooter for a fictional Hollywood studio named General Consolidated Pictures. The job of a "troubleshooter," according to one of the Lennox tales, was to "iron out whatever bottlenecks developed in the production schedule," said bottlenecks involving actors and actresses mixed up in crimes such as crooked gambling, blackmail and murder. Ballard wrote 27 Lennox stories for *Black Mask*, from 1933-1942.

Lennox's appearances didn't stop with *Black Mask*. Ballard also wrote five novels featuring the character. In the first book, *Say Yes to Murder* (1942, aka *The Demise of a Louse*), Lennox investigates the murder of an alcoholic actor named Leon Heyworth, who Lennox finds under the bed of a well known actress. In *Murder Can't Stop* (1946), a bed is again the story's catalyst—only this time the dead body is found in Lennox's own bed, at a secluded mountain lodge where Lennox is staying. *Dealing Out Death* (1948) sends Lennox to Las Vegas at the beginning of that city's days as America's gambling mecca. The last two Lennox novels were *The Murder in Hollywood* (1951) and *Lights, Camera, Murder* (1960), which were published under Ballard's pseudonym John Shepherd.

As Neil MacNeil, Ballard wrote a series about a pair of Scottish private eyes named Tony Costaine and Bert McCall. The Costaine and McCall series takes a different tone than the tough-as-nails, *Black Mask*-inspired Lennox series. Costaine and McCall are very much a product of their time, 1958-1966—the easygoing, swinging era of the Rat Pack, the *Playboy* lifetsyle, and cocktail music. Tony Costaine is the tall, dark and handsome one of the pair. But no mere meathead, Costaine graduated first from Dartmouth and then Columbia Law School, and worked for both the FBI and the OSS (which later became the CIA). Bert McCall is more of a roughneck and handles the physical aspects of the job. McCall stands at a hulking 6'5" and 265 pounds, but like Costaine, he is no dummy. He served in the FBI and OSS with Costaine, and is a virtuoso on the bagpipes. As a team, Costaine and McCall are witty, cool and cocky. They are also killers—ladykillers, of course. Altogether, Ballard wrote seven Costaine/McCall PBOs for Gold Medal. Notable examples are *Death Takes an Option* (1958), *Third On a Seesaw* (1959), *Two Guns for Hire* (1959) and *Hot Dam* (1960).

As Harrison Hunt, Ballard co-wrote *Murder Picks the Jury* (1947) with fellow pulp/mystery writer Norbert Davis.

Between the 1950's and '60's, Ballard wrote over 60 Westerns, using both his own name and the pseudonyms John Hunter, Parker Bonner, Sam Bowie, Jack Slade and Clay Turner. He also wrote scripts for Western TV shows, including *Death Valley Days, Shotgun Slade, Cowboy G-Men* and *The Adventures of Wild Bill Hickock.*

**Further Reading:**
*Bill Lennox series (complete):*
SAY YES TO MURDER (1942, as
DEMISE OF A LOUSE, as by John Shepherd, 1962)
MURDER CAN'T STOP (1946)
DEALING OUT DEATH (1948)
LIGHTS, CAMERA, MURDER (1960, as by John Shepherd)
MURDER LAS VEGAS STYLE (1967)

*Lieutenant Max Hunter series:*
PRETTY MISS MURDER (1961)
THE SEVEN SISTERS (1962)
THREE FOR THE MONEY (1963)

WALK IN FEAR (1952)
CHANCE ELSON (1958)

**As Neil MacNeil**
*Tony Costaine and Bert McCall series (complete):*
DEATH TAKES AN OPTION (1958)
THIRD ON A SEESAW (1959)
TWO GUNS FOR HIRE (1959)
HOT DAM (1960)
THE DEATH RIDE (1960)
MEXICAN SLAY RIDE (1962)
THE SPY CATCHERS (1966)

**As Harrison Hunt**
DEATH PICKS THE JURY (1947, with Norbert Davis)

---

**If you like W. T. Ballard,** you might like: George Harmon Coxe, Frank Gruber

# Bill S. Ballinger

(born William Sanborn Ballinger; also wrote as Frederic Freyer, B. X. Sanborn).
Born in Oskaloosa, Iowa, 1912. Died in Tarzana, California, 1980.

Bill S. Ballinger wrote innovative suspense novels using shifting first-person/third-person points-of-view.

After graduating from the University of Wisconsin in 1934, Ballinger moved to New York and worked in advertising and radio. His first pair of novels, *The Body in the Bed* (1948) and *The Body Beautiful* (1949), feature Chicago-based private detective, Barr Breed. The Breed novels are good examples of the postwar hardboiled dick, but Ballinger had not yet created his multiple-viewpoints technique.

Three novels often cited as being notable examples of Ballinger's shifting narrative technique are *Portrait in Smoke* (1950, a.k.a. *The Deadlier Sex*), *The Tooth and the Nail* (1955) and *The Wife of the Red-Haired Man* (1957).

In *Portrait in Smoke*, Danny April, the owner of a collection agency, comes across an old photo of a local beauty queen named Krassy Almauniski. Danny falls in love with Krassy's image and becomes obsessed with tracking her down. The first-person chapters tell the story of Danny's search, starting in the Chicago slums where Krassy grew up, and leading him up the socio-economic ladder, eventually to the world of the Chicago opera. The third-person chapters tell the story of Krassy's rise from rags to riches, and the nastiness involved in that rise, which results in Danny's discovery that Krassy might not be as sweet and innocent as he had believed. *Portrait in Smoke* was filmed in 1956 as *Wicked As They Come*, starring Philip Carey and Arlene Dahl.

In *The Tooth and the Nail*, the first-person chapters are about magician Lew Mountain's vengeance-seeking search for his wife's killer. The third-person chapters are about the killer's murder trial; the identity of the accused is withheld from the reader until the end.

In *The Wife of the Red-Haired Man*, a woman's first husband (previously thought dead) kills the woman's second husband. The woman and her first husband flee together, with a police detective in hot pursuit. The first-person chapters are from the police detective's point-of-view, and take us on his journey to track down the couple. The third-person chapters detail the couples' efforts to remain free.

Later in his career, Ballinger created a half-Spanish, half-Native American CIA agent named Joaquin Hawks. The Hawks novels are adventure tales set in exotic locales such as Indonesia, Bangkok and Saigon. Titles include *The Chinese Mask* (1965), *The Spy in Bangkok* (1965) and *The Spy in the Java Sea* (1966).

Ballinger wrote teleplays for *Alfred Hitchcock Presents, The Outer Limits, Ironside, Cannon* and *Kolchak: The Night Stalker*, among others. He won an Edgar award from the Mystery Writers of America in 1960, for his TV adaptation of the Stanley Ellin short story "The Day of the Bullet," which was shown on *Alfred Hitchcock Presents*.

In later years, Ballinger was Associate Professor of Writing, California State University, Northridge (1977-1979).

**Further Reading:**
*Barr Breed series (complete):*
THE BODY IN THE BED (1948)
THE BODY BEAUTIFUL (1949)

PORTRAIT IN SMOKE (1950)
THE DARKENING DOOR (1952)
RAFFERTY (1953)
THE TOOTH AND THE NAIL (1955)
THE LONGEST SECOND (1957)
THE WIFE OF THE RED-HAIRED MAN (1957)
FORMULA FOR MURDER (1958)
NOT I, SAID THE VIXEN (1965)
THE SOURCE OF FEAR (1968)
THE LOPSIDED MAN (1969)

*Joaquin Hawks series (complete):*
THE CHINESE MASK (1965)
THE SPY IN BANGKOK (1965)
THE SPY IN THE JUNGLE (1965)
THE SPY AT ANGKOR WAT (1966)
THE SPY IN THE JAVA SEA (1966)

---

**If you like Bill S. Ballinger,** you might like: Helen Nielsen, Milton K. Ozaki

# Ann Bannon

(born Ann Weldy). Born in Joliet, Illinois, 1932.

Ann Bannon was an early paperback pioneer—a lesbian who wrote lesbian-themed books for lesbians. That might sound redundant, but throughout the 1950's and '60's, most of the paperbacks about lesbians were written by heterosexual men *for* heterosexual men—packaged and marketed to provide titillation, as well as a voyeuristic look into (as the salacious cover copy liked to whisper) the "forbidden world" of the "third sex."

Bannon experienced a traditional upbringing and attended the University of Illinois at Champaign-Urbana, graduating with a degree in French. In spite of feeling "different" during her childhood, and beginning to recognize her own sexuality while in college, Bannon was married during the 1950's, and went on to have two children.

In the early 1950's, Bannon read lesbian author Vin Packer's (real name Marijane Meaker) novel, *Spring Fire* (1952)—a story about two sorority sisters who fall in love. The novel struck a chord in Bannon and she wrote a letter to Meaker, asking for advice about how she might get her own story of a lesbian love affair published. Meaker invited Bannon to New York and introduced her to Gold Medal editor, Richard Carroll. He read Bannon's clunky, elephantine, 600 page rough draft—a story about various women in Bannon's sorority whom she admired—and advised her to edit the manuscript and focus on a subplot concerning the relationship of two sorority sisters. Bannon took Carroll's advice, and when she re-submitted the book, Gold Medal accepted it and published it without changing a word. Titled *Odd Girl Out* (1957), the story focused on the love affair between sorority sisters, Beth (the older, more experienced of the two) and Laura (the younger, less worldly-wise). At the story's end, Beth decides on a heterosexual relationship with an earlier college sweetheart. Endings like this were the norm for homosexual-themed books during the 1950's— in order for the books not to be banned as pornography, one of the two characters had to either go crazy, turn "straight," or commit suicide.

Bannon's next novel, *I Am a Woman* (1959), introduced Bannon's series character, a "butch" lesbian named Beebo Brinker. Beebo was smart, strong, experienced and independent. In the story, Laura (who, at the end of *Odd Girl Out*, has decided to move to New York to find her place in the world) experiences the homosexual lifestyle of Greenwich Village, and begins an intense relationship with Beebo. In *Women In the Shadows* (1959), Laura experiences conflict in her relationship with Beebo and marries a homosexual friend named Jack; the novel also tackles the subjects of interracial relationships and gay and lesbian parenthood. *Beebo Brinker* (1962), a "prequel" to *Odd Girl Out*, introduces a young Beebo, arriving in New York fresh off the bus from Wisconsin. Beebo meets Jack (from previous Bannon novels), who introduces her to the gay bars of Greenwich Village. She falls in love with an in-the-closet movie star named Venus Bogardus and travels with Venus to California, but must stay hidden behind Venus's pseudo-heterosexual lifestyle. Beebo eventually rejects this role, and returns to New York and the lifestyle where she can stay true to her sexual identity.

Throughout the 1950's, '60's and '70's, Bannon remained married, but her novels and inner turmoil sparked constant battles with her husband. She finally divorced in the early 1980's.

Ann Bannon stopped writing novels in 1962 to pursue a doctorate in linguistics from Stanford University. She became a professor and eventually an associate dean at California State University, Sacramento. During the late 1990's, a resurgence of interest in Bannon's novels began. Excerpts were included in numerous lesbian fiction anthologies, and serious critical attention was given to her work. In 1997, Bannon retired from teaching and began touring the country, visiting paperback-collecting shows and lecturing at universities about her writings and experiences.

**Further Reading:**
ODD GIRL OUT (1957)
I AM A WOMAN (1959)
WOMEN IN THE SHADOW (1959)
JOURNEY TO A WOMAN (1960)
BEEBO BRINKER (1962)

---

If you like Ann Bannon, you might like: Vin Packer, Patricia Highsmith

# Robert Leslie Bellem

(also wrote as Ellery Watson Calder, Walt Bruce, Franklin Charles, Anthony Gordon, John Grange, Jerome Severs Perry, John A. Saxon, Harley L. Court, Nelson Kent, Hugh McKnight, Kenneth A. Nelson, Harcourt Weems). Born in Philadelphia, Pennsylvania, 1902. Died in Los Angeles, California, 1968.

Robert Leslie Bellem's breezy, "spicy" Dan Turner pulp tales were the precursors to Richard S. Prather's series of sexy paperback novels featuring Shell Scott, as well as the paperback mysteries of Carter Brown.

Bellem was inspired by crime fighting heroes when young–his father was a tough, no-nonsense railroad detective. Beginning in the 1920's Bellem worked as a newspaperman all over the United States: Philadelphia, Atlantic City, Miami, Tulsa, Albuquerque; he finally wound up in Santa Monica, California, where he found work as a movie extra.

Between Dan Turner's first appearance in *Spicy Detective* in April, 1934, and his final appearance in *Hollywood Detective* in 1950, Turner was featured in more than two hundred stories. His stories appeared in every issue of *Spicy Detective* from 1934 to 1947, and also had his own magazine, *Dan Turner, Hollywood Detective*, during the 1940's. The Spicy line of pulp magazines also included *Spicy Mystery*, *Spicy Adventure* and *Spicy Western*. The text of their stories was accompanied by illustrations of beautiful girls constantly wrestling to keep on their flimsy clothing. In terms of content, there aren't many characters with a larger libido and a more salacious eye than the hero in a Spicy story; no matter how desperate his mission, he always has time to pause for an amorous interlude with a beautiful woman.

Prose style is everything in a Dan Turner story. While the character of Turner differs little from hundreds of hard-boiled dicks, Bellem has invented an endless amount of linguistic idiosyncrasies for his hero. Guns don't fire–they bark, cough, sneeze and belch. Women are "wrens," "frills," "frails" and "cupcakes." The act of murder is "killery," "bumpery" and "croakery."

As for Dan's favorite items? His preferred nomenclature is "perky pretty-pretties," "creamy bon-bons," "thems and thoses," "tiddlywinks" or "whatchacallems." The Turner stories take place in a 1930's B-movie, alternate-universe version of Hollywood, populated by fictional studios such as Titanic, Paravox, Paratone and Supertone, and by characters who sport alliteration-laden names such as Constance Calvert, Roland Ruthvan, Lola Lawrence, Stan Sweetson, Maizie Murdock and Dixie Dunnagan.

In a career that spanned more than twenty-five years, Bellem cranked out more than three thousand stories in every conceivable pulp genre, under both his own name and an assortment of pseudonyms. He also wrote several novels, among them two under his own name, *Blue Murder* (1938) and *The Window with the Sleeping Nude* (1950), and three in collaboration with Cleve F. Adams, *The Vice Czar Murders* (1941, as by Franklin Charles), *No Wings on a Cop* (1950, as by Adams), and *Shady Lady* (1955, as by Adams).

When the pulps died out in the early 1950's, Bellem wrote scripts for TV shows such as *The Lone Ranger*, *The Adventures of Superman*, *Captain Midnight*, *Dick Tracy* and *77 Sunset Strip*.

**Further Reading:**
BLUE MURDER (1938)
THE VICE CZAR MURDERS (1941; as Franklin Charles; with Cleve F. Adams)
HALF-PAST MORTEM (1947, as John A. Saxon)
THE WINDOW WITH THE SLEEPING NUDE (1950)
NO WINGS ON A COP (1950, expanded from a story by Cleve F. Adams)
SHADY LADY (1955; expanded from a story by Cleve F. Adams; with W. T. Ballard)

---

**If you like Robert Leslie Bellem,** you might like: Carter Brown, Richard S. Prather

# A. I. "Buzz" Bezzerides

(born Albert Isaac Bezzerides, also wrote as Al Bezzerides). Born in Samsum, Turkey, 1908. Emigrated to Fresno, California while an infant. Died in Los Angeles, California, 2007.

This is the story of two men named Bezzerides.

First there's the story of Buzz Bezzerides the writer. Bezzerides wrote three novels: *The Long Haul* (1938), the story of brothers Nick and Paul Benay, independent truckers who work long hours for little pay, shuttling goods between Oakland and Los Angeles, routinely getting ripped off by shady bosses; *There is a Happy Land* (1942), the story of Vern Cope, who's fed-up with his grueling job as a migrant laborer, and yearns for a place where, as the song says, "It's summertime, and the living is easy"; and *Thieves' Market* (1949), the story of Nick Garcos's effort to avoid the fate of his recently deceased father, who had worked back-breaking jobs in produce markets for corrupt bosses who paid nickels-and-dimes.

Bezzerides also wrote the screenplays for a number of classic film noirs (*On Dangerous Ground*, *Kiss Me Deadly* and his own adaptation of *Thieves' Market*, renamed *Thieves' Highway*), and was the co-creator of TV's long-running show, *The Big Valley*.

And then there's the story of Buzz Bezzerides the fighter.

The story of Buzz Bezzerides the fighter is the story of Buzz Bezzerides in Hollywood. It's a story that exposes the same kind of corrupt and conniving bosses that Bezzerides wrote about in his novels. It's a story that names the names. That's down and dirty. A story that might be called Tinseltown Confidential.

On producers:

"Writers never understand: producers are the goddamndest crooks you ever saw. And they think that writing is *shit*." ("The Thieves Market: A. I. Bezzerides In Hollywood," article and interview by Lee Server, *The Big Book of Noir*, page 116)

"The writers eat at their own table. They didn't like to associate with producers. Nobody wanted them around, picking your brain. They'd take your ideas. Even take your conversation. I remember one day at the writers' table sitting next to [producer] Jerry Wald. I was working with him and we were talking about [Bezzerides' script idea] and Wald says, 'Jesus Christ, Buzz, that's a cliché.' And I say, 'Jerry, everything is a cliché. You're born, you live, die, all clichés. It's what you do with the clichés that's important.' A couple weeks later at the writers' table, somebody's talking about a meeting with Jerry Wald. Jerry wants some old bit in the script, and the writer told him it's the oldest cliché in the book. And what did Jerry say? 'Life's a cliché! You're born, you live...' That's a producer for you." (Ibid., pg. 117)

"[Jack] Warner boasted, "I've got the best writer in the world [William Faulkner], and I pay him peanuts." (*Heartbreak and Vine: The Fate of Hardboiled Writers In Hollywood*, by Woody Haut, pg. 166)

On studio shenanigans:

"I wrote a book about truckers called *The Long Haul*. Warner Bros. wanted to buy it... And we went to see Mark Hellinger, the producer. As we walked into his office, Hellinger took something off the table and put it underneath something else. I saw the title, *They Drive By Night*... Then I read in the trades that Warner Bros. is making a picture about truckers and so forth, based on *The Long Haul*, and its going into production. So that's when I find out that they'd already done a script. Jerry Wald's written *They Drive By Night* using my novel and using the ending of another story, *Bordertown*. They used it without my permission, before they even bought it." (*The Big Book of Noir*, page 116)

On being at the mercy of the higher-ups during the production of *Thieves' Highway*:

"Then the director, [Jules] Dassin says, 'For the [female lead], I want Valentina Cortesa, so rewrite it for her.' He was going with her... So we go to [20th Century Fox's production head, Darryl F. Zanuck's] office. He's got a yes-man standing there, lips puckered to kiss Zanuck's ass. And Zanuck goes like this—holds his hand out, and the flunky immediately puts a Coke in his hand... Now in my story the father is dead at the beginning. The kid starts trucking because he's trying to make his father's life valid. The first thing Zanuck says is, 'I want a new beginning. I want the father still alive. He's crippled, that's why the kid's trucking.' It was bullshit... The picture didn't do real well. There were good things in it, but it wasn't the story I wanted to do. I had the producer's chickenshit changes, the director's girlfriend, and Zanuck's ideas. I only knew that story from my life, my book, my script. But that didn't matter. Oh, I tell you, once you give in a little bit you're finished." (Ibid, page 121)

On being the low-man-on-the-totem pole in Hollywood:

"They don't listen to writers!" (*Heartbreak and Vine*, pg. 171)

Many years later, A. I. Bezzerides, the writer and the fighter, must have felt that at least he'd won a battle, if not the war, when director Robert Aldrich phoned him shortly before Aldrich died in 1983. "He told me he'd been wondering how the hell he had shot *Kiss Me Deadly* in 20 days. So he had taken out the script and reread it. He said, 'Now I know. It's all there. It's in the script.'" (*The Big Book of Noir*, pg. 122)

**Further Reading:**
THE LONG HAUL (1938; aka THEY DRIVE BY NIGHT)
THERE IS A HAPPY LAND (1942)
THIEVES' MARKET (1949)

---

**If you like A. I. Bezzerides,** you might like: Daniel Mainwaring, Mickey Spillane, Edward Anderson

# *Robert Bloch*

(also wrote as Tarleton Fiske, Collier Young). Born in Chicago, Illinois, 1917. Died
in Los Angeles, California, 1994.

 Robert Bloch was a master of macabre wit. Bloch best
characterized this approach himself with his oft-quoted
line, "I have the heart of a small boy; I keep it in a jar
on my desk." Equally adept at writing crime, horror, or
science fiction, Bloch is of course most well known for
his novel and its subsequent movie adaptation, *Psycho*.

Bloch's interest in fiction writing began early. He
started reading the classic fantasy/horror pulp *Weird*
*Tales* when he was ten years old, and a few years later, he wrote a letter to
one of *Tales'* premier writers, H.P. Lovecraft. Lovecraft was so impressed
with young Bloch's letter that he and Bloch corresponded with each other
for the next five years, starting in 1932 and lasting until Lovecraft's
untimely death in 1937. Bloch was only seventeen when he sold his first
short story to *Weird Tales*. His early short stories showed Lovecraft's influence, but Bloch quickly began to develop his own style, infusing many of
his horror stories with gallows humor and wicked wit.

Bloch wrote hundreds of short stories for the pulps between 1935-1947,
including stories for magazines such as *Weird Tales, Amazing, Strange Stories,*
*Dime Mystery Magazine* and *Thrilling Mystery*. He wrote his most well known
short story, "Yours Truly, Jack the Ripper," in 1943. "Ripper" is narrated by
John Carmody, a psychiatrist living in Chicago. John meets Sir Guy Hollis
of the British Embassy, who has a theory about the Ripper— Hollis
believes the Ripper did not grow old and is, in fact, living among them in
Chicago. Hollis enlists Carmody's help to prove his theory and capture the
killer. By the end of the story, Hollis discoverers whether his theory is true
or not. By this time in Bloch's career, his prose was almost completely
shorn of Lovecraft's winding, twisting sentence structure, as well as
Lovecraft's interest in ancient rites and primordial myths. Bloch had
developed his own style—more terse and direct, and his stories dealt with
matters contemporary and psychological.

During his apprenticeship writing short stories, Bloch worked for an
advertising agency as a copywriter, starting in 1943. He also wrote 39
episodes of a radio show called *Stay Tuned for Terror*, from 1944-1945, and
wrote gags for radio comedians, as well.

In 1947, Bloch published his first novel, *The Scarf*. It was a doozy. The
novel starts out with these lines: "Fetish? You name it. All I know is, I've
had to have it with me. Ever since I was a kid at Horton High, I had to
have it. Ever since..." The story is about Daniel Morley, who appears nor-

mal on the surface, but who has a peculiar way of using his red scarf when it comes to breaking up with girlfriends. Daniel decides to become a novelist and screenwriter but, unable to think up original stories, he writes about what he knows best—women he's strangled. The story is told in the first-person, from Daniel's point of view, and Bloch shows acute insight into the twisted highways and byways of Daniel's warped mind. *The Scarf* is widely considered one of Bloch's best novels.

Bloch's next notable book was *The Kidnaper*, published in 1954. The story is another chilling first-person narrative about a cold, clinical psychopath. Steve Collins is a small-time grifter who enlists his girlfriend to help him kidnap the young daughter of a wealthy industrialist for a large ransom. But Steve's unpredictable temper causes the child's death, and he desperately tries to continue the charade in hopes of still collecting the ransom. As with *The Scarf*, Bloch gives this story a surface of normality, and the sociopath's narrative voice is smooth and breezy, as if he could be your friendly neighborhood mailman.

And then came Norman Bates.

Actually, and then came Ed Gein, the man whose real life Bloch used to loosely base his novel *Psycho* (1959). Gein was a 40-year old farmer in Wisconsin who lived with his mother until she died in 1945. As a child, Gein's mother drilled it through his head that all women, except herself, were no better than prostitutes. She quoted passages from the Old Testament related to death and murder, and endlessly harangued young Gein about God's wrath and vengeance. After his mother died, he remained isolated on the remote farm for 12 more years. But in 1957, authorities discovered he had exhumed corpses from local graveyards and fashioned trophies and keepsakes from their bones and skin. Upon further investigation into Gein's farm, authorities found a recently-murdered woman, four noses, human skin used as furniture upholstery, a bowl made from a skull, a pair of lips on a string, and other perverse paraphernalia.

Bloch watched the case unfold on television and read about it in the newspapers, then weaved the tale of 50 year-old, overweight, shy and introverted Norman Bates, who ran the Bates Motel and lived in an old house on the property with his, uh, "mother." *Psycho* is narrated in the third person, but Bloch nevertheless shows the same insight into Bates's psychopathology that he showed in *The Scarf* and *The Kidnaper*.

And once Alfred Hitchcock, screenwriter Joseph Stefano, actor Anthony Perkins, and actress Janet Leigh got together to make the movie, the rest was history.

Bloch became very in-demand around Hollywood. He wrote *Straight-Jacket* (1964) and *The Night Walker* (1964) for frightmeister Willam Castle. He wrote scripts for Britain's Amicus horror anthology movies: *Torture Garden*

(1967), *The House That Dripped Blood* (1970) and *Asylum* (1972). He wrote numerous teleplays for *Alfred Hitchcock Presents*, *Thriller* and *Night Gallery*, among others.

Bloch was the recipient of a multitude of awards and honors during his lifetime. He was Guest of Honor at the World Science Fiction Convention in 1948. He won a Hugo Award in 1959, the Mystery Writers of America's Edgar Allan Poe award in 1960 and the World Fantasy Convention Award in 1975. From 1970-71 he served as the President of the Mystery Writers of America.

Pleasant dreams.

**Further Reading:**
THE SCARF (1947, as THE SCARF OF PASSION, 1948; revised edition, 1966)
THE KIDNAPPER (1954)
SPIDERWEB (1954)
THE WILL TO KILL (1954)
SHOOTING STAR (1958)
TERROR IN THE NIGHT AND OTHER STORIES (1958, short stories)
PSYCHO (1959)
THE DEAD BEAT (1960)
PLEASANT DREAMS–NIGHTMARES (1960, short stories; as NIGHTMARES, 1961)
FIREBUG (1961)
THE COUCH (1962, movie novelization)
YOURS TRULY, JACK THE RIPPER: TALES OF HORROR (1962, short stories)
ATOMS AND EVIL (1962, short stories)
THE EIGHTH STAGE OF FANDOM: SELECTIONS FROM 25 YEARS OF FAN WRITING (1962, non-fiction)
TALES IN A JUGULAR VEIN (1965, short stories)
THE STAR STALKER (1968)
FEAR TODAY–GONE TOMORROW (1971, short stories)
NIGHT-WORLD (1972)
THE KING OF TERRORS (1977, short stories)
SUCH STUFF AS SCREAMS ARE MADE OF (1979, short stories)
PSYCHO II (1982)
PSYCHO HOUSE (1990)
ONCE AROUND THE BLOCH (1993, autobiography)

If you like Robert Bloch, you might like: Fredric Brown, Cornell Woolrich, William Lindsay Gresham

# Lawrence Block

(also wrote as B. L. Lawrence, Benjamin Morse, Jill Emerson, Sheldon Lord, Andrew Shaw, John Warren Wells, Lee Duncan, Paul Kavanagh, Chip Harrison, William Ard, Ben Christopher, Ann Campbell Clarke, Liz Crowley, Lesley Evans, John Dexter, Don Holliday). Born in Buffalo, New York in 1938.

MWA Grandmaster Lawrence Block has a career, much like friend and contemporary Donald E. Westlake, that perfectly bridges the world of the paperback original novel and contemporary hardcover crime fiction. From paperback sleaze to standalone novels to the creation of no fewer than *five* different series, from numerous short stories to essays and books about the writing process, Block has done it all, and done it well, for more than fifty years.

Starting with the soft-core *Carla* (Midwood, 1958), Block wrote similar books for about a decade. Interspersed with these were standalone crime and adventure novels such as *The Specialists* (1960), *Mona* (1961) and *The Girl With the Long Green Heart* (1966), but it was with his series books that he has become so popular. In 1966 Block published the first of his Evan Tanner series, based on an adventurer who had lost the ability to sleep when shrapnel damaged the sleep center of his brain during the Korean War. *The Thief Who Couldn't Sleep* (1966) kicked off the series of eight books (with 28 years elapsing between the seventh and eighth books) and has Tanner heading off to Turkey in search of a hidden cache of gold. The second to last book, *Me Tanner, You Jane* (1970), has Tanner in a newly created African country attempting to track the missing ruler, recently absconded with the nation's treasury.

This same year Block began his second series, writing under the name "Chip Harrison," which also turned out to be the name of the books' hero. The books have the slightly suggestive and juvenile names like *No Score* (1970), *Chip Harrison Scores Again* (1971), *Make Out With Murder* (1974) and *The Topless Tulip Caper* (1975). The series started out with a young, aroused Chip constantly trying to gain experience with the opposite sex, and gradually morphed into a sort of Rex Stout/Nero Wofe pastiche with Chip playing the part of Wolfe's Archie after he went to work for a private detective.

In 1976 we get *The Sins of the Father* (1976), the much more mature beginning to what is arguably Block's most popular and significant series, indeed, what has to be a serious contender for the best PI series ever written. The Matt Scudder books feature a former policeman who is also a committed alcoholic, as he scrapes through life after a tragedy on the job took an innocent life. Passing time through a succession of bars and after-hours joints, Scudder becomes something of an unlicensed private investigator, a man who does favors for people who tend to reward him with cash when he's through.

As interesting as the stories and mysteries are themselves, it's the character of Scudder who is the real star. He has his friends, like saloon-keeper Mick Ballou, once rumored to carry a rival's severed head around in a bowling ball bag, and Elaine, a local prostitute who helps tether him to life outside of booze. Along with Scudder's guilt, the early books take us through his struggles with cases as he occasionally suffers blackouts and beatings, as he visits neighborhood churches, faithfully tithing his unofficial "fees." Scudder ages as the series goes on, eventually going from binges to AA meetings while still meeting the challenges of living his old life, maintaining his old friends, and trying to forgive himself for his past.

The fifth Scudder novel, *8 Million Ways To Die* (1982) was made into a film of the same name starring Jeff Bridges, Rosanna Arquette and Andy Garcia. It was director Hal Ashby's last feature film and had a screenplay written by Oliver Stone. Unfortunately, the location was changed from New York City to Los Angeles and the story became somewhat muddled in the process. The tenth entry, 1992's *A Walk Among the Tombstones*, is currently being filmed on location in New York and stars Liam Neeson as Scudder.

*Burglars Can't Be Choosers* (1977) was the first entry in Block's "burglar" series about bookseller Bernie Rhodenbarr. Much like friend and sometimes collaborator Donald E. Westlake's dual-natured creations (the ultra-hardboiled Parker—in his series written as by Richard Stark—and his lighter, comicly styled Dortmunder series), Block's Rhodenbarr is a thief for hire whose jobs never quite seem to go as planned. Where the Scudder books capture the grit and grime of the streets of New York, the Rhodenbarr books take place among the lights and the posh because, of course, that's where the things worth stealing are. There are currently thirteen "burglar" books. In 1987, Bernie was turned into "Bernice" Rhodenbarr in the Hugh Wilson-directed Whoopi Goldberg vehicle, *Burglar*.

Beginning in 1998, Block brought out a new series regular, the stamp-collecting assassin-for-hire named John Paul Keller. Keller lives a quiet, solitary kind of life until every so often the phone rings and he's given an assignment from a person in White Plains…. The run begins with *Hit Man* (1998) and is actually a series of interconnected short stories. Perhaps even more so than with Matt Scudder or Bernie Rhodenbarr, the Keller books' charm lies with the characteristics of their protagonist. Keller leads a quiet, unassuming life, sees a psychiatrist as he copes with the violent side of his nature, collects his stamps and finds pleasures in the physical aspects of the towns that he visits on his assignments. Block is able to keep Keller, a man who kills people for a living, a sympathetic and interesting character.

In addition to the standalone novels and series novels, Block has also written a number of short stories about attorney Martin Ehrengraf, a man willing to use any trick he can find to get his clients off the hook. Many of these were collected in book form in 1994's *Ehrengraf for the Defense*. As John Warren Wells, Block gave us a number of short novels supposedly based on actual psychological case files concerning different sorts of sexual adventures. And in 2002, 84 of Block's short stories were collected in the massive compilation, *Enough Rope*.

In recent years, Block has not only acknowledged his authorship of his early soft core books, he has allowed and encouraged their publication, often in hardcover limited print editions. In 2010 Subterranean Press published an omnibus edition of Block's and Westlake's sleaze collaborations called *Hellcats and Honeygirls*. Also in 2010, Creeping Hemlock Press brought out "Andrew Shaw's" first book, *Campus Tramp*. In 2011 Hard Case Crime released *Getting Off*, a new book written as by Jill Emerson, another of Block's bylines from his softcore days. And again by Hard Case Crime, in 2012 they released a "double" version of books as by "Sheldon Lord" and "Ben Christopher": *Strange Embrace/69 Barrow Street*. Embracing the digital movement, Block has also been active in releasing virtually his entire backlist in electronic format.

Having tried to retire from writing and failing on several occasions, Block is nonetheless still producing books today, well into his seventies.

**Further reading:**

CARLA (1958)

CANDY (1960)

THE SPECIALISTS (1960)

$20 LUST (1961)

THE CASE OF THE PORNOGRAPHIC PHOTOS (1961)

DEATH PULLS A DOUBLECROSS (1961)

MONA (1961)

SIN HELLCAT (1962)

A MADWOMAN'S DIARY (1962)

WARM AND WILLING (1964)

ENOUGH OF SORROW (1965)

THE GIRL WITH THE LONG GREEN HEART (1965)

DEADLY HONEYMOON (1967)

AFTER THE FIRST DEATH (1969)

SUCH MEN ARE DANGEROUS (1969)

THREESOME (1970)

THIRTY (1970)

THE TRIUMPH OF EVIL (1971)

A GIRL CALLED HONEY (1960)

A STRANGE KIND OF LOVE (1960)

KEPT (1960)

RONALD RABBIT IS A DIRTY OLD MAN (1971)
SENSUOUS (1972)
THE TROUBLE WITH EDEN (1973)
NOT COMIN' HOME TO YOU (1974)
A WEEK AS ANDREA BENSTOCK (1975)
ARIEL (1979)
CODE OF ARMS (1982)
INTO THE NIGHT (1987)
RANDOM WALK (1988)
THE PERFECT MURDER (1991)
THE LOST CASES OF ED LONDON (2001)
SMALL TOWN (2002)
TERROR'S ECHO (2005)
LUCKY AT CARDS (2007)
A DIET OF TREACLE (2008)
KILLING CASTRO (2009)
APRIL NORTH (2010)
COMMUNITY OF WOMEN (2010)
GETTING OFF (2011)
STRANGE EMBRACE/69 BARROW STREET (2012)

*Evan Tanner series (complete):*
THE THIEF WHO COULDN'T SLEEP (1966)
THE CANCELLED CZECH (1966)
TANNER'S TWELVE SWINGERS (1967)
TWO FOR TANNER (1967)
TANNER'S TIGER (1968)
HERE COMES A HERO (1968)
ME TANNER, YOU JANE (1970)
TANNER ON ICE (1998)

*Chip Harrison series (complete):*
NO SCORE (1970)
CHIP HARRISON SCORES AGAIN (1971)
MAKE OUT WITH MURDER (1974)
THE TOPLESS TULIP CAPER (1975)

*Matt Scudder series (complete):*
THE SINS OF THE FATHER (1976)
IN THE MIDST OF DEATH (1976)
TIME TO MURDER AND CREATE (1977)
A STAB IN THE DARK (1981)
EIGHT MILLION WAYS TO DIE (1982)

WHEN THE SACRED GINMILL CLOSES (1986)
OUT ON THE CUTTING EDGE (1989)
A TICKET TO THE BONEYARD (1990)
A DANCE AT THE SLAUGHTERHOUSE (1991)
A WALK AMONG THE TOMBSTONES (1992)
THE DEVIL KNOWS YOU'RE DEAD (1993)
A LONG LINE OF DEAD MEN (1994)
EVEN THE WICKED (1996)
EVERYBODY DIES (1998)
HOPE TO DIE (2001)
ALL THE FLOWERS ARE DYING (2005)
A DROP OF THE HARD STUFF (2011)

*Bernie Rhodenbarr series (complete):*
BURGLARS CAN'T BE CHOOSERS (1977)
THE BURGLAR IN THE CLOSET (1978)
THE BURGLAR WHO LIKED TO QUOTE KIPLING (1979)
THE BURGLAR WHO STUDIED SPINOZA (1980)
THE BURGLAR WHO PAINTED LIKE MONDRIAN (1983)
LIKE A THIEF IN THE NIGHT (1983)
THE BURGLAR WHO DROPPED IN ON ELVIS (1990)
THE BURGLAR WHO TRADED TED WILLIAMS (1994)
THE BURGLAR WHO THOUGHT HE WAS BOGART (1995)
THE BURGLAR IN THE LIBRARY (1997)
THE BURGLAR WHO SMELLED SMOKE (1997)
THE BURGLAR IN THE RYE (1999)
THE BURGLAR ON THE PROWL (2004)

*Keller series (complete):*
HIT MAN (1998)
HIT LIST (2000)
HIT PARADE (2006)
HIT AND RUN (2008)
HIT ME (2013)

*Short story collections:*
ENOUGH ROPE (2002)
ONE NIGHT STANDS AND LOST WEEKENDS (2008)

---

**If you like Lawrence Block,** you might like: Donald E. Westlake, Ed McBain/Evan Hunter

# Leigh Brackett

(also wrote as George Sanders). Born in Los Angeles, California, 1915. Died in Lancaster, California, 1978.

 When director Howard Hawks was looking for a writer to collaborate with William Faulkner on the screenplay adaptation of Raymond Chandler's *The Big Sleep*, he remembered a tough, hardboiled crime novel he had recently read—*No Good from a Corpse*, written by Leigh Brackett. Assuming the author to be a man, Hawks told his secretary, "Get this guy, Brackett." When the "guy" appeared in Hawks's office, the movie director was surprised to discover that Brackett was "a rather attractive girl who looked like she had just come from a tennis match. She looked as if she wrote poetry." (*Heartbreak and Vine: The Fate of Hardboiled Writers in Hollywood*, by Woody Haut, pg. 193)

Leigh Brackett was born in Los Angeles, California, and grew up in Santa Monica. As a teenager, she read science fiction and adventure pulps—favorite writers included Edgar Rice Burroughs, Robert E. Howard and C(atherine) L.(ucille) Moore.

Brackett sold her first short story, "Martian Quest," to *Astounding Science Fiction* in 1940. She wrote scores of stories for pulps such as *Super-Science Stories*, *Planet Stories* and *Comet Stories*. Her tales were sword-and-sorcery swashbucklers with titles like "The Dragon-Queen of Jupiter," "Interplanetary Reporter," "The Vanishing Venusians," and "Teleportress of Alpha C." They were short on "hard science" and long on vivid action—which was the way her readers liked them.

Brackett admired the work of Raymond Chandler and in 1944, she wrote her own Chandleresque mystery novel, the aforementioned *No Good from a Corpse*. In the story, private detective Edmond Clive searches Los Angeles to find the killer of an ex-girlfriend. Along the way, he contends with rich and spoiled playboys, a blackmailer, various thugs and a progressively mounting number of corpses. The novel successfully captured Chandler's portrayal of a world-weary knight, as well as the tone of his lyrical, evocative prose:

> "She was wearing a white raincoat with the hood thrown back. There were raindrops caught in her long black hair, but the drops in her thick lashes never came out of a Los Angeles sky."

Brackett's other crime-oriented novels include *Stranger at Home* (1946, ghost-written for actor George Sanders), a story about Hollywood resident Michael Vickers, who disappears for four years, is presumed dead, and returns to find his would-be killer or killers; *An Eye for an Eye* (1957, which later became the basis for the TV series, *Markham*), the story of a bitter, divorced man who kidnaps his ex-wife's lawyer for revenge; and the crime novel many critics believe is Brackett's best, *The Tiger Among Us* (1957), the story of mild-mannered suburbanite Walter Sherris, who becomes an enraged, vengeance-seeking vigilante after being robbed and brutally beaten by a gang of juvenile delinquents. *The Tiger Among Us* was filmed in 1962, its title changed to *13 West Street*; it starred Alan Ladd.

Throughout her career, Brackett continued to devote her writing to science fiction. *The Starmen* (1952) chronicles the adventures of the only race able to endure interstellar travel. In *The Sword of Rhiannon* (1953), an archaeologist's discovery of the mythical Sword of Rhiannon sends him back in time to the planet Mars, where he becomes a barbarian gladiator. *The Long Tomorrow* (1955) is set in a fascist, post-apocalyptic America where scientific knowledge is forbidden.

In Hollywood, Brackett became one of Howard Hawks's favorite screenwriters. Ironically, this "rather attractive girl" who "looked like she wrote poetry" worked on the screenplays for several of Hawks's action-packed, male bonding movies: *Rio Bravo* (1959, starring John Wayne, Dean Martin and Ricky Nelson), *Hatari!* (1962, starring Wayne and an ensemble cast) and *El Dorado* (1966, starring Wayne, Robert Mitchum and James Caan).

Brackett dealt with Raymond Chandler's material again, twenty-seven years after *The Big Sleep*, when she wrote the screenplay for director Robert Altman's adaptation of *The Long Goodbye* (1973, starring Elliot Gould and Sterling Hayden; opinions are fiercely divided by Chandler fans as to this adaptation's merit).

Brackett's last work was on the screenplay for *The Empire Strikes Back* (1980, released posthumously).

Quite a list of accomplishments for the girl "who looked like she had just come from a tennis match."

Further Reading:
NO GOOD FROM A CORPSE (1944)
STRANGER AT HOME (1946, ghost written for George Sanders)
THE STARMEN (1952)                    THE SWORD OF RHIANNON (1953)
THE BIG JUMP (1955)                   THE LONG TOMORROW (1955)
THE TIGER AMONG US (1957)             AN EYE FOR AN EYE (1957)
RIO BRAVO (1959, movie novelization)
THE COMING OF THE TERRANS (1967, short stories)
THE BEST OF LEIGH BRACKETT (1977, short stories)

---

If you like Leigh Brackett, you might like: Raymond Chandler, Helen Nielsen

# *Malcolm Braly*

Born in Portland, Oregon, 1925. Died Baltimore, Maryland, 1980.

 Malcolm Braly—along with Iceberg Slim, Eddie Bunker and Al Nussbaum—was one of a handful of real-life ex-cons who found success as a crime novelist.

Abandoned by his parents at a young age, Braly was shuffled between foster homes and reform schools. When he was eighteen years old he was convicted for a series of burglaries, and spent the next twenty years in and out of prisons such as Folsom and San Quentin.

Braly's first three novels were written while he was still in prison, and were published by Gold Medal. Knox Burger, Gold Medal's editor at the time, believed Braly's life was salvageable, and he wrote letters to the young convict, praising his talent and encouraging him to stay on the straight-and-narrow once he got paroled.

Braly's first book was *Felony Tank* (1961). The front cover blurb reads: "This is what it's like to be thrown in jail for the first time, to grow up hard and cool almost overnight, in the gray metal guts of the FELONY TANK." *Felony Tank* won the Mystery Writers of America's prestigious Edgar award for best first novel.

*Shake Him Till He Rattles* (1963), Braly's second book, is set in the world of beatniks, vagabonds and jazz players in San Francisco. In this atmosphere of free-flowing narcotics, ex-con and current sax player Lee Cabiness finds himself the prey of narcotics officer Lieutenant Carver. Carver becomes obsessed with the idea that Cabiness alone is responsible for this permissive new atmosphere, and the lieutenant relentlessly stalks Cabiness, trying to destroy him by any means necessary.

After Braly's parole, he moved to New York and worked for Knox Burger at Gold Medal. He started off organizing files, was promoted to manuscript reader, and was eventually made associate editor—all in the space of four months.

*On the Yard* (1967) is considered Braly's classic by many critics. Set in prison, the book's main two characters are "Chilly" Willy, a violent offender who bosses the prison's black market in drugs, and Paul, a man torn apart by his conscience for the murder of his wife. The *Publishers Weekly* reviewer wrote: "The expertly drawn ensemble cast and institutional insight may remind readers of *One Flew Over the Cuckoo's Nest*—Braly does for prisons what Kesey did for the insane asylum." *On the Yard* was successfully filmed in 1978. Braly wrote the screenplay.

Braly's final book was autobiographical: *False Starts: A Memoir of San Quentin and Other Prisons* (1973), details how Braly's years in prison trained him to be institutionalized and to have trouble adjusting to life outside the walls.

Unfortunately, Braly had been out of prison only fifteen years when he was killed in a car accident.

**Further Reading:**
FELONY TANK (1961)
SHAKE HIM TILL HE RATTLES (1963)
IT'S COLD OUT THERE (1966)
ON THE YARD (1967)
THE MASTER (1973, movie novelization of *Lady Ice*)
FALSE STARTS: A MEMOIR OF SAN QUENTIN AND OTHER PRISONS (1973, autobiography)
THE PROTECTOR (1979, movie novelization)

---

**If you like Malcolm Braly,** you might like: W. R. Burnett, Eddie Bunker, John Bright

# *Gil Brewer*

(also wrote under the names Al Conroy (with Marvin Albert), Eric Fitzgerald, Bailey Morgan, Elaine Evans, Morgana Hill, Marc Mixer, Dee Laye, Alex Sexton, Viola Vixen, Anita Sultry, Connie Everett, Luke Morgann, Billy Marks, Mark Bailey, Harry Arvay; ghosted for writers Day Keene, Ellery Queen, Hal Ellson, Don Pendleton). Born in Cauandaigua, New York, 1922. Died in St. Petersburg, Florida, 1983.

 Gil Brewer's life and career was a series of peaks and valleys. The noir master wrote more than fifty novels during his lifetime—at one point, five of his books were on the racks at once. But during another period, he didn't write a word for four years. He socialized with a large coterie of fellow writers while living in Florida, including Day Keene, Talmage Powell, Harry Whittington and Jonathan Craig; they talked fiction writing late into the night. But he was also a loner, shunning publicity, turning down interviews and other opportunities to promote his work. He once wrote a book in three days, and wrote another in five. But there were times when he sat at the typewriter, staring at blank paper, waiting for words that never came.

Brewer came from a poor background and was largely self-educated. He served overseas in the Army during World War II and afterwards worked in a gas station, canning factory and as a bookseller.

Brewer's paperback career started with a bang. His third novel, *13 French Street* (1951), sold over a million copies. The book tells a classic noir "triangle" story, involving Alex, Verne (Alex's sick Army buddy) and Verne's predatory wife, Petra. The book balances lean, terse prose with raw emotional power. Brewer also hit it big when he scored Capt. Joseph T. Shaw, renowned editor of *Black Mask* magazine during its heyday, as his literary agent.

Mystery writers and reviewers cite *The Red Scarf* (1958) and *A Killer is Loose* (1954) as two of Brewer's best paperbacks. In *The Red Scarf*, Roy Nichols, a motel owner desperately in need of money, hitches a ride with Noel Teece and Vivian Rise. While in the car, Roy learns about a briefcase full of money belonging to the Mob. The rest of the story is about Roy's attempts to keep the money for himself, while still running his motel. *A Killer is Loose* tells the story of Ralph Angers, an unhinged Korean War veteran. The narrator, Steve Logan, is a down-on-his-luck ex-cop who makes the mistake of saving Angers' life, thus becoming his buddy. When Angers goes on a killing spree in a quiet suburban neighborhood, Logan must track him down while keeping the surrounding community oblivious to the dangerous hunt taking place.

Brewer's other notable paperbacks include *Satan is a Woman* (1951), *The Brat* (1957), *Little Tramp* (1957), *The Vengeful Virgin* (1958), *Nude On Thin Ice* (1960) and *The Three-Way Split* (1960). As might be evident from some of these titles, Brewer specialized in the "femme fatale" and, similar to the novels of James M. Cain, showed the exhilarating yet destructive effects of the webs of lust and greed woven by these predatory women.

Gil Brewer waged a lifelong battle with the bottle. He was first hospitalized during the 1960's and throughout the decade, went through a cycle of recovering and backsliding. In 1970, he totalled his Porsche, sustaining severe injuries. Now Brewer not only had alcoholism to contend with, but an addiction to pain-killing medication, as well. Much of his time thereafter was spent in bed, recuperating and trying to write more novels. Most of his writing during that time was rejected as unmarketable, though he was able to sell some "sleaze" novels for adults-only publishers, as well as find some ghostwriting assignments.

Brewer's health and finances continued to deteriorate, and he finally lost the battle in 1983.

**Further Reading:**

13 FRENCH STREET (1951)             SATAN IS A WOMAN (1951)
SO RICH, SO DEAD (1951)             FLIGHT TO DARKNESS (1952)
HELL'S OUR DESTINATION (1953)
A KILLER IS LOOSE (1954)
AND THE GIRL SCREAMED (1956)
THE ANGRY DREAM (1957, published as THE GIRL FROM HATEVILLE, 1958)
THE MOB SAYS MURDER (1958, as Albert Conroy)
THE BRAT (1957)                     LITTLE TRAMP (1957)
THE RED SCARF (1958)
THE VENGEFUL VIRGIN (1958)
WILD (1958)
WILD TO POSSESS (1959)
THE THREE-WAY SPLIT (1960)
BACKWOODS TEASER (1960)
NUDE ON THIN ICE (1960)
APPOINTMENT IN HELL (1961)
A TASTE OF SIN (1961)
MEMORY OF PASSION (1963)
THE HUNGRY ONE (1966)
SIN FOR ME (1967)
APPOINTMENT IN CAIRO (1970, TV novelization, *It Takes a Thief*)

---

**If you like Gil Brewer,** you might like: James M. Cain, Harry Whittington

## Carter Brown

(real name Alan Geoffrey Yates; also wrote as Tom Conway, Paul Valdez, Caroline Farr, Peter Carter Brown, Peter Carter-Brown, Raymond Glenning, Sinclair MacKellar, Dennis Sinclair). Born in London, England, 1923. Became Australian citizen in 1948. Died in Australia, 1985.

Along with Peter Cheyney, James Hadley Chase and Hank Janson, Carter Brown was one of the most successful overseas imitators of the American hardboiled crime story. He wrote scores of PBOs from 1953-1981, which sold in the tens of millions. Most of his books are set in or around Los Angeles—an area Brown never visited, but learned about from books and movies.

The Carter Brown paperbacks are light, breezy, humorous stories—a brief respite from the hyperbolically violent adventures of Mike Hammer and company. In a different way, the Carter Brown books follow directly in the footsteps of their American forefathers by including plenty of girls, girls, girls! In fact, no female is introduced in a Brown book without her breasts also being introduced and described in the same paragraph. The Brown paperbacks sold over ten million copies and he knocked-out over 150 of them using this formula. And no wonder. Girls, girls, girls—what a formula!

Before Yates could earn a living as a full time writer, he worked as a sound recorder for Gaumont-British films in London (1946-48), then worked in public relations for Qantas Airways in Sydney, Australia (1951-53). Early in his writing career, Yates wrote crime stories, horror and westerns for magazines such as *Thrills Incorporated* using the unlikely pen name of Tex Conrad. Yates's first book was published in 1953, *Venus Unarmed*. Initially published only in Australia, U.S. publisher New American Library soon brought Yates's stories to the states. For their U.S. releases, many of the Carter Brown book covers were lushly, lavishly and lasciviously illustrated by Barye Phillips and Robert McGinnis.

Yates wrote numerous series characters. Al Wheeler is a homicide lieutenant in Los Angeles. Rick Holman is a Hollywood private eye who often saves blackmailed film starlets. Larry Baker is a Hollywood script writer who becomes involved in the kind of bizarre cases that can only happen in faddish and fanatical Southern California. PI Mavis Seidlitz is described as "tops in the numbers game (38-23-37)" and a "sexpert in the art of self-defense."

Many of Brown's titles are puns or plays-on-words: *Lament for a Lousy Lover; Strip Without Tease; Blonde On the Rocks; Nude—With a View; Curves for the Coroner; Murder by Miss-Demeanor; Blonde, Beautiful and—Blam!; Hi-Jack for a Jill; A Corpse for Christmas; No Blonde is an Island.*

Yates was an intelligent and sophisticated man, and in the Carter Brown books he often mixes highbrow culture with lowbrow by referring to famous films, novels or works of art. (In *The Dame* he quotes John Keats.) He was also a family man, married to Denise Sinclair Mackellar; they had one daughter and three sons.

**Further Reading:**
*Danny Boyd series:*

CUTIE WINS A CORPSE (1957)          SIREN SIGNS OFF (1958)
TEMPT A TIGRESS (1958)               THE DREAM IS DEADLY (1960)
THE SAVAGE SALOME (1961)           NYMPH TO THE SLAUGHTER (1963)
THE BLACK LACE HANGOVER (1966)

*Rick Holman series:*
ZELDA (1961)
MURDER IN THE HARLEM CLUB (1962)
BLONDE ON THE ROCKS (1963)
THE WIND-UP DOLL (1965)
NUDE WITH A VIEW (1965)
THE GIRL FROM OUTER SPACE (1965)
BLONDE ON A BROOMSTICK (1966)
THE DEADLY KITTEN (1967)
A GOOD YEAR FOR DWARFS? (1970)

*Mavis Seidlitz series:*
HONEY, HERE'S YOUR HEARSE (1955)
A BULLET FOR MY BABY (1955)
THE LOVING AND THE DEAD (1959)
LAMENT FOR A LOUSY LOVER (1960)
THE BUMP AND GRIND MURDERS (1964)
SEIDLITZ AND THE SUPER-SPY (1967)
AND THE UNDEAD SING (1974)

*Al Wheeler series:*
THE CORPSE (1958)
THE LOVER (1959)
THE MISTRESS (1959)
THE WANTON (1959)
THE UNORTHODOX CORPSE (1961)

**If you like Carter Brown,** you might like: Michael Avallone, Henry Kane

## *Fredric Brown*

(also wrote as John S. Endicott, Felix Graham, Jack Hobart, Allen Morse, Bob Woehlke). Born in Cincinnati, Ohio, 1906. Died in Tucson, Arizona, 1972.

Fredric Brown was notable for his experimentation in the mystery and sci-fi genres. His stories contain multiple narrators, invented language, symbolism, allegory and paradoxes aplenty. His short stories, in particular, were noted for their ingenuity, and he wrote masterful surprise endings like a magician pulling rabbits out of a hat. Last, but certainly not least, was Brown's humor. Always, the humor.

Brown's writing career began in 1938. He wrote more than 200 stories for pulps such as *Black Mask, Thrilling Mystery, Detective Tales, Astounding Science Fiction, Unknown Worlds* and *Weird Tales,* among others. Some of his short story titles show off his penchant for word-play ("Pardon My Ghoulish Laughter," "A Little White Lye," "Compliments of a Fiend") and black humor ("Who Was That Blonde I Saw You Kill Last Night?", "I'll Slit Your Throat Again, Kathleen"). Despite a long roster of short story credits, it was still necessary for him to supplement his income, and he worked full time as a proofreader for the *Milwaukee Journal.*

Brown decided to take a crack at a full time writing career during the mid-1940's. He moved to New York and wrote *The Fabulous Clipjoint* (1947), a Chicago-set PI novel about the uncle-nephew team of Am (short for Ambrose) and Ed Hunter. When Ed's father is murdered, he and uncle Ambrose search for the killer, traveling through Chicago's underbelly of cheap bars, sleazy carnies, tempting tramps and an array of tough thugs. The book won the Edgar award from the Mystery Writers of America. Brown could now devote himself full time to writing.

Highlights among Brown's other crime-related novels include *The Screaming Mimi* (1948), a "Beauty and the Beast" allegory about a reporter's search for a Jack the Ripper-style killer (made into a noirish movie in 1948, starring Anita Ekberg); *Knock Three-One-Two* (1959), a story about a psychopathic killer told from eight different points-of-view; and *Night of the Jabberwock* (1950), the story of a hard-drinking newspaper editor who may or may not be involved in strange events straight out of *Alice in Wonderland.* Collections of Brown's criminous short stories include *Mostly Murder* (1953) and *The Shaggy Dog and Other Murders* (1963).

Among Brown's sci-fi novels, notable examples include *What Mad Universe* (1949), the story of sci-fi pulp editor Keith Winston, who experiences a parallel New York where aliens and humans are at war with each other; in *Martians, Go Home* (1955), a group of peeping-tom aliens disrupt daily life with their mischievous hijinks. Two excellent sci-fi short story collections are *Nightmares and Geezenstacks* (1961) and *Daymares* (1968).

During the 1950's, numerous short stories of Brown's were adapted for popular TV anthology shows such as *Tales of Tomorrow*, *Thriller* and *Alfred Hitchcock Presents*.

Brown moved to Taos, New Mexico, in the late forties due to respiratory problems. He had a heart attack in the early 1960's and was not able to do much writing up to his death in 1972.

A curio: novelist/philosopher Ayn Rand, author of *The Fountainhead* and *Atlas Shrugged*, was a fan of Brown's work, calling him "an unusually ingenious writer."

**Further Reading:**
*Ed and Am Hunter series (complete):*

| | |
|---|---|
| THE FABULOUS CLIPJOINT (1947) | THE DEAD RINGER (1948) |
| THE BLOODY MOONLIGHT (1949) | COMPLIMENTS OF A FIEND (1950) |
| DEATH HAS MANY DOORS (1951) | THE LATE LAMENTED (1959) |
| MRS. MURPHY'S UNDERPANTS (1963) | |

MURDER CAN BE FUN (1948; as A PLOT FOR MURDER, 1949)
THE SCREAMING MIMI (1949)
WHAT MAD UNIVERSE (1949)
HERE COMES A CANDLE (1950)
NIGHT OF THE JABBERWOCK (1951)
THE CASE OF THE DANCING SANDWICHES (1951)
THE FAR CRY (1951)
SPACE ON MY HANDS (1951, short stories)
THE DEEP END (1952)
WE ALL KILLED GRANDMA (1952)
MADBALL (1953)
MOSTLY MURDER (1953, short stories)
HIS NAME WAS DEATH (1954)
MARTIANS, GO HOME (1955)
THE LENIENT BEAST (1956)
ROGUE IN SPACE (1957)
THE OFFICE (1958)
HONEYMOON IN HELL (1958, short stories)
KNOCK THREE-ONE-TWO (1959)
THE FIVE-DAY NIGHTMARE (1962)
THE SHAGGY DOG AND OTHER MURDERS (1963, short stories)
DAYMARES (1968, short stories)

---

**If you like Fredric Brown,** you might like: Robert Bloch, Kendell Foster Crossen, Henry Kuttner

## Howard Browne

(also wrote as John Evans, Alexander Blade, Lawrence Chandler, Ivar Jorgensen, Lee Francis). Born in Omaha, Nebraska, 1908. Died in San Diego County, California, 1999.

Howard Browne, creator of Paul Pine, private eye, expressed his early affinity for pulp fiction thusly: "While my high school teachers were extolling the virtues and values of reading the classics, I was out behind the barn deep in *Flynn's Detective Weekly* and similar character-warping pulp magazine publications...The English mysteries, with their accent on clues instead of character, left me cold: the fact that 'Lady Van de Meers lorgnette was found four yards west of the sundial, proving the butler was in East Hampton on the night of the murder' might be fine for a puzzle buff, but not something designed to keep me up nights. In short, I'll take Raymond Chandler over Agatha Christie, Robert Parker over S.S. Van Dine. Any day." (*Twentieth-Century Crime & Mystery Writers*, pgs. 137-138)

All through Browne's life, even while not writing pulp fiction, he was working in some capacity within its sphere. From 1941-1951 he worked as managing editor, both in Chicago and New York, for the Ziff-Davis pulps (which published *Mammoth Detective, Mammoth Mystery, Amazing Stories* and *Fantastic Adventures*, among others). He wrote numerous short stories for these pulps, as well. For *Mammoth Detective*, he wrote about investigators with the unlikely names of Lafayette Muldoon (a real estate company troubleshoooter) and Wilbur Peddie (a bowler-wearing, polite-mannered skip tracer for the Tinsley Department Store).

While Hammett had Spade and the Op, and Chandler had Philip Marlowe, Browne's private dick was Paul Pine. Browne freely admits Chandler's influence: "The writing style of my first books was heavily influenced, to put it mildly, by Raymond Chandler... In fact, if there had been no 'Philip Marlowe' there could've been no 'Paul Pine.'" (*Twentieth-Century Crime & Mystery Writers*, pg. 138)

But Browne's Paul Pine was no mere imitation, no flat "two-dimensional" version that was all style and no substance. For example, Pine tackles cases revolving around subject matter Marlowe never touches: lesbianism in *Halo in Brass* and child molestation in *The Taste of Ashes*. There's also one other little item that made Paul Pine his own man: Browne was a hell of a writer. There were four completed Paul Pine novels. (A fifth, uncompleted novel, *The Paper Gun*, was published by Dennis McMillan, together with the only Paul Pine short story, "So Dark for April.") The first three (all written under the Evans pseudonym) were *Halo in Blood* (1946), *Halo for Satan* (1948) and *Halo in Brass* (1949). The fourth, *The Taste of Ashes* (1957, published under Browne's own name), was deeper, more complex, and the characters were more believable and better developed than in the earlier books. It's widely considered Browne's best novel—Browne's own *The Long Goodbye*, if you will.

Browne wrote a couple non-Pine books, as well. *Thin Air* (1954) is about a man's search for his wife, who has suddenly disappeared. *Pork City* (1988) is the fact-based story of the murder of Jake Lingle, a *Chicago Tribune* reporter who was on Al Capone's payroll.

During the 1950's and '60's, Browne wrote (under his own name) for the television shows *Playhouse 90*, *Bourbon Street Beat*, *Hawaiian Eye*, *Maverick*, *77 Sunset Strip*, *The Virginian* and *Kraft Suspense Theatre*, among others. He wrote screenplays (again, under his own name) for *Portrait of a Mobster* (1961), *The St. Valentine's Day Massacre* (1967) and *Capone* (1975 version).

**Further Reading:**
*Paul Pine series (as John Evans; complete):*
HALO IN BLOOD (1946)
HALO FOR SATAN (1948)
HALO IN BRASS (1949)
THE TASTE OF ASHES (1957, as Howard Browne)
THE PAPER GUN (1985, unfinished)

IF YOU HAVE TEARS (1947, as John Evans; published as LONA, 1952)
THIN AIR (1952)
PORK CITY (1988)

---

**If you like Howard Browne,** you might like: Raymond Chandler, William Campbell Gault

# W. R. Burnett

(William Riley Burnett, also wrote as John Monahan, James Updyke). Born in Springfield, Ohio, 1899. Died in Santa Monica, California, 1982.

Listen here, you mugs. I'm gonna tell you about a guy what used to be a pal of mine, see? W. R. Burnett. I used to call him Big Bill.

Lemme introduce myself. Cesare Enrico Bandello. Little Caesar, see? I helped Big Bill get his start in this racket. He wrote a book about me and did it score big. It was the goods, all right.

Big Bill started off in the sticks and was gettin' nowhere fast. He was living in Ohio and he wrote more than a hundred stories, but he didn't sell a one. Not a word, see? He even got married. The sap. Take it from Rico: dames are o.k. when you got the itch. But if you hang around'em too long, you get so you can dish it out but you just can't take it no more.

Big Bill finally wised up and came to Chi-town in 1927. He started working as a desk clerk at the Northmere Hotel. He met some of my best pals there. Hustlers. Hoods. Hoboes. A swell bunch of guys, see?

That's how Big Bill came to write that book about me, *Little Caesar*, in 1929. It told all about what a swell guy I was, and how I always took care of the three most important things in life: myself, my hair, and my gat. It told how I started off in the small time, but took over a gang from Sam Vittori, who got so he could dish it out but just couldn't take it no more. Speaking of my gang, you couldn't meet a more regular bunch of guys. Killer Pepe. Scabby. Bat Carillo. Otero. And a guy named Joe Massara. He was our front man. Could put on the monkey suit and get into the swellest joint in the city. But he ended up turning sissy and falling for a dame. The sap.

All the swells out in Hollywood went crazy over the book, and they made a movie of it with Eddie Robinson. I think they shoulda let me play myself, but Eddie was o.k. I liked the way he flicked the ashes off his cigar. Real class.

Big Bill made a bundle of dough, and wrote more books about tough birds like me. He wrote *High Sierra* in 1940, about a yegg named Roy Earle, who's part of a gang that holds up one of them high-class hotels in California. He wrote *The Asphalt Jungle* in 1949, a book about a gang, all specialists in their fields, who try to pull off the biggest caper of their lives. In *Nobody Lives Forever*, a slick con-man and his cronies try to bilk a rich dame out of her dough. All them books was made into movies. They were the goods, all right.

Big Bill wrote other books, too, but they were kind of sissy stuff. He wrote *Dark Hazard*, about a bird named Jim Turner who's supposed to be a tough gambler. But Rico's gonna wise you up about this story, so listen here: not only does this Turner mug fall for a dame, but for a racetrack dog, as well. Chee, what a sap!

He also wrote a book called *Captain Lightfoot*. I ain't read it, but with a title like that, it's gotta be for sissies.

Big Bill worked on even more movies than he did books. He knew where the dough was, and I don't mean maybe. Some of the best were *Scarface* (1932), *The Beast of the City* (1932), *This Gun for Hire* (1942), *Wake Island* (1942) and *Nobody Lives Forever* (1946). That last title kind of sums things up, as Big Bill couldn't see none too good in his later years and then was planted six feet under in 1982. Make no mistake about it, though: Big Bill Burnett was the goods, alright.

**Further Reading:**
LITTLE CAESAR (1929)
IRON MAN (1930)
THE SILVER EAGLE (1931)
DARK HAZARD (1933)
KING COLE (1936)
HIGH SIERRA (1940)
NOBODY LIVES FOREVER (1943)
TOMORROW'S ANOTHER DAY (1945)
THE ASPHALT JUNGLE (1949)
STRETCH DAWSON (1950)
LITTLE MEN, BIG WORLD (1951)
VANITY ROW (1952)
BIG STAN (1953, as John Monahan)
CAPTAIN LIGHTFOOT (1954)
UNDERDOG (1957)
ROUND THE CLOCK AT VOLARI'S (1961)
THE COOL MAN (1968)

---

**If you like W. R. Burnett,** you might like: Peter Rabe, Fletcher Flora, Malcolm Braly, Dashiell Hammett, James M. Cain

# James M. Cain

Born in Annapolis, Maryland, 1892. Died in University Park, Maryland, 1977.

 James Mallahan Cain, one of the best writers of tough, terse, telegraphic-style prose and dialogue, originally wanted to be an opera singer. This ambition (luckily, for all readers) did not pan out. After graduating from *Washington College*, Cain climbed the journalistic ladder and became an accomplished journalist for 14 years, beginning in 1917. He started as a reporter at the *Baltimore American*, moved on to the *Baltimore Sun*, and graduated to high editorial positions in New York, briefly working as managing editor of a newly-formed magazine called *The New Yorker*.

Cain's first published book was a non-fiction analysis of U.S. policy called *Our Government* (1930).

Although Cain's journalism career was successful, he was unhappy with it and yearned to write fiction. He moved to Hollywood and, with the help of an agent, was hired as a screenwriter by Paramount in 1931. Soon after his arrival, some friends suggested that Cain write a novel. Cain was toying with the idea of writing crime fiction, and the true-crime story of Ruth Snyder and Judd Gray was still fresh in the public consciousness. Snyder, a married woman, got involved in a romantic relationship with Gray, and they murdered Snyder's husband for the insurance money. Snyder and Gray were caught, convicted, and executed in 1928. Cain put the fiction and non-fiction ideas together, along with his spare, journalistic writing style, and came up with *The Postman Always Rings Twice* (1934). The novel is about Cora, a young and beautiful woman married to an older man and working in their roadside café, and Frank Chambers, a drifter. As in the Snyder-Gray case, Cora and Frank begin an affair and murder Cora's husband for the insurance money.

The book was groundbreaking on many levels. Cain's writing style was pared-down and stark, but with dashes of a kind of pulp poetry. The narration was first person, told by Frank in a confessional, intimate style. The characters were everyday people in everyday places. The content was tawdry, sordid, tabloid:

> I took her [Cora] in my arms and mashed my mouth up against hers...
> "Bite me! Bite me!" [Cora said]
> I bit her. I sunk my teeth into her lips so deep I could feel the blood spurt into my mouth. It was running down her neck when I carried her upstairs.

*Postman*'s story foundation—the young stud and hot dame killing the older husband for the insurance money—has become a template for innumerable radio plays, short stories, novels, movies and even comic books. Because of censorship regulations within the film industry, *Postman* didn't make it to the screen until 1946. It was finally made into a film noir by MGM, starring John Garfield and Lana Turner; remade in 1981, starring Jack Nicholson and Jessica Lange, with a screenplay by David Mamet.

Cain's next book-length story was similar to *Postman*, but this time the main character was a life-insurance salesman himself. *Double Indemnity* (1936) was even more pared-down (no "he said" or "she said") than *Postman*, and was set in suburban Southern California. It was first serialized in *Liberty* magazine, then was published in book form in 1943. It was made into a classic film noir in 1944, starring Fred MacMurray and Barbara Stanwyck, directed by Billy Wilder, and written by Wilder and one of Cain's fellow masters of hardboiled fiction, Raymond Chandler.

Cain ratcheted up the sex and violence in his next novel, *Serenade* (1937). The story is about a bisexual opera singer and a Mexican prostitute, and includes a torrid lovemaking scene in a Mexican church, the use of sacramental wine in an iguana stew, and, of course, murder. Critics and the Catholic Church were in an uproar and publicly lashed out at the book for its sordid content. *Serenade* was made into a worth missing, sanitized, musical melodrama starring Mario Lanza in 1956.

Cain shifted gears in *Mildred Pierce* (1941). The story was told in third-person, focusing on a mother-daughter relationship rather than one between man and woman, and had no murders (although in the movie version, a murder was created to bookend the story's beginning and end). Mildred Pierce is a single mother during the Depression, who works her way up from being a waitress to owning a successful chain of restaurants. Mildred's daughter is an opportunistic, spoiled brat, who looks down on her mother's working class status, and desires to mingle in elite social circles. The many conflicts between mother and daughter form the core of the book. The book was made into an excellent, atmospheric film noir in 1945, earning Joan Crawford an Oscar for her portrayal of Mildred, and directed by master-of-all-genres Michael Curtiz.

Throughout Cain's career, reviewers and critics labeled his writing "hardboiled," but Cain thought otherwise:

"I make no conscious effort to be tough, or hardboiled, or grim, or any of the things I am usually called. I merely try to write as the character would write, and I never forget that the average man, from the fields, the streets, the bars, the offices and even the gutters of his country, has acquired a vividness of speech that goes beyond anything I could invent, and that if I stick to this heritage, this logos of the American countryside, I shall attain a maximum of effectiveness with very little effort." (Cain's preface to *Double Indemnity*)

**Further Reading:**
THE POSTMAN ALWAYS RINGS TWICE (1934)
SERENADE (1937)
MILDRED PIERCE (1941)
LOVE'S LOVELY COUNTERFEIT (1942)
CAREER IN C MAJOR AND OTHER STORIES (1943)
THREE OF A KIND: CAREER IN C MAJOR, THE EMBEZZLER, DOUBLE INDEMNITY (1944)
PAST ALL DISHONOR (1946)
SINFUL WOMAN (1948)
THE MOTH (1948)
JEALOUS WOMAN (1950)
THE ROOT OF HIS EVIL (1952, published as SHAMELESS, 1958)
GALATEA (1953)
MIGNON (1962)
THE MAGICIAN'S WIFE (1965)
THE BABY IN THE ICEBOX AND OTHER SHORT FICTION (1981)

---

**If you like James M. Cain,** you might like: Gil Brewer, Horace McCoy

# Paul Cain

aka Peter Ruric (real name George Carroll Sims). Born in Iowa, 1906. Died in Los Angeles, CA 1966.

 If you looked at the single publicly available photo of Paul Cain (the name he used for prose works), Peter Ruric (the name he used on screenplays like *The Black Cat*, directed by Edgar G. Ulmer and starring Boris Karloff and Bela Lugosi), or George Sims, you might have seen a precursor to the Beats: slender-frame, hair longer than the style for the 1930's, and a blonde goatee. If you listened to Cain/Ruric/Sims expound upon his life, you might have heard he had been a Dada painter, a boatswain's mate, and a gynecologist; that he had written stories named *Hypersensualism: A Practical Philosophy for Acrobats* or The *Ecstasy Department* (this was the reply he gave to a writer seeking biographical information; neither of the two stories were found to exist). If you've read Cain's novel, *Fast One*, or his collection of short stories, *Seven Slayers* (all originally published in *Black Mask*), you might have been reminded of one of the better low-budget film noirs or, you might have discovered, as Raymond Chandler did, that you were reading "some kind of high point in the ultra hardboiled manner."

George Sims was a mystery man, and where his personal life was concerned, a W.C. Fields-ian teller of tall tales. Though few facts are known about Sims's life, this is what's known: from the mid-1930's until his death, he traveled extensively between Hollywood, New York, Europe and North Africa. He also married at least three times. In 1940, his first marriage made the Los Angeles papers when his wife leapt three stories from their Hollywood apartment after a drunken quarrel. She survived, but her jump, not surprisingly, ended the marriage. The identity of his second wife is unknown—but relatives remember being told she was either a script writer or an Italian actress. In the early 1950's, he moved to Mallorca, Spain—a sun-soaked haven for penniless writers. There he married an American student. The couple drifted to North Africa before moving to Laguna Beach, California. They had two sons, then divorced in the late 1950's. Sims's last public works were *The Tasting Machine* (published as by Peter Ruric) in *Gourmet* magazine in 1949, and another story for the same publication in 1951.

When asked about Cain/Ruric/Sims in an interview with Peter Bogdanovich, director Edgar G. Ulmer said, "He was a young man who had come out from New York, and I met him; a very intelligent boy who should've been a great playwright but got lost." (*Who the Devil Made It:*

*Conversations with Legendary Film Directors*, Peter Bogdanovich)
**Further Reading:**
FAST ONE (1933)
SEVEN SLAYERS (1946, short stories)

---

**If you like Paul Cain,** you might like: Frederick Nebel, Dan J. Marlowe

# Erskine Caldwell

Born in Coweta County, Georgia, 1903. Died in Paradise Valley, Arizona, 1987.

Erskine Caldwell has been called the "master of rural ribaldry," and he wrote sweaty, steamy, sexy books about the lives and loves of poor Southern white farmers and their clans. His characters had names like Jeeter Lester, Pluto Swint, Buck Walden, Ellie Mae, Darling Jill and Sister Bessie Rice. He was accused of being a Communist, a corrupter of morals, and a traitor to the South. His novels, *Tobacco Road* and *God's Little Acre*, were huge sellers, hugely controversial, and incisively critiqued racism, bigotry, and the rural South's economic system. Though these books were originally published in hardcover during the 1930's, when they were reprinted in the late 1940's they broke sales records within the burgeoning paperback industry, spawning a sub-genre of backwoods-themed novels written by PBO pros such as Harry Whittington and Charles Williams.

Erskine Caldwell was born in Georgia, and his father was a Presbyterian minister who moved from church to church all over the American South. The family rarely lived for more than six months in the same place; Caldwell was mainly taught by his mother, a schoolteacher. During these years he acquired invaluable knowledge about impoverished sharecroppers, knowledge which he later utilized in his stories.

Caldwell's first novel was *Tobacco Road* (1932). He peopled the novel with grotesques, perhaps as a metaphor to express the decay poverty brings— Ellie Mae is an eighteen year-old girl with a severe cleft lip; Sister Bessie Rice's face has no nose bone, and as a result, when looking straight at her face, a person can see into her nostrils, like a pig. The Jeeter Lester family's extreme poverty comes about due to the industrialization of production and the population's migration into cities. But Jeeter has lived on the same piece of land since birth, and he, with pride, refuses to move to the city to make a better life for him and his family. The purchase of a new car provides the catalyst for much of the damage, destruction and death within the Jeeter Lester clan.

*Tobacco Road*'s sales were slow at first, but as word-of-mouth spread, so did the groundswell of controversy. Many southerners denounced the novel as exaggerated, needlessly cruel, an affront to the gentility of the region, and even pornographic. Residents of other regions banned the book and the authorities seized copies. The controversy no doubt helped the book become a bestseller, and helped Caldwell become a famous man. *Tobacco Road* was adapted for the stage and ran for over seven-and-a-half years, still one of the longest-running plays in Broadway history. When the book was reprinted in paperback form, it sold six million copies.

Caldwell's next sensational novel was *God's Little Acre* (1933). The story is about family patriarch Ty Ty Walden's delusional search to find buried gold under his farm's useless soil. Walden has two beautiful daughters, two lazy sons, and a lusty, nubile daughter-in-law. Themes in the novel include the plight of workers deprived of union protection and the misuse of land and other natural resources.

The storm of controversy caused by *Tobacco Road* was only a drizzle compared to *God's Little Acre*—it was censored by the Georgia Literary Commission, banned in Boston, and attacked by the New York Society for the Suppression of Vice; Caldwell himself was arrested in New York while on a book signing tour. However, many of the reviews echoed the *Saturday Review of Literature*'s: "A beautifully integrated story of the barren southern farm and the shut southern mill, and one of the finest studies of the southern poor white which has ever come into our literature." When reprinted in paperback, as was the case with *Tobacco Road*, *God's Little Acre* was a multi-million seller.

*God's Little Acre* was filmed 1958, and though not a particularly well made movie, it was graced with a one-of-a-kind, bizarro cast: Robert (*film noir* actor extraordinaire) Ryan, Buddy (low-brow-comedian-who-talks-like-he-has-marbles-in-his-mouth) Hackett, Tina ("Ginger" of *Gilligan's Island*) Louise, Jack (*Hawaii 5-0*) Lord and Michael (*I Was a Teenage Werewolf*) Landon. It was directed by Anthony Mann (*Winchester'73*, *The Naked Spur*), and the music was supplied by the famed Elmer Bernstein.

Caldwell continued writing successfully and consistently, and produced 23 more novels, 150 short stories, 12 nonfiction collections, and 2 books for young adults. Whatever your opinion of Caldwell's books, their influence on the success of the blossoming paperback industry is indisputable.

**Further Reading:**
TOBACCO ROAD (1932)            GOD'S LITTLE ACRE (1933)
GEORGIA BOY (1943)             TRAGIC GROUND (1944)
A HOUSE IN THE UPLANDS (1946)  THIS VERY EARTH (1948)
A PLACE CALLED ESTHERVILLE (1949)
LOVE AND MONEY (1954)
GULF COAST STORIES (1956, short stories)
JENNY BY NATURE (1961)
THE LAST NIGHT OF SUMMER (1963)

---

**If you like Erskine Caldwell,** you might like: John Faulkner, John Thompson, Harry Whittington

# R. V. Cassill

(real name Ronald Verlin Casill; also wrote as Owen Aherne). Born in Cedar Falls, Iowa, 1919. Died in Providence, Rhode Island, 2002.

 R. V. Cassill was something of a literary schizophrenic: a well-respected academic who was lauded as "a man of letters" by *The New York Times*, and whose mainstream novels' thematic concerns include "the correspondences between the interior world—of desire and anxiety—and the public world of power." He also wrote sleaze PBOs with titles such as *A Taste of Sin: A Novel of Insidious Temptation*, *The Wife Next Door* and the lesbian-themed *Dormitory Women*.

Cassill graduated from the University of Iowa with a B.A. in 1939 (Phi Beta Kappa) and an M.A. in 1947. He attended the Sorbonne in Paris as a Fulbright fellow, 1952-53. He was a professor at the prestigious University of Iowa's Writers' Workshop, whose list of graduates include Flannery O'Conner, and whose faculty members have included Kurt Vonnegut and Philip Roth. He was an associate professor, 1966-71, and professor of English, 1972-83, at Brown University, in Providence, Rhode Island.

Cassill's approach to writing sleaze paperbacks was simple and direct: "The formula for writing a cheap, sensational novel is...take a cheap, sensational idea...and write it as well as you possibly can." ("The Writer's Craft: Stephen King, R. V. Cassill, and writing as well as you possibly can", by Tad Richards, www.examiner.com.) Some of his sleaze paperbacks and their taglines include 1954's *Left Bank of Desire* ("They pursued pleasures forbidden even in Paris"); 1956's *The Hungering Shame* ("Four men, a lonely road—and a girl"); 1959's *The Wife Next Door* ("They met like two comets in the night—the bored and reckless man, the lush and willing woman"); and 1961's *Night School* ("In this class, the students taught the teacher...").

Cassill's mainstream novels include *Eagle On the Coin* (1950), about racial equality; *Clem Anderson* (1961), about a failed writer; *Dr. Cobb's Game* (1970), about the Profumo sex scandals in Britain in the early 1960's; and *After Goliath* (1985), about King David of the Old Testament.

The periodicals where Cassill published short stories and articles also reflect the broad spectrum of his literary pursuits. From 1955-1979, he wrote short stories and articles for mainstream slicks, *Esquire* and *The Saturday Evening Post*; early-60's softcore *Playboy* imitators, *Dude* and *Gent*; and the more hardcore magazine, *Penthouse*.

**Further Reading:**
THE EAGLE ON THE COIN (1950)
DORMITORY WOMEN (1953)
THE LEFT BANK OF DESIRE (1955)
A TASTE OF SIN (1955)
A HUNGERING SHAME (1956)
THE WOUND OF LOVE (1956)
NAKED MORNING (1957)
THE BUCCANEER (1958)
LUSTFUL SUMMER (1958)
THE WIFE NEXT DOOR (1960)
CLEM ANDERSON (1960)
MY SISTER'S KEEPER (1961)
NIGHT SCHOOL (1961)
NURSES' QUARTERS (1962)
PRETTY LESLIE (1963)
THE PRESIDENT (1964)
DOCTOR COBB'S GAME (1969)
THE GOSS WOMEN (1974)
HOYT'S CHILD (1976)
LABORS OF LOVE (1980)
FLAME (1980)
AFTER GOLIATH (1985)
THE UNKNOWN SOLDIER (1991)
------------------------------------------------------------

**If you like R. V. Cassill,** you might like: Orrie Hitt, Richard Himmel

# Raymond Chandler

Born in Chicago, Illinois, 1888. Moved to England in 1895. Returned to U.S. in 1912. Died in La Jolla, California, 1959.

Raymond Chandler may be the best known writer of crime fiction of all time. Along with Dashiell Hammett, he is credited with giving birth to the enduring popularity of the crime fiction we read today.

If we know Chandler at all, we know the familiar stories. We know how he grew up in England, and of his early, unsuccessful efforts at writing romantic poetry. We know of his faithful marriage to Cissy, a woman seventeen years his senior. We know that when he moved back to the U.S. (Los Angeles, California, specifically) he worked his way up to an executive position in the oil industry but was fired in 1933, both because of the Depression and because of his heavy drinking. We know he didn't write his first crime-related story (*Blackmailers Don't Shoot*, 1933) until he was forty-five years old, and that his first novel (*The Big Sleep*, 1939) wasn't published until he was fifty. We know that movie director Billy Wilder hired Chandler to co-write the screenplay of Wilder's upcoming film, *Double Indemnity*. We know of Wilder and Chandler's acrimonious relationship, and that Chandler wrote letters to Paramount executives, fussily demanding that Wilder not "swish under Mr. Chandler's nose or to point in his direction the thin, leather-handled malacca cane which Mr. Wilder was in the habit of waving around," and that Wilder not "give Mr. Chandler orders of an arbitrary or personal nature such as 'Ray, will you open the window?' or 'Ray, will you shut the door, please.'"

We know Chandler was a slow worker, polishing his stories fastidiously, and that he only published seven novels during his lifetime: *The Big Sleep* (1939), *Farewell, My Lovely* (1940), *The High Window* (1942), *The Lady in the Lake* (1943), *The Little Sister* (1949), *The Long Goodbye* (1953) and *Playback* (1958). We know the main character was Philip Marlowe, private eye. We know about the classic movies made from his books, like *The Big Sleep* and *Murder, My Sweet*, and the film noir screenplays Chandler wrote or co-wrote, like *Double Indemnity*, *The Blue Dahlia*, and *Strangers On a Train*. We know Chandler's (and by extension, Marlowe's) cynicism was a mask to shield his wounded romanticism. We know Chandler could be a snob, an elitist, and, in today's terms, "anal retentive," and that even though he railed so hard against greed, dishonesty and corruption in the world, he was such a nitpicker, and his moral standards were so impossibly high, he probably wouldn't have been happy in any kind of a world. We know that when his wife Cissy died in 1954, the sixty-six year-old Chandler (already an alcoholic) began drinking even more and his health, both mental and physical, drastically deteriorated. Last but not least, we know Raymond Chandler was a master.

So what makes Raymond Chandler so memorable? What's made so many writers cite Chandler as a major influence? What made Hollywood come a-calling? What makes Chandler so quotable? What makes the name Philip Marlowe and the title *The Big Sleep* still familiar today?

Is it the plots? Colorful characters like General Sternwood, Amthor, and Moose Malloy? Atmospheric descriptions of Los Angeles during the 1940's? The wit? The one-of-a-kind similes and metaphors? The incisive critiques of hypocrisy among the wealthy? Is it Marlowe himself?

It is undoubtedly *the voice*.

The voice of Chandler—whether in his fiction or non-fiction, his dialogue or his descriptions, his prose stories or his screenplays—is what sticks in the mind. The voice of Chandler's makes such an impression that novice writers find themselves imitating it without half realizing it. The voice is precise, cool, and in control. The voice is the voice we wish we had.

> "Down these mean streets a man must go who is not himself mean, who is neither tarnished nor afraid...He must be a complete man and a common man and yet an unusual man...He must be the best man in his world and a good enough man for any world." — "The Simple Art of Murder"

> "It was a blonde. A blonde to make a bishop kick a hole in a stained glass window." —*Farewell, My Lovely*

> "If my books had been any worse I should not have been invited to Hollywood and if they had been any better I should not have come."
> —*Selected Letters of Raymond Chandler*

> "Even on Central Avenue, not the quietest dressed street in the world, he looked about as inconspicuous as a tarantula on a slice of angel food."
> —*Farewell, My Lovely*

> "I needed a drink. I needed a lot of life insurance. I needed a vacation. I needed a home in the country. What I had was a hat, a coat and a gun."
> —*Farewell, My Lovely*

"I don't mind if you don't like my manners. They're pretty bad. I grieve over them during the long winter nights."
—*The Big Sleep*

"There are blondes and blondes and it is almost a joke word nowadays...There is the soft and willing alcoholic blonde who doesn't care what she wears as long as it is mink or where she goes as long as it is the Starlight Roof and there is plenty of dry champagne... There is the pale, pale blonde with anemia of some non-fatal but incurable type. She is very languid and very shadowy and she speaks softly out of nowhere and you can't lay a finger on her because in the first place you don't want to and in the second place she is reading the Wasteland or Dante in the original, or Kafka or Kierkegaard or studying Provençal...And lastly there is the gorgeous show piece who will outlast three kingpin racketeers and then marry a couple of millionaires at a million a head and end up with a pale rose villa at Cap d'Antibes, an Alfa Romeo town car complete with pilot and co-pilot, and a stable of shopworn aristocrats, all of whom she will treat with the affectionate absentmindedness of an elderly duke saying good night to his butler." —*The Long Goodbye*

"What did it matter where you lay once you were dead? In a dirty sump or in a marble tower on top of a high hill. You were dead, you were sleeping the big sleep, you were not bothered by things like that. Oil and water were the same as wind and air to you. You just slept the big sleep, not caring about the nastiness of how you died or where you fell." —*The Big Sleep*

"To say goodbye is to die a little." —*The Long Goodbye*

**Further Reading:**
THE BIG SLEEP (1939)
FAREWELL, MY LOVELY (1940)
THE HIGH WINDOW (1942)
THE LADY IN THE LAKE (1943)
THE LITTLE SISTER (1949)
THE LONG GOODBYE (1953)
PLAYBACK (1958)
POODLE SPRINGS (1989, completed by Robert B. Parker)

*Short story collections:*
FIVE MURDERS (1944)
FIVE SINISTER CHARACTERS (1945)
FINGER MAN AND OTHER STORIES (1946)
RED WIND (1946)
SPANISH BLOOD (1946)

*Essay:*
THE SIMPLE ART OF MURDER (1950)

-----------------------------------------------------------------

**If you like Raymond Chandler,** you might like: Dashiell Hammett, Howard Browne

# *James Hadley Chase*

(born René Brabazon Raymond; also wrote as James L. Docherty, Ambrose Grant, Raymond Marshall, R. Raymond). Born in London, England, 1906. Died in Corseaux, Switzerland, 1985.

James Hadley Chase was one of about a dozen other Brits (including Peter Cheyney, Hank Janson, and "Griff") who took the style and substance of the American hardboiled crime novel and made it his own, becoming internationally famous in the process. These men rarely, if ever, visited the United States, their preferred sources being atlases and encyclopedias. Yet after their work became wildly popular in Europe, it found spectacular success during the postwar paperback boom in America as well, and reprints could be found on the racks right alongside books by Mickey Spillane and Jim Thompson.

Chase's literary career got off to a screaming start right out of the gate with the publication of his first novel, the controversial *No Orchids for Miss Blandish* (1939, first published in the U.S. as *The Villain and the Virgin*). The genesis for the book came after Chase read James M. Cain's *The Postman Always Rings Twice*, as well as U.S. news reports about the infamous Midwestern criminals Ma Barker and her sons. Blending Cain's style with the reported exploits of the Barker gang, Chase came up with a story about a wealthy young socialite who is kidnapped and held for ransom, then mentally and physically abused as she is forced to act as one of the gang's unwilling wife.

The novel caused an instant sensation, both in terms of sales and in terms of public outcry. Numerous regions throughout England banned the book, claiming its sexual brutality was pornographic. In 1944, during the height of WWII, George Orwell wrote an article reporting that, "several people, after reading *No Orchids* have remarked to me, 'It's pure Fascism,'" an opinion with which Orwell concurred. On the other hand, Orwell wrote that *No Orchids* is "not, as one might expect, the product of an illiterate hack, but a brilliant piece of writing, with hardly a wasted word or a jarring note anywhere." (*Cult Fiction*, by Andrew Calcutt and Richard Shephard, pg. 59)

Readers apparently thought the book was brilliantly written, as well—sales had reached half a million copies by the time of Orwell's article. The book was filmed under its original title in the UK in 1948, and again in the U.S. in 1971 as *The Grissom Gang*, directed by noir specialist Robert Aldrich.

Many of Chase's other novels retained the tough and terse style of James M. Cain. Like *Blandish*, some were controversial, with flashy titles like *Kiss My Fist!* (1939, aka *The Dead Stay Dumb*), *Twelve Chinks and a Woman* (1940, the title changed in later printings to the less inflammatory *Twelve Chinamen and a Woman*) and *The Marijuana Mob* (1950). Chase created numerous series characters, including California-based PI Vic Malloy (*You're Lonely When You're Dead* (1949), *Figure It Out for Yourself* (1950)); ex-commando Martin "Brick-Top" Corridon (*Mallory* (1950), *Why Pick On Me?* (1951, written as by Raymond Marshall)); playboy adventurer, former WWII pilot, Don Micklem (*Mission to Venice* (1954), *Mission to Siena* (1955)); CIA agent Mark Girard (*This is for Real* (1965), *You Have Yourself a Deal* (1966)).

Chase was incredibly prolific, and wrote more than ninety books throughout his forty-five year career.

**Further Reading:**
NO ORCHIDS FOR MISS BLANDISH (1939; as
  THE VILLIAN AND THE VIRGIN, 1948)
THE DEAD STAY DUMB (1939; as KISS MY FIST!, 1952)
TWELVE CHINKS AND A WOMAN (1940; revised edition, as
  12 CHINAMEN AND A WOMAN, 1950)
MISS SHUMWAY WAVES A WAND (1944)
I'LL GET YOU FOR THIS (1946)
THE FLESH OF THE ORCHID (1948)
YOU NEVER KNOW WITH WOMEN (1949)
YOU'RE LONELY WHEN YOU'RE DEAD (1950)
FIGURE IT OUT FOR YOURSELF (1950; as THE MARIJUANA MOB, 1952)
STRICTLY FOR CASH (1951)
THE FAST BUCK (1952)
THE DOUBLE SHUFFLE (1952)
I'LL BURY MY DEAD (1953)
THIS WAY FOR A SHROUD (1953)
SAFER DEAD (1954; as DEAD RINGER, 1955)
YOU'VE GOT IT COMING (1955)
THERE'S ALWAYS A PRICE TAG (1956)
NOT SAFE TO BE FREE (1958; as
  THE CASE OF THE STRANGLED STARLET, 1958)
WHAT'S BETTER THAN MONEY? (1960)
COME EASY–GO EASY (1960)
JUST ANOTHER SUCKER (1961)
A LOTUS FOR MISS QUON (1961)
I WOULD RATHER STAY POOR (1962)
TELL IT TO THE BIRDS (1963)
THE SOFT CENTRE (1964)
THIS IS FOR REAL (1965)
THE WAY THE COOKIE CRUMBLES (1965)

YOU HAVE YOURSELF A DEAL (1966)
HAVE THIS ONE ON ME (1967)
BELIEVED VIOLENT (1968)

---

**If you like James Hadley Chase,** you might like: Peter Cheyney, James M. Cain

# Peter Cheyney

(born Reginald Southouse Cheyney, also wrote as Lyn Southney, Harold Brust).
Born in London, England, 1896. Died in London, England, 1951.

 Peter Cheyney's early jobs included work as a song-
writer and journalist. As a reporter, Cheyney acquired
first-hand knowledge of London's notorious West End
and its criminal underworld. He was known for writing by dictation, and his first fictional works were
short stories he wrote for British magazines during the
early 1930's. Set in England, most of these featured
series character Alonzo MacTavish—a suave, debonair,
"gentleman crook," whose personality was patterned after Leslie
Charteris's The Saint.

Cheyney began his fictional tour of the United States in 1936, with the
publication of *This Man is Dangerous*. The book featured Cheyney's most popular character, a tough, wise-cracking, New York-based FBI agent named
Lemmy Caution. Lemmy narrated his adventures in the first-person; his
narrative voice was a combination of Edward G. Robinson's portrayal of
Little Caesar, and the comedic con men who populated Damon Runyon's
(*Guys and Dolls*) stories. In *Don't Get Me Wrong* (1939), Lemmy is ruminating
about a former romance:

> "She was a honey, that dame. She had everything. She was sorta
> petite an' clingin' but she was a very forceful character, like the time
> when she tried to stick a meat skewer in my eye for slingin' a hot
> look at the local school marm. Love can be hell. But maybe you heard
> about that."

Lemmy was featured in a total of 10 novels, including *Dames Don't Care*
(1937), *Can Ladies Kill?* (1938) and *I'll Say She Does* (1946). He was also featured
in a number of French films starring American actor Eddie Constantine.
Lemmy's profile was exponentially raised when he was featured in French
New Wave director Jean-Luc Godard's film, *Alphaville* (1965).

Cheyney also created a series character named Slim Callaghan.
Cheyney set these in his homeland, and made Slim an Englishman. In contrast to the loopiness of the Caution books, the Callaghan series was more
straightforward, tough, and hardboiled. Callaghan himself was along the
lines of Hammett's Sam Spade: he's a ladies' man, has a love/hate relationship with the police, and will bend the law when he deems it necessary.
Slim's first appearance was in *The Urgent Hangman* (1938); other notable
titles include *Dangerous Curves* (1939), *They Never Say When* (1944) and *Uneasy
Terms* (1946).

**Further Reading:**
(dates and titles are for British publications)

*Lemmy Caution series (complete):*
THIS MAN IS DANGEROUS (1936)
POISON IVY (1937)
DAMES DON'T CARE (1937)
CAN LADIES KILL? (1938)
DON'T GET ME WRONG (1939)
YOU'D BE SURPRISED (1940)
YOUR DEAL, MY LOVELY (1941)
NEVER A DULL MOMENT (1942)
YOU CAN ALWAYS DUCK (1943)
I'LL SAY SHE DOES! (1945)

*Slim Callaghan series (complete):*
THE URGENT HANGMAN (1938)
DANGEROUS CURVES (1939)
YOU CAN'T KEEP THE CHANGE (1940)
IT COULDN'T MATTER LESS (1941)
SORRY YOU'VE BEEN TROUBLED (1942)
THE UNSCRUPULOUS MR. CALLAGHAN (1943)
THEY NEVER SAY WHEN (1944)
UNEASY TERMS (1946)

DARK DUET (1942)
SINISTER ERRAND (1945)
DARK HERO (1946)
TRY ANYTHING TWICE (1948)
NO ORDINARY CHEYNEY (1948, short stories and sketches)
LADIES WON'T WAIT (1951)

---

**If you like Peter Cheyney,** you might like: James Hadley Chase, Henry Kane

## George Harmon Coxe
Born in Olean, New York, 1901. Died in Old Lyme, Connecticut, 1984.

George Harmon Coxe's most popular character was Flashgun Casey, whose official capacity was as a newspaper photographer at crime scenes, but who inevitably found himself involved in solving crimes due to clues in his photos. During the 1930's-1960's, Casey was a crossover sensation, appearing in pulps, novels, movies, radio and TV. He even had a brief comic book series.

Born in New York, Coxe attended Purdue University in 1920 and Cornell University in 1921. Between 1922-1927, he was a reporter for the *Santa Monica Outlook* and the *Los Angeles Express* in California, and for the *Utica Observer Dispatch* and the *Elmira Star-Gazette* in New York.

Before starting his writing career, Coxe was an avid fan of the pulps, and noticed plenty of crime-solving newspaper reporters, but no photographers in that role. Hence, Flash Casey was born. Casey initially works for *The Boston Globe*, then later for the *Boston Express*. Casey is a rough, hard-drinking, hot-tempered Irishman. Critic J. Randolph Cox sums up a typical Casey plot: "Casey is after a news story in pictures, the opposition (the criminals) don't want him to get those pictures, and the police don't want him to interfere. Casey's interference, of course, delivers the criminals to the police." (*Twentieth Century Crime & Mystery Writers*, pg. 254.)

Casey appeared in over twenty stories in *Black Mask*, in a collection of short stories called *Flash Casey, Detective* (1946), and in five novels: *Silent Are the Dead* (1942), *Murder for Two* (1943), *Error of Judgment* (1961), *The Man Who Died Too Soon* (1962) and *Deadly Image* (1964).

Coxe, in a number of his novels, took Flashgun Casey's occupation and unofficial status as a PI, and revamped the character, naming him Kent Murdock. Murdock, also Boston-based, has several traits which distinguish him from Casey: where Casey has street smarts, Murdock has a more formal education. Murdock is also more sophisticated, urbane, and better mannered. These traits allow him to become involved in crimes amongst Boston's upper-class blue-bloods. In a number of the books, Murdock is married, and he and his wife, Joyce, work as a team. Murdock first appeared in *Murder With Pictures* (1935), which was also Coxe's first novel. Other notable titles include *The Camera Clue* (1937), *Mrs. Murdock Takes a Case* (1947), *Focus On Murder* (1954) and *The Reluctant Heiress* (1965), among others.

Coxe also created three official private detectives: Max Hale, Sam Crombie and Jack Fenner. He wrote numerous stand-alone crime novels, as well.

Overall, Coxe wrote over 150 short stories, nearly 65 novels, and numerous screenplays, radio plays, and teleplays. He was elected president of the

Mystery Writers of America in 1952 and won the MWA's Grand Master
Award in 1964.

**Further Reading:**
*Flash Casey series (complete):*
SILENT ARE THE DEAD (1942)
MURDER FOR TWO (1943)
FLASH CASEY, PHOTOGRAPHER (1946, short stories)
ERROR OF JUDGEMENT (1961, published as ONE MURDER TOO MANY, 1969)
THE MAN WHO DIED TOO SOON (1962)
DEADLY IMAGE (1964)

*Kent Murdock series:*
MURDER WITH PICTURES (1935)      THE CAMERA CLUE (1937)
FOUR FRIGHTENED WOMEN (1939)
MRS. MURDOCK TAKES A CASE (1941)
THE CHARRED WITNESS (1942)
THE FIFTH KEY (1947)
THE HOLLOW NEEDLE (1948)
LADY KILLER (1949)
THE WIDOW HAD A GUN (1951)
FOCUS ON MURDER (1954)
THE BIG GAMBLE (1958)
THE LAST COMMANDMENT (1960)
THE RELUCTANT HEIRESS (1965)

*Sam Crombie series (complete):*
THE FRIGHTENED FIANCEE (1950)
THE IMPETUOUS MISTRESS (1958)

*Max Hale series (complete):*
MURDER FOR THE ASKING (1939)
THE LADY IS AFRAID (1940)

NO TIME TO KILL (1941)
MURDER IN HAVANA (1943)
THE GROOM LAY DEAD (1944)
THE MAN WHO DIED TWICE (1951)
NEVER BET YOUR LIFE (1952)

---

**If you like George Harmon Coxe,** you might like: W. T. Ballard, Stewart
Sterling

# Jonathan Craig

(born Frank E. Smith). Born in 1919. Died in 1984.

Jonathan Craig made a significant contribution to the world of the PBO with his series of ten police procedurals featuring Detective Pete Selby of Manhattan's 6th Precinct. Like fellow crime writer Ed McBain, who created the 87th Precinct series, Craig's series of police procedurals were set in New York City (although McBain used the fictional name Isola for his setting). But whereas McBain's series followed the exploits of the entire 87th Precinct, Craig's series focused on main character Pete Selby. To Craig's credit, the debut of his series (*The Dead Darling*, 1955) pre-dated McBain's by nearly a year.

A blurb on the front of *The Case of the Beautiful Body* (1957) sets up the general procedure for storylines in the series:

> "She was beautiful and she was dead — then Detective Selby learned how evil she had been"

The stories begin with the discovery of the dead body of a beautiful (usually nude) woman. As Selby and his partner, Stan Rayder, weave their way through clues, they gradually learn the victim was an amoral woman who manipulated and blackmailed numerous men—thus creating a situation where a large pool of suspects have numerous reasons for wanting her dead.

Craig's writing style for the 6th Precinct series is terse and direct. The fast-paced, ping-pong, back-and-forth tempo for the interrogations was said to have been inspired by *Dragnet*. Notable entries in the series are *Morgue for Venus* (1956), *Case of the Cold Coquette* (1957), *The Case of the Beautiful Body* (1957) and *Case of the Nervous Nude* (1959). All books in the 6th Precinct series were published by paperback publisher Gold Medal.

Two of Craig's non-series books have been singled out by mystery writers and critics as must-reads: *Alley Girl* (1954, aka *Renegade Cop*) is a "rogue cop" book; mystery historian Gary Lovisi calls it "a nasty little shocker." *So Young, So Wicked* (1957) tells the story of a fifteen year-old, Lolita-like tramp who has been blackmailing members of a local crime syndicate.

Throughout the 1950's, '60's and early '70's, Craig wrote scores of short stories for *Manhunt*, *Pursuit*, *Accused*, *Alfred Hitchcock Mystery Magazine*, *Shell Scott Mystery Magazine* and *Mike Shayne Mystery Magazine*.

**Further Reading:**
*6th Precinct series (complete):*
THE DEAD DARLING (1952)
MORGUE FOR VENUS (1956)
CASE OF THE COLD COQUETTE (1957)
THE CASE OF THE BEAUTIFUL BODY (1957)
CASE OF THE PETTICOAT MURDER (1958)
CASE OF THE NERVOUS NUDE (1959)
CASE OF THE VILLAGE TRAMP (1959)
CASE OF THE LAUGHING VIRGIN (1960)
CASE OF THE SILENT STRANGER (1964)
CASE OF THE BRAZEN BEAUTY (1966)

RED-HEADED SINNER (1953)
ALLEY GIRL (1954; as RENEGADE COP, 1959)
COME NIGHT, COME EVIL (1957)
SO YOUNG, SO WICKED (1957)

---

**If you like Jonathan Craig,** you might like: Evan Hunter/Ed McBain, Milton K. Ozaki

## *Kendell Foster Crossen*

(also wrote as Richard Foster, Bennett Barlay, M. E. Chaber, Christopher Monig, Kent Richards, Ken Crossen, Clay Richards). Born in Albany, Ohio, 1910. Died in Los Angeles, California, 1981.

Ken Crossen was the creator of the popular investigator Milo March, as well as the creator of the only Buddhist super-hero to grace the pages of a pulp magazine, the Green Lama.

Crossen was educated at Rio Grande College, in Ohio, and afterward was a member of the WPA Writer's Project, a New Deal program instituted by President Roosevelt during the Great Depression. Crossen also spent time working as an insurance investigator, an experience that would come in handy during the writing of his Milo March series. In 1936, he was the editor of one of the most popular detective pulps of the era, *Detective Fiction Weekly*. He pursued fiction writing as well, and his first story was published in *DFW* in 1939—"The Aaron Burr Murder Case."

In 1940, in an attempt to compete with pulp hero the Shadow, Crossen created the Green Lama, a practicing Buddhist who had acquired superhuman powers through his Buddhist studies, as well as scientific knowledge such as the use of radioactive salts that, when ingested, gave him the ability to "shock" his foes by his very touch. Crossen wrote fourteen Lama stories for *Double Detective* pulp magazine under the name Richard Foster, and also contributed stories when the character began appearing in comic books in 1944.

For his novels, Crossen's most popular series character was Milo March, featured in more than twenty books beginning with *Hangman's Harvest* in 1952, and lasting until *Born to be Hanged* in 1973. March, a former CIA agent, was employed by Intercontinental Insurance Agency; he was a high living connoisseur of fine wine and fine women who bopped around the globe on missions locating missing persons or valuable objects. A particular March adventure which has achieved iconic status is the paperback edition of *The Splintered Man* (1957), which sports a classic "hypo needle" cover, and is one of the earliest novels to feature the use of LSD. In 1958, there was a Milo March movie, *The Man Inside*, a UK production, starring Jack Palance, Anita Ekberg, and Anthony Newley.

Crossen created other series characters, as well. Brian Brett, an insurance investigator, appeared in four books, including *The Burned Man* (1956) and *Abra-Cadaver* (1958), as by Christopher Monig. Pete Draco was a two-fisted Miami-based private eye, featured in *Bier for a Chaser* (1959) and *Two Late for Mourning* (1960). Chin-Kwang Kham, a Green Lama variation, was featured in *The Laughing Buddha Murders* (1944) and *The Invisible Man Murders* (1945).

**Further Reading:**
MURDER OUT OF MIND (1945)
YEAR OF CONSENT (1954)
THE REST MUST DIE (1959)

*The Green Lama series:*
THE GREEN LAMA: THE COMPLETE PULP ADVENTURES, VOL. 1-3 (2011-2012)

*Kim Locke series:*
THE BIG DIVE (1959)
THE TORTURED PATH (1957)
THE GENTLE ASSASSIN (1964)

**As Christopher Monig**
*Brian Brett series:*
ONCE UPON A CRIME (1959)
THE LONELY GRAVES (1960)

**As M. E. Chaber**
*Milo March series:*

| | |
|---|---|
| HANGMAN'S HARVEST (1952) | NO GRAVE FOR MARCH (1953) |
| AS OLD AS CAIN (1954) | THE MAN INSIDE (1954) |
| THE SPLINTERED MAN (1955) | THE BURNED MAN (1956) |
| A LONELY WALK (1956) | ABRA-CADAVER (1958) |
| THE GALLOWS GARDEN (1958) | |
| A HEARSE OF ANOTHER COLOR (1958) | |
| SO DEAD THE ROSE (1959) | JADE FOR A LADY (1962) |
| SOFTLY IN THE NIGHT (1963) | SIX WHO RAN (1964) |
| UNEASY LIES THE DEAD (1964) | WANTED: DEAD MEN (1965) |
| THE DAY IT RAINED DIAMONDS (1966) | |
| A MAN IN THE MIDDLE (1967) | |
| WILD MIDNIGHT FALLS (1968) | |
| THE FLAMING MAN (1969) | |
| GREEN GROW THE GRAVES (1970) | |
| THE BONDED DEAD (1971) | |
| BORN TO BE HANGED (1973) | |

**If you like Kendell Foster Crossen,** you might like: Stephen Marlowe, Lester Dent

# Dan Cushman

Born in Marion, Michigan, 1909. Died in Great Falls, Montana, 2001.

Paperback publisher Gold Medal marketed Dan Cushman's PBOs (this description could apply just as well to Cushman's novels for other publishers) as "tales of high adventure and exotic romance." His tough-guy heroes were gun runners and soldiers-of-fortune with names like Rocky Forbes, Frisco Dougherty and "Armless" O'Neil. They pursued gold and girls—the gold was buried treasure, the girls were exotic maidens such as the woman on the cover of *The Half-Caste* who was described as "like a tropic night...dark, smooth, and glowing...and behind lay the subtle hint of—savagery!" The stories were set in strange, foreign lands such as the Congo, Bangkok, the Java Sea and the Orient. Books Cushman wrote in this vein include 1951's *Naked Ebony* ("In this part of Africa you called no man a friend, no woman your own and trusted only your gun"); 1951's *Jewel of the Java Sea* ("Hide your gold and your women! Here comes Frisco Dougherty"); 1954's *The Fabulous Finn* ("In titanic brawls, in historic ben-ders, in roaring pursuit of good-looking dames, it was Machi vs. Hannegan—two lusty giants born to battle, mostly each other"); and 1955's *Port Orient* ("Back of the bamboo curtain was gold—and three tough yanks to steal it").

Cushman grew up in Montana, near the Rocky Boy's Indian Reservation. After graduating from the University of Montana, he held jobs as a geologist's assistant and prospector. He began his writing career as a reporter for the *Big Sandy Mountaineer* and the *Great Falls Tribune*. In the late '40's, he wrote short stories featuring the western pulp hero, The Pecos Kid, for the popular pulp, *The Pecos Kid Western*. Other pulps Cushman wrote for include *Jungle Stories*, *Action Stories*, *Frontier Stories*, *Dime Western*, *Lariat Story Magazine* and *Zane Grey Western Magazine*.

Cushman wrote more than twenty-five Westerns. His most successful was *Stay Away, Joe* (1953), a satirical novel about Big Joe Champlain, a Native American whose family lives on a reservation in Montana. The book's por-trayal of American Indians, especially that of Big Joe, a lusty rogue, aroused controversy in Montana, and the Indian novelist James Welch vetoed the inclusion of an excerpt in a popular Montana anthology. But Richard A. Lupoff, in *The Great American Paperback*, praises the book as "a fine and sensitive novel." *Stay Away, Joe* was made into a successful Broadway musical in 1958, the title changed to *Whoop-Up!* In 1968, the novel was filmed under its original title, with Elvis Presley in the lead role. Critics uniformly rate the movie as one of Elvis's worst; one reviewer com-pared the level of its comedy to an episode of *F-Troop*.

Cushman's non-fiction includes *The Great North Trail* (1966), about the route from Asia across Alaska to the plains of Texas; *Cow Country Cookbook* (1967); and an autobiography, *Plenty of Room and Air* (1975).

In 1998, Cushman received the H. G. Merriam Award for Distinguished Contributions to Montana Literature.

**Further Reading:**
MONTANA, HERE I BE (1950)
JEWEL OF THE JAVA SEA (1951)
NAKED EBONY (1951)
SAVAGE INTERLUDE (1952)
THE RIPPER FROM RAWHIDE (1953)
STAY AWAY, JOE (1953)
TIMBERJACK (1953)
THE FABULOUS FINN (1954)
TONGKING! (1954)
PORT ORIENT (1955)
THE SILVER MOUNTAIN (1957)
THE FORBIDDEN LAND (1958)
THE HALF-CASTE (1960)
THE CON MAN (1960)
ON THE MAKE (1962)
4 FOR TEXAS (1963, movie novelization)
OPIUM FLOWER (1963)
NORTH FORK TO HELL (1964)
THE GREAT NORTH TRAIL (1966, non-fiction)
THE LONG RIDERS (1967)
COW COUNTRY COOKBOOK (1967, non-fiction)

_____

**If you like Dan Cushman,** you might like: David Dodge, A. S. Fleischman

# Carroll John Daly

(also wrote as John D. Carroll). Born in Yonkers, New York, 1889. Died in Los Angeles, California, 1958.

Though you may have assumed it was Dashiell Hammett who was the originator of the hardboiled private detective story, it was in fact a now forgotten writer named Carroll John Daly.

In his youth, Daly was drawn to the newly emerging art form which would come to be known as the cinema, and after attending the American Academy of Dramatic Arts in New York City, he worked as an usher, projectionist, assistant manager (and eventually manager) of one of the first movie houses in Atlantic City.

Daly's private eye, and the prototype for countless PIs to come, made his initial appearance in a June 1, 1923 *Black Mask* story titled, "Knights of the Open Palm." Race Williams, private eye, narrated his own adventures using a slangy colloquy, introducing himself as "a middleman–just a halfway house between the dicks and the crooks...I do a little honest shooting once in a while–just in the way of business. But my conscience is clear; I never bumped off a guy what didn't need it."

Williams is tough, cynical, wisecracking, aggressive, and, at times, brutal. Something of a vigilante, dealing out his own brand of justice, he often shoots first and asks questions later. Daly developed his unique creation by taking the character of the lone gunfighter from popular dime novels and transplanting him to the city–creating, in effect, an "urban cowboy."

Daly and Williams were enormously popular. Daly's name on the cover of a pulp meant an increase in sales by fifteen percent. In 1930, the editor of *Black Mask* conducted a poll among readers to see who their favorite writer was–Carroll placed first, runner-up was Erle Stanley Gardner and placing a distant third was Dashiell Hammett.

The relentless narrative drive of his stories doubtless contributed to their popularity, while among Daly's weaknesses were thin characterizations. Throughout the 1920's and '30's, Race Williams appeared in fifty-three stories in *Black Mask*, as well as a number of stories in *Dime Detective*; he was also featured in seven novels.

In Daly's personal life, he was far removed from the rough-and-tumble ways of his superstar pulp hero. He lived in suburban White Plains, New York, and traveled into the asphalt jungle of Manhattan as little as possible. His idea of vigorous activity was walking the length of the fifty-foot lot in front of his house, and he needed to live in a scrupulously climate-controlled environment. Daly also had a pathological fear of dentists (but don't we all?).

Later in life, while other writers had moved on to writing for the movies or television, Daly's popularity waned, and he was restricted to writing for comic books. Ironically, in the late 1940's his creation spawned a sensation within the burgeoning paperback industry, when a young man named Frank Morrison Spillane updated the Race Williams character and created his own ass-kicking vigilante, a private detective named Mike Hammer. Spillane even sent Daly a letter of gratitude, writing, "Yours was the first and only style of writing that ever influenced me in any way. Race was the model for Mike; and I can't say more in this case than imitation being the most sincere form of flattery."

**Further Reading:**
*Race Williams series:*
THE SNARL OF THE BEAST (1926)
THE HIDDEN HAND (1929)
THE TAG MURDERS (1930)
TAINTED POWER (1931)
THE THIRD MURDERER (1931)
THE AMATEUR MURDERER (1933)
MURDER FROM THE EAST (1935)

THE WHITE CIRCLE (1926)
THE MAN IN THE SHADOWS (1928)
MURDER WON'T WAIT (1933)
EMPEROR OF EVIL (1937)

---

**If you like Carroll John Daly,** you might like: Frederick Nebel, Mickey Spillane

# Jada M. Davis

(also wrote as Jada Davis). Born Texas, 1919. Died in 1996.

 Jada Davis was one of eleven children born to a struggling family in West Texas. As a child, Jada, along with his brothers and sisters, were sent out to pick cotton to help make ends meet; as Davis told it, the Great Depression didn't mean a whole lot of change to their life. A reader of what material he could get hold of, when a neighbor gave him an armload of old books he was finally exposed to the books and writers he would come to admire.

Reading and writing became Davis's escape mechanism and he sold his first story to *Liberty* magazine when he was just 15 years old. He submitted his first novel to Random House at 18. He had been making extra money selling short pieces to magazines and newspapers when he joined the Army in the 1930's, training in the deserts of the Southwest. When World War II broke out, Davis contracted tuberculosis and ended up sitting out the war in a sanitarium. Afterwards, still wanting to make a contribution, he allowed himself to be bombarded with radiation as part of some military medical experiments.

Once out of the service, Davis worked as a writer and editor for newspapers around the West Texas area. In 1953 he sold his first novel to Fawcett Red Seal, the hardboiled classic *One For Hell*. The story is based on real life events and features one Willa Ree, a boxcar drifter looking for a place to make a buck–a place with oil, because oil meant money. With only a dime in his pocket Ree wanders into a café and finds Ben Halliday, or rather, Halliday finds Ree. Halliday is looking for a certain kind of man, the kind who can look after himself but also take certain kinds of orders. In Ree, Halliday thinks he's hit it just right.

Ree has notions of his own, however. He takes Halliday up on his job to become a policeman in town but it isn't long before Halliday and the men he represents come to know exactly what they've found in Willa Ree: an uncontrollable force of nature that is way more than they've bargained for.

Davis's second published book was for Avon, 1956's *The Outraged Sect*, also based on real events. This book is in some ways a mirror image to *One For Hell*. *Sect* is the story of a good man fighting bad men and runaway prejudice in a small town bent on driving out "the Sect," a pacifistic religious group the townspeople just don't understand. World War II is still going on and the rumor of the Sect's refusal to salute the American flag rubs most of the town the wrong way. Small acts of violence become bigger and tension escalates as one man, newspaperman Book Morris, tries to talk sense into the increasingly difficult townspeople. Morris ends up putting his own life on the line, a lone man against an entire town, as he tries to save a young woman's life and defuse the blind hatred raging through the land.

Unfortunately, these were the only two books Davis published in his lifetime. He turned down an offer to develop his writing career in New York, and instead took a job with Southwestern Bell, ending up as a senior executive in public relations. But he never stopped writing. In an interview with *Paperback Quarterly* (vol. 1, no. 2), Davis says he's "written fifteen novels, but have only *five* I really like." He also says he likes two of them "better than" *One For Hell* and *The Outraged Sect*.

One of these may be *So Curse the Day*, the story of Dun Lattner, another drifter through the American Southwest, looking for something he'll probably never find. At least not without the kind of trouble he's looking to avoid. Here Davis gives us the classic wealthy bad girl, the kind of woman a man like Lattner thinks he can control but never really can, mostly because he'll never have the kind of money it always seems to take. There's the good girl he'd like desperately to be worthy of, but he's at war with his own nature, and he can never believe in himself the way she always will. At the heart of it is Lattner's own cynical ego, and though he tries to go straight, to be the kind of man his girl wants him to be, he can't help but take the easy way out when a wealthy matron named Nora takes him in and is willing to reward him for his company. This is classic noir straight out of James M. Cain territory, and is very close to the level of *One For Hell*.

The other is likely *Midnight Road* (forthcoming from Stark House Press, 2014). While not as hardboiled a crime novel as *One For Hell* or *So Curse the Day*, it is nevertheless Davis's overwhelming tour de force. A coming of age story, *Midnight Road* tells the story of a boy from a poor family, 15 year-old Jeff Carr who folks claim looks a whole lot more like the easy-going Kenty Hooker than his own mother's husband.

Not only does Jeff have to deal with his tense family situation, he gets involved with the violent and unpredictable family of Old Trails, as mean a cuss as there was around those parts. His daughter, though, was wonderful, the love of Jeff's life. One of her brothers was a torment and a bully, and the other was forced to live under the porch to escape Old Trails' constant beatings.

With attempted murder, hidden secrets and family scandals, Davis shows he's as adept at writing complex characters and family situations as he is at keeping the reader absorbed with constant nail-biting tension.

Before his death in 1996, Davis said that he "hope[d] to retire early and resume the career I should never have abandoned." If only that had come true.

**Further Reading:**
ONE FOR HELL (1953)
THE OUTRAGED SECT (1956)
MIDNIGHT ROAD (2014)

---

**If you like Jada M. Davis,** you might like: Jim Thompson, James M. Cain

# Norbert Davis

(also, in collaboration with W. T. Ballard wrote as Harrison Hunt, also wrote as Cedric Titus). Born in Morrison, Illinois, 1909. Died in Harwick, Massachusetts, 1949.

One of the funniest mystery writers ever was Norbert Davis. His novel *Sally's in the Alley* (1943) may rank alongside such literary comic and satirical gems as Evelyn Waugh's *The Loved One* and Jerzy Kosinsky's *Being There*.

The word most often associated with Davis's brand of humor is "whimsical" (definition: playful; lighthearted or amusing). Another word would be "deadpan" (def: form of comic delivery in which humor is presented in a casual, monotone, or very serious, matter-of-fact voice). In other words, Davis doesn't call attention to his humor. He doesn't "slyly wink" at the reader, as if to say, "Ha ha ha. See how funny I am?" His protagonists often make sardonic comments to other characters without the other characters even realizing they've just been ridiculed.

Norbert Davis was studying law at Stanford University in California when he first sold a story to *Black Mask* ("Reform Racket," June 1932). By the time he graduated, he was firmly entrenched as a successful pulp magazine writer, and he decided to abandon law for fiction writing. He went on to sell crime stories to *Dime Detective*, *Detective Fiction Weekly*, *Detective Tales* and *Double Detective*. He wrote adventure stories, love stories and westerns, as well.

Davis created numerous memorable series characters for the pulps: Max Latin, Just Plain Jones, Bail Bond Dodd and Ben Shaley. In 1940, in a two-part story for *Argosy*, Davis introduced the two characters who would become the comic high-point in his career: Doan and Carstairs. Doan is a short, fat private detective. Carstairs is a Great Dane that Doan won in a poker game. As for character traits, Doan never seems to run out of creative ways to antagonize as many people as possible. His boss at the detective agency says Doan is "the most dangerous little devil I've ever seen, and he's all the worse because of that half-witted manner of his. You never suspect what he's up to until it's too late." As for Carstairs, he is truly a unique creation, with a lot more sense than many so-called "humans." Carstairs behaves as if he is in every way superior to Doan, and he often is; he doesn't approve of Doan's drinking, and he stubbornly refuses to acquiesce to Doan's commands when he feels he is in the right, which is pretty much all the time.

Davis's first Doan and Carstairs novel was *The Mouse in the Mountain* (1943, aka *Dead Little Rich Girl*). In the story, Doan and Carstairs travel to Los

Altos, Mexico to convince an American fugitive not to return to the U.S. and give himself up. The story also includes three murders, numerous villains, and a an earthquake that cuts the mountainous little village of Los Altos off from the rest of Mexico.

The second Doan and Carstairs novel was *Sally's in the Alley*. In this book, two government agents persuade Doan to find an ore deposit important to the war effort, which is located in a small town on the state line of California and Nevada. The target of most of the novel's satire comes in the form of Harriet Hathaway, a soon-to-become WAAC who evangelistically pesters anyone who crosses her path to contribute every bit of mind, body, and soul to the war effort.

In the last Doan and Carstairs novel, *Oh, Murderer Mine* (1946), the comedy is broader and more farcical, the wit a bit less sharp-edged. In this book, the pair are hired by Heloise of Hollywood, a 54 year-old cosmetics maven, to keep an eye on her husband, a handsome and virile meteorologist at a local college who is half her age. The target of much of the book's satire is university life.

It's a cliché that most funnymen have a dark side. Unfortunately, in Norbert Davis's case, this was true. In the late '40's, Davis abandoned writing for the pulps and yearned to write for the more prestigious and higher paying slick magazines. Some writers speculate Davis became depressed because of his lack of success in this regard, although he did sell twelve stories to *The Saturday Evening Post* between 1944-1949. He also had a confluence of bad events which added to his woes: marital problems, the death of his agent, a cancer diagnosis. In July of 1949, Davis drove to a vacation resort on Cape Cod, ran a hose from his car's exhaust pipe to a room in the house where he was staying, and took his own life.

**Further Reading:**
THE MOUSE IN THE MOUNTAIN (1943; as DEAD LITTLE RICH GIRL, 1945)
SALLY'S IN THE ALLEY (1943)
OH, MURDERER MINE (1946)

**As Harrison Hunt**
MURDER PICKS THE JURY (1947, with W.T. Ballard)

---

**If you like Norbert Davis,** you might like: Frank Gruber, Fletcher Flora

# Richard Deming

(also wrote as Max Franklin, Halsey Clark, Nick Morino, Richard Hale Curtis, Richard Deeming, Emily Moor, Lee Davis Willoughby, Ellery Queen). Born in Des Moines, Iowa, 1915. Died in 1983.

Richard Deming came of age during the late 1940's and early 1950's, just when pulps like *Black Mask* and *Dime Detective* were dying out, and smaller format "digests" like *Manhunt* and *Mike Shayne Mystery Magazine* were beginning. He wrote nearly 150 short stories for both the pulps and the digests.

Deming attended Washington University in St. Louis and the University of Iowa. He served in the United States Army for four years during World War II and was discharged in 1945 with the rank of Captain.

Deming was working for the Red Cross in New York when he started writing pulp stories featuring his first series character, Manville "Manny" Moon. In the Hammett and Chandler tradition, Manny is tough, honest and quick-witted. One aspect of Moon that distinguishes him from other private detectives is the fact that, due to a war injury, he has an artificial leg. But Moon can still more than hold his own: he's an expert shot and has a black belt in judo. Deming provides local color to the Manville stories by way of Moon's "office," which is in a Mexican restaurant. The Moon tales have a strong narrative drive, a realistically described low-rent atmosphere and crackling dialogue. Deming wrote four Manny Moon novels: *The Gallows in My Garden* (1952), *Tweak the Devil's Nose* (1953), *Whistle Past the Graveyard* (1954) and *Juvenile Delinquent* (1958).

Deming also wrote a series of books about Matt Rudd, a vice cop in the fictional Southern California city of St. Cecilia. The Rudd novels are police procedurals; St. Cecilia is a city steeped in sin and filled with numerous organized crime rackets. The Rudd novels are *Vice Cop* (1961), *Anything But Saintly* (1963) and *Death of a Pusher* (1964).

Deming, using both his own name and the pseudonym Max Franklin, wrote more than 20 novelizations for TV shows such as *Dragnet*, *The Mod Squad*, *Starsky and Hutch*, *Charlie's Angels* and *Vegas*.

**Further Reading:**
*Manny Moon series (complete):*
THE GALLOWS IN MY GARDEN (1952)
TWEAK THE DEVIL'S NOSE (1953, as HAND-PICKED TO DIE, 1956)
WHISTLE PAST THE GRAVEYARD (1954)
JUVENILE DELINQUENT (1958)

*Matt Rudd series (complete):*
VICE COP (1961)
ANYTHING BUT SAINTLY (1963)
DEATH OF A PUSHER (1964)

DRAGNET: THE CASE OF THE COURTEOUS KILLER (1958, TV novelization)
DRAGNET: THE CASE OF THE CRIME KING (1959, TV novelization)
KISS AND KILL (1960)
HIT AND RUN (1960)
BODY FOR SALE (1962)
THIS GAME OF MURDER (1964)
THE MOD SQUAD: A GROOVY WAY TO DIE (1968, TV novelization)
THE MOD SQUAD: THE SOCK-IT-TO-EM MURDERS (1969, TV novelization)

**As Max Franklin**
(TV novelizations)
STARSKY AND HUTCH: KILL HUGGY BEAR (1976)
STARSKY AND HUTCH: THE PSYCHIC (1977)
CHARLIE'S ANGELS: ANGELS ON A STRING (1977)
CHARLIE'S ANGELS: ANGELS IN CHAINS (1977)

**As Ellery Queen**
DEATH SPINS THE PLATTER (1962)
WIFE OR DEATH (1963)
LOSERS (1966)
SHOOT THE SCENE (1966)
WHY SO DEAD? (1966)

------------------------------------------------------------

**If you like Richard Deming,** you might like: Frederick Nebel, Dashiell
Hammett

# Lester Dent

(also wrote as Harmon Cash, Tim Ryan, Kenneth Roberts, Kenneth Robeson, H. O. Cash, Harold A. Davis, Robert Wallace, C. K. M. Scanlon, George H. Wilcoxson, Johnny Wiley, Cliff Howe, Ralph Powers, Robert Lewis). Born in La Plata, Missouri, 1904. Died in La Plata, Missouri, 1959.

Lester Dent is best known for the long-running series of Doc Savage pulp adventure novels which he wrote under the pseudonym Kenneth Robeson, and for his unusual detectives–Click Rush, the Gadget Man; Lee Nace, the Blond Adder; and Foster Fade, the Crime Spectacularist.

In 1929, Dent, a telegraph operator working for the Associated Press out of the offices of the *Tulsa World*, sold his first pulp story, "Pirate Cay," to *Top Notch*. A year later, he worked as a contract writer for *Sky Riders* and *Scotland Yard*, until the Depression killed off both pulps.

As a freelancer, Dent then mastered several pulp genres–western, aviation and detective. His work brought him to the attention of Street & Smith, who contacted him to write a Shadow novel, *The Golden Vulture* (written in 1932 and revised by Maxwell Grant and published in 1938), before hiring him to inaugurate their new *Doc Savage Magazine*.

Although Street & Smith business manager Henry W. Ralston and editor John L. Nanovic came up with the original idea of a bronze superman named Doc Savage who travels the world fighting evil, Dent gave the character personality. Doc was raised by his father, a wealthy adventurer, following the death of his mother when he was a toddler. Trained from childhood to follow a demanding exercise regimen, he became a perfect physical specimen. He was tutored by experts in various fields and his knowledge became encyclopedic.

He gathered together a crew of five assistants who were experts in their own fields. "Monk" Mayfair was a roughneck who was also a world-renowned chemist. "Renny" Renwick, who enjoyed punching out door panels with his massive fists, was an engineer. "Long Tom" Robert worked wonders with electricity. "Johnny" Littlejohn was a brilliant archeologist. "Ham" Brooks, who carried a sword cane, was an astute lawyer.

Doc Savage (nicknamed "the Man of Bronze" because of the hue of his skin, hair and eyes) and his comrades, financed by gold reserves from a hidden Central American mine, were assigned to go "from one end of the world to the other, looking for excitement and adventure, striving to help those who need help; to punish those who deserve it."

Dent, under the name Kenneth Robeson, wrote his first Doc Savage story, "The Man of Bronze," in March of 1933, and almost immediately the circulation of *Doc Savage Magazine* reached 200,000. It soon caught up to *The Shadow*, topping out around 300,000 per month. The series lasted until 1949, with 181 issues, of which 159 were written by Dent.

In 1964, five years after Dent's death, Bantam Books began reprinting the Doc Savage tales in paperback with unexpected success. Doc Savage was also featured in the 1975 movie, *Doc Savage: The Man of Bronze*, starring Ron Ely.

In his personal life, Dent shared traits with his larger than life pulp characters. Physically imposing at 6'2" and weighing over 200 pounds, he possessed vast arcane knowledge and was a master of assorted skills—pilot, radio operator, electrician, and architect (he designed his own house from scratch). He loved exploring deserts, sailing tropic waters, and diving for sunken treasure.

After the cancelation of *Doc Savage Magazine* in 1949, Dent supervised his family's dairy farm in his hometown of La Plata, Missouri, and wrote a few novels for the burgeoning paperback market. *Cry at Dusk* (1952, Gold Medal) is the story of former college football hero Johnny Marks's search for his uncle's killer while a dark secret from Johnny's past seeks to overtake him. The daring for its time story deals with homosexuality and sadomasochism. *Lady in Peril* (1959, Ace) is the story of Mitchell Loneman's search for his wife, who has gone missing while investigating the murder of her brother, a whistleblower who testified about the dirty dealings of a statewide food-pricing racket.

Another notable achievement of Dent's is that, in the mid-1930's, he sold two stories, "Sail" and "Angelfish," to *Black Mask*. In 1936, he wrote an article for the *Writer's Digest Yearbook* about his formula for a short story master plot which, according to Dent, had never failed to produce a sale if written accordingly.

**Further Reading:**
DEAD AT THE TAKE-OFF (1946; as HIGH STAKES, 1953)
LADY TO KILL (1946)
LADY AFRAID (1948)
LADY SO SILENT (1951)
CRY AT DUSK (1952)
LADY IN PERIL (1959)

---

**If you like Lester Dent,** you might like: Edward S. Aarons, Kendell Foster Crossen

# Thomas B. Dewey

(also wrote as Tom Brandt, Cord Wainer; not to be confused with Thomas Dewey, "racket busting" New York District Attorney and former presidential candidate). Born in Elkhart, Indiana, 1915. Died in Tempe, Arizona, 1981.

Thomas B. Dewey created three memorable series characters during the Golden Age of paperbacks: Singer Batts, Pete Schofield and Dewey's most popular creation, a private eye who went simply by the name of "Mac."

Dewey graduated from Kansas State Teachers College in 1936, and did graduate work at the University of Iowa, 1937-38. From 1938-1942, he was an editor at Storycraft Inc., a correspondence school in Hollywood. He was an administrative and editorial assistant for the State Department in Washington DC (1942-45), worked in advertising in Los Angeles from 1945-1952, made a living as a full time novelist from 1952-1971 and was an assistant professor of English at Arizona State University, 1971-77.

Whew. No shirker, this Thomas B. Dewey.

Dewey introduced Singer Batts in *Hue and Cry* (1944). Batts is a small-town Midwestern hotel owner, Shakespearean scholar, and amateur sleuth. Dewey provides Batts with plenty of idiosyncrasies: Batts searches for his soul mate by writing to lonely-hearts clubs, intensively researches historical murder cases, and refuses to have his reading interrupted before finishing a chapter, no matter what's happening around him. The Batts novels are narrated by Joe Spinder, the manager of the hotel and the tougher, more level-headed of the pair, who frequently has to help pull Batts out of one scrape after another. The three other Batts novels are *As Good as Dead* (1946), *Mourning After* (1950) and *Handle With Fear* (1951).

Dewey also wrote a series of books featuring private detective Pete Schofield and his wife, Jeanne. The frequent banter between Pete and Jeanne is reminiscent of Dashiell Hammett's Nick and Nora Charles. Notable titles in the series include *The Golden Hooligan* (1961), a story involving a dead bullfighter; *Go,Honeylou* (1962), where Pete searches for a kidnapped 19 year-old sexpot; and the book which most reviewers call the best of the series, *Only On Tuesdays* (1964), which includes the death of a pin-up model, a mysterious dachshund found in Pete's bedroom closet and a frenzied sailboat race to Catalina Island.

In 1947, Dewey wrote a book featuring the series character he is best known for, a Chicago-based PI known simply as "Mac." In Mac's first appearance, *Draw the Curtain Close* (aka *Dame in Danger*), he describes himself as:

> "...just a guy. I go around and get in jams and then try to figure a way out of them. I work hard. I don't make very much money and

most people insult me one way or another. I'm thirty-eight years old, a fairly good shot with small arms, slow-thinking but thorough, and very dirty in a clinch."

Mac has been called one of the most believable and humane PI's in crime fiction. He is reluctant to use either his gun or his fists, but will do so when the situation demands it, or in self-defense; he doesn't merely solve his clients' cases, but provides moral support and sympathy as well; and perhaps most notable of all, Mac *feels*, and is not afraid to show it— pain, loss, sorrow, loneliness. Notable books include *The Mean Streets* (1955), where Mac goes undercover as a high school teacher to search for the leader of a violent teenage gang that's terrorizing the community; *Deadline* (1966), where Mac has four days to save an innocent man from the electric chair and find the real killer; and the book which is widely regarded as Dewey's best, *A Sad Song Singing* (1963), where Mac is hired by a teenaged singer to find her guitar playing boyfriend. Altogether, Dewey wrote 17 novels featuring Mac.

Dewey's "Mac" novel, *Every Bet's a Sure Thing* (1953), served as the basis for an episode of *Cannon*, titled "Death's a Double-Cross" (1971).

Further Reading:

*Singer Batts series (complete):*
HUE AND CRY (1944; as ROOM FOR MURDER, 1950)
AS GOOD AS DEAD (1946)
MOURNING AFTER (1950)
HANDLE WITH FEAR (1951)

*Mac series:*
DRAW THE CURTAIN CLOSE (1947; as DAME IN DANGER, 1958)
EVERY BET'S A SURE THING (1953)
THE MEAN STREETS (1955)
THE BRAVE, BAD GIRLS (1956)
YOU'VE GOT HIM COLD (1958)
THE CASE OF THE CHASED AND THE UNCHASTE (1959)
HOW HARD TO KILL (1962)
A SAD SONG SINGING (1963)
DON'T CRY FOR LONG (1964)
PORTRAIT OF A DEAD HEIRESS (1965)
DEADLINE (1966)
DEATH AND TAXES (1967)

*Pete Schofield series:*
AND WHERE SHE STOPS (1957)
GO TO SLEEP JEANNIE (1959)
TOO HOT FOR HAWAII (1960)
THE GOLDEN HOOLIGAN (1961)
GO, HONEYLOU (1962)
THE GIRL WITH THE SWEET PLUMP KNEES (1963)
ONLY ON TEUSDAYS (1964)
THE GIRL IN THE PUNCHBOWL (1964)
NUDE IN NEVADA (1965)

MY LOVE IS VIOLENT (1956)
HUNTER AT LARGE (1961)
CAN A MERMAID KILL? (1965)
A SEASON FOR VIOLENCE (1966)

---

**If you like Thomas B. Dewey,** you might like: William Campbell Gault, William Ard, Bill Pronzini

# H. Vernor Dixon

(real name Harry Vernor Dixon. Born 1908, died in 1984.)

 H. Vernor Dixon tried for something a little more literary than was the norm for Gold Medal PBOs during the 1950's and early '60's. His suspenseful, noirish novels offer incisive critiques of the culture of the wealthy— their decadence, their vacuousness, and a sense of purposelessness in their lives which leads them to chase after increasingly heightened sensations (Dixon titled one of his books *The Pleasure Seekers*). Dixon's protagonists are men on the outside—rugged, amoral layabouts whose only ambition is to crash the gates of the upper-crust and live the good life—and their primary goal is to achieve, as Dixon titled another of his books, *Something for Nothing*.

The women in Dixon's books are slumming socialites attracted to the primitive virility of the Stanley Kowalski-like "hero"; to snare him is to win a prize, a trophy—the back cover copy of *That Girl Marian* encapsulates this point of view: "Millionairess Nets Fisherman." As for Dixon's culture at large, the hoi polloi, they find themselves attracted to Dixon's alpha males, admiring a ruthlessness that surpasses even their own.

Dixon grew up in Sacramento, and most of his books are set in Northern California—in Carmel, Monterey, and other coastal towns near San Francisco. From 1939-50 he published stories in slick magazines such as *Collier's, Cosmopolitan* and *The Saturday Evening Post*.

The owner of the "Reading California Fiction" website makes a Great Gatsby comparison with Dixon's fiction, and posits that Dixon has created a "Gatsby trilogy," with his novels *Something for Nothing* (1950), *To Hell Together* (1951) and *Deep is the Pit* (1952). The blurb for Dixon's early novel, *Laughing Gods* (1935), seems to point this way, touting the book as a "Moralistic novel of the jazz age." A contemporary review of *Something for Nothing* from *The Saturday Review* lends weight to this argument: "The seamier side of sunny California opens up to reveal...various forms of heady over-indulgence, and an abyss of criminal filth." It would be interesting to know if Vernor's obsession with the wealthy is based on any of his own real-life experiences or observations, but no additional biographical information could be found.

In Dixon's novel, *Too Rich to Die* (1953) he veers from his usual formula as a playboy leaves his purposeless, dissolute lifestyle and takes a grunt job as a cook on a fishing boat in an attempt to find something more "real" and down to earth.

Dixon's books are thicker than normal PBO fare. Whereas most paperbacks during the 1950's were either 128, 160, or 190 pages, five of Dixon's books were between 240 and 280 pages, most likely due to Dixon's ambitions to create social critiques. Dixon wrote a total of sixteen novels, fourteen of which were PBOs, nine for Gold Medal.

**Further Reading:**
LAUGHING GODS (1935)
SOMETHING FOR NOTHING (1950)
TO HELL TOGETHER (1951)
DEEP IS THE PIT (1952)
TOO RICH TO DIE (1953)
UP A WINDING STAIR (1953)
A LOVER FOR CINDY (1954)
THE HUNGER AND THE HATE (1955)
CRY BLOOD (1956)
KILLER IN SILK (1956)
THAT GIRL MIRIAM (1962)
THE PLEASURE SEEKERS (1963)
THE RAG PICKERS (1966)

---

**If you like H. Vernor Dixon,** you might like: W. R. Burnett, Fletcher Flora

# David Dodge

Born in Berkeley, California, 1910. Died in San Miguel Allende, Mexico, 1974.

David Dodge wrote the novel *To Catch a Thief*, which was made into the famous movie directed by Alfred Hitchcock. Throughout his career, Dodge's books were notable for their glamorous and romantic international locales and in addition to fiction, wrote a number of bestselling travel books.

Dodge was born in Berkeley, California, and moved to Southern California after his father's early death in an automobile accident. When Dodge was sixteen years old, he quit school, took a job as a bank messenger in Los Angeles and started taking night school classes at the American Institute of Banking. By 1937, he had quit the banking business, moved back to Northern California, and was working as a Certified Public Accountant.

His novel writing career started when he bet his wife Elva that he could write a better mystery novel than the one she was currently reading. He wrote a book featuring James "Whit" Whitney, an accountant who inadvertently becomes involved in a murder mystery. The book, *Death and Taxes*, was published in 1941, and Dodge won $5 from his wife. (I'm assuming the book she was reading wasn't *The Maltese Falcon* or *The Big Sleep*, but we'll probably never know.) Whit had a partner and love interest in that book, Kitty MacLeod, and reviewers compared Whit and Kitty to Hammett's Nick and Nora Charles because of *Death's* breezy tone, witty dialogue, and Whit and Kitty's large consumption of alcohol. Dodge wrote three more books featuring Whit and Kitty: *Shear the Black Sheep* (1943), *Bullets for the Bridegroom* (1944, in which Whit and Kitty are married), and *It Ain't Hay* (1946, which sports a classic cover showing a red-garbed figure of death and a giant marijuana cigarette).

During World War II, Dodge served in the Navy. Upon his release, he and his wife and daughter traveled through many Latin American countries. These experiences provided Dodge with the material for a second series character, adventurer and private detective Al Colby. The tone of the Colby novels differs from the breezy air of the Whitney novels—Colby is a tough and rugged adventurer; the stories are suspense-filled and take place in exotic locales. The first Colby book was *The Long Escape* (1948), where Colby has to track down a runaway husband from Mexico to Santiago, Chile. The other Colby books are *Plunder in the Sun* (1949), where Colby is hired to find a lost Inca treasure in Peru; and *The Red Tassel* (1950), where Colby fights saboteurs and witch doctors in the Bolivian Andes. *Plunder in the Sun* was made into a successful movie in 1953 starring Glenn

Ford, written by crime writer Jonathan Latimer and directed by John Farrow.

After the Colby series, Dodge focused on stand-alone novels and suspense stories. These include *To Catch a Thief* (1952), in which a retired cat burglar, to clear himself, is forced to track down a copycat (no pun intended) thief; *Angel's Ransom* (1956), a story about a yacht captain who faces murderous kidnappers; and *Carambola* (1960), a story about a mining engineer who must smuggle his ex-wife's current husband across the Pyrenees from Spain to France.

**Further Reading:**
*Whit Whitney series (complete):*
DEATH AND TAXES (1941)
SHEAR THE BLACK SHEEP (1942)
BULLETS FOR THE BRIDEGROOM (1944)
IT AIN'T HAY (1946)

*Al Colby series (complete):*
THE LONG ESCAPE (1948)
PLUNDER OF THE SUN (1949)
THE RED TASSEL (1950)

HOW GREEN WAS MY FATHER: A SORT OF TRAVEL DIARY
   (1947, non-fiction)
HOW LOST WAS MY WEEKEND: A GREENHORN IN GUATEMALA
   (1948, non-fiction)
TO CATCH A THIEF (1952)
THE POOR MAN'S GUIDE TO EUROPE (1953, non-fiction)
ANGEL'S RANSOM (1956)
LOO LOO'S LEGACY (1960)
CARAMBOLA (1961)
THE RICH MAN'S GUIDE TO THE RIVERIA (1962, non-fiction)
THE POOR MAN'S GUIDE TO THE ORIENT (1965, non-fiction)
FLY DOWN, DRIVE MEXICO (1968, non-fiction, revised as
   THE BEST OF MEXICO BY CAR, 1969)
HOOLIGAN (1969)

---

**If you like David Dodge,** you might like: Howard Hunt, Dan Cushman

# Hal Ellson

(not to be confused with Harlan Ellison). Born 1910. Died in Brooklyn, New York, 1994.

Hal Ellson was one of the mainstays of juvenile delinquent fiction during the late 1940's-'60's.

Ellson's thoughts first turned to writing during the 1940's, while he was working in the psychiatric adolescent ward at Bellevue Hospital. "It was a time when the New York neighborhoods were filled with these teenage gangs...I saw all kinds of mixed up and crazy things at that job and I took my notebook everywhere I went. I made lots of notes and a lot of the stuff in my books was just writing down what these young people said." (*Over My Dead Body*, by Lee Server, pg 91.)

The novel that gained Ellson the most attention was his first, *Duke* (1949). The story of a fifteen year old Harlem gang leader, Duke's activities included pimping, pushing drugs, rape and murder. Ellson wrote Duke's story in the first person, allowing the reader to get into the warped mind of the character:

> "I'd get dreaming I could go in a bank and have a bullet-proof on and grab everything and have all the women in the world. I wanted to be a Superman. I wanted to rob a squad car with riot guns, snatch them up and shoot my name on the wall."

*Duke* received detailed analytical reviews from prestigious periodicals like *The Saturday Review* and from socially conscious writers like Nelsen Algren, who attributed Duke's rage to "spiritual isolationism," brought about by American culture's investment in technological advances (such as Thunderjets and napalm) designed to defend against foreign invaders, at the expense of neglecting its own homegrown at-risk youth. ("Bitter Physics of the Deprived," by Nelson Algren, *The Saturday Review*, July 4, 1953)

After the success of *Duke*, Ellson became privy to even more inside information about juvenile gangs and their misdeeds. "After *Duke* came out they'd be lined up waiting to talk to me, kids accused of a couple of murders, saying 'Want to hear a good story?'" (*Encyclopedia of Pulp Fiction Writers*, pg. 89.)

Ellson's follow-up novel, *Tomboy* (1950), is a female version of *Duke*, featuring a girl gang leader. *Tomboy* was filmed as *Wasteland* (1960), a French production directed by Marcel Carne. In 1952, *Tomboy*, along with books by John Steinbeck and John Faulkner, was branded by a special congressional house committee as being "objectionable literature" and "obscene and gruesome," though no further action was taken. Ironically, the first edition of *Tomboy* boasted a supportive introduction by censorship advocate and arch-enemy of 1950's comic book publishers, Dr. Fredric Wertham.

Ellson continued writing juvenile delinquent related novels for the rest of his career, including *I'll Fix You* (1956), *Jailbait Street* (1959), *Stairway to Nowhere* (1959), *The Knife* (1961) and *Nightmare Street* (1965).

Ellson wrote short stories for *Manhunt*, *The Saint Detective Magazine*, *Shell Scott Mystery Magazine*, *Off Beat Detective Stories*, *Alfred Hitchcock's Mystery Magazine* and *Pursued*.

**Further Reading:**
DUKE (1949)
TOMBOY (1950)
THE GOLDEN SPIKE (1952)
SUMMER STREET (1953)
ROCK (1955)
TELL THEM NOTHING (1956, short stories)
I'LL FIX YOU (1956)
THIS IS IT (1956)
JAILBAIT STREET (1959)
A KILLER'S KISS (1959)
STAIRWAY TO NOWHERE (1959)
A NEST OF FEAR (1961)
THE KNIFE (1961)
NIGHTMARE STREET (1965)
GAMES (1967, movie novelization)
THAT GLOVER WOMAN (1967)
BLOOD ON THE IVY (1971)

---

**If you like Hal Ellson,** you might like: Irving Shulman, Wenzell Brown

# John Faulkner

(real name John Wesley Thompson Falkner, III). Born in Ripley, Mississippi, 1901. Died in Oxford, Mississippi, 1963.

 John Faulkner must have known just how James, the younger brother of Jesus, felt. Big brother Bill was the darling of the literary establishment, winning the Nobel Prize for Literature in 1950. So John Faulkner spent his first 40 years doing his damnedest to stay out of brother William's shadow—at various times he was an assistant civil engineer, a commercial airline pilot and a farmer. But the writing muse finally caught up with him, and in 1951 he published his first paperback for Gold Medal, *Cabin Road*.

The book painted a satirical portrait of the bawdy, earthy, uneducated backwoods folk who lived on an isolated patch of land in Mississippi. Gold Medal's blurb described the book thusly: "You will howl with delight over the female problems of Jones Peabody, of the Government Man, of Uncle Good and his 'girls,' of the Ex-Senator, and a list of earthy, uninhibited males and females such as you have never met before on earth or in heaven."

John's ribald tale of backwoods antics was successful, and Gold Medal asked for more. John wrote a sequel called *Uncle Good's Girls*, then wrote three more paperbacks highlighting similar characters: *Sin Shouter of Cabin Road*, *Ain't Gonna Rain No More*, and *Uncle Good's Weekend Party*. The ironically named "Uncle Good" was an amoral hillbilly who made his living pimping his daughters, Jewel Mae and Orta June, for fifty cents each. These books were also successful, and Faulkner's books for Gold Medal sold more than 2 million copies.

Ultimately, John never completely stopped following in the footsteps of big brother Bill—he died in 1963, only a year after his more famous sibling's passing.

**Further Reading:**

MEN WORKING (1941)                    DOLLAR COTTON (1942)
CHOOKY (1948)                         CABIN ROAD (1951)
UNCLE GOOD'S GIRLS (1952)             SIN SHOUTER OF CABIN ROAD (1954)
AIN'T GONNA RAIN NO MORE (1957)
UNCLE GOOD'S WEEKEND PARTY (1959)

----------------------------------------------------------------

**If you like John Faulkner,** you might like: Erskine Caldwell, Charles Williams

# Kenneth Fearing

(also wrote as Kirk Wolff, Donald F. Bedford). Born in Oak Park, Illinois, 1902.
Died in New York, New York, 1961.

Kenneth Fearing was a writer with a wide range of literary talents. He was a staff writer for *Time* magazine, a renowned poet whose talents were compared to Carl Sandburg's, and a founding member of the literary magazine *The Partisan Review*. But what will be of most interest to noir fiction fans are his five mystery novels, particularly *The Big Clock*.

Fearing developed his talent for writing early, and while attending the University of Wisconsin at Madison he wrote for and edited his school's literary journal. In 1925, he moved to Greenwich Village and became involved in shaping that culture's literary and bohemian lifestyle. He also became active in left wing causes during that time. In the early-mid 1930's, Fearing began writing short stories for the "spicy" pulps using the pseudonym Kirk Wolff. He wrote for pulps such as *French Nightlife Stories, Tattle Tales, Spicy Stories, Snappy Stories* and others.

Fearing's first crime novel was the psychological thriller *Dagger of the Mind* (1941, reprinted as *Cry Killer!* by Avon in 1958). The basic story is a murder mystery set in an artists' colony. Fearing himself repeatedly attended Yaddo, the famous writers' colony in Sarasota Springs, New York. Fearing took the opportunity to satirize many of the colony's people and their idosyncrasies. In a *New York Times* review, Isaac Anderson wrote, "Here are gathered some of the most eccentric and unconventional characters that can possibly be imagined.... Taken as a whole, this book is not so much a mystery story as a study in abnormal psychology—an absorbing one at that—although the mystery element is by no means negligible."

Fearing is most well known among crime and mystery fans for his novel *The Big Clock* (1946). On the surface, the story is about George Stroud, a reporter for *Crimeways*, one of the many magazines published by Janoth Enterprises. One night, George inadvertently witnesses his boss, despotic Earl Janoth, murdering his mistress. Complications arise when Janoth realizes someone has witnessed the murder (although he doesn't know who), and he organizes the staff of Janoth Enterprises to search his mammoth office building, claiming he wants to find the killer, but in actuality hoping to find the *witness*, who Janoth secretly plans to do away with. And who is the man assigned to lead this search force? George Stroud.

But the novel goes much deeper than what is apparent from the plot synopsis. George Stroud finds his creativity stifled by the culture of mechanization and routine at Janoth Enterprises. "The Big Clock," a fixture at

Janoth Enterprises and a character itself, is used to illustrate how the tick-tock routine at Janoth can grind away an individual's heart and soul. When published, the novel was a hit, and in 1948 was made into a seminal film noir, with a screenplay by veteran crime writer Jonathan Latimer, starring Ray Milland as Stroud and Charles Laughton as the ruthless and tyrannical Earl Janoth. In 1997, the Library of America reprinted *The Big Clock* in *Crime Novels: American Noir of the 1930's and 40's*, placing it alongside such noir masterpieces as James M. Cain's *The Postman Always Rings Twice*, Cornell Woolrich's *I Married A Dead Man* and Horace McCoy's *They Shoot Horses, Don't They?*, among others.

Fearing's other noirish novels were *The Loneliest Girl in the World* (1951), *The Generous Heart* (1954) and *The Crozart Story* (1960). He also wrote a few short stories for the crime digests *Manhunt, Ed McBain's Mystery Book* and *Mike Shayne Mystery Magazine*.

**Further Reading:**
DAGGER OF THE MIND (1941; as CRY KILLER!, 1958)
CLARK GIFFORD'S BODY (1942)
THE BIG CLOCK (1946)
THE LONELIEST GIRL IN THE WORLD (1951; as THE SOUND OF MURDER, 1952)
THE GENEROUS HEART (1954)
THE CROZART STORY (1960)

If you like Kenneth Fearing, you might like: Dorothy B. Hughes, Peter Rabe

# G. G. Fickling

(real names Forrest E. "Skip" Fickling and Gloria Fickling). Forrest Fickling—born
in Long Beach, California, 1925. Died in Laguna Beach, California, 1998. Gloria
Fickling—presently living in California.

Forrest and Gloria Fickling jumped
on the Mickey Spillane bandwagon,
along with numerous other mystery
writers, during the mid-1950's. The
difference was that instead of blast-
ing enemies with a.45 caliber, the
Fickling's PI, Honey West, wielded
her 38-22-36 measurements.

Before creating Honey West, Forrest was a journalist and sports broad-
caster; Gloria was a fashion magazine editor. They got the idea for Honey
when their friend, writer Richard S. Prather (of Shell Scott fame), suggested they write a story about a sexy female private eye. But rather than the
hardboiled, tough-as-nails adventures of private eyes such as Mike
Hammer, the Honey West tales were a tongue-in-cheek blend of zany
humor. Their first Honey West book was *This Girl for Hire* (1957). The book
was an instant success.

There were 11 Honey West books published altogether. Titles include:
*Girl On the Loose* (1958), *Honey in the Flesh* (1959), *Dig a Dead Doll* (1961), and the
final book in the series, *Honey On Her Tail* (1971).

Honey West became something of a craze during the mid-60's. *Honey
West* was a successful TV series, starring the lithe and lovely Anne Francis.
There was a Honey West board game, a Honey West doll and a soundtrack
for the Honey West TV show. Honey even starred in a one-shot comic book.

In addition to Honey, the Ficklings wrote three books featuring private
eye Erik March: *Naughty But Dead* (1962), *The Case of the Radioactive Redhead*
(1963) and *The Crazy Mixed-up Nude* (1964). The March books did not meet
with the same success. In an interesting side note, March made a "guest
appearance" in a Honey West novel, *Stiff as a Broad* (1971).

Interesting trivia: The Ficklings appeared as contestants on Groucho
Marx's quiz show, *You Bet Your Life*.

**Further Reading:**
*Honey West series (complete):*
THIS GIRL FOR HIRE (1957)
A GUN FOR HONEY (1958)
GIRL ON THE LOOSE (1958)
HONEY IN THE FLESH (1959)

GIRL ON THE PROWL (1959)
KISS FOR A KILLER (1960)
DIG A DEAD DOLL (1960)
BLOOD AND HONEY (1961)
BOMBSHELL (1964)
STIFF AS A BROAD (1971, Erik March appearance)
HONEY ON HER TAIL (1971)

*Erik March series (complete):*
NAUGHTY BUT DEAD (1962)
THE CASE OF THE RADIOACTIVE REDHEAD (1963)
THE CRAZY MIXED-UP NUDE (1964)

---

If you like G. G. Fickling, you might like: Carter Brown, Henry Kane

# Jack Finney

(born Walter Braden Finney). Born in Milwaukee, Wisconsin, 1911. Died in
Greenbrae, California, 1995.

Jack Finney's claim to fame was his classic science fiction novella, "The Body Snatchers" (1955), and its equally classic movie adaptation, *Invasion of the Body Snatchers*
(1956). But Finney was no one-shot wonder, and a number of his other suspense and science fiction books have
garnered well-deserved cult followings.

Finney attended Knox College in Galesburg, Illinois,
graduating in 1934. Shortly afterward, Finney moved to
New York and found work at an advertising agency. His first short story,
"The Widow's Walk" (1946), won a contest sponsored by *Ellery Queen's
Mystery Magazine*, and the story was published in that digest the same year.
He then began publishing stories in publications like *The Magazine of Fantasy
and Science Fiction*, as well as in slick magazines like *Collier's* and *The Saturday
Evening Post*.

Finney's early science fiction and fantasy short stories are collected in
*The Third Level* (1956).

Finney's most famous story, "The Body Snatchers," was first serialized
in *Collier's*, and then released as a Dell First Edition paperback. The story is
about a race of aliens who replace the citizens of an idyllic small town
with "pod people"—perfect physical duplicates—while the citizens are
sleeping. The small town's family physician, Miles Bennell, catches wind
of the situation, and with the help of an old flame, struggles to stay awake
and warn the townspeople who have not yet been duplicated. Yet Bennell
is continually confronted by "pod people" who try to convince him to join
them, that the life of a pod person is a life of peace and ease, that war and
pain will end, and that their new race offers harmony and unity.

Reviewers and critics interpret the story's meaning many different
ways. Some claim it's a parable about a Communist takeover of a sleeping
America. Others claim just the opposite—that the story is an indictment
against McCarthyism and paranoia about anyone who is "different" or
"alien." And still others claim it's a warning against suburban conformity.
Finney himself disavowed all these interpretations, and responded that he
was merely trying to create popular entertainment. The novella was re-
titled *Invasion of the Body Snatchers* for later printings. Don Siegel directed
the first film version in 1956, and the story was later filmed, less successfully, in 1978.

Finney wrote other notable books as well. His first published novel was
*Five Against the House* (1955), a caper story about five college students who

planned to rob a Nevada casino. Later in 1955, the story was adapted into
an excellent crime thriller starring Kim Novak and Brian Keith. Finney's
*Assault On a Queen* (1959) was a very different kind of caper novel—modern
pirates plan to resurrect a sunken submarine in order to rob the *Queen
Mary*.

Finney scored another of his numerous cult hits with *The Night People*
(1977). The story is about two hipper-than-thou boyfriend/girlfriend couples from San Francisco. Bored with lives they consider mundane, they
begin to plan and execute pranks. Over time, they up the ante and the
pranks become progressively more and more dangerous. Eventually, the
couples cause a massive traffic jam on the Golden Gate Bridge, and project
images from monster movie into the air to create chaos and for their own
amusement.

Finney had explored the concept of time travel in many of his early
short stories, but his tour de force on this subject was his novel *Time and
Again* (1970). The story is about Simon Morley, an advertising agency artist.
Morley is approached by an Army major to participate in a secret government project. He agrees, and through the program he travels back in time
to the New York of the 1880's. What makes the book so memorable is
Finney's wistfully romantic tone, and his detailed recreation of turn-of-
the-century trolleys, horse drawn carriages and gaslights. To add to the
book's sense of authenticity, Finney included numerous photographs of
New York during the 1880's.

The book struck the same wistfully romantic tone in its readers as it
did in its author. For twenty-five years they clamored for a sequel, so
Finney wrote *From Time to Time* (1996, published posthumously). In this
book, Simon Morley travels to 1911 where he becomes involved with events
both personal and political—he tries to prevent WWI and the sinking of
the *Titanic*. The book was well received, but most fans agreed it didn't sur-
pass the original. Still, even being on par with the original was no small
feat.

Finney won the Life Achievement Award at The World Fantasy
Convention in 1987.

Further Reading:
FIVE AGAINST THE HOUSE (1954)
THE BODY SNATCHERS (1955; revised, as
  INVASION OF THE BODY SNATCHERS, 1961)
THE HOUSE OF NUMBERS (1957)
THE THIRD LEVEL (1957, short stories)
ASSAULT ON A QUEEN (1959)
GOOD NEIGHBOR SAM (1963)
I LOVE GALESBURG IN THE SPRINGTIME: FANTASY AND TIME STORIES
  (1963, short stories)
TIME AND AGAIN (1970)
FROM TIME TO TIME (1996)

---

If you like Jack Finney, you might like: Richard Matheson, Elmore Leonard

# *Bruno Fischer*

(also wrote as Russell Gray, Harrison Storm, Jason K. Storm). Born in Berlin, Germany in 1908; immigrated to the United States in 1913. Died in Mexico, 1992.

Bruno Fischer came of age during the 1930's, during the thriving era of the pulps. In particular, he made a name for himself writing stories for the "weird menace" pulps, using the pseudonym Russell Gray. These stories were brutal tales of women enduring gruesome acts of torture, often at the hands of mad scientists. Fischer's stories had titles such as "Fresh Fiancés for the Devil's Daughter," "Daughters of Lusting Torment," "Lovely Ladies for the Butcher," and "Girl's Enslaved in Glass"; they appeared in pulps such as *Dime Mystery Magazine, Terror Tales,* and *Sinister Stories.* Although many pulp magazines, due to their over-the-top nature, are often viewed as campy by modern readers, the detailed descriptions of torture in the "weird menace" pulps can, even today, be unsettling: "The whipping I had received from Tala Mag was nothing compared to what the servant Clops did to Portia with those hot irons...After a while one of her large breasts melted away under the iron as if it had been ice. There was no blood, for the heat cauterized as it burned. Clops shifted the iron to a fresh spot; momentarily it sizzled as it touched the clammy perspiration covering agonized flesh. Then the stench of burning flesh grew heavier." ("Fresh Fiancés for the Devil's Daughter," *Marvel Tales,* May 1940)

Fischer graduated from the Rand School of Social Sciences, which was established by the American Socialist Party in 1906. He became a sports reporter for the Long Island *Daily Press* (1929-1931), then worked at the *Labor Voice* (1931-32), a socialist newsletter. He went on to edit the *Socialist Call* (1934-36), the official weekly for the Socialist Party.

Fischer published his first novel, *So Much Blood,* in 1939. He found his biggest success during the 1950's, writing paperback originals—*House of Flesh* (1950), a story about a man's encounter with a femme fatale and her brood of savage dogs, sold nearly two million copies. Another notable book is *So Wicked My Love* (1954), a story about a man who gets involved with a murderous sexpot. Fischer has described his most typical novels as being about "ordinary people in extraordinary situations."

Fischer wrote a series featuring Ben Helm, a private detective who works as a criminologist when he's not investigating. The Helm novels are: *The Dead Men Grin* (1945), *More Deaths Than One* (1947), *The Restless Hands* (1949), *The Silent Dust* (1950) and *The Paper Circle* (1951).

Fischer's life was far removed from the brutality of his fiction. Politically active, he held memberships in the Social Democrats and the

Workmen's Circle (the Jewish socialist fraternity). He also corresponded with Dr. Hannah Arendt, the famous political philosopher, on various Jewish relief organizations. Fischer even ran as a Socialist candidate for the New York state senate in 1938. When not writing his own books, he served editorial stints at Macmillan's Collier Books (a paperback house) and Arco Publishing Company (a textbook house).

He spent his later years living at Camp Three Arrows, a socialist cooperative in Putnam County, New York.

**Further Reading:**
*Ben Helm series (complete):*
THE DEAD MEN GRIN (1945)
MORE DEATHS THAN ONE (1947)
THE RESTLESS HANDS (1949)
THE SILENT DUST (1950)
THE PAPER CIRCLE (1951, as STRIPPED FOR MURDER, 1953)

THE HORNET'S NEST (1944)
QUOTH THE RAVEN (1944, as THE FINGERED MAN, 1953)
THE PIGSKIN BAG (1946)
KILL TO FIT (1946)
THE BLEEDING SCISSORS (1948)
HOUSE OF FLESH (1950)
FOOLS WALK IN (1951)
THE LADY KILLS (1951)
THE FAST BUCK (1952)
RUN FOR YOUR LIFE (1953)
SO WICKED MY LOVE (1954)
MURDER IN THE RAW (11957)
SECOND-HAND NUDE (1959)
THE GIRL BETWEEN (1960)
THE EVIL DAYS (1974)

**As Russell Gray**
THE LUSTFUL APE (1950, published as by Bruno Fischer, 1959)

---

**If you like Bruno Fischer,** you might like: Paul Cain, Gil Brewer, Day Keene

## *Steve Fisher*

(also wrote as Stephen Gould, Grant Lane). Born in Marine City, Illinois, 1912. Died in Canoga Park, California, 1980.

Steve Fisher is an excellent example of a "journeyman" writer—he was equally adept at writing detective stories, military tales, "spicy" romances, aviator adventures and "yellow peril" yarns. His stories contain all the best elements of pulp: larger than life characters, fast-paced action and melodrama aplenty. Incredibly prolific, he wrote five hundred short stories, thirty novels, twelve stage plays, forty-two screenplays and numerous teleplays during a career lasting from the 1930's-1980's.

Fisher came from a middle-upper class background. He was in military school until he turned sixteen, then ran away and joined the U.S. Navy. He served in the Navy for four years, and published his first short stories in naval magazines such as *Our Navy* during this time.

In 1934, Fisher moved to New York to try his hand at writing for the burgeoning pulp markets. Shortly after arriving, he met pulp writer Frank Gruber and the two struck up a friendship. (Gruber recounts their friendship in his excellent memoir, *The Pulp Jungle*, 1967.) Gruber helped open the door to the pulp market for Fisher, and Fisher published stories in pulps as diverse as *Black Mask*, *Dare-Devil Aces*, *Saucy Romantic Adventures*, *The Mysterious Wu Fang*, *G-Men*, *Don Winslow of the Navy* and *Detective Tales*, among many others.

Fisher scored a bullseye with his crime novel *I Wake Up Screaming* (1941). Set in Hollywood, the story is a noirish tale about a male screenwriter named "Peg" who falls in love with Vicky, a beautiful woman who Peg is helping break into the movies. When Vicky is murdered, Peg becomes the main suspect and he is forced into a frantic cat and mouse game by a sadistic police detective named Ed Cornell (the last name was a tribute to writer Cornell Woolrich, a friend of Fisher's). The book was made into a successful film noir the same year, starring Victor Mature, Betty Grable and Laird Cregar (although the setting was changed from Hollywood to New York). It was filmed again in 1953 under the title *Vicki*.

Fisher became a highly in-demand screenwriter and wrote screenplays for some of Hollywood's most successful film noirs: *Johnny Angel* (1945, starring George Raft), *The Lady in the Lake* (1946, starring Robert Montgomery, based on the novel by Raymond Chandler), *Dead Reckoning* (1947, starring Humphrey Bogart and Lizabeth Scott), *Song of the Thin Man* (1947, starring William Powell and Myrna Loy, based on characters created by Dashiell Hammett), *I Wouldn't Be in Your Shoes* (1948, based on the story by Cornell

Woolrich), *Roadblock* (1951, starring Charles McGraw, adapted from a story by Geoffrey Homes, aka Daniel Mainwaring), *Las Vegas Shakedown* (1955, starring Dennis O'Keefe) and *I, Mobster* (1958, starring Steve Cochran, directed by Roger Corman).

He wrote for major studios such as Warner Brothers, as well as "Poverty Row" outfits like Monogram Pictures. He wrote teleplays for *Peter Gunn, Tales of Wells Fargo, U.S. Marshal, Have Gun—Will Travel, 77 Sunset Strip, Ripcord, Combat, Fantasy Island* and *Starsky and Hutch*.

Other Fisher novels include *Homicide Johnny* (1940, as by Stephen Gould, reprinted as by Steve Fisher, 1950), a story about a small town homicide detective and a librarian's murder investigation; *Giveaway* (1954), about a teenager who tries to scam free prizes from TV quiz shows; and *No House Limit* (1958), a story about an independent casino owner trying to keep from being squeezed out of business by the Syndicate.

Altogether, Fisher's amazingly prolific career lasted more than fifty years.

**Further Reading:**
SPEND THE NIGHT (1935, as by Grant Lane)
SATAN'S ANGEL (1936)
MURDER OF THE ADMIRAL (1936, as by Stephen Gould)
MURDER OF THE PIGBOAT SKIPPER (1937)
THE NIGHT BEFORE MURDER (1939)
HOMICIDE JOHNNY (1940, as by Stephen Gould)
I WAKE UP SCREAMING (1941; revised, 1960)
WINTER KILL (1946)
THE SHELTERING NIGHT (1952)
TAKE ALL YOU CAN GET (1955)
NO HOUSE LIMIT (1958)
IMAGE OF HELL (1961)
SAXON'S GHOST (1969)
THE BIG DREAM (1970)
THE HELL-BLACK NIGHT (1970)

---

**If you like Steve Fisher,** you might like: Frank Gruber, Day Keene

# A. S. Fleischman

(also wrote as Sid Fleischman, Max Brindle). Born in Brooklyn, New York, 1920. Died in Santa Monica, California, 2010.

 Albert Sidney Fleischman started out with the ambition to become a magician. He published his first book, *Between Cocktails* (1939), which detailed various magic tricks, when he was only nineteen. He joined the Navy during WWII, and sold his first short story to *Liberty* magazine while in the service. After the war, Fleischman wrote for the *Toronto Star Weekly* and then wrote his first two mystery novels, *The Straw Donkey Case* (1948) and *Murder's No Accident* (1949), published by low-budget publisher Phoenix Press.

Fleischman's first paperback for Gold Medal was *Shanghai Flame* (1951), an adventure novel. Also for Gold Medal: *Look Behind You, Lady* (1952), *Danger in Paradise* (1953) and *Malay Woman* (1954,) Most of Fleischman's Gold Medal novels are set in Oriental locales, an environment he felt was conducive to intrigue, mystery and suspense. Fleischman's most successful novel for Gold Medal was *Blood Alley* (1955), a story about a skipper who is shanghaied into taking a group of villagers to Hong Kong. It was made into a successful movie starring John Wayne and Lauren Bacall, and directed by William Wellman; Fleischman wrote the screenplay. In 1960, Fleischman wrote *Yellowleg*, a western set during the 1870's. A heist cum revenge story, it won the Spur Award from the Western Writers of America. Fleischman adapted it for the screen and it was filmed as *The Deadly Companions* (1961), which was director Sam Peckinpah's first feature film.

After Gold Medal's *The Venetian Blonde* (1963), Fleischman turned exclusively to writing children's books, many of which incorporated his love of magic and the old west. Between 1962 and 2009, he published more than forty children's books, winning the Newbery Medal for *The Whipping Boy* (1986), the *Boston Globe* Horn Book Award for *Humbug Mountain* (1978) and was the United States nominee for the international Hans Christian Andersen Award in 1994. He published his autobiography, *The Abracadabra Kid: A Writer's Life*, in 1996; the book covers his Gold Medal years in some detail.

Further Reading:
THE STRAW DONKEY CASE (1948)
MURDER'S NO ACCIDENT (1949)
SHANGHAI FLAME (1951)
LOOK BEHIND YOU, LADY (1952)
DANGER IN PARADISE (1953)
MALAY WOMAN (1954)
COUNTERSPY EXPRESS (1954)
BLOOD ALLEY (1955)
YELLOWLEG (1960)
THE VENETIAN BLONDE (1963)

---

If you like A. S. (Sid) Fleischman, you might like: Dan Cushman, Richard Powell

# Fletcher Flora

Born in Parsons, Kansas, 1914. Died in 1968.

Fletcher Flora's novels are filled with wit, irony, and black humor. The best word to describe Flora's writing style might be "sardonic." His stories are likely to remind you of those marvelously wicked Roald Dahl short stories, or of many of the wry episodes of TV's *Alfred Hitchcock Presents.*

Flora spent his early years in Kansas. In 1943, he was drafted into the U.S. Army and, unfortunately, sustained major injuries. He received numerous shrapnel wounds in both legs and in his right arm. These injuries dogged Flora throughout his life. After his release from the Army, he became an education advisor in the Department of the Army at Fort Leavenworth, Kansas, from 1945 until 1963.

Flora started writing short stories in 1952, just as pulps like *Dime Detective* were dying out and digests like *Manhunt* were beginning. He wrote more than fifty short stories for the digests—many of his wry tales of murder appeared in *Alfred Hitchcock's Mystery Magazine.*

An excellent example of Flora's use of black humor is *Skulldoggery* (1967). The story is about a group of greedy relatives who believe they're going to inherit $10 million when the family patriarch dies. When they discover the money is instead left to the patriarch's chihuahua with the provision that the inheritance will pass to the relatives should the dog and all her pups die, the relatives plot the chihuahua's demise. Flora's writing style in *Skulldoggery* owes a tip of the hat to the work of Oscar Wilde. In another example of black humor, *Killing Cousins* (1961), a married woman has an affair with her husband's cousin and, when her husband confronts her and dares her to shoot him, she does—and immediately afterward proceeds to finish attending to more important matters, such as polishing her nails. The rest of the story concerns the comic complications of what to do with the dead body.

Flora's notable books in the hardboiled vein include *The Hot Shot* (1956), *Leave Her to Hell* (1958) and *Park Avenue Tramp* (1958).

Further Reading:
STRANGE SISTERS (1954)
DESPERATE ASYLUM (1955; published as WHISPER OF LOVE, 1958)
THE HOT SHOT (1956)
THE BRASS BED (1956)
LET ME KILL YOU, SWEETHEART (1958)
LEAVE HER TO HELL (1958)
WHISPERS OF THE FLESH (1958)
PARK AVENUE TRAMP (1958)
TAKE ME HOME (1959)
WAKE UP WITH A STRANGER (1959)
KILLING COUSINS (1960)
MOST LIKELY TO LOVE (1960)
THE SEDUCER (1961)
THE IRREPRESSIBLE PECCADILLO (1962)
SKULLDOGGERY (1967)
HILDEGARDE WITHERS MAKES THE SCENE (1969, with Stuart Palmer)

---

If you like Fletcher Flora, you might like: Jonathan Latimer, H. Vernor
Dixon

# Jay Flynn

(born John M. Flynn; also wrote as J. M. Flynn, Jack Slade). Born in 1927. Died in Connecticut, 1985.

According to mystery writer/reviewer Bill Pronzini, Jay Flynn's characters were like the man: "tough, hard-living, heavy-drinking, woman-chasing, blarney-spouting, scatterbrained, occasionally inept, and yet completely likeable Irishmen." (*American Pulp*, edited by Ed Gorman, Bill Pronzini, and Martin H. Greenberg, p. 284) Flynn wrote more than twenty crime and adventure related PBOs between 1958-76.

Early in his career, Flynn worked as a crime reporter for the *Portland Express* (Maine) and *San Jose Mercury*. His first books were noirish paperbacks that were part of the Ace Doubles series, including *The Deadly Boodle* (1958), *Drink with the Dead* (1959), *The Hot Chariot* (1960), *The Girl from Las Vegas* (1961) and *The Screaming Cargo* (1962).

From 1959-62, Flynn wrote a series of five books about a character named McHugh—a secret agent who somewhat oddly doubled as a bar owner in San Francisco. Called by Pronzini a "two-fisted Irish-American James Bond," McHugh tends to his bar, The Door, until a phone call from the Pentagon's General Burton Harts sends the secret agent into action in foreign locales such as Mexico and the Caribbean.

In *McHugh* (1959), our hero searches for an electronics expert that neither the FBI nor the mob want found. *It's Murder, McHugh* (1960) sends our boy to Mexico on the trail of stolen jet fighters and AWOL pilots. McHugh confronts a tropical island dictator in *Viva McHugh* (1960). All the McHugh books were written as by Jay Flynn. Two non-series books, *Terror Tournament* (1959, as by J.M. Flynn) and *The Action Man* (1961, as by Jay Flynn), are well regarded caper stories. *The Action Man* was made into a French/Italian movie in 1967, starring Jean Gabin and Robert Stack.

During the 1970's, Flynn descended several rungs down the PBO ladder and wrote softcore books for "sleaze" publisher Belmont-Tower; he also worked in an editorial capacity for the company. He wrote "sexed-up" (the term is Pronzini's) westerns about a World War I-era operative of the Gallows Detective Agency, Jim Bannerman, in *Bannerman* (1976) and *Border Incident* (1976); sexed-up adventure tales featuring a drifter named Venable; and sexed-up, violent cop melodramas featuring San Francisco police sergeant Joe Rigg in *Blood On Frisco Bay* (1976) and *Trouble is My Business* (1976). After two years with Belmont-Tower, he was fired from his editorial capacity because of drinking on the job, and his novels, the quality of which was becoming progressively unwieldy, were rejected.

Flynn quit writing in the late '70's and lived on the skid row section of Richmond, Virginia. He became a bootlegger assisting in the selling of illegal white lightning hooch (ironically, his 1959 novel, *Drink with the Dead*, is about a treasury agent who exposes a bootlegging operation) then took a legit job as a security guard. He battled his drinking demons off and on for the next few years, and died of cancer in a VA hospital.

**Further Reading:**
*McHugh series (complete):*
McHUGH (1959)
IT'S MURDER, McHUGH (1960)
A BODY FOR McHUGH (1960)
VIVA McHUGH (1960)
THE FIVE FACES OF MURDER (1962)

THE ACTION MAN (1961)
BLOOD ON FRISCO BAY (1976)
TROUBLE IS MY BUSINESS (1976)
BANNERMAN (1976)
BORDER INCIDENT (1976)

**As J.M. Flynn**
THE DEADLY BOODLE (1958)
DRINK WITH THE DEAD (1959)
TERROR TOURNAMENT (1959)
THE HOT CHARIOT (1960)
RING AROUND A ROGUE (1960)
ONE FOR THE DEATH HOUSE (1961)
THE GIRL FROM LAS VEGAS (1961)
DEEP SIX (1962)
THE SCREAMING CARGO (1962)
SURFSIDE SIX (1962, TV novelization)
WARLOCK (1976)
DANGER ZONE (1977)

---

**If you like Jay Flynn,** you might like: Kendell Foster Crossen, Stephen Marlowe

## *Sam Fuller*

(Samuel Fuller). Born in Worcester, Massachusetts, 1912. Died in Hollywood, California, 1997.

Sam Fuller the pulp novelist is the same person as Sam Fuller the movie director, Sam Fuller the actor, Sam Fuller the crime reporter, and Sam Fuller the war hero. According to Fuller, his "life was work and work was life."

Sam Fuller was a larger than life figure, an adventurer, a "character." He chomped his cigar, spoke in a raspy voice, had a craggy and leathery face, and while directing his movies he frequently shot a .45 into the air. But Fuller was not an angry man. Anyone who's seen interviews or documentary footage of Fuller can tell that he thoroughly enjoyed being Sam Fuller, and thrived on telling tales, whether tall or true. When asked "What is cinema?" during his cameo appearance in Jean-Luc Godard's *Pierrot le Fou*, Fuller's answer could equally apply to his movies, his acting, his crime reporting, his war experiences and his novels: "Love, hate, violence, death...In a word, emotion."

Fuller started his slam-bang career at age 17 as the youngest crime reporter for the tabloid style newspaper the *New York Graphic*. His reporting covered the most gritty scenes New York had to offer: riots, robberies, muggings, murders, and executions.

Fuller started writing pulp novels during the mid-1930's. They were explosively sensationalistic in both substance and style. In *Burn, Baby, Burn* (1935), a pregnant woman is scheduled to be executed which, by extension, would kill her innocent, unborn child. *Test Tube Baby* (1936) is about the then startling concept of artificial insemination. *Make Up and Kiss* (1938) is an exposé about a high-stakes financial scam at a major cosmetics firm.

Fuller's most successful and well known novel is *The Dark Page* (1944). The book is set in the world of tabloid journalism, a world Fuller knew well. The story is about newspaper editor Carl Chapman. Chapman is married, but his former wife Charlotte, who he never divorced, shows up and threatens to expose him. They get into a heated argument in Charlotte's apartment, and Chapman knocks her down, accidentally killing her. The rest of the book involves Chapman's efforts to avoid being found out by his own star reporter, Lance McCleary, who is investigating Charlotte's death for a newspaper story he's writing. *The Dark Page* was made into an excellent movie called *Scandal Sheet* (1952), though oddly enough it wasn't directed by Fuller but by Phil Karlson.

The remainder of Fuller's books were novelizations of his movies and of unfinished movie projects. They retained his same direct, punchy, in your face style.

Sam Fuller was a true original. Pick up one of his books, grab a stogie and take a couple of puffs for old Sam.

**Further Reading:**
BURN, BABY, BURN (1935)
TEST TUBE BABY (1936)
THE DARK PAGE (1944)
SCANDAL SHEET (1952)
THE BIG RED ONE (1980)
A THIRD FACE: MY TALE OF WRITING, FIGHTING AND FILMMAKING
   (2002)

---

If you like Sam Fuller, you might like: David Goodis, Frank Gruber

## *Peggy Gaddis*

(born Erolie Pearl Gaddis; also wrote as Gail Jordan, Georgia Craig, Perry Lindsay, James Clayford, Peggy Dern, Joan Tucker, John Tucker, Joan Sherman, Roberta Courtland, Sylvia Erskine, Luther Gordon, Gerald Foster, Carolina Lee). Born in Gaddistown, Georgia, 1895. Died in Tucker, Georgia, 1966.

Peggy Gaddis was a one-time former Hollywood scenarist who was also an indefatigable storyteller. Writing at a book-a-month pace for years, she turned out over 300 novels, including hardcovers, "nurse" novels, romances and books for young readers. She was also a pulp writer who specialized in two pulp subgenres: "love" pulps and "spicy" pulps. The love pulps had titles like *Love Story, Exciting Love, Ideal Love* and *Thrilling Love*. The love pulps catered to readers (mostly women) who wanted stories of sweet and sentimental romance. The heroines blushed and their emotions gushed, and their virginity was to be protected at all costs.

The spicy pulps included *Breezy Stories, Paris Nights, Saucy Movie Tales* and *Ginger Stories*. The spicy pulps catered to readers (mostly men) who wanted a heroine to do anything that would give the writer an opportunity to describe a shapely leg or curve, which was pretty much *anything*—reading a newspaper, sharpening a pencil; no activity was too mundane to be linked to sex. These heroines were often adventuresses who used their bodies to achieve money, power, or revenge. The stories included incidents of premarital sex, extramarital sex, and even wife-swapping. However, don't get the wrong idea: as shocking as these stories may have been for their time, pulp writer William Campbell Gault, interviewed decades later, claimed: "They were supposed to be hot stuff, but the stories were about as sexy as church." (*Danger is My Business*, by Lee Server, page 85.)

Gaddis published her first novel in 1935—her first six, in fact. They were published by the low budget outfit Godwin books and were of the spicy variety: *Eve in the Garden, Unfaithful?, Shameless, Wedding Night, One More Woman* and *Respectable?* Gaddis published these under her own name, but later in the 1930's, she reserved that byline for her sweet and innocent love novels such as *Heart's Retreat* (1936), *Tomorrow's Roses* (1938) and *Love is Always New* (1938).

She continued writing pulpy novels of racy romance but used the pseudonyms Perry Lindsay, James Clayford and Gail Jordan to produce such lust drenched classics as *Passion in the Pantry* (1941), *The Private Life of a Street Girl* (1950), *Divorce Bait* (1950) and *Sin Cinderella* (1948).

Late in the 1950's and throughout the '60's, Gaddis published, under her own name and the pseudonym Peggy Dern, a series of "nurse" novels that were quite iconoclastic for the time. She wrote about "career girls" during an era when women were expected to be homebodies. The protagonists were independent-minded women who were sympathetic and compassionate, yet had the pluck and toughness to carve out their own niche in a male dominated world. Titles include *Kerry Middleton, Career Girl* (1959), *Nurse Christine* (1962), *Betsy Moran, R.N.* (1961), *Nurse Angela* (1965) and *Nurse's Dilemma* (1966).

**Further Reading:**
DOCTOR MERRY'S HUSBAND (1947)
LEOTA FOREMAN, RN (1957)
BELOVED INTRUDER (1958)
A LITTLE LOVE (1959)
NURSE AT SPANISH CAY (1962)
THE JOYOUS HILLS (1965)

---

**If you like Peggy Gaddis,** you might like: Jimmy Gifford, Orrie Hitt, some Harry Whittington

## Erle Stanley Gardner

(also wrote as A. A. Fair, Carleton Kendrake, Charles J. Kenny, Charles J. Kenney, Kyle Corning, Charles M. Green, Les Tillray, Robert Parr, Robert Park, Grant Holiday). Born in Malden, Massachusetts, 1889. Died in Temecula, California, 1970.

Erle Stanley Gardner's Perry Mason ranks as one of the most popular mystery series characters of all time. On television during the 1950's, Raymond Burr became a superstar playing the character, and *Perry Mason* became as well known and iconic as *Superman* or *I Love Lucy*.

Oddly enough, the bespectacled Gardner started out as a real life tough guy. Although born in Massachusetts, Gardner spent much of his childhood traveling with his father (a mining engineer) through rough and rocky regions of Oregon, California and the Klondike. As a teen, Gardner was a professional boxer and also promoted a number of matches (although they were unlicensed). He attended Valparaiso University in Indiana to study law, but was expelled for punching out a professor. Amazingly, without ever finishing college, Gardner continued to study law on his own, and passed the California state bar exam in 1911.

Starting in the 1920's, while practicing law during the day, Gardner began writing short stories for the pulps at night. Throughout the decade, Gardner sold hundreds of stories to the most popular pulps, including *Black Mask* and *Argosy*. Gardner was so prolific that in 1932, writing for only 1-2 cents per word, he earned $20,000.

In 1933, Gardner quit his law practice to write full time, and published his first Perry Mason novel, *The Case of the Velvet Claws*. During the first dozen or so adventures of defense attorney Mason, Gardner's writing style and presentation of Mason's character was hardboiled and heavily influenced by his *Black Mask* writing. Later Mason books took on a slicker style, and many were first serialized in *The Saturday Evening Post*. The Mason novels were written with lickety-split pacing, terse character descriptions and vigorous verbal jousting during the courtroom scenes. The cast of supporting characters throughout the series included Mason's assistant Paul Drake, secretary Della Street and, on the other side of the bar, police lieutenant Tragg and district attorney Hamilton Burger. Some notable titles singled out by mystery critics include *The Case of the Sleepwalker's Niece* (1936), *The Case of the Black-Eyed Blonde* (1944), *The Case of the Lazy Lover* (1947) and *The Case of the Daring Decoy* (1957). Altogether, 82 Perry Mason novels were published, the last being *The Case of the Postponed Murder* (1973, published posthumously).

Under the name A. A. Fair, Gardner also wrote 29 novels featuring the private detective team of Bertha Cool and Donald Lam. Bertha Cool, the agency's owner, was middle-aged, tough, sarcastic and obese. Her partner, Donald Lam, was young, slim and brainy. The Cool and Lam books contain more humor than the Mason novels; "screwball" mysteries, they might be called. Notable titles include *Owls Don't Blink* (1942), *Crows Can't Count* (1946), *Top of the Heap* (1952) and *Some Slips Don't Show* (1957).

Gardner also wrote a few novels about small town prosecutor Doug Selby (the flip side of defense attorney Mason), as well as numerous other series characters in his short stories for the pulps.

He won the Mystery Writers of America Edgar Allen Poe award in 1952, and the Grand Master award in 1961.

**Further Reading:**
*Perry Mason series:*
THE CASE OF THE VELVET CLAWS (1933)
THE CASE OF THE LUCKY LEGS (1934)
THE CASE OF THE CURIOUS BRIDE (1934)
THE CASE OF THE STUTTERING BISHOP (1936)
THE CASE OF THE LAME CANARY (1937)
THE CASE OF THE SHOPLIFTER'S SHOE (1938)
THE CASE OF THE PERJURED PARROT (1939)
THE CASE OF THE HAUNTED HUSBAND (1941)
THE CASE OF THE CARELESS KITTEN (1942)
THE CASE OF THE DROWSY MOSQUITO (1943)
THE CASE OF THE BLACK-EYED BLONDE (1944)
THE CASE OF THE BORROWED BRUNETTE (1946)
THE CASE OF THE LAZY LOVER (1947)
THE CASE OF THE NEGLIGENT NYMPH (1950)
THE CASE OF THE GRINNING GORILLA (1952)
THE CASE OF THE GLAMOROUS GHOST (1955)
THE CASE OF THE DARING DECOY (1957)
THE CASE OF THE SHAPELY SHADOW (1960)
THE CASE OF THE MISCHIEVOUS DOLL (1963)
THE CASE OF THE WORRIED WAITRESS (1966)

**As A. A. Fair**
*Cool and Lam series:*
THE BIGGER THEY COME (1939)
GOLD COMES IN BRICKS (1940)
OWLS DON'T BLINK (1942)
CATS PROWL AT NIGHT (1943)

CROWS CAN'T COUNT (1946)
FOOLS DIE ON FRIDAY (1947)
SOME WOMEN WON'T WAIT (1953)
YOU CAN DIE LAUGHING (1957)
SOME SLIPS DON'T SHOW (1957)
KEPT WOMEN CAN'T QUIT (1960)
UP FOR GRABS (1964)
ALL GRASS ISN'T GREEN (1970)

---

**If you like Erle Stanley Gardner,** you might like: Harold Q. Masur, Ellery Queen, Lester Dent

# David J. Garrity

(also wrote as Garrity, Dave J. Garrity). Born, 1923. Died, 1984.

In 1948, Mickey Spillane's debut novel, *I, The Jury*, changed the landscape of American crime fiction. When the book was first published in hardcover in 1947, it sold only reasonably well, but with the publication of the paperback edition a year later, sales skyrocketed, and Spillane becomes a national sensation. He became to the publishing industry what Madonna is to the music industry and Quentin Tarantino is to the film industry.

Spillane's influence was such that he was able to help his buddy, Dave Gerrity, get his own hardboiled fiction published. Gerrity thought he could write tough guy novels like the Mick, if the Mick would only help him out a little. Gerrity explained: "You sit at Spillane's table for a couple of hours and drink beer with him and you could steal enough of his throwaway ideas to write twenty books." (*Encyclopedia of Pulp Fiction Writers*, by Lee Server, pg. 111)

Gerrity proved that he indeed *could* write books (though the number turned out to be eight, not twenty—a still admirable amount), and Spillane helped Gerrity get his first book published by Gold Medal. *Kiss Off The Dead* (1960) was published as by "Garrity" (someone at Gold Medal must have thought that using only the surname would sound more hardboiled). The story is about Max Carey, an ex-cop on the run after being accused of murdering his wife. In the tradition of the Mick, Carey is the first person narrator, his patter is plenty hardboiled, and there's enough blood and guts to go around for everyone.

Gerrity's second book, *Cry Me A Killer* (1961), acknowledged Spillane with the dedication, "With a tip of the hat to the Mick."

Gerrity's most interesting book, in terms of the Spillane-Garrity connection, was *Dragon Hunt* (1967, as by Dave J. Garrity). It was Gerrity's only PI novel and Spillane's mark is literally all over the book. The back cover shows a photo of Gerrity hanging out with "close friend" and "world famous writer" Mickey Spillane. A blurb on the cover sounds like the voiceover narration for one of the Mick's beer commercials: "Mickey thinks it's the greatest." A Spillane blurb on the cover reads, "Guts, action...the kind of stuff I like to read." The most interesting Spillane related aspect of the book is that one of the main supporting characters is none other than Mike Hammer. Throughout the book, Gerrity's PI, Peter Braid, calls Hammer and asks for advice. Hmmm...I wonder if that paralleled Gerrity and Spillane's real life writer-to-writer relationship. Ya think?

Gerrity also wrote two novels about the world of race car driving, *The Hot Mods* (1969) and *Rim Of Thunder* (1973), and three novels centered around organized crime, *The Never Contract* (1975), *The Plastic Man* (1976) and *The Numbers Man* (1977).

The Gerrity books are a special treat for anyone looking to explore the influence of Spillane on 1950's and '60's hardboiled fiction. And the fact that Gerrity's books continued to successfully sell shows that he was not a bad scribe in his own right.

**Further Reading:**
**As Dave J. Garrity**
DRAGON HUNT (1967)
THE HOT MODS (1969)
RIM OF THUNDER (1973)

**As Garrity**
KISS OFF THE DEAD (1960)
CRY ME A KILLER (1961)

**As David J. Garrity**
THE NEVER CONTRACT (1975)
THE PLASTIC MAN (1976)
THE NUMBERS MAN (1977)

---

**If you like David J. Gerrity,** you might like: Mickey Spillane, Frank Kane

# William Campbell Gault

(also wrote as Will Duke, Roney Scott, Larry Sternig, William C. Gault). Born in Milwaukee, Wisconsin, 1910. Died in 1995.

William Campbell Gault blended crime fiction with his love of sports. His stories featured athletes of all stripes: football players, boxers, race car drivers and even golfers.

Gault graduated from the University of Wisconsin. He served with the U.S. infantry, 1943-45, and after returning from the war, he found work as a mailman, aircraft assembler, waiter and hotel manager. He start-ed his writing career by selling short stories to the pulps beginning in 1936. Not in detective pulps like *Black Mask* or *Dime Detective* however, but in "spicy" pulps such as *Paris Nights* and *Scarlett Adventuress*. During the next three years, Gault broke into sports pulps like *Ace Sports* and *All-American Football*. He started writing stories for the detective pulps in 1940 and con-tinued until the late 1950's. When the pulps died out and digests had taken over, Gault's criminous stories were published in *The Saint* and *Manhunt*. Altogether, Gault wrote more than 300 short stories.

Gault's first novel was *Don't Cry for Me* (1952). The main character, Pete Worden, a WWII veteran and former football quarterback, is on the run after a dead body is found in his apartment. Fellow mystery writer Fredric Brown wrote that *Don't Cry for Me* "is not only a beautiful chunk of story but, refreshingly, it's about *people* instead of characters, people so real and vivid that you'll think you know them personally. Even more important, this boy Gault can *write*, never badly and sometimes like an angel." (*1001 Midnights*, by Bill Pronzini and Marcia Muller, pg.293). The book was awarded a Best First Novel Edgar by The Mystery Writers of America.

Gault combined his interest in sports and crime fiction and created private eye, ex-LA Rams football player, Brock "The Rock" Callahan. Callahan is worlds apart from the typical 1950's Spillane-esque private eye: he knows he's big and tough so he feels no need to prove it; he's down to earth; and he has a steady relationship with his girlfriend, interior deco-rator Jan Bonnet. The Callahan novels are uniformly excellent. A *New York Times* review called Callahan, "one of the major private detectives created in American fiction since Chandler's Philip Marlowe." Notable Callahan titles include *Day of the Ram* (1956), where Brock investigates the blackmail-ing of an ex-Rams teammate; *The Convertible Hearse* (1957), where Brock investigates a "hot-car" racket; and *County Kill* (1962), where Brock helps an 11 year-old boy clear his father of a murder charge. Gault featured Callahan in fourteen books.

Gault's second series character was private eye Joe Puma. Puma was more rough around the edges and "blue collar" than Callahan. Whereas Callahan's cases often revolved around some of California's wealthiest and most socially well connected people, Puma's universe was populated by low rent lowlifes on society's fringe—a whorehouse madam, professional wrestlers, a religious cult leader. Puma's first appearance was in a non-series novel, *Shakedown* (1953, as by Roney Scott); he appeared in seven other books, as well as seven short stories. Notable Puma adventures include *Night Lady* (1958), *Sweet Wild Wench* (1959) and *The Hundred Dollar Girl* (1961).

Throughout the '50's, Gault had been writing sports oriented Young Adult novels as well as crime novels. After 1962, Gault quit writing mysteries and focused exclusively on YA books. He explained:

"My Edgar winner—*Don't Cry for Me*—came out in 1952 and was out of print two months later. In 1952 I also wrote a juvenile novel, *Thunder Road*, which is still in print. So, one has to eat." (*Twentieth-Century Crime & Mystery Writers, Third Edition*, pg. 427)

Twenty years later, in 1982, Gault revived Callahan for seven more novels. One of these novels, *The Cana Diversion* (1982), provides a unique premise as Callahan investigates the murder of a fellow detective—Gault's own Joe Puma.

Further Reading:
*Brock Callahan series:*
RING AROUND ROSA (1955; as MURDER IN THE RAW, 1956)
DAY OF THE RAM (1956)
THE CONVERTIBLE HEARSE (1957)
COME DIE WITH ME (1959)
VEIN OF VIOLENCE (1961)
COUNTY KILL (1962)
DEAD HERO (1963)
THE BAD SAMARITAN (1982)
THE CANA DIVISION (1982, Joe Puma appearance)
DEATH IN DONEGAL BAY (1984)
CAT AND MOUSE (1988)

*Joe Puma series:*
SHAKEDOWN (1953, as by Roney Scott)
END OF A CALL GIRL (1958)
NIGHT LADY (1958)
SWEET WILD WENCH (1959)
THE WAYWARD WIDOW (1959)
MILLION DOLLAR TRAMP (1960)
THE HUNDRED-DOLLAR GIRL (1961)

DON'T CRY FOR ME (1952)
THE BLOODY BOKHARA (1953)
THE CANVAS COFFIN (1953)
BLOOD ON THE BOARDS (1953)
RUN, KILLER, RUN (1954)
SQUARE IN THE MIDDLE (1957)
DEATH OUT OF FOCUS (1959)
THE SWEET BLOND TRAP (1959)

**As Will Duke**
FAIR PREY (1956)

_____

**If you like William Campbell Gault,** you might like: Thomas B. Dewey, William Ard

# David Goodis

(also wrote as Logan Clayborne, David Crewe, Lance Kermit, Ray P. Shotwell and there are believed to be two to four unidentified ones). Born in Philadelphia, Pennsylvania, 1917. Died, Philadelphia, Pennsylvania 1967.

 Crime writer Ed Gorman noted that David Goodis "didn't write novels, he wrote sucide notes." In light of that sentiment, which is commonly held among Goodis aficionados, it seems reasonable to conclude that Goodis's life was perhaps as melancholy as his work.

But what about the other David Goodises?

The David Goodis, for example, who appears (in Lee Server's book, *Over My Dead Body*) in a beautifully photographed black and white portrait, standing arm in arm between Humphrey Bogart and Lauren Bacall, a reserved but noticeable smirk on his face, during the filming of his novel, *Dark Passage*? Goodis wasn't the first literary light to make the sojourn west and rub shoulders with Hollywood royalty—preceding him were such literary lights as F. Scott Fitzgerald, Dorothy Parker, James M. Cain, newspaperman Ben Hecht and playwright Clifford Odets. David Goodis: fast-rising star/sensitive writer from "back east."

Or what about the David Goodis who (according to Geoffrey O'Brien's introduction to the Black Lizard series of Goodis's novels), while in one of Hollywood's most chi-chi night clubs, stuffed the red cellophane strips from Lucky Strike cigarette packs up his nostrils to simulate a nosebleed? Or the Goodis who would borrow a friend's old bathrobe and would hit the Hollywood night life pretending to be an exiled White Russian prince? Or the Goodis who, while in some of the movie palaces of the day, would scream in pain while pretending to be caught in a revolving door, or would roll down the steps as if the victim of an accident? David Goodis: prankster.

Or what about this Goodis: the David Goodis who (according to author James Sallis in his book *Difficult Lives: Jim Thompson—David Goodis—Chester Himes*) roamed through ghetto bars and clubs late at night, seeking out black women to spend time with and indulge his fantasy life. David Goodis: Fetishest?

Sallis (in *Difficult Lives*) titled his chapter about Goodis, "David Goodis: Life in Black And White." But did David Goodis really live a life in black and white? Didn't Goodis—the many David Goodises—live a life (or lives, if you will) where he explored and experienced all colors of the spectrum? Didn't Goodis live a life among various shades of color, quickly darting from one shade to another, perhaps in an effort to keep people from analyzing him, pigeonholing him, categorizing him, and judging him?

Even during the past 2-3 years, new information about Goodis—his life, his relationships with women, his hobbies, his moods and his circle of friends—has come to light which has contradicted earlier reports and which has shed light on more facets of Goodis.

So the question remains: who is the real David Goodis?

For the record, here is what is known about the life and work of David Goodis.

David Loeb Goodis grew up in Philadelphia, Pennsylvania. He graduated with a degree in journalism from Temple University in 1938, and published his first novel, Retreat from Oblivion, shortly thereafter. The novel—a story about a group of twentysomethings and their relationships—was successful neither with the critics nor the public.

Goodis then moved to New York and instead of trying another literary effort, started writing for the pulps: Battle Birds, Captain Combat, Dare-Devil Aces, Air War, Double-Action Detective, Gangland Detective Stories, Hooded Detective. Between 1940 and 1945, Goodis wrote for all these and more, employing a score of pseudonyms. He also wrote for the radio shows House of Mystery, Superman, and Hop Harrigan of the Airwaves during this time.

In 1946, Goodis scored a bullseye with his second novel, Dark Passage. The story is about wrongly convicted Vincent Parry, who escapes from prison and has his face changed through plastic surgery. He finds an ally in Irene Jansen, and together they track down the real criminal.

When an author hits it big, Hollywood comes a-calling, and Warner Brothers hired Goodis as a staff writer. Warners also turned Dark Passage into a successful movie starring Humphrey Bogart and Lauren Bacall in 1947, although the screenplay was not written by Goodis, but by the film's director, Delmer Daves. Goodis toiled in Hollywood for four years but his only screenplay to be made into a movie was The Unfaithful (1947), starring Ann Sheridan as a woman who tries to convince her husband and lawyer that she killed a mysterious intruder in self defense. The Unfaithful was a fine remake of 1940's The Letter, which had starred Bette Davis in the Sheridan role.

Goodis wrote three novels while in Hollywood. Nightfall (1947) is the story of Jim Vanning, a suspected bank robber who's on the run from both cops and crooks. Nightfall is smoothly written and presents an edge of your seat atmosphere of suspense and paranoia; it was made into a successful movie in 1957, starring Aldo Ray and Anne Bancroft, and directed by Out of the Past director Jacques Tourneur. Behold This Woman (1947) focuses on a ruthless, shrewish, manipulative married woman named Clara Ervin, and her power over her husband. Goodis scholars suggest that the protagonist's relationship to Clara Ervin was a thinly disguised version of Goodis's own short-lived marriage to Elaine Astor.

The last novel Goodis wrote while in Hollywood was Of Missing Persons

(1950). An anomaly for Goodis, this was a police procedural, more along the lines of *Dragnet* than "the wounded and the slain" souls of Goodis's most characteristic works.

Achieving only limited success in Hollywood, Goodis hightailed it back to Philadelphia in 1950, and wrote the books he is best known for.

From 1951 onward, Goodis's books were, for the most part, variations on a few common themes. The Goodis protagonist achieves fame and fortune (as concert pianist, artist, pop singer), rejects fame and fortune, and spends the rest of his time slowly drinking his life away. It was also common for Goodis to write about two types of women. One type is near anorexic, frail and alcoholic. The Goodis protagonist invariably falls in love with this woman, wanting to save her from herself. The other type of woman is obese, profanity spouting and physically abusive (both to men and women). The Goodis protagonist allows himself to be bullied and manipulated by this type of woman. The last theme running throughout most of Goodis's novels is that the protagonist, who while rarely a professional criminal, becomes entangled with a criminal gang and forms familial ties with the gang's members.

As to specific books: *Cassidy's Girl* (1951) is a story about a disgraced airline pilot wrongly blamed for a fatal crash, who now drinks away his days and nights, fights with his wife Mildred, and falls in love with an alcoholic named Doris. *The Burglar* (1953), one of Goodis's most precisely written books, is about a criminal gang that slowly falls apart after a botched robbery. *Black Friday* (1954) is about a once well known artist who gets involved with a gang of criminals. In *Street of No Return* (1954) a once successful crooner gets involved with a gang of criminals and becomes a reluctant hero by helping to stop a race riot—only to return, at book's end, to the same dead end life on a street corner where he and two fellow winos had been drinking. *Down There* (1956, re-titled *Shoot the Piano Player* for Francois Truffaut's 1962 film version), is a tale about Eddie, a former concert pianist who now contentedly pounds the keys in a sleazy bar, until his hoodlum brother bursts in, begging for Eddie's help from the criminals that are after him.

David Goodis died in 1967, just two months shy of his 50th birthday. But with his death, as with so many events in his life, the facts are muddy. During the past few years, however, David Goodis's acquaintances, friends and relatives have come forward to share not only their stories, but first hand source material such as photographs, letters and even Goodis's death certificate. There is an annual GoodisCon that started in 2007.

At this website, http://www.davidgoodis.com/page1/page1.html, you'll find the following enlightening items, among others:

• Numerous photographs of David Goodis with his friends that span the age of 17 into his 40's. There are even some photos of Goodis and his friends having fun at a party, dressed up as doctors and nurses about to perform a fake operation on a patient.

• A photograph of Elaine Astor Goodis (David's wife during his short-lived marriage) along with Goodis at a restaurant, and information about his marriage to "the mysterious Elaine."

• Letters written between Goodis and friends during the latter part of his life, where he makes it clear he knows he isn't long for this world.

• Photographs and the story behind David's mentally and physically disabled brother, Herbie, who David took care of—spending much time, money, and energy to support.

• Anecdotes about Goodis playing pool with his friend, Dutch Silver.

• More details about Goodis's mysterious death (listed on the death certificate as "cerebral vascular accident").

• Goodis's lawsuit against TV's *The Fugitive*, which Goodis believed ripped off the plot of *Dark Passage*.

• The "lost works" of David Goodis.

**Further Reading:**
RETREAT FROM OBLIVION (1939)    DARK PASSAGE (1947)
NIGHTFALL (1947; as THE DARK CHASE, 1953)
BEHOLD THIS WOMAN (1947)    OF MISSING PERSONS (1950)
CASSIDY'S GIRL (1951)    OF TENDER SIN (1952)
STREET OF THE LOST (1952)    THE BURGLAR (1953)
THE MOON IN THE GUTTER (1953)    BLACK FRIDAY (1954)
THE BLONDE ON THE STREET CORNER (1954)
STREET OF NO RETURN (1954)
THE WOUNDED AND THE SLAIN (1955)
DOWN THERE (1956; as SHOOT THE PIANO PLAYER, 1962)
FIRE IN THE FLESH (1957)    NIGHT SQUAD (1961)
SOMEBODY'S DONE FOR (1967)

---

**If you like David Goodis,** you might like: Cornell Woolrich, Patricia Highsmith

# William Lindsay Gresham
Born in Baltimore, Maryland, 1909. Died in New York, New York, 1962.

William Lindsay Gresham was immersed and fascinated by carnival life, and he wrote both fiction and non-fiction about that world. His novel *Nightmare Alley*, as well as the movie of the same name, are today acknowledged as cult classics.

Gresham's family moved to New York when he was young. It was during visits to Coney Island where Gresham first encountered and was fascinated by carnival freak shows. While in his 20's, Gresham moved to Greenwich Village, where he was known as something of a bohemian. During the 1930's he joined the Communist Party, and in 1937, when a close friend died in the Spanish Civil War, Gresham went to Spain and fought against General Franco and the fascists.

When Gresham returned to New York he was depressed and drank heavily, leading to an attempted suicide. But he came out of his funk, and worked as a magician, copywriter and magazine editor. He began writing both short stories and articles.

Then he had an idea for a novel. He thought back to his experiences observing carnival sideshows, as well as back to his time during the Spanish Civil War, where he'd met a man named Joseph Halliday who'd worked in carnivals. Halliday gave Gresham the inside scoop about carny culture, feeding Gresham as much information as Gresham's voracious appetite could devour. Halliday had also introduced the word "geek" to Gresham. A geek was a hopeless alcoholic who the carnival owner could persuade, with the promise of a drink, to crawl around in his own feces and bite the heads off chickens.

Gresham took his experiences, knowledge and imagination and wrote *Nightmare Alley* (1946). The story is about the rise and fall of a young opportunistic huckster named Stan Carlisle. Stan works in a traveling carnival and learns the tricks of the various cons and scams. In particular, he learns about the "mentalist" trade, a scam where the mentalist can "read the mind" of someone in the audience. Stan becomes a mentalist himself but decides he wants to make it bigger so he leaves the carnival and starts his own "spook racket," where he bilks the wealthy by convincing them he can contact their dead loved ones. He meets and falls in love with Dr. Lilith Ritter, a sophisticated and intelligent psychiatrist; it is she who precipitates Stan's fall.

The book was an immediate success and was made into an excellent film noir in 1947. Former pretty boy Tyrone Power actively lobbied for the chance to play the against type role of the scheming and scamming Stan Carlisle. He won the part and gave a deviously noirish performance along with colorful character actors Joan Blondell, Mike Mazurki and Helen Walker. During the 1980's and '90's, quite a buzz was created around the movie because it was not available to be released on videotape due to legal rights issues. It was finally released on DVD in 2005.

Gresham wrote only three more books. *Limbo Tower* (1949) is set in a hospital and centers around the diseased and dying patients. *Monster Midway* (1953) is Gresham's non-fiction account of the carny world—its freaks and geeks, its hustlers and hucksters, its lingo, and its tricks of the various trades. *Houdini: The Man Who Walked Through Walls* (1959) is a biography of the famous magician.

Gresham learned he had tongue cancer in 1962. He was an alcoholic who had drunk most of his money away, his physical health was rapidly deteriorating and he became depressed and despondent. He checked into a fleabag hotel later that same year and committed suicide.

Gresham's books *Nightmare Alley* and *Monster Midway* continue to provide a fascinating look at a culture on the margins of society.

**Further Reading:**
NIGHTMARE ALLEY (1946)
LIMBO TOWER (1949)
MONSTER MIDWAY: AN UNINHIBITED LOOK AT THE
   GLITTERING WORLD OF THE CARNY (1954, non-fiction)
HOUDINI: THE MAN WHO WALKED THROUGH WALLS (1959, non-fiction)

---

**If you like William Lindsay Gresham,** you might like: Robert Edmon Alter, Cornell Woolrich

# *Frank Gruber*

(also wrote as Stephen Acre, Charles K. Boston, John K. Vedder, C. K. M. Scanlon).
Born in Elmer, Minnesota, 1904. Died in Santa Monica, California, 1969.

Frank Gruber was a workhorse. He wrote more than three hundred stories for the pulps, more than sixty novels and over two hundred screenplays and teleplays. Gruber specialized in creating quirky characters and placing them in even quirkier situations. Gruber's protagonists were mostly amateur sleuths who tended to stumble into crime cases rather than actively seek them. The tone of Gruber's stories is often humorous, somewhat akin to the stories of his friend and fellow writer, Norbert Davis. His plots are fast-paced and his settings are often low-rent and seedy, not unlike places Gruber inhabited during his early days peddling stories to the pulps.

Perhaps Gruber's most fascinating book is his non-fiction memoir, *The Pulp Jungle*, one of the few first-hand, novel-length accounts of what is was like working for the pulp markets in New York during the 1930's—an account that includes Gruber's encounters with fellow pulp scribes Steve Fisher, Cornell Woolrich, Dashiell Hammett and Raymond Chandler.

Gruber moved to New York in 1933, and published his first pulp story, "Strangler's Glory," in *Underworld Magazine* that same year. Over the next thirty-six years, Gruber published a torrent of stories in pulps and men's digests in titles as diverse as *Black Mask*, *Detective Tales*, *Dr. Yen Sin*, *Ranch Romances*, *Western Trails*, *Zane Grey's Western Magazine* and *Ellery Queen's Mystery Magazine*. He also wrote the "non-hero" stories that accompanied the main story in pulps such as *The Shadow*, *The Spider*, *Secret Agent X*, and *The Whisperer*.

Gruber created three memorable series teams. First up was Oliver Quade and Charlie Boston (a name Gruber later chose for one of his pseudonyms). Oliver Quade is a self-proclaimed "human encyclopedia" with a photographic memory. He's a book salesman, and travels around the country with sidekick Charlie Boston trying to hawk his 1200 page tome, *Compendium of Human Knowledge*. The ten Quade-Boston stories all originally appeared, with the exception of the first story (which appeared in *Thrilling Detective*) in the pages of *Black Mask* during the 1930's and '40's. They were later collected in book form in *Brass Knuckles* (1966). In 1939 an Oliver Quade movie was made, titled *Death of a Champion*, starring character actor Lynne Overman as Quade, and co-scripted by mystery writer Stuart Palmer, creator of "Hildegarde Withers."

Gruber next created the team of Johnny Fletcher and Sam Cragg. Fletcher is, technically, a salesman, traveling door to door to sell his "self-help" booklet, *Every Man a Samson*. But in reality he is a grifter and a con man, using his wits to plan scams and get rich quick schemes. Cragg is Fletcher's "Samson," a muscle-bound mug who flexes his biceps as "living proof" that Fletcher's booklet lives up to its promises. Cragg also functions as Fletcher's bodyguard, and often has to get them both out of scrapes that Fletcher has gotten them into. Gruber wrote twelve novels featuring Fletcher and Cragg, starting with *The French Key* (1940) and ending with *Swing Low Swing Dead* (1964). *The French Key* was made into a movie in 1946, starring Albert Dekker as Fletcher, Mike Mazurki (who played Moose Malloy in *Murder, My Sweet*) as Cragg, and scripted by Gruber.

Gruber's Simon Lash, who debuted in *Simon Lash, Private Detective* (1941), is, unlike Quade-Boston and Fletcher-Cragg, an honest to goodness private detective. But like Quade and Fletcher, Lash is also a bibliophile, who thrives on devouring stories about the old West. Lash is an ex-lawyer, an ex-soldier and a cranky curmudgeon who barely tolerates the existence of other people, including his assistant, Eddie Slocum. Gruber wrote three books about Lash and Slocum. Besides the aforementioned debut novel, the other titles are *The Buffalo Box* (1942) and *Murder'97* (1948). Once again, a Gruber character appeared in his own movie. Based on *Simon Lash, Private Detective*, the film was titled *Accomplice* (1946), starred Richard Arlen as Lash and Tom Dugan as Slocum, and was co-scripted by Gruber.

Gruber published his memoir, *The Pulp Jungle*, in 1967. Part of the book was about his struggling early days: he made tomato soup for free at the automat using a bowl of ketchup and hot water, he was regularly locked out of his room because he couldn't pay the rent, his stories were frequently rejected, and he was frequently lonely. Another part of the book was about Gruber's indefatigable drive to succeed. Recalling a year where he produced 800,00 words, he noted:

"This is an enormous amount of writing, any way you slice it. The manual labor involved in typing eight hundred thousand words a year is considerable. I flogged the typewriter day and night, I flogged it in the early hours of the morning, I beat at it, late at night. I worked Saturdays and Sundays." (*The Pulp Jungle*, pg. 13)

Some of Gruber's stories were rejected more than twenty times before selling; he sent each rejected story to a new magazine the day the rejection slip arrived. But *The Pulp Jungle* is more than just a personal memoir. It's also a history of New York City during the Depression, a history of *Black Mask* magazine, and a history of the writers Gruber encountered— some who "made it," and some who didn't.

In addition to his crime writing, Gruber wrote a biography of Zane

Grey and created three Western TV series: *The Texan, Tales of Wells Fargo* and *Shotgun Slade* (unusual in that it was about a private detective in a Western setting).

**Further Reading:**
*Johnny Fletcher and Sam Cragg series (complete):*
THE FRENCH KEY (1940; as THE FRENCH KEY MYSTERY, 1942; as ONCE OVER DEADLY, 1956)
THE LAUGHING FOX (1940)
THE HUNGRY DOG (1941; as THE HUNGRY DOG MURDERS, 1943; as DIE LIKE A DOG, 1957)
THE NAVY COLT (1941)
THE TALKING CLOCK (1941)
THE GIFT HORSE (1942)
THE MIGHTY BLOCKHEAD (1942; as THE CORPSE MOVED UPSTAIRS, 1964)
THE SILVER TOMBSTONE (1945; as THE SILVER TOMBSTONE MYSTERY, 1959)
THE HONEST DEALER (1947)
THE WHISPERING MASTER (1947)
THE SCARLET FEATHER (1948; as THE GAMECOCK MURDERS, 1949)
THE LEATHER DUKE (1949; as A JOB OF MURDER, 1950)
THE LIMPING GOOSE (1954; as MURDER ONE, 1973)
SWING LOW, SWING DEAD (1964)

*Simon Lash series (complete):*
SIMON LASH, PRIVATE DETECTIVE (1941)
THE BUFFALO BOX (1942)
MURDER 97 (1948; as THE LONG ARM OF MURDER, 1956)

THE LAST DOORBELL (1941, as by John K. Vedder; as KISS THE BOSS GOODBYE, as by Frank Gruber, 1954)
THE YELLOW OVERCOAT (1942, as by Stephen Acre; as FALL GUY FOR A KILLER, as by FRANK GRUBER, 1955)
THE FOURTH LETTER (1947)
FORT STARVATION (1953)
QUANTRELL'S RAIDERS (1954)
BRASS KNUCKLES (1966, short stories, featuring Oliver Quade)
THE PULP JUNGLE (1967, autobiography)

---

**If you like Frank Gruber,** you might like: Norbert Davis, Steve Fisher

# Brett Halliday

(born Davis Dresser; also wrote as Asa Baker, Matthew Blood, Kathryn Culver, Don Davis, Hal Debrett, Anthony Scott, Anderson Wayne). Born in Chicago, Illinois, 1904. Died in Montecito, California, 1977.

Davis Dresser's private detective, Mike Shayne, although not as well known today, is as much of an American institution as Erle Stanley Gardner's Perry Mason. Shayne's novel-length adventures have sold over thirty million copies; he appeared in hundreds of short stories; he was successfully featured on radio shows, in films, and in a television series; and he had his own digest, *Mike Shayne Mystery Magazine*, which lasted for nearly thirty years.

Before starting his career as a writer, Dresser led a rough and tumble life. As a young boy, he poked out his left eye on a barbed wire fence, and wore an eye patch for the rest of his life. When he was 14 years old, he ran away to join the Army. He served for two years before his real age was discovered and he was discharged. After graduating high school, he worked the oil fields of Texas and California.

Using the name Brett Halliday, Dresser published his first Mike Shayne novel in 1939, *Dividend On Death*. Shayne is a tough, redheaded Irishman, who uses his fists and brains more than his gun. Perhaps Shayne's most distinguishing characteristics are his straightforwardness and logic. According to Dresser, "I think the most important characteristic in [Shayne's] spectacular success as a private eye is his ability to drive straight forward to the heart of the matter without deviating one iota for obstacles or confusing side issues. He has an absolutely logical mind which refuses to be sidetracked." (*Four and Twenty Bloodhounds*, an anthology edited by Anthony Boucher.)

The Shayne novels have a recurring cast of characters: Shayne's wife Phyllis (who appeared in the early novels but was killed off after eight books, in *Blood On the Black Market*, 1943); Timothy Rourke, a crime reporter and Mike's drinking buddy; secretary Lucy Hamilton; Chief of Police Will Gentry, Mike's supporter and close friend; and Chief of Detectives Peter Painter, Mike's thorn in the side and ever present antagonist.

Notable titles in the Shayne series include *Murder Wears a Mummer's Mask* (1943, aka *In a Deadly Vein*), set in a ghost town in Colorado; *This is It, Michael Shayne* (1950), involving the death of a scandal reporter; and *She Woke To Darkness* (1954), where Brett Halliday himself is a character attending a Mystery Writers of America convention.

Dresser wrote approximately fifty Shayne novels, finally abandoning the series with *Murder and the Wanton Bride* (1958). Afterward, the Shayne series continued, ghost-written under the Brett Halliday pseudonym. Writers Ryerson Johnson and Robert Terrell penned the remaining novels, and Mike Avallone, Richard Deming, Dennis Lynds, James Reasoner and a host of others wrote the novelettes which appeared in *Mike Shayne Mystery Magazine*. The final Shayne novel appeared in 1976, and the digest's run ended in 1985.

The Shayne movie series started with *Michael Shayne: Private Detective* (1940), starring Lloyd Nolan, based on the novel, *The Private Practice of Michael Shayne*. 20th Century Fox featured Nolan in six more Shayne films, ending with *Time to Kill* (1942; interestingly, it was based partly on Raymond Chandler's *The High Window*). Low-budget studio PRC resurrected the series in 1946, starring Hugh "Leave It to Beaver" Beaumont as Shayne. A TV series starred Richard Denning, from 1960-61.

**Further Reading:**
*Mike Shayne series:*
DIVIDEND ON DEATH (1939)
THE PRIVATE PRACTICE OF MICHAEL SHAYNE (1940)
BODIES ARE WHERE YOU FIND THEM (1941)
THE CORPSE CAME CALLING (1942; as THE CASE OF THE WALKING CORPSE, 1943)
MICHAEL SHAYNE'S LONG CHANCE (1944)

| | |
|---|---|
| MURDER IS MY BUSINESS (1945) | MARKED FOR MURDER (1945) |
| COUNTERFEIT WIFE (1947) | A TASTE FOR VIOLENCE (1949) |

THIS IS IT, MICHAEL SHAYNE (1950)

| | |
|---|---|
| FRAMED IN BLOOD (1951) | WHAT REALLY HAPPENED (1952) |
| SHE WOKE TO DARKNESS (1954) | DEATH HAS THREE LIVES (1955) |
| STRANGER IN TOWN (1955) | THE BLONDE CRIED MURDER (1956) |

WEEP FOR A BLONDE (1957)
MURDER AND THE WANTON BRIDE (1958)

**As Asa Baker**
MUM'S THE WORD FOR MURDER (1938)
THE KISSED CORPSE (1939)

**As Matthew Blood**
THE AVENGER (1952, with Ryerson Johnson)
DEATH IS A LOVELY DAME (1954, with Ryerson Johnson)

---

**If you like Brett Halliday,** you might like: Marvin Albert, Bart Spicer, Frank Kane

# Donald Hamilton

(born Donald Bendtgsson). Born in Uppsala, Sweden, 1916. Emigrated to the U.S.
in 1924. Died in Ipswich, Massachusetts, 2006.

 Donald Hamilton created Matt Helm, professional
assassin for a secret government agency. According to
critic Anthony Boucher, Hamilton "brought to the spy
novel the authentic hard realism of Dashiell Hammett,
and his stories are as compelling, and probably as close
to the sordid truth of espionage, as any now being
told." (*Encyclopedia of Mystery and Detection*, by Chris
Steinbrunner and Otto Penzler, pg. 195)
Hamilton brought a well-thought-out point of view to genre fiction,
which perhaps lent weight to the storytelling skills praised by Boucher:

> "Crime/mystery fiction and the kind of suspense/action novels
> in which I specialize...[have] been around since the invention of
> language. Is Jason going to make it home with the Golden Fleece? Is
> Achilles going to get revenge for the death of Patroclus? Is Matt Helm
> going to get revenge for the death of Eleanor Brand, meanwhile sav-
> ing Latin America for the forces of good as opposed to the forces of
> evil? The themes are universal; only the presentation varies."
> (*Twentieth-Century Crime & Mystery Writers*, pg. 492)

Hamilton didn't start off with Helm. He began his professional writing
career in 1946, publishing short stories in *Collier's*, and soon wrote his first
novel, *Date with Darkness* (1947), a story of counter-espionage. *Night Walker*
(1954) is a noirish tale about a Navy lieutenant who wakes up in the hospital with a different identity. Hamilton also wrote Westerns: *Smoky River*
(1954), *Mad River* (1956) and *The Big Country* (1957, made into a movie in 1958,
starring Gregory Peck and Charlton Heston, directed by William Wyler).

In 1960, with the publication of *Death of a Citizen*, Hamilton created the
character he was most famous for. The "citizen" in the title who dies is
Helm himself. In the book, we learn that, while serving in the Army during World War II, Helm was given the code name "Eric" and recruited into
a counterintelligence group so secret that even other government entities
didn't know of its existence. In the beginning of the book, fifteen years
have passed since the war, and Helm is married with children, is an avid
outdoorsman and is a successful writer and photographer. Throughout the
story, we see the layers of Helm's present identity fall away like snake
skins as he transforms back into the highly trained, deadly assassin
known as "Eric."

Also appearing in this novel is a female agent with the code name "Tina," a fierce, bloodthirsty woman who served on a dangerous mission with Helm during the war. The other main character in the book is Mac, the man who gives the orders and who seems not to have aged a day since Helm has first known him. The plot is full of manipulation, lies, deceit, and double- and triple-crosses aplenty.

Hamilton wrote 25 Matt Helm novels, including *The Wrecking Crew* (1961), *Murderer's Row* (1962), *The Silencers* (1962), *The Ravagers* (1964), *The Devastators* (1965), *The Menacers* (1968) and *The Poisoners* (1971), among others. A major aspect that kept the series fresh was the continuity throughout the series: Helm/Eric faces dilemmas and decisions that cause him to grow and mature.

In terms of Helm's character traits, Hamilton describes him thusly: "A) He's actually a pretty good guy. B) He kills." (*Twentieth-Century Crime & Mystery Writers*, pg. 492)

Though surely an oversimplification, this description points to the fact that Helm is a through and through professional—he has a job to do, he strictly adheres to a moral code, and he cannot be bought.

During the late 1960's, *The Silencers, The Ambushers, Murderer's Row* and *The Wrecking Crew* were made into movies starring Dean Martin as Matt Helm. They were intended as parodies of both James Bond-type super spy movies and of Dean Martin's laid back persona.

Further Reading:
*Matt Helm series:*
DEATH OF A CITIZEN (1960)
THE WRECKING CREW (1960)
THE REMOVERS (1961)
MURDERER'S ROW (1962)
THE SILENCERS (1962)
THE RAVAGERS (1964)
THE SHADOWERS (1964)
THE DEVASTATORS (1965)
THE BETRAYERS (1966)
THE MENACERS (1968)
THE INTERLOPERS (1969)
THE POISONERS (1971)
THE INTRIGUERS (1972)
THE INTIMIDATORS (1974)
THE TERMINATORS (1975)
THE RETALIATORS (1976)
THE TERRORIZERS (1977)

DATE WITH DARKNESS (1947)
THE STEEL MIRROR (1948)
MURDER TWICE TOLD (1950)
NIGHT WALKER (1954)
SMOKY VALLEY (1954)
LINE OF FIRE (1955)
ASSIGNMENT: MURDER (1956; as ASSASSINS HAVE STARRY EYES, 1966)
THE BIG COUNTRY (1957)
ON GUNS AND HUNTING (1970, non-fiction)

---

**If you like Donald Hamilton,** you might like: Edward S. Aarons, Earl Norman

# Dashiell Hammett

(born Samuel Dashiell Hammett; also wrote as Peter Collinson, Mary Jane Hammett). Born in St. Mary's County, Maryland, 1894. Died in New York, New York, 1961.

This author profile could be called "The Strange Case of Dashiell Hammett." Here are some "clues" that are as random as Hammett's life:

He was (and remains) the "gold standard" for hard-boiled crime fiction, yet all his crime related short stories and novels were written in only eleven years, from 1923-1934, after which he published nothing new for the next twenty-seven years, though his daughter said Hammett never stopped writing, he just stopped finishing (*Dashiell Hammett: A Daughter Remembers*, Jo Hammett, De Capo Press, 2001).

His various health problems included alcoholism, gonorrhea, pneumonia, and tuberculosis, which permanently damaged his lungs.

He served patriotically in WWI, which was where he contracted TB, and then enlisted again for WWII, at the age of 47(!). He joined the communist party in the 1930's (as did so many writers), and continued to support left wing and civil rights causes throughout his life.

His intelligence, insight and wit were obvious, yet he dropped out of school when he was only 14 years old to help support his family.

He was one of the few writers of PI fiction who had actual experience as a private detective, having worked for the famous Pinkerton agency.

During the anti-communist fervor of the 1950's, he refused to testify at the trial of numerous defendants accused of conspiracy against the U.S. government. Hammett had to serve five months in prison for contempt of court, even though he was 57 years old and frail from health problems at the time.

This hardboiled master wrote a comic strip, *Secret Agent X-9*, drawn by Flash Gordon artist Alex Raymond.

The characters in Hammett's novel *The Thin Man* were partially based on his real-life relationship with author Lillian Hellman.

He only wrote five novels—*Red Harvest* (1929, featuring a nameless private detective called the Continental Op), *The Dain Curse* (1929, again featuring the Op), *The Maltese Falcon* (1930, Sam Spade), *The Glass Key* (1931, featuring non-PI Ned Beaumont) and *The Thin Man* (1934, featuring Nick and Nora Charles; Nick is a retired PI who comes out of retirement). He wrote over twenty short stories featuring the Continental Op, many of which were collected in *The Continental Op* (1945), *Hammett Homicides* (1946), *Nightmare Town* (1948) and *The Big Knockover* (1966). He also wrote three short stories featuring Sam Spade; these were collected in *The Adventures of Sam Spade and Other Stories* (aka, *A Man Called Spade*, 1945). The majority of his short stories were written for the "gold standard" of detective pulps, *Black Mask*, and except for *The Thin Man*, all his novels were originally serialized or appeared as separate stories in that seminal pulp.

He wrote the screen story for an early gangster movie, *City Streets* (1931, starring Gary Cooper); and in one of his few post-1934 writing forays, he was nominated for an Academy Award for his screenplay for *Watch On the Rhine* (1943), a movie about espionage during WWII, based on Lillian Hellman's stage play.

For Hammett completists, he even had three poems published— "Caution to Travelers" (in *The Lariat*, November 1925 issue), "Goodbye to a Lady" (in *Stratford Magazine*, June 1927) and "Curse in the Old Manner" (in *The Bookman*, September 1927 issue).

He became rich from the movie, radio, and TV shows adapted from his stories and characters. Yet near the end of his life he needed financial assistance from his friend/lover/companion Lillian Hellman, and when he died from lung cancer in 1961 he was near penniless, his only income being a social security check less than $120 a month.

**Further Reading:**
RED HARVEST (1929)
THE DAIN CURSE (1929)
THE MALTESE FALCON (1930)
THE GLASS KEY (1931)
THE THIN MAN (1934)

*Short story collections:*
THE ADVENTURES OF SAM SPADE AND OTHER STORIES (1944; as A MAN CALLED SPADE 1945)
THE CONTINENTAL OP (1945)
THE RETURN OF THE CONTINENTAL OP (1945)
HAMMETT HOMICIDES (1946)
DEAD YELLOW WOMEN (1947)
NIGHTMARE TOWN (1948)
THE CREEPING SIAMESE (1950)
WOMAN IN THE DARK (1951)
A MAN NAMED THIN AND OTHER STORIES (1962)
THE BIG KNOCKOVER: SELECTED STORIES AND SHORT NOVELS (1966)

---

**If you like Dashiell Hammett,** you might like: Raoul Whitfield, Frederick Nebel

# *Arnold Hano*

(also wrote as Gil Dodge, Matthew Gant, Ad Gordon, Mike Heller; ghostwriter for William Gargan). Born in New York City in 1922. Currently lives in Laguna Beach, California.

 Hano began his writing career in 1930 on a mimeographed newspaper he and his brother published when they were seven and ten years old. From here he made the leap to his first professional job as a copy boy at the *New York Daily News* in 1941. The next year he enlisted in the Army and served in the Pacific until 1946. After the war, Hano became a high school English teacher and editor of a Dept. of Labor newsletter before joining Bantam as a western editor, eventually becoming managing editor. After being fired at Bantam for trying to unionize their shop, Hano was hired by Magazine Management to start Lion Books, which he ran as editor-in-chief from 1949-1954. Here he created the seminal noir paperback publisher, often providing story ideas as well as developing the careers of authors like Jim Thompson, Richard Matheson, David Karp and David Goodis.

During this time, Hano tried his hand at writing his own thrillers, most of them written pseudonymously to avoid any conflict with his editorship at Lion. These were usually rather dark stories about twisted, angry men. These tarnished knights appeared as doomed assassins (*Flint*, 1957), disgraced baseball players (*The Big Out*, 1951), insecure blackmailers (*So I'm a Heel*, 1957) and haunted gunslingers (*The Last Notch*, 1958). The majority of his novels were westerns, but a few—like *So I'm a Heel*, *The Executive* (1964) and *Queen Street* (1963)—were given a contemporary setting. Hano also wrote biographical novels on Paul Gaugin (*The Flesh Painter*, 1955) and Sam Houston (*The Raven and the Sword*, 1960), as well as many sports biographies.

The book he is most known for is *A Day in the Bleachers*, originally published in 1955 and still in print today. This is Hano's inning-by-inning account of Game 1 of the 1954 World Series, which as its fabled centerpiece features the famous catch-and-throw of center fielder Willie Mays. It is considered a classic of baseball literature, a celebration of Hano's favorite sport.

In 1955, Arnold Hano moved with his wife Bonnie and their daughter Laurel to Laguna Beach, California. In 1963, he received the Sidney Hillman Award for magazine writing and was also named Magazine Sportswriter of the Year. Hano has since taught writing at the University of Southern California, Pitzer College and the University of California, Irvine. Still going at age 90, he writes a monthly column for an environmental organization, while currently engaged in writing his autobiography, *Hack*.

**Further Reading:**
THE BIG OUT (1951)
THE EXECUTIVE (1964)
A DAY IN THE BLEACHERS (1955)

*As Gil Dodge*
FLINT (1957)

*As Matthew Gant*
VALLEY OF ANGRY MEN (1953)
THE MANHUNTER (1957)
THE LAST NOTCH (1958)
THE RAVEN AND THE SWORD (1960)
QUEEN STREET (1963)

*As Ad Gordon*
THE FLESH PAINTER (1955)
SLADE (1956)

*As Mike Heller*
SO I'M A HEEL (1957)

---

**If you like Arnold Hano,** you might like: Jim Thompson, Clifton Adams, David Karp

## *Patricia Highsmith*

(born Mary Patricia Plangman; also wrote as Claire Morgan; moved to Europe in 1963 and lived abroad for the rest of her life). Born in Fort Worth, Texas, 1921. Died in Locarno, Switzerland, 1995.

Patricia Highsmith became well known for her spectacular debut novel, *Strangers On a Train*, which became the basis for the Alfred Hitchcock film, and for her series of books about homicidal sociopath Tom Ripley. Although she wrote mostly crime fiction, Europeans view her work as transcending the genre, and rank her alongside such psychological and existential writers as Camus, Kafka and Dostoevsky.

Highsmith graduated from New York's Barnard College in 1942. Oddly, for this writer of such dark and brooding tales, Highsmith initially wrote for comic books. Although she wrote for such fantasy-laden superheroes as Spy Smasher and Captain Midnight, she also wrote non-fiction comic book profiles for historical figures such as Einstein, Galileo and Sir Isaac Newton. She wrote for the comics from 1942-1948, living in New York and Mexico during various times.

Highsmith's first novel, *Strangers On a Train*, was published in 1950. Architect Guy Haines and spoiled, psychopathic Charles Bruno meet on a train, never having seen each other before. They get to talking. Guy hates his wife, Bruno hates his father. Bruno proposes a solution: Bruno will kill Guy's wife, Guy will kill Bruno's father. Neither man has a motive for killing the proposed victim, so neither will be suspected. Guy doesn't take the suggestion seriously, but Bruno does—hence, Guy is drawn further and further into the insanity of Bruno's world. The novel presents an incisive examination of secrets, lies and obsession. The book was an instant success and was made into a movie in 1951, starring Farley Granger and Robert Walker, co-written by Raymond Chandler, and directed by Alfred Hitchcock.

Highsmith's first book about Tom Ripley was *The Talented Mr. Ripley* (1955). Ripley is a unique character in fiction—one of the first "anti-heroes." Ripley is blithe, a smooth talker, and can easily schmooze with society's upper crust. Yet inwardly he is vacant and hollow, and fears an inner death from a lack of identity, lack of feeling, and lack of purpose. To alleviate those fears, Tom engages in two activities throughout the series: he is a thief who commits literal identity theft, and he is a serial killer. In this first book, Ripley meets and kills Dickie Greenleaf. He then literally "becomes" Greenleaf. He steals Greenleaf's name, clothes, speaking style and mannerisms. Throughout the rest of the story we learn just how vacant Ripley is. He purposely puts himself in situations where he might be caught. He enjoys danger and taking risks. Without the element of danger, Ripley/Greenleaf becomes bored. It becomes a game to Ripley, and his continued audaciousness shows how he attempts to fill his inner void.

Throughout the series, Ripley engages in more identity theft and commits more murders, yet becomes more spiritually bereft, as he justifies his own crimes by comparing them with the evil he sees in society. The other Ripley novels are *Ripley Under Ground* (1970), *Ripley's Game* (1974), *The Boy Who Followed Ripley* (1980) and *Ripley Under Water* (1991). Starting in 1999, the first three Ripley books were made into fairly successful films: *The Talented Mr. Ripley* (1999) starred Matt Damon as Ripley, *Ripley's Game* (2002) starred John Malkovich and *Ripley Under Ground* (2005) starred Barry Pepper.

Highsmith also wrote an excellent non-fiction book, *Plotting and Writing Suspense Fiction* (1966), which sheds light on her own writing process, as well as being an excellent manual for budding crime writers.

Highsmith was a lesbian, and homosexuality is a subtext which runs through most of her books, though they are usually underscored with male homosexuality. She wrote one novel dealing explicitly with lesbians, *The Price of Salt* (1953, as by Claire Morgan), about a relationship between a married woman and a shop girl. She also had a long term relationship with writer Marijane Meaker (aka Vin Packer), which Meaker wrote about in her memoir, *Highsmith: A Romance of the 1950's.*

In 1957 Highsmith won *The Grand Prix de Littérature Policière* and in 1964 the British Crime Writers Association awarded her a Silver Dagger. In 1979 she received the Grand Master award from the Swedish Academy of Detection.

**Further Reading:**
*Tom Ripley series (complete):*
THE TALENTED MR. RIPLEY (1955)
RIPLEY UNDER GROUND (1970)
RIPLEY'S GAME (1974)
THE BOY WHO FOLLOWED RIPLEY (1980)
RIPLEY UNDER WATER (1991)

STRANGERS ON A TRAIN (1950)
THE PRICE OF SALT (1952, as Claire Morgan)
THE BLUNDERER (1954; as LAMENT FOR A LOVER, 1956)
DEEP WATER (1957)
A GAME FOR THE LIVING (1958)
MIRANDA THE PANDA ON THE VERANDA (1958, children's book)
THE SWEET SICKNESS (1960)

THE CRY OF THE OWL (1962)
THE TWO FACES OF JANUARY (1964)
THE GLASS CELL (1964)
THE STORY-TELLER (1965)
PLOTTING AND WRITING SUSPENSE FICTION (1966, non-fiction)
THOSE WHO WALK AWAY (1967)
THE TREMOR OF FORGERY (1969)
THE SNAIL-WATCHER AND OTHER STORIES (1970, short stories)
A DOG'S RANSOM (1971)
EDITH'S DIARY (1977)
PEOPLE WHO KNOCK AT THE DOOR (1985)
LITTLE TALES OF MISOGYNY (1986, short stories)

---

**If you like Patricia Highsmith,** you might like: David Goodis, Peter Rabe, Vin Packer

# Chester Himes
Born in Jefferson City, Missouri, 1909. Died in Moravia, Spain, 1984.

 Chester Himes didn't start out as a writer. In fact, he didn't start out as much of anything. When he became a writer, and an accomplished one, he was not acclaimed in his homeland. He did not get invited to Hollywood to earn fat paychecks writing screenplays or to wine and dine with movie stars at ritzy nightclubs such as Ciro's and The Mocambo. A small part of the reason may have been because of Himes's angry and contentious attitude.

But the main reason was because he was black. And not ashamed of it.

Chester Himes came from a middle class background. In 1928, he went to prison for armed robbery (he was released in 1936). It was in prison, of all places, where Himes first turned toward literary pursuits. "When I could see the end of my time inside," Himes wrote, "I bought myself a typewriter and taught myself touch typing. I'd been reading stories...in *Black Mask* and I thought I could do them just as well...All you have to do is tell it like it is." (*Twentieth-Century Crime and Mystery Writers*, pg. 539)

Himes's early novels were not of the hardboiled, criminous variety. His first book, *If He Hollers Let Him Go* (1945), was autobiographical in nature and dealt with the racism he encountered while trying to find work in the Los Angeles defense industry during WWII. "It was the look on people's faces when you asked 'em about a job," Himes wrote. "Most of 'em didn't say outright they wouldn't hire me. They just looked so goddamned startled that I'd even asked." (*If He Hollers Let Him Go*, pg. 9).

Other books in this vein were *Lonely Crusade* (1947), *First Stone* (1953), *The Third Generation* (1954) and *The Primitive* (1955). They were all powerfully written accounts of the racism Himes encountered at various times and places in America. When first published they were not particularly successful—critics and the public found their expressions of hostility too raw.

Frustrated with his career and fed up with racism in America, Himes followed in the footsteps of other black literary expatriates such as Richard Wright and James Baldwin and moved to Europe. He wandered around in different countries for a few years before finally settling in Paris in the mid-1950's. A French editor, Marcel Duhamel, contacted Himes and asked him to write a series of detective novels for the French *Serie Noire* line of American crime fiction. Himes, by now almost broke, happily agreed.

Duhamel gave Himes suggestions about what kind of writing his publisher wanted: "Like motion pictures. Always the scenes are visible...We don't give a damn who's thinking what—only what they're doing...Don't worry about it making sense. That's for the end. Give me 220 typed pages." (*Encyclopedia of Pulp Fiction Writers*, by Lee Server, pg. 140)

Himes took the suggestions, and came up with the following:

> The setting: Harlem—dirty, impoverished, chaotic. The heroes: two police detectives, Coffin Ed Johnson and Gravedigger Jones—violent, unpredictable, and profanely funny. The plots: big cons or big capers. The tone: fast-paced, action-packed, raucous—with large dollops of absurdity and deadpan humor.

In terms of the fact that these books were genre fiction, they were not potboilers where Himes abandoned writing about his observations about racism in America. Rather, in the same way that writer Rod Serling was able to both cloak and express his personal and political issues within the sci-fi genre for his TV series *The Twilight Zone*, Himes did likewise with crime fiction.

Himes titled his first novel for the Gallimard *Serie Noir* line, *For Love of Imabelle* (1957). The book was a financial and critical success, and won *The Grand Prix de Littérature Policière* in 1958. In 1991 the book was made into a successful movie called *A Rage in Harlem*; later printings bear this title. Himes was off and running.

The rest of the series follows Jones and Johnson as they "prowl the streets... connecting with a broad network of junkies, stool pigeons, whores, and pimps, doing what they can to maintain law and order by bashing heads and making deals." (*The Big Book of Noir*, pg. 275.) The remaining Jones and Johnson novels are *The Crazy Kill* (1959), *The Real Cool Killers* (1959), *All Shot Up* (1960), *The Big Gold Dream* (1960), *Cotton Comes To Harlem* (1965; made into a movie in 1970, starring Godfrey Cambridge and Raymond St. Jacques, directed by Ossie Davis), *The Heat's On* (1966; filmed as *Come Back, Charleston Blue* in 1972, starring Cambridge and St. Jacques) and *Blind Man with a Pistol* (1969).

In Himes's later years, he wrote two more autobiographical novels: *The Quality of Hurt* (1972) and *My Life of Absurdity* (1976). He made a few return trips to America, but lived the rest of his life in coastal Spain.

Further Reading:
*Coffin Ed Johnson and Grave Digger Jones series (complete):*
FOR LOVE OF IMABELLE (1957; as, A RAGE IN HARLEM, 1965)
THE CRAZY KILL (1959)
THE REAL COOL KILLERS (1959)
ALL SHOT UP (1960)
THE BIG GOLD DREAM (1960)
COTTON COMES TO HARLEM (1965)
THE HEAT'S ON (1966; as COME BACK, CHARLESTON BLUE, 1970)
BLIND MAN WITH A PISTOL (1969)

IF HE HOLLERS LET HIM GO (1945)
LONELY CRUSADE (1947)
CAST THE FIRST STONE (1952)
THE THIRD GENERATION (1954)
THE PRIMITIVE (1956)
PINKTOES (1961)
RUN, MAN, RUN (1966)
THE QUALITY OF HURT (1972, autobiography)
MY LIFE OF ABSURDITY (1976, autobiography)

---

**If you like Chester Himes,** you might like: Ed Lacy, Richard Wright, Langston Hughes, James Baldwin

# Richard Himmel

Born in Chicago, Illinois, 1920. Died in Palm Beach, Florida, 2000.

 Richard Himmel's PBO, *I'll Find You* (1950), was one of the first ten books published by fledgling newcomer Fawcett Gold Medal, and contributed to that publisher's now-legendary success. Further books by Himmel continued to buoy the company's growth, and during Gold Medal's first six years, Himmel's *I Have Gloria Kirby* (1951), along with Vin Packer's *Spring Fire* and Charles Williams' *Hill Girl*, was one of only twelve novels to sell over a million copies. Himmel wrote eight novels for GM, from 1951-58.

Himmel came from a well to do background—his father was a prosperous Chicago-based radio distributor. He attended the University of Chicago, majoring in English and Journalism, where he was inspired and influenced by *Our Town* playwright Thornton Wilder, who Himmel studied under and who became Himmel's personal friend. Himmel's first novel, *Soul of Passion* (1950), was a "spicy" romance about the relationship between widow Kit Greer and her dead husband's best friend.

Himmel's books tended to lean in one of two directions. He wrote hardboiled detective stories featuring Johnny Maguire in six novels, including the aforementioned *I'll Find You* (also published as *It's Murder, Maguire*, 1962) and *I Have Gloria Kirby*, as well as *The Chinese Keyhole* (1951), *Two Deaths Must Die* (1954) and *The Rich and the Damned* (1958). His other books were near-sleaze novels such as 1952's *Beyond Desire* ("Would he ever have the strength to resist her?") and 1955's *Cry of the Flesh* ("If the devil had a daughter, Marion would be her name").

Himmel was a charismatic and colorful character. Besides being an internationally renowned interior designer whose famous clients included Muhammad Ali, he was a discotheque owner and abstract-expressionist painter who, according to his obituary, possessed an "ebullient personality" and was a "witty and charming fixture on the local [Palm Beach] social scene."

**Further Reading:**

*Johnny Maguire series:*

I'LL FIND YOU (1950; as, IT'S MURDER, MAGUIRE, 1962)
THE CHINESE KEYHOLE (1951)
I HAVE GLORIA KIRBY (1951)
TWO DEATHS MUST DIE (1954)
THE RICH AND THE DAMNED (1958)

SOUL OF PASSION (1950; as STRANGE DESIRES, 1954)
BEYOND DESIRE (1952)
THE SHARP EDGE (1952)
CRY OF THE FLESH (1954)
THE SHAME (1959)

---

**If you like Richard Himmel,** you might like: Wade Miller, Orrie Hitt

## Dolores Hitchens

(also wrote as D. B. Olsen, Dolan Birkley, Noel Burke). Born in San Antonio, Texas, 1907. Died in San Antonio, Texas, 1973.

 Traditionally, the consensus among fans of hardboiled fiction is that Leigh Brackett's *No Good from a Corpse* is the best hardboiled detective novel written by a woman. But mystery writer and critic Bill Pronzini claims that Dolores Hitchens' *Sleep with Slander* "is the best hardboiled private-eye novel written by a woman—and one of the best written by anybody." (1001 *Midnights*, by Bill Pronzini and Marcia Muller, pg. 371.)

Dolores Hitchens was born in Texas but spent much of her life in California, Oregon and Washington state. She worked as a nurse and a teacher before starting her writing career. Her first book was *The Clue in the Clay* (1938, as by D. B. Olsen). Her second book, *The Cat Saw Murder* (1939, also written as by Olsen), began a successful series of 12 novels featuring elderly but inquisitive amateur sleuth Rachel Murdock and her crime solving cat, Samantha. These novels were early entries in the sub-genre of "cat mysteries" popularized by later writers such as Lillian Jackson Braun. Recurring characters in the novels are Rachel's stick in the mud, spinsterish sister, Jennifer, and police detective Stephen Mayhew. Notable Murdock titles include *The Cat Wears a Noose* (1944), *Cats Have Tall Shadows* (1948) and *The Cat Wears a Mask* (1949). The Murdock novels are lighthearted and diverting entertainments.

Beginning in 1955, Hitchens wrote a series of five novels in collaboration with her husband, Bert (a railroad detective), featuring a squad of Los Angeles area railroad cops. These books were grittier and more hardboiled than the Murdock series. Hitchens' "railroad cop" novels featured a different set of cops, although detective John Farrell, an alcoholic struggling with the reality of a wife who's left him and taken their child with her, appeared in three of the novels. The five books are *F.O.B. Murder* (1955), *One-Way Ticket* (1956), *End of the Line* (1957), *The Man Who Followed Women* (1959) and *The Grudge* (1963).

*Sleep with Slander* (1960), the book highly praised by Pronzini, is in actuality the second of two books Hitchens wrote which featured private detective Jim Sader. The story is set in Long Beach, California, where Sader is hired to locate a child who, five years earlier, was given away to a private couple, rather than put up for adoption by a legitimate agency. Sader, in the tradition of Raymond Chandler's Philip Marlowe, is a world weary knight, although he allows himself more emotional involvement than Marlowe. Throughout his investigation, Sader discovers grim family skeletons, including insanity, child abuse, rape and murder. In Sader's debut, *Sleep with Strangers* (1956), he is hired by a beautiful femme fatale to find her missing mother. Pronzini, in *1001 Midnights*, ranks this book a notch below *Slander* because of some patches of sentimentality and a shaky ending.

Hitchens' novel *Fool's Gold* (1958) became the basis for French "New Wave" director Jean-Luc Godard's movie *Bande a Part* (1964, released as *Band of Outsiders* in the U.S.).

**Further Reading:**
*Jim Sader series (complete):*
SLEEP WITH STRANGERS (1955)      SLEEP WITH SLANDER (1960)

STAIRWAY TO AN EMPTY ROOM (1951)
TERROR LURKS IN DARKNESS (1953)
FOOLS' GOLD (1958)                    THE WATCHER (1959)
THE ABDUCTOR (1962)
THE MAN WHO CRIED ALL THE WAY HOME (1966)

*With Bert Hitchens:*
F.O.B. MURDER (1955)                  ONE-WAY TICKET (1956)
END OF THE LINE (1957)
THE MAN WHO FOLLOWED WOMEN (1959)
THE GRUDGE (1963)

**As D.B. Olsen**
*Rachel Murdock series:*
THE CAT SAW MURDER (1939)
THE ALARM OF THE BLACK CAT (1942)
CAT'S CLAW (1943)
CATSPAW FOR MURDER (1943)
THE CAT WEARS A NOOSE (1944)
CATS DON'T SMILE (1945)
CATS DON'T NEED COFFINS (1946)
CATS HAVE TALL SHADOWS (1948)
THE CAT WEARS A MASK (1949)
DEATH WEARS CAT'S EYES (1950)
THE CAT AND CAPRICORN (1951)
THE CAT WALK (1953)
DEATH WALKS ON CAT FEET (1956)

---

**If you like Dolores Hitchens,** you might like: Leigh Brackett, Stuart Palmer

# Orrie Hitt

(also wrote as Kay Addams, Joe Black, Roger Normandie, Charles Verne, Nicky Weaver). Born in Colchester, New York, 1916. Died in Montrose, New York, 1975.

 Orrie Hitt was the epitome of the "paperback writer." He cranked out one hundred and fifty novels during his fifteen year career (some were written in as little as two weeks), pounding the keys of his battered typewriter, chain smoking Winstons and chugging cup after cup of iced coffee.

Hitt grew up in Forestburgh, New York, a small town upstate. When he was eleven-years-old, his father committed suicide, so Orrie and his mother worked for a hunting lodge to make ends meet. His first professional writing sale came while he was still in high school—he sold non-fiction articles about hunting to outdoor magazines. He joined the Army during WWII and after the war, worked as an insurance salesman, hotel desk clerk, radio station DJ and as a jack-of-all-trades handyman. He later drew on these experiences for his novels.

Hitt's first book was *I'll Call Every Monday* (1953), a James M. Cain-like tale of an insurance salesman and young married woman who plot to kill her wealthy husband.

The men in Orrie Hitt's books were typically 6'1", 190 lb., square-jawed he-man types with names like Dutch, Arch, Rip, Brick, Buck and Slade. Hitt's women were 38-19-36, good girls gone bad, with names like Sheba, Sherry, Honey, Candy, Cherry and Lola. Hitt wrote for adults-only "sleaze" publishers like Beacon and Midwood, and his work covered all the topics typically written about for the sleaze publishers: peeping toms (*I Prowl By Night*, 1961, *The Peeper*, 1959, *Lust Prowl*, 1964), the smut picture racket (*Trapped*, 1958, *Sin Doll*, 1959, *Naked Model*, 1962, *Mail Order Sex*, 1962), vacation resort hijinks (*Hotel Hostess*, 1960, *Hotel Confidential*, 1958, *Summer of Sin*, 1961, *The Love Season*, 1961), suburban indiscretions (*Suburban Wife*, 1958, *Suburban Trap*, 1961, *Suburban Interlude*, 1960, *The Cheat*, 1958, *Never Cheat Alone*, 1960), juvenile delinquents (*Wild Oats*, 1958, *The Torrid Teens*, 1960, *Wayward Girl*, 1960), backwoods passions (*Dirt Farm*, 1961, *Ellie's Shack*, 1958), nudist camps (*Nudist Camp*, 1957, *The Naked Flesh*, 1962, *My Wild Nights with Nine Nudists!*, 1963), and lesbian themed (*Warped Desire*, 1960, *Queer Patterns*, 1959, *Three Strange Women*, 1960, *The Strangest Sin*, 1961).

In order for the sleaze publishers to print books about such subject matter and not be arrested for obscenity, they marketed their books as socially redeeming "exposés," the cover blurbs trumpeting the stories as "frank," "revealing," "candid," "unblushing" and "dealing honestly with a taboo subject."

In contrast to the sin drenched lives of his characters, Hitt was a lifelong family man, faithfully married to one woman, who raised four children while living in upstate New York.

**Further Reading:**
I'LL CALL EVERY MONDAY (1953)
SHE GOT WHAT SHE WANTED (1954)
SHABBY STREET (1954)
UNFAITHFUL WIVES (1956)
THE SUCKER (1957)
NUDIST CAMP (1957)
PUSHOVER (1957)
TRAILER TRAMP (1957)
SUBURBAN WIFE (1958)
WILD OATS (1958)
AFFAIRS OF A BEAUTY QUEEN (1958)
GIRL'S DORMITORY (1958)
SHEBA (1959)
CARNIVAL GIRL (1959)
THE PEEPER (1959)
EX-VIRGIN (1959)
WAYWARD GIRL (1960)
THE TORRID TEENS (1960)
CALL ME BAD (1960)
THE LADY IS A LUSH (1960)
THE CHEATERS (1960)
FRIGID WIFE (1961)
VIRGINS NO MORE (1961)
HOT BLOOD (1961)
DIPLOMA DOLLS (1961)
TWISTED LOVERS (1961)
EASY WOMEN! (1961; as INFLAMED DAMES, 1963; as LOVE SEEKERS, 1964; as JENKINS' LOVERS, 1965)
PEEPING TOM (1961)
DIAL "M" FOR MAN (1962)
TORRID CHEAT (1962)
LIBBY SIN (1962)
PASSION HOSTESS (1962)
CAMPUS TRAMP (1962)
VIOLENT SINNERS (1962)
ABNORMAL NORMA (1962)
MAN-HUNGRY FEMALE (1962; as MORE!MORE!MORE!, 1964)

TORRID WENCH (1963)
STRIP ALLEY (1963)
NUDE DOLL (1963)
LOOSE WOMEN (1963)
AN AMERICAN SODOM (1963)
THE COLOR OF LUST (1964)
LUST PROWL (1964)
WOMAN'S WARD (1966)
WHILE THE CITY SINS (1967)
PANDA BEAR PASSION (1968)
NUDE MODEL (1970)

**As Kay Addams**
QUEER PATTERNS (1959)
LUCY (1960)
THREE STRANGE WOMEN (1960)
WARPED DESIRE (1960)
THE STRANGEST SIN (1961)
THE AUTOBIOGRAPHY OF KAY ADAMS (1962, aka THE SECRET
PERVERSIONS OF KAY ADDAMS)
MY SECRET PERVERSIONS (1962, aka HIDDEN HUNGERS)
MY WILD NIGHTS WITH NINE NUDISTS! (1963, reprinted as NOCTURNAL
NUDISTS)

**As Joe Black**
UNNATURAL URGE (1962)

**As Roger Normandie**
RUN FOR COVER (1957; as RACE WITH LUST, 1959)
WEB OF EVIL (1957)
THE LION'S DEN (1957; as TORMENTED PASSIONS, 1959)

**As Charles Verne**
MR. HOT ROD (1957)
THE WHEEL OF PASSION (1957)

**As Nicky Weaver**
LOVE, BLOOD AND TEARS (1963)
LOVE OR KILL THEM ALL (1963)

---

**If you like Orrie Hitt,** you might like: James M. Cain, Harry Whittington

# Elisabeth Sanxay Holding

Born in Brooklyn, New York, 1889. Died in New York, New York, 1955.

Elisabeth Sanxay (pronounced "*sanks-ay*") Holding wrote what Anthony Boucher characterized as "psychological novels of suspense." Her stories explore conflict within close family relationships, where murder is the catalyst for the main character to reevaluate those relationships.

Holding grew up in Brooklyn and was educated in a number of middle-upper class private schools. When she married British diplomat George E. Holding in 1913, she traveled extensively throughout South America, the West Indies and Bermuda. Upon her husband's retirement, Holding returned to New York.

Holding's first novels were romantic fiction, among them *Invincible Minnie* (1920), *Rosaleen Among the Artists* (1921) and *The Shoals of Honor* (1926). When the Great Depression hit in 1929, she turned to the more lucrative field of mystery fiction, starting with *Miasma* (1929). She published nineteen suspense novels, ending with *Widow's Mite* (1953). Many of these novels were also serialized in national magazines, and almost all were published in paperback and foreign editions, as well as by mystery book clubs. In paperback, Dell published several of her novels in the '50's, and Mercury published a few in digest form. During the 1960's, Ace Books published twelve of her books as Ace Doubles. She published short stories in magazines ranging from *McCall's*, *American Magazine* and *Ladies' Home Journal*, to *Alfred Hitchcock's Mystery Magazine*, *The Saint*, *Ellery Queen's Mystery Magazine* and *The Magazine of Fantasy & Science Fiction*. She even wrote a children's book, *Miss Kelly* (1947), the story of a cat who could understand and speak human, and who comes to the aid of a terrified tiger.

Notable novels include: *Dark Power* (1930), about a penniless woman who is taken in to the home of a distant uncle and has to contend with a nest of dangerously dysfunctional relatives; *Lady Killer* (1942), where a woman on a cruise ship struggles to save a fellow passenger from being murdered by her husband; and *Net of Cobwebs* (1945), the story of an amnesiac seaman suffering traumatic nightmares about his torpedoed ship.

Holding's best known work is perhaps *The Blank Wall* (1947). The story centers on Lucia Holley, a middle-class wife and mother whose daughter's sleazy boyfriend is found dead under circumstances that may implicate the daughter. When Lucia covers up incriminating evidence, she is blackmailed by the boyfriend's criminal cohorts. The book was made into an excellent, underrated film noir in 1949, starring Joan Bennett (in a change of type from the femme fatales she played in *Scarlet Street* and *Woman in the*

*Window*) and James Mason. It was remade in 2001 as The Deep End, star-ring Tilda Swinson.

No less a personage than Raymond Chandler wrote that Holding was "the top suspense writer of them all."

**Further Reading:**
MIASMA (1929)
DARK POWER (1930)
THE DEATH WISH (1934)
THE UNFINISHED CRIME (1935)
THE STRANGE CRIME IN BERMUDA (1937)
THE OBSTINATE MURDERER (1938)
THE GIRL WHO HAD TO DIE (1940)
WHO'S AFRAID? (1940)
SPEAK OF THE DEVIL (1941)
KILL JOY (1942; as MURDER IS A KILL-JOY, 1946)
LADY KILLER (1942)
THE OLD BATTLE AX (1943)
NET OF COBWEBS (1945)
THE INNOCENT MRS. DUFF (1946)
MISS KELLY (1947)
THE BLANK WALL (1947)
TOO MANY BOTTLES (1951; as THE PARTY WAS THE PAY-OFF, 1953)
THE VIRGIN HUNTRESS (1951)
WIDOW'S MITE (1953)

---

If you like Elisabeth Sanxay Holding, you might like: Dorothy B. Hughes, Fletcher Flora

# Dorothy B. Hughes
(born Dorothy Belle Flanagan). Born in Kansas City, Missouri, 1904. Died in
Ashland, Oregon, 1993.

 In a genre largely dominated by men, Dorothy B.
Hughes wrote noirish suspense novels which were
often more gripping than a number of her male coun-
terparts'.

Hughes graduated from the University of Missouri
with a BA in journalism in 1924. She did graduate work
at the University of New Mexico and Columbia
University in New York. Beginning in the 1930's, she
reviewed mystery fiction for the *Albuquerque Tribune*, the *Los Angeles News*,
the *Los Angeles Mirror* and the *New York Herald-Tribune*. In 1950, she received
an Edgar award for her reviews.

Hughes first novel, *The So Blue Marble* (1941), combined suspense and
fantasy. In the story, a fashion designer is drawn into a search for a small
marble with ancient supernatural powers, and encounters violence and
brutality along the way. *The Fallen Sparrow* (1942) is another notable book.
Kit McKittrick, having fought against the fascists in the Spanish Civil War,
returns home to New York to search for the killer of a long time friend,
but is forced to contend with a group of spies as well as dealing with
haunting memories of being tortured in a Spanish prison. *The Fallen
Sparrow* was made into an edge of your seat thriller in 1943 starring John
Garfield. In *Ride the Pink Horse* (1946), "Sailor," a hood from Chicago, has
trailed a senator who is on the run after having set up his wife's murder.
Sailor catches up with the senator in Santa Fe, New Mexico, and wants
money or he'll talk. Hughes sets the novel during Fiesta week, a time of
lively festivals and rituals, which serves as an ironic counterpoint to
Sailor's and the senator's dark deeds. In 1947, the book was made into an
excellent film noir starring Robert Montgomery.

Hughes's *In a Lonely Place* (1947) is an early, incisive novel about a serial
killer and is perhaps her best book. Dix Steele is a WWII veteran who
moves to Los Angeles. He is mainly a loner (though, chameleon-like, he
can wear the mask of civility and fit in with whoever he spends time
with) who prowls the Santa Monica beach area late at night searching for
women to attack. A wrench is thrown into Dix's works when he looks up
an old Army buddy, Brub Nicolai. When Dix and Brub meet, Dix is surprised to find that Brub is a detective with the Los Angeles Police
Department. The magnetism of the book comes from how well Hughes
penetrates into Dix's psyche. It's as if Hughes had written a true crime
account of Ted Bundy thirty years before the fact. *In a Lonely Place* was

made into a classic film noir starring Humphrey Bogart and Gloria Grahame, directed by Nicholas Ray. Though the book and movie have very little in common, the movie is excellent in its own right.

With the exception of *The Expendable Man* (1963), Hughes stopped writing novels in 1952. Her ill mother was living with her, and Hughes's own children were having babies and needed help caring for them. However, Hughes didn't give up writing entirely. She reviewed books and movies for the *Los Angeles Times* and wrote a critically acclaimed study of Erle Stanley Gardner titled *The Case of the Real Perry Mason* (1979). In 1978, she was named Grand Master by the Mystery Writers of America.

**Further Reading:**
THE SO BLUE MARBLE (1940)
THE CROSS-EYED BEAR (1940)
THE BAMBOO BLONDE (1941)
THE FALLEN SPARROW (1942)
THE BLACKBIRDER (1943)
THE DELICATE APE (1944)
JOHNNY (1944)
DREAD JOURNEY (1945)
RIDE THE PINK HORSE (1946)
IN A LONELY PLACE (1947)
THE CANDY KID (1950)
THE DAVIDIAN REPORT (1952; as, THE BODY ON THE BENCH, 1955)
THE EXPENDABLE MAN (1963)
ERLE STANLEY GARDNER: THE CASE OF THE REAL PERRY MASON (1978, non-fiction)

---

**If you like Dorothy B. Hughes,** you might like: Horace McCoy, Leigh Brackett

# Howard Hunt

(born Everette Howard Hunt; also wrote as E. Howard Hunt, Gordon Davis, Robert Dietrich, David St. John, P. S. Donoghue, John Baxter). Born in Hamburg, New York, 1918. Died in Miami, Florida, 2007.

Yes, E. Howard Hunt, writer of hardboiled crime fiction, is the same E. Howard Hunt who, as consultant to President Richard M. Nixon, was part of the group of men responsible for the Watergate break in. However, throughout the 1950's and '60's, Hunt wrote tightly paced, gripping crime and spy fiction for Gold Medal, Dell and other top flight paperback houses. His books sold well and were well regarded within the mystery writers' community. Not only that, but early in his writing career, Hunt was published in the prestigious *New Yorker* and won a Guggenheim Fellowship in Creative Writing.

Maybe Hunt should have stuck to his day job.

Hunt graduated from Brown University. He served in the United States Naval Reserve during World War II, wrote narration for the *March of Time* newsreel series, and was a war correspondent for *Life* magazine.

Hunt's first novel for Gold Medal (using his own name but dropping his first initial, "E.") was *The Violent Ones* (1950). Paul Cameron, an ex-G.I, flies to France to help an old friend find a cache of hidden gold. The story is suspense filled, the characters are amoral, and the prose is hardboiled—the archetypical Gold Medal novel. In *The Judas Hour* (1951), a skid row alcoholic is kidnapped and taken to a communist training camp, where a beautiful Soviet agent uses mind control methods to try to convert him to side with communist Russia. Other crime related Gold Medal books under Hunt's own name include *Whisper Her Name* (1952) and *Lovers are Losers* (1953)—"She was too evil to live and too beautiful to die."

Under the name Gordon Davis, Hunt started his Gold Medal run with *I Came to Kill* (1955). In *House Dick* (1961), hotel detective Pete Novak, while investigating a murder, hides the corpse and chooses not to notify the police. *Where Money Waits* (1965) is about Washington attorney Pat Conroy, who had been involved in the botched Bay of Pigs invasion to assassinate Fidel Castro, and is now recruited to recover funds collected for that mission.

Mystery writers and critics think that some of Hunt's best writing appears in the paperbacks written under the pseudonym Robert Dietrich. The Dietrich books feature series character Steve Bentley, a Washington-based CPA who assists the police in tracking down racketeers and murderers. Though an accountant, Bentley's attitude and behavior is more akin to that of a hardboiled PI. In perusing some of the Bentley novels, it's interesting to come across Hunt's narrator offering observations that we now know to be "inside information" about Washington....

> "Washington...On the surface the Nation's Capital, Grecian and gray, with teeming hives of government workers. No liquor sold after midnight. No whore houses and no gambling halls. On the surface. Scrape away a little of the worn patina and you find as many forbidden delights as a Hong Kong pimp can offer. Plus a per capita crime rate larger than any city in the U.S...A citizenry without votes, and kept voteless because Negroes are in the majority." (*Curtains for a Lover*, 1962)

...as well as making prophetically ironic statements in light of Hunt's future role in Watergate:

> "Let's say the mood changed. Mood's a fragile thing, Morgan. Like morality. Once stretched it's never quite the same again." (*Curtains for a Lover*)

Notable Bentley titles include 1959's *End of a Stripper* ("Her nude body was on display for the last time—in the morgue"), 1960's *Murder On Her Mind* ("She was a lush-bodied Latin chanteuse with a song on her lips, passion in her heart and...Murder On Her Mind") and 1961's *Angel Eyes* ("She died the way she lived—in the heat of passion").

Under the name David St. John, Hunt wrote a series of spy thrillers featuring CIA agent Peter Ward: *On Hazardous Duty* (1965), *The Venus Probe* (1966) and *Diabolus* (1971).

After the Watergate scandal, Hunt's novels, rather than fading into the woodwork, became *more* popular, and books he had written under pseudonyms were reprinted under his own name, their covers trumpeting blurbs such as: "a novel by THE FORMER CIA AGENT AND WATERGATE CONSPIRATOR."

Hunt spent four years in prison and upon his release in 1977 he jumpstarted his writing career anew—he wrote memoirs, mainstream political thrillers and created a new series character, a rogue DEA agent named Jack Novak. His resuscitated writing career successfully lasted twenty-five years.

Who says crime doesn't pay?

Further Reading:
MAELSTROM (1948, as CRUEL IS THE NIGHT, 1955)
BIMINI RUN (1949)
THE VIOLENT ONES (1950)
DARK ENCOUNTER (1950)
THE JUDAS HOUR (1951)
WHISPER HER NAME (1952)
LOVERS ARE LOSERS (1953)

**As Gordon Davis**
I CAME TO KILL (1953)
HOUSE DICK (1961)
COUNTERFEIT KILL (1963)
RING AROUND ROSY (1964)
WHERE MURDER WAITS (1965)

**As Robert Dietrich**
*Steve Bentley series (complete):*
MURDER ON THE ROCKS (1957)
THE HOUSE ON Q STREET (1959)
END OF A STRIPPER (1959)
MISTRESS TO MURDER (1960)
MURDER ON HER MIND (1961)
ANGEL EYES (1961)
STEVE BENTLEY'S CALYPSO CAPER (1961)
CURTAINS FOR A LOVER (1961)
MY BODY (1962)

ONE FOR THE ROAD (1954)
THE CHEAT (1954)
BE MY VICTIM (1956)

---

**If you like Howard Hunt,** you might like: David Dodge, Dan J. Marlowe

# *Evan Hunter*

(born Salvatore Lombino; also wrote as Ed McBain, Richard Marsten, Curt Cannon, Hunt Collins, Ezra Hannon, John Abbott, Dean Hudson). Born in New York City, New York, 1926. Died in Weston, Connecticut, 2005.

Salvatore Lombino was Evan Hunter, who was Ed McBain, who was Richard Marsten, who was Curt Cannon, who was Hunt Collins, who was Ezra Hannon, who was John Abbott, and who was Dean Hudson, but wouldn't admit it. Got all that straight?

As Salvatore Lombino, he grew up in East Harlem and the Bronx. He served in the Navy during WWII, and it was during that time his interest in writing began. After WWII, he attended Hunter College as an English major, minoring in Drama and Education. When he graduated in 1950 he taught at the Bronx Vocational High School, but the experience was so disheartening he quit after 17 days. For a brief period afterward, Lombino worked for AAA. The turning point in his life came when he answered a want ad from the Scott Meredith Literary Agency. He was given a job as editor, and the beginning of his relationship with Scott Meredith was the beginning of his professional writing career.

As Evan Hunter (Lombino legally changed his name to Hunter in 1952), he found fame and fortune with the publication of his novel *The Blackboard Jungle* (1954), and the subsequent movie adaptation, starring Glenn Ford and Sidney Poitier. *The Blackboard Jungle* was based partly on Hunter's teaching experience. *Second Ending* (1956) was a gripping book about dope and jazz musicians. The famous crime/mystery digest *Manhunt* published several of his short stories. Hunter also wrote non-crime related novels. *Streets of Gold* (1974; Hunter's personal favorite) was about a blind jazz musician. *Let's Talk* (2005) was a non-fiction account of his battle with cancer. He also wrote several screenplays and teleplays, including the screenplay for Alfred Hitchcock's *The Birds* (1963).

As Ed McBain he wrote his most well known books, the 87thPrecinct series. The 87th Precinct books are about a detective squad located in the fictional city of Isola, a thinly-disguised version of Manhattan. The protagonist for the series would generally be considered Steve Carella, a diligent and conscientious member of the squad. But this is somewhat misleading as the 87th Precinct books really feature an ensemble cast. Lieutenant Byrnes is the respected chief of the squad, Cotton Hawes is the son of a Protestant minister, Meyer Meyer is a Jew who dealt with prejudice while growing up in a gentile neighborhood, Arthur Brown is an impatient black cop, Andy Parker is a sadistic cop, Bert Kling is the youngest member of the squad, and the list goes on.

McBain did extensive research into the realities of day to day police investigative methods. He wrote approximately fifty books in the series and kept the stories fresh by alternating the cast of characters from book to book, by experimenting with different methods of storytelling instead of relying on a repetitive formula, and by seamlessly weaving irony, humor, sex, pathos and tragedy into the stories. Notable titles include *The Mugger* (1956), *The Pusher* (1956), *Killer's Wedge* (1959), *The Heckler* (1960), *Ax* (1964), *Fuzz* (1968, later made into a movie starring Burt Reynolds) and *Lightning* (1984), among many others.

Later in his career, McBain wrote a series of novels featuring Florida lawyer Matthew Hope, who became involved in murders and various crimes through his clients. The titles, such as *Goldilocks* (1977), are all named after various nursery rhymes; the titles serve as ironic counterpoints to the books' brutality and violence. Other Matthew Hope novels are *Rumpelstiltskin* (1981) and *Beauty and the Beast* (1982), among others.

As Richard Marsten, he wrote sci-fi novels for young adults, including *Danger, Dinosaurs!* (1953) and *Rocket To Luna* (1953). He also wrote non-series crime novels like *Vanishing Ladies* (1957), *Even the Wicked* (1958) and *Big Man* (1959). Along with the Hunter byline, McBain published numerous Marsten stories in *Manhunt*. Often, stories under both names appeared in the same issue.

As Curt Cannon he wrote about what is perhaps his most hardboiled character—alcoholic, down and out, pissed off, ex-PI Matt Cordell, who wanders through skid row in the Bowery. Cannon wrote only one Cordell novel, *I'm Cannon for Hire* (1958, early printings named both the author and the character Curt Cannon; the Matt Cordell name came later). He also published *I Like 'Em Tough* (1958), a collection of all the Cannon/Cordell short stories, which originally appeared in (can you guess?) *Manhunt*.

As Hunt Collins he wrote two early novels. *Cut Me In* (1954) is a mystery set in the movie business and features the murder of a prominent literary agent. *Tomorrow's World* (1956) is a futuristic dystopian novel about the battle between the sex- and drug-loving "Vikes" and the conservative and realistic "Rees." And it must have just been a coincidence, but somehow Hunt Collins also slipped a story or two into *Manhunt*.

As Ezra Hannon, he wrote one novel, *Doors* (1975), featuring master burglar Alex Hardy. Sorry, no *Manhunt* stories from Mr. Hannon

As James Abbott, he also wrote one novel. *Scimitar* (1992) is a story of political intrigue about an assassin who's hired by one head of state to kill another.

And as for Dean Hudson.... Ah, yes, the elusive Mr. Hudson. The name Dean Hudson is the beginning of a fascinating story for all Lombino-Hunter-McBain-Marsten-Cannon-Collins-Hannon-Abbott-philes. In brief, "Dean Hudson" was a house name for Nightstand Books, Bedside Books,

Corinth Books and other publishers that sold soft core "adults only" books
with titles such as *Las Vegas Lust*, *Wall Street Wanton* and *Showcase for Sin*.
Many now well known writers penned books under the Hudson name, as
well as other pseudonyms, not wishing their work for "sleaze" publishers
to be known to the public. Hunter was one of them. The story of Evan
Hunter as Dean Hudson has enough intrigue, shadowy figures, under the
table dealings, sex and drugs, denials and admissions and then denials
again, and shell game shenanigans to fill three or four noirish novels of
its own. The best reference is a link to the website of Dean Hudson/Evan
Hunter's editor, Earl Kemp:

http://efanzines.com/EK/eI24/index.htm

When you open the link, click on the entry called "The Whitewash
Jungle" and you'll be taken to Earl Kemp's story regarding the Hunter-
Hudson connection.

**Further Reading:**
THE EVIL SLEEP! (1952)
THE BLACKBOARD JUNGLE (1954)
SECOND ENDING (1956)
STRANGERS WHEN WE MEET (1958)
A MATTER OF CONVICTION (1959)
MOTHERS AND DAUGHTERS (1961)
A HORSE'S HEAD (1967)
EVERY LITTLE CROOK AND NANNY (1972)

**As Ed McBain**
*87th Precinct series:*
COP HATER (1956)
THE MUGGER (1956)
THE PUSHER (1956)
THE CON MAN (1957)
KILLER'S CHOICE (1957)
KILLER'S PAYOFF (1958)
KILLER'S WEDGE (1959)
GIVE THE BOYS A GREAT BIG HAND (1960)
THE HECKLER (1960)
SEE THEM DIE (1960)
TEN PLUS ONE (1963)
AX (1964)
EIGHTY MILLION EYES (1966)

FUZZ (1968)
HAIL, HAIL, THE GANG'S ALL HERE! (1971)
SADIE WHEN SHE DIED (1972)"
LET'S HEAR IT FOR THE DEAF MAN (1972)
HAIL TO THE CHIEF (1973)

**As Richard Marsten**
ROCKET TO LUNA (1953)
DANGER: DINOSAURS! (1953)
RUNAWAY BLACK (1954)
MURDER IN THE NAVY (1955) (later published as DEATH OF A NURSE, by
Ed McBain, 1968)
EVEN THE WICKED (1958)
BIG MAN (1959)

**As Curt Cannon**
I LIKE 'EM TOUGH (1958, short stories)
I'M CANNON — FOR HIRE (1958)

**As Hunt Collins**
CUT ME IN (1954)
TOMORROW AND TOMORROW AND TOMORROW (1956)

**As Ezra Hannon**
DOORS (1975)

**As Dean Hudson**
LAS VEGAS LUST (1961)
WALL STREET WANTON (1961)
CASTING COUCH (1961)
PASSION MAN (1962)
PASSION SUBURB (1962)

---

**If you like Evan Hunter,** you might like: Jonathan Craig, William P.
McGivern, Wade Miller

# John Jakes

(also wrote as William Ard, Alan Payne, Jay Scotland, Darius John Granger, Allen Wilder, John Lee Gray). Born in Chicago, Illinois, 1932. Presently dividing his time between South Carolina and Florida.

Before finding mainstream success with his 1970's saga *The Kent Family Chronicles* and his 1980's *The North and South Trilogy*, John Jakes spent over twenty years writing more than 200 western, sci-fi and mystery short stories for the pulps, and more than 60 paperback originals in those same genres.

Jakes started his freshman year at Northwestern University studying acting, but when he sold his first short story at the age of 18, he decided to switch from the stage to the page. He transferred to DePauw University to enroll in their creative writing program and graduated in 1953—by that time having sold many more stories to pulps such as *Amazing* and *Fantastic Adventures*. He earned an MA in American Literature from Ohio State University in 1954, and upon graduation, found a day job as a copywriter—first for a pharmaceutical company and then for numerous ad agencies. At night, he kept toiling away at his fiction.

Jakes sold his first novel when he was 21. *Gonzaga's Woman* (1953) was a thriller about the vice racket. It was first published as a double by Royal Books, along with the reprinting of a Talbot Mundy novella, *Affair in Araby*. *Gonzaga's Woman* was later republished by one of the most well known soft core paperback houses, Beacon books. He wrote *The Devil Has Four Faces* in 1958, a story about a detective with the unusual name Marco Polo Smith, who is on the hunt for a Nazi refugee hiding in Chicago. Jakes also created a series about a quirky, unlicensed private detective, Johnny Havoc. Although Havoc is only 5'1", he has an extra-large libido. But his diminutive stature doesn't seem to bother Johhny. With his flaming red hair, his cockiness, his guts, and with the help of police Detective FitzHugh Goodpasture, Johnny always manages to get his man. Or woman, which he much prefers. The Havoc novels are energetic and comedic. Jakes wrote three Havoc books: *Johnny Havoc* (1960), *Johnny Havoc Meets Zelda* (1962, aka *Havoc for Sale* and *Johnny Havoc and the Siren in Red*) and *Johnny Havoc and the Doll Who Had "It"* (1963, aka *Holiday for Havoc*).

Jakes also ghostwrote books for William Ard's Lou Largo series after Ard's early death at the age of 37. Largo is a no-nonsense, sarcastic ex-Marine turned private eye. Jakes's first book in the series was *Make Mine Mavis* (1961), where Largo helps singer Tommy Topper escape from sadistic Las Vegas gangster Jan O'Hara. In *And So To Bed* (1962), Largo travels

through the seedier areas of New York and encounters a grossly obese
crook, a blind and bitter used bookstore owner, a prostitute and a girl who
gets her kicks popping peyote. In *Give Me This Woman* (1963), Largo is hired
by a gangster to high-tail it to Niagara Falls to bring back his independent-
minded daughter.

As Alan Payne, Jakes wrote two books which were part of the Ace
Double series: *Murder, He Says* (1958) and *This'll Slay You* (1958).

Though Jakes later went on to bigger (though not necessarily better)
things, all fans of crime fiction should be grateful for the twenty years he
toiled in the vintage paperback jungle.

**Further Reading:**
*Johnny Havoc series (complete):*
JOHNNY HAVOC (1960)
JOHNNY HAVOC MEETS ZELDA (1962)
JOHNNY HAVOC AND THE DOLL WHO HAD "IT" (1963)

GONZAGA'S WOMAN (1953)
A NIGHT FOR TREASON (1956)
WEAR A FAST GUN (1956)
THE DEVIL HAS FOUR FACES (1958)
THE IMPOSTER (1959)
STRIKE THE BLACK FLAG (1961)
ARENA (1963)
G.I. GIRLS (1963)
MAKING IT BIG (1967)
SIX GUN PLANET (1970)

---

**If you like John Jakes,** you might like: Harry Whittington, Frank Gruber

# *Richard Jessup*

(also wrote as Richard Telfair, Carey Rockwell, October Smith). Born in Savannah, Georgia, 1925. Died in Nokomis, Florida, 1982.

Before Richard Jessup struck it rich with *The Cincinnati Kid*, he wrote crime novels, westerns and spy thrillers for paperback publishers Gold Medal and Dell.

Jessup's first novel, *The Cunning and the Haunted* (1954), which recounts a boy's brutal upbringing in an orphanage, was based on his own experiences. He was placed in an orphanage when he was three months old and ran away during his teens. The book was made into a movie titled *The Young Don't Cry* (1957) starring Sal Mineo. Jessup wrote the screenplay.

Jessup's next novel, *A Rage to Die* (1955), dealt with corrupt politicians and urban vice. One of Jessup's most hardboiled novels, *Wolf Cop* (1961), tells the story of Tony Serella, a cop obsessed with meting out vigilante justice, no matter how harsh the tactics, and whose law enforcement methods become increasingly brutal as his obsession engulfs his life.

As Richard Telfair, Jessup wrote a western series featuring gunslinger Wyoming Jones: *Wyoming Jones* (1958), *Day of the Gun* (1958), *The Secret of Apache Canyon* (1959), *Wyoming Jones for Hire* (1959) and *Sundance* (1960). Jessup also wrote westerns under his own name, beginning with *Cheyenne Saturday* (1957). One of his most notable westerns was *Chuka* (1961). Set during the 1870's, the story is about a gunfighter named Chuka and his battles at Fort Clendennon—a place infamously nicknamed Fort Hell. *Chuka* was made into a movie in 1967 and starred Rod Taylor and Ernest Borgnine. Jessup again wrote the screenplay.

Jessup, under the name Telfair again, wrote a series of spy novels featuring Monty Nash, an agent who worked for the Department of Counter Intelligence. Nash is an uber-hardass whose independent, argumentative streak gets under the skin of his superiors. In the first Nash adventure, *The Bloody Medallion* (1959), Nash's partner has been murdered and Monty seeks revenge. In *Scream Bloody Murder* (1960), Nash must stop/confront a smuggling operation. In *The Slavers* (1961), Nash searches for the kidnapped daughter of a rich Arab king. *Monty Nash* became a TV series for a season during 1971-72 and starred Harry Guardino as Nash.

Jessup's most popular book was also his first hardcover, *The Cincinnati Kid* (1963). *Kid* is about a young, hotshot poker player who wants to dethrone a legendary old pro nicknamed "The Man." *The Cincinnati Kid* was made into a successful movie in 1965, starring Steve McQueen and Edward G. Robinson. It was directed by Norman Jewison from a script by Ring Lardner, Jr. and Terry Southern.

Further Reading:
THE CUNNING AND THE HAUNTED (1954)
A RAGE TO DIE (1955)
CRY PASSION (1956)
NIGHT BOAT TO PARIS (1956)
CHEYENNE SATURDAY (1957)
LOWDOWN (1958)
THE DEADLY DUO (1959)
PORT ANGELIQUE (1961)
WOLF COP (1961)
CHUKA (1961)
THE CINCINATTI KID (1963)

**As Richard Telfair**
*Monty Nash series (complete):*
THE BLOODY MEDALLION (1959)
THE CORPSE THAT TALKED (1959)
SCREAM BLOODY MURDER (1960)
GOOD LUCK, SUCKER (1961)
THE SLAVERS (1961)

*Wyoming Jones series (complete):*
WYOMING JONES (1958)
DAY OF THE GUN (1958)
THE SECRET OF APACHE CANYON (1959)
WYOMING JONES FOR HIRE (1959)
SUNDANCE (1960)

---

**If you like Richard Jessup,** you might like: Marvin Albert, Cleve F. Adams

# Frank Kane

(also wrote as Frank Boyd). Born in Brooklyn, New York, 1912. Died in Long Island, New York, 1968.

Frank Kane's series featuring private detective, Johnny Liddell, debuted at the beginning of the action-packed Spillane era. Puzzle plots, locked door mysteries, and ratiocination were out, and tough talking guys, double dealing dames and rock 'em sock 'em action were in.

Kane worked as a reporter and editor for several New York newspapers during the 1930's. From the mid-late '40's, he wrote scripts for the popular radio shows *The Shadow, Gangbusters* and *The Fat Man.*

Kane's first Johnny Liddell novel was *About Face* (1947). Liddell has a sexy red-haired secretary named Pinky, and he frequents a local bar named Mike's Deadline Café. Although New York-based, a number of Johnny's cases take him out of the familiar urban environs of the city. *Poisons Unknown* (1953) takes Johnny to New Orleans. The setting of *Crime of Their Life* (1962) is a Caribbean cruise ship. Two of the books take Johnny outside the United States altogether. He slugs his way through Vienna in *Fatal Undertaking* (1964) and travels through France in *Maid in Paris* (1966).

Kane's Liddell tales were noted for their hard-hitting action. According to writers Robert A. Baker and Michael T. Nietzal, "Every novel has between two and ten killings, three or more fist fights, brawls and/or knifings, two to eight head bashings and at least one to three kidnappings. Just about every object in the Sears Fall Catalog is used as a weapon to cause breaks and bruises on the human anatomy." (*Private Eyes: 101 Knights,* by Baker and Nietzal, pg. 162.)

Kane's prose style is spare and concise, keeping description to a minimum. He supplied his stories with an air of authenticity by utilizing the inside information of his brother, a member of the NYPD. The Liddell novels lasted from 1947-1967, and had sold 5,000,000 copies by Kane's death in 1968.

Kane wrote 23 teleplays for the 1958-59 season of *Mickey Spillane's Mike Hammer,* starring Darren McGavin. As Frank Boyd, he wrote a novelization of the noir-drenched TV show *Johnny Staccato.* One of his non-series novels, *Key Witness* (1956), about a middle class man who witnesses a gang killing in Harlem, was made into an edge of your seat thriller in 1960, starring Jeffrey Hunter and Dennis Hopper, directed by noir specialist Phil Karlson.

Kane published numerous short stories in *Manhunt, Mike Shayne Mystery Magazine* and *The Saint.*

**Further Reading:**
*Johnny Liddell series:*
ABOUT FACE (1947; as DEATH ABOUT FACE, 1948; as THE FATAL FOURSOME, 1958)
GREEN LIGHT FOR DEATH (1949)
SLAY RIDE (1950)
BULLET PROOF (1951)
DEAD WEIGHT (1951)
BARE TRAP (1952)
POISONS UNKNOWN (1953)
GRAVE DANGER (1954)
RED HOT ICE (1955)
A REAL GONE GUY (1956)
JOHNNY LIDDELL'S MORGUE (1956, short stories)
THE LIVING END (1957)
TRIGGER MORTIS (1958)
A SHORT BIER (1960)
TIME TO PREY (1960)
THE MOURNING AFTER (1961)
STACKED DECK (1961, short stories)
CRIME OF THEIR LIFE (1962)
RING-A-DING-DING (1963)
JOHNNY COME LATELY (1963)
HEARSE CLASS MALE (1963)
FINAL CURTAIN (1964)
ESPRIT DE CORPSE (1965)
MARGIN FOR TERROR (1967)

KEY WITNESS (1956)
LIZ (1958)
SYNDICATE GIRL (1958)
THE LINE-UP (1959, tv novelization)
JUKE BOX KING (1959)
THE FLESH PEDDLERS (1959, as by Frank Boyd)
JOHNNY STACCATO (1960, TV novelization, as by Frank Boyd)

---

**If you like Frank Kane,** you might like: Brett Halliday, Mickey Spillane

## Henry Kane

also wrote as Kenneth R. McKay, Mario J. Sagola, Katherine Stapleton, Anthony McCall, Ellery Queen). Born in New York City, New York, 1918. Died 1988.

 Henry Kane parodied the hardboiled, Mickey Spillane style of writing so popular in detective paperbacks during the 1950's and '60's. His writing blended the wit and sarcasm of Raymond Chandler with the wacky, parodic prose stylings of Robert Leslie Bellem. Kane's most prominent private detective (private "richard," according to Kane) is Peter Chambers. Kane featured Chambers in thirty-five novels, novelettes and short story collections, beginning with *A Halo for Nobody* (1947, aka *Martinis and Murder*) and ending with *Kill for the Millions* (1972).

Chambers' adventures are usually set in New York. His secretary, Miranda Foxworth, is "built like an old-fashioned icebox but colder." Pete frequents Trennan's Dark Morning Tavern, a local bar. Chambers characterizes himself as, "A wise guy private eye. Talks hard with the tough guys, purrs with the ladies. All the girls fall for him. You know, like what you read about." One of Chambers' distinguishing traits is his sense of humor and love for word play. Notable Chambers titles include *Until You are Dead* (1951), *Too French and Too Deadly* (1955), *Death of a Flack* (1961) and *Unholy Trio* (1967, aka *Better Wed Than Dead*), among many others.

Here's Chambers, waiting in his office for an assignment to come in:

> "The call came through at one o'clock of an afternoon which was running its own special preview of Indian Summer. It was muggy and sweaty and hotter than a cooch-grinder wriggling through an audition for a rhythm show in Vegas. My legs were up on the desk and I was dreamily debating a visit to a lady graphologist who had begun to prick at my libido." (*Death On the Double*, 1957)

In 1969, with the sexual revolution beginning and censorship regulations loosening, Peter Chambers joined right in, and became one of the first X-rated private eyes. These novels were published by Lancer books, a soft core publishing house, and began with *Don't Call Me Madame* (1969). Later titles include *The Shack Job* (1969), *The Glow Job* (1971) and *The Tail Job* (1971).

Henry Kane also wrote three books about a private detective named McGregor, beginning with *The Midnight Man* (1965). McGregor is a former NYPD inspector, weighs 250 pounds, is sophisticated and literate and loves good food, wine and women—though not necessarily in that order.

McGregor is a more mature, less wisecracking version of Peter Chambers.

Kane wrote a number of standalone titles. These tended to be darker and more noirish than the Chambers books. Excellent titles include *Edge of Panic* (1950), a man-on-the-run story; *Death for Sale* (1957, aka *Sleep Without Dreams*) about a husband who hires a hit man to murder his wife and then wants to cancel the deal; and *My Darlin' Evangeline* (1961), about a bank clerk who is set up as the fall guy for a robbery by his unfaithful wife and her boyfriend.

Kane wrote screenplay adaptations for two of Ed McBain's 87th Precinct novels: *Cop Hater* (1958) and *The Mugger* (1958). He wrote teleplays for *Martin Kane, Private Eye* and *Johnny Staccato*.

**Further Reading:**
*Peter Chambers series:*
A HALO FOR NOBODY (1947; as MARTINIS AND MURDER, 1956)
ARMCHAIR IN HELL (1948)
HANG BY YOUR NECK (1949)
UNTIL YOU ARE DEAD (1951)
TOO FRENCH AND TOO DEADLY (1955)
WHO KILLED SWEET SUE? (1956)
THE NAME IS CHAMBERS (1957, short stories)
DEATH IS THE LAST LOVER (1959)
DEATH OF A FLACK (1961)
NEVER GIVE A MILLIONAIRE AN EVEN BREAK (1963)
DON'T CALL ME MADAME (1969)
THE SCHACK JOB (1969)
THE GLOW JOB (1971)
THE TAIL JOB (1971)

*Inspector McGregor series:*
THE MIDNIGHT MAN (1965)
CONCEAL AND DISGUISE (1966)
LAUGHTER IN THE ALEHOUSE (1968)

EDGE OF PANIC (1950)
THE DEADLY FINGER (1957)          THE PRIVATE EYEFUL (1959)
PETER GUNN (TV novelization)      RUN FOR DOOM (1962)
MY DARLIN' EVANGELINE (1961)
HOW TO WRITE A SONG (1962, non-fiction)
TWO MUST DIE (1963)               FRENZY OF EVIL (1966)

**If you like Henry Kane,** you might like: Peter Cheyney, John Jakes

# David Karp

(also wrote as Wallace Ware, Adam Singer). Born in New York City, New York, 1922. Died in Pittsfield, Massachusetts, 1999.

David Karp's novels tackled controversial social issues and dealt with fascist, dystopian societies.

Karp came from a low income background and grew up in New York City. He served in the military from 1942-1946. After his release from the service, he found work writing for radio.

Karp first tackled social issues with the publication of his novel, *Hardman* (1952). Jack Hardman, a cunning juvenile delinquent, smooth talks his way out of trouble with the courts by blaming his actions on his "bad environment." In a unique twist for a JD novel, a Judge mentors Hardman into channeling his anger and violent feelings into writing, whereupon the brutal youth becomes a best-selling author. In yet another twist, the Judge discovers that Hardman's bad environment might not be what made him into a ruthless criminal, after all.

Karp explored totalitarian societies with his novel, *One* (1953, a.k.a. *Escape to Nowhere*). The story is set in the future, where "the State" has created a culture of conformity, and eliminated dissension by using a system of surveillance, re-education and brainwashing. Professor Burden, a college professor, considers himself a loyal citizen of the State, but suddenly finds himself declared a heretic, and is held captive and treated to the State's re-education process. Writer and critic Cyril Connelly wrote thusly about *One*: "The publishers have bracketed this novel with *Darkness at Noon*, *Nineteen Eighty-Four* and *Brave New World*, which I at first thought presumptuous; but now, after reading it, I am inclined to agree." *One* was filmed as a television episode for both *The Kraft Television Theatre* in 1955 and for *Matinee Theater* in 1957. In both instances, the teleplay was written by Karp.

Karp's next book to tackle the issue of control and conformity was *The Brotherhood of Velvet* (1953), which depicts a secret organization (somewhat akin to Yale University's infamous Skull and Bones society) that places people in key government positions, and thoroughly controls the lives of its members. Jim Watterson, who gained his $50,000 a year job through his connections in the Brotherhood, is ordered to make public some scandalous information which would destroy the career of Watterson's best friend. When Watterson tries to buck the Brotherhood, he finds his own life and career in jeopardy.

*The Brotherhood of Velvet* was made into a TV movie in 1970 starring Glenn Ford, the title having been changed to *The Brotherhood of the Bell*. Karp again wrote the teleplay, and was nominated for an Emmy award under the category Outstanding Writing Achievement in Drama — Original Teleplay. He was nominated on two other occasions, as well.

Karp worked extensively in television. During "The Golden Age of Television," his teleplays were compared with those of top writers Paddy Chayefsky (*Marty*), a pre-Twilight Zone Rod Serling (*Patterns, Requiem for a Heavyweight*) and Reginald Rose (*Twelve Angry Men*). TV programs he wrote for include *Studio One, Playhouse 90, The Defenders, I Spy* and *The Untouchables*, among many others.

**Further Reading:**
THE BIG FEELING (1952; as THE GENTLE THIEF, as by Wallace Ware, 1967)
CRY FLESH (1952; as THE GIRL ON CROWN STREET, as by Wallace Ware, 1967)
HARDMAN (1952; as by Wallace Ware, 1967)
BROTHERHOOD OF VELVET (1953)
PLATOON (1953, as by Adam Singer)
ONE (1953; as ESCAPE TO NOWHERE, 1955)
THE DAY OF THE MONKEY (1955)
ALL HONORABLE MEN (1956)
LEAVE ME ALONE (1957)
ENTER SLEEPING (1960, aka SLEEPWALKERS)
THE LAST BELIEVERS (1964)

---

If you like **David Karp,** you might like: Benjamin Appel, H. Vernor Dixon

## *Harry Stephen Keeler*

Born in Chicago, Illinois, 1890. Died in Chicago, Illinois, 1967.

 Looking for something a little different? Something weird, wild, wacky, freaky, zany, nutty, cracked, harebrained, screwball or madcap? Looking for a writer whose lunacy falls somewhere on the literary spectrum between Ed Wood and Thomas Pynchon?

You've come to the right place. Welcome to the world of Harry Stephen Keeler.

Keeler lived most of his life in Chicago. He graduated from the Armour Institute (now called the Illinois Institute of Technology) with a degree in electrical engineering. Early jobs included work as an electrician in a steel mill and as editor of *10 Story Book* magazine, 1919—1940.

Keeler wrote more than 70 novels. His first book was *The Voice of the Seven Sparrows* (1924). His last book published in America was *The Case of the Transposed Legs* (1948). He wrote five additional books which were published only in England, the last in 1953. For the last fourteen years of his life, he wrote books which were published in Spain and Portugal (*The Case of the Crazy Corpse* was published as *O Caso do Cadaver Endiabrado*). Books that were never published during his lifetime have now been published by independent publishers. Keeler wrote one of the longest mystery novels ever published—*The Box from Japan* (1932), weighing in at a hefty 765 pages.

Keeler specialized in the "webwork" plot, whereby he wove multiple (sometimes nearly a hundred) unrelated plot threads which, by strange coincidences, were all tied together by the story's end.

Between the covers of a single Keeler novel you might find any or all of the following: circus freaks; trepanning (the practice of drilling holes in the skull for supposed therapeutic purposes); insane asylums; complex mathematical equations; Eastern philosophy; multiple ethnic dialects; character names such as Screamo the Clown, Legga the Human Spider, and millionaire Balhatchet Barkstone; and rants against social evils such as racism, capital punishment and the mistreatment of cats.

To get the full impact of Keeler's whacked-out genius, you need a sample of the Master's prose, thus:

> "Quiribus Brown, 7½ foot high giant, ascending the narrow low-ceilinged staircase that led upstairs to the 'Restaurant of the 99 Blackbirds Returning to Nest, Prop. Hung Fung Lee', in Chicago's Chinatown, realized that this heavily adorned and ornate place, smelling of weird though fragrant incense, must undoubtedly have

been constructed, and was being run, for the delectation of people visiting Chinatown for a thrill." (*The Case of the Flying Hands*)

In 1969, mystery writer and critic Francis M. Nevins, Jr. wrote a series of articles about Keeler for the *Journal of Popular Culture*. These articles eventually led to Keeler's rediscovery and current cult following. Bill Pronzini also featured Keeler's work in his book, *Son of Gun in Cheek: An Affectionate Guide to More of the 'Worst' in Mystery Fiction*, which highlighted various authors whose writing occupied a kind of so-bad-they're-good zone.

Keeler's novel *Sing Sing Nights* (1928), was used to "suggest" two low budget movies: *Sing Sing Nights* (1934) and *The Mysterious Mr. Wong* (1935, starring Bela Lugosi). An IMDB reviewer called the movie version of *Sing Sing Nights* "worse than a death sentence."

Further Reading:
THE VOICE OF THE SEVEN SPARROWS (1924)
FIND THE CLOCK (1925)
THE SPECTACLES OF MR. CAGLIOSTRO (1926)
SING SING NIGHTS (1927)          THIEVES' NIGHTS (1929)
THE GREEN JADE HAND (1930)      THE BOX FROM JAPAN (1932)
THE FACE OF THE MAN FROM SATURN (1933)
THE MYSTERY OF THE FIDDLING CRACKSMAN (1934)
THE RIDDLE OF THE TRAVELING SKULL (1934)
THE SKULL OF THE WALTZING CLOWN, TEN HOURS, THE DEFRAUDED
YEGGMAN (1935-37, three volumes)
THE MYSTERIOUS MR. I. (1937)
Y. CHEUNG, BUSINESS DETECTIVE (1939)
THE MAN WITH THE MAGIC EARDRUMS (1939)
THE MAN WITH THE CRIMSON BOX (1940)
THE MAN WITH THE WOODEN SPECTACLES (1941)
THE PEACOCK FAN (1941)          THE VANISHING GOLD TRUCK (1941)
THE LAVENDER GRIPSACK (1941)
THE BOOK WITH THE ORANGE LEAVES (1942)
THE CASE OF THE TWO STRANGE LADIES (1943)
THE SEARCH FOR X-Y-Z (1943)
THE CASE OF THE 16 BEANS (1945)
THE CASE OF THE MYSTERIOUS MOLL (1945)
THE CASE OF THE BARKING CLOCK (1947)
THE CASE OF THE TRANSPOSED LEGS (1948)

---

If you like Harry Stephen Keeler, you might like: Michael Avallone, George Baxt

# Day Keene

(real name Gunard Hjerstedt; also wrote as Lewis Dixon, William Richards, Daniel White, John Corbett, Donald King). Born in Chicago, Illinois, 1904. Died in North Hollywood, California, 1969.

 Day Keene was an expert plotter. He could take an old plot and, through narrative twists and turns, make it seem new again. His protagonists were often thrust into a seemingly impossible situation, but always remained believable, no matter how outlandish the plot twists. His talent covered the bases and he wrote radio scripts, short stories for the pulps, paperback originals and a few hardcovers.

Keene started out as an actor, playing repertory theatre during the 1920's. During the 1930's he wrote for the radio shows *Little Orphan Annie* and *Kitty Keene Inc.*, about a female private eye. During the 1940's, his name appeared on the covers of such top crime pulps as *Black Mask*, *Dime Detective* and *Detective Tales*. But his heyday was during the 1950's when he wrote approximately 35 paperback originals for publishers such as Gold Medal, Graphic, Avon, Ace and others.

Some of his noteworthy books are *Framed in Guilt* (1949), a tightly plotted story of blackmail and murder involving a Hollywood screenwriter; *Notorious* (1954, no relation to the Hitchcock film), about Ed Ferron, ex-con and owner of a carnival, who gets involved with a beautiful blonde and becomes framed for murder; *The Big Kiss-Off* (1954), about Cade Cain, a returning POW who had begun living a quiet and peaceful life aboard his boat in the Gulf, but who, suddenly one day, finds six bodies in the muddy tide; *Home is the Sailor* (1952), about "Swede" Nelson, who just wants to settle down and buy a farm, but who becomes entangled with young widow and femme fatale Corliss Mason and gets entangled in her devious schemes; *Who Has Wilma Lathrop?* (1955), about Jim Lathrop, whose wife disappears and who, while searching for her, discovers she's not who she appeared to be, as well as becoming a murder suspect himself.

Keene stopped writing crime fiction sometime during the '60's, but in his later years, he successfully wrote mainstream, *Peyton Place*-type novels. Altogether, his output included more than fifty novels and more than a hundred short stories.

Movies based on Keene's books include *Joy House* (1964), a French production starring Alain Delon and Jane Fonda, based on his 1954 novel of the same name; and the Elvis movie, *The Trouble with Girls* (1969), based on Keene's 1960 novel, *Chautauqua*. He wrote some episodes for the TV shows *Burke's Law* and *Hawaiian Eye*.

In regards to his name change from Hjerstedt to Keene, friend and writer Talmage Powell said in an interview: "When Day began writing for the magazines, he went up to the office of the editor who told him, 'This name is absolutely impossible. I would like to cover-mention this story, but I am not going to put that name on the cover of the magazine. Why don't you pick out a good pen name to work under?' On the spur of the moment, Day remembered that his mother's maiden name was Daisy Keeney. Day thought to himself that 'If I can't use my father's name, I will use my mother's.' He contracted her name to Day Keene. That became his legal name." (Mystery file.com, Al Tonik interview with Talmage Powell)

A curiosity from *Seed of Doubt* (1961): "The explosive, shocking novel about artificial insemination."

**Further Reading:**
FRAMED IN GUILT (1949)
MY FLESH IS SWEET (1951)
TO KISS OR KILL (1951)
HUNT THE KILLER (1952)
HOME IS THE SAILOR (1952)
IF THE COFFIN FITS (1952)
WAKE UP TO MURDER (1952)
MRS. HOMICIDE (1953)
THE BIG KISS-OFF (1954)
DEATH HOUSE DOLL (1954)
HOMICIDAL LADY (1954)
JOY HOUSE (1954)
NOTORIOUS (1954)
SLEEP WITH THE DEVIL (1954)
WHO HAS WILMA LATHROP? (1955)
MURDER ON THE SIDE (1956)
BRING HIM BACK DEAD (1956)
DEAD DOLLS DON'T TALK (1959)
MIAMI 59 (1959)
SO DEAD MY LOVELY (1959)
THE BRIMSTONE BED (1960)
PAYOLA (1960)
CHATAUQUA (1960, with Dwight Vincent)
SEED OF DOUBT (1961)
CARNIVAL OF DEATH (1965)

If you like Day Keene, you might like: Gil Brewer, Harry Whittington

# Ed Lacy

(born Leonard Zinberg; also wrote as Steve April). Born in New York City, New York, 1911. Died in New York City, New York, 1968.

During an era of segregated schools, bathrooms and buses, Ed Lacy was one of the earliest writers of mystery fiction to create a black private eye.

Lacy's real name was Leonard Zinberg. He was a white man married to a black woman and lived in New York City where, cliché or not, some of his best friends really *were* black. Lacy was also an avid boxing fan, and boxers often featured prominently in his novels and short stories.

Lacy's first novel was *Walk Hard—Talk Loud* (1940, as by Len Zinberg). It was originally published as a mainstream novel by Bobbs-Merrill, and is a story about black Andy Whitman, an amateur boxer about to turn pro, and Lou Ross, the white boss/gangster of the fight racket who tries to stop Whitman's rise. The book was reprinted as a paperback by Lion books in 1950. Lacy's novels *Go for the Body* (1954) and *The Big Fix* (1960) are also about the fight game.

Lacy's most well known and well developed character, although he appears in only two books, is black private detective Toussaint Marcus Moore (known as "Touie" to his friends). Moore is a 234 lb., ex-WWII vet who lives in Harlem. In the first Moore book, *Room to Swing* (1957), Moore trails a killer to Bington, Ohio, and through the course of his investigation, clashes with the small town's white community. *Room to Swing* won the Mystery Writers of America's Edgar award for 1958. The second Moore book, *Moment of Untruth* (1964), takes Moore to Mexico, where he's traveled to find the killer of a wealthy woman's husband. A wrench is thrown in the works when Moore finds himself becoming sympathetic to the killer. The sport of bullfighting is featured prominently in the book.

Lacy wrote numerous books about other detectives as well. Lee Hayes, a black NYC police detective and former boxer, appeared in *Harlem Underground* (1965) and *In Black and Whitey* (1967). Barney Harris is a PI hired by a murdered cop's wife to find her husband's killer and expose police corruption in *The Best That Ever Did It* (1955). Marty Bond, an alcoholic detective for a seedy hotel, is the protagonist in *The Men from the Boys* (1956). Hal Darling, in *Strip for Violence* (1953), is only 5'1" but is a judo expert and former flyweight boxer.

Lacy had over one hundred short stories and non-fiction essays published in magazines as diverse as *The New Republic*, *The New Yorker*, *Esquire*, *Manhunt*, *Alfred Hitchcock's Mystery Magazine*, *The Man from U.N.C.L.E.*, *Argosy* and *Sir!* During the late '50's/early '60's, a few of his stories were adapted for episodes of *Alfred Hitchcock Presents*, *Naked City* and *Markham*.

Lacy died of a heart attack at the early age of 56.

Further Reading:
*Toussaint Moore series (complete):*
ROOM TO SWING (1957)
MOMENT OF UNTRUTH (1964)

*Lee Hayes series (complete):*
HARLEM UNDERGROUND (1965)
IN BLACK AND WHITEY (1967)

WALK HARD–TALK LOUD (1940, as by Len Zinberg)
WHAT D'YA KNOW FOR SURE (1947, as by Len Zinberg; as STRANGE
DESIRES, 1948)
SIN IN THEIR BLOOD (1952)
STRIP FOR VIOLENCE (1953)
GO FOR THE BODY (1954)
THE BEST THAT EVER DID IT (1955; as VISA TO DEATH, 1956)
THE MEN FROM THE BOYS (1956)
LEAD WITH YOUR LEFT (1957)
BREATHE NO MORE, MY LADY (1958)
SHAKEDOWN FOR MURDER (1958)
BLONDE BAIT (1959)
THE BIG FIX (1960)
A DEADLY AFFAIR (1960)
THE FREELOADERS (1961)
TWO HOT TO HANDLE (1963)
PITY THE HONEST (1965)
THE BIG BUST (1969)

---

**If you like Ed Lacy,** you might like: Chester Himes, Don Tracy

# Jonathan Latimer

Born in Chicago, Illinois, 1906. Died in La Jolla, California, 1983.

 Jonathan Latimer was a writer of several notable distinctions. He wrote a series of successful "screwball" mysteries featuring private detective Bill Crane. He wrote a novel in 1941 that was considered so "obscene," an unexpurgated edition wasn't published in the United States until 1982. He also wrote a healthy serving of well regarded film noirs.

Latimer graduated Phi Beta Kappa from Knox College in Galesburg, Illinois, in 1929. From 1929-1935 he worked the crime beat for Chicago's *Herald Examiner*. While covering his territory, Latimer came across such top gangland bosses as Al Capone and Bugs Moran.

Latimer's first novel was *Murder in the Madhouse* (1935). It was the first in a series of five books featuring private detective Bill Crane. The tone of the Crane novels was akin to that of Hammett's *The Thin Man*—Crane and his fellow operatives, Tom O'Malley and Doc Williams, spend as much time eating, drinking and being merry as they do solving cases. Witty banter and gallows humor are trademarks of the Crane novels. The other books in the series are *Headed for a Hearse* (1935, filmed as *The Westland Case* in 1937), *The Lady in the Morgue* (1936, made into a movie in 1938, starring Preston Foster), *The Dead Don't Care* (1938, filmed as *The Last Warning* in 1938, starring Foster) and *Red Gardenias* (1939).

Latimer published his best and most infamous novel in 1941, *Solomon's Vineyard*. Karl Craven, private detective and apotheosis of the term "hardboiled," is hired to rescue a young heiress from a dangerous religious cult. In a brief introductory statement to the reader, Craven warns:

> "This is a wild one. Maybe the wildest yet. It's got everything but an abortion and a tornado."

And falling under the category of "everything" includes: a shootout in a steam bath, a knifing in a whorehouse, sadomasochistic sex, grave-robbing and necrophilia.

*Soloman's Vineyard* was originally published only in England. At that time, its first sentence read, "From the way her buttocks looked under the black silk dress, I knew she'd be good in bed." When the book was published in the U.S. in 1950, its title was changed to *The Fifth Grave* and its first sentence was changed to: "From the way she looked under the black silk dress, I knew she'd be a hot dame." The novel was heavily edited and toned down throughout, until it was finally released unexpurgated in 1982.

Latimer moved to California in the late 1930's and wrote screenplay adaptations of a number of classic crime novels, including *The Glass Key* (1942, based on the Dashiell Hammett novel), *The Big Clock* (1948, based on the Kenneth Fearing novel), *Night Has a Thousand Eyes* (1948, based on the Cornell Woolrich novel) and the adventure-mystery *Plunder of the Sun* (1953, based on the David Dodge novel).

He also wrote more than thirty episodes of *Perry Mason*.

**Further Reading:**
*Bill Crane series (complete):*
MURDER IN THE MADHOUSE (1935)
HEADED FOR A HEARSE (1935)
THE LADY IN THE MORGUE (1936)
THE DEAD DON'T CARE (1938)
RED GARDENIAS (1939; as SOME DAMES ARE DEADLY, 1955)

THE SEARCH FOR MY GREAT UNCLE'S HEAD (1937, as Peter Coffin)
SOLOMON'S VINEYARD (1941–UK edition; as THE FIFTH GRAVE, 1950)
SINNERS AND SHROUDS (1955)
BLACK IS THE FASHION FOR DYING (1959)

_____

**If you like Jonathan Latimer,** you might like: Craig Rice, Norbert Davis

# *Elmore Leonard*

(also wrote as Leonard Elmore, Emmett Long, Elmo Scribbles). Born in New Orleans, Louisiana, 1925.

 Elmore Leonard is one of the last working writers who started publishing in the pulps, moved into paperback originals, and is still turning out hardcover bestsellers today. Known for his clear, realistic dialogue, his books are said to read like movies and indeed he has had plenty of work produced in Hollywood, much of it from his own screenplays.

Born in New Orleans, Leonard moved to Detroit at the age of 9 and later spent time in the southwest. He served in the Naval Reserve and became an advertising man turning out ads and film scripts for brands like Chevrolet and the Encyclopedia Britannica.

He sold his first story in 1951, a western called "Trail of the Apache" to *Argosy*. Though sales of westerns began to decline in the '50's, Leonard sold thirty more stories to pulps like *Dime Western* and *Zane Grey's Western*, and wrote five novels during that time. Two of the short stories were sold to Hollywood and made into movies: *The Tall T*, 1957, from "The Captives," which starred Randolph Scott, and *3:10 to Yuma* (1957) starring Burt Lancaster and Van Heflin (from "Three-Ten to Yuma"). Leonard was paid ninety dollars for the story version of *Yuma* and four thousand for the sale to Hollywood. It was later remade in 2007 starring Russell Crowe and Christian Bale.

Leonard, known as "Dutch" to his friends, sold other westerns to Hollywood, including *Hombre* (1961), and *Valdez Is Coming* (1970), starring Burt Lancaster, and after the sale of *Hombre* in 1966 was able to let go of his advertising agency and write full time. It was the money from Hollywood that allowed him to continue writing until the book sales themselves eventually reached a certain level. As a novelist, Leonard was a true 40-year overnight success, but that was still to come.

His first western novel was written in 1953, *The Bounty Hunters*. Four more westerns followed before he published his first crime novel, 1969's *The Big Bounce*, about a caper planned by an alcoholic and a millionaire's plaything. It was published by Gold Medal after being rejected some 84 times as being "too grim." This was followed by *The Moonshine War* (1969), another caper novel set in Prohibition times about a bunch of city sophisticates trying to steal a load of Kentucky moonshine. From here Leonard was on his way, steadily writing his novels but making his real money from his sales to Hollywood, including writing the screenplays for many of his own books and story ideas.

Leonard has written more than forty novels, as well as short story collections, screenplays based on his work, original screenplays, and even a serialized novel in the *New York Times*. His penchant for realistic and smooth dialogue led Hollywood to his door, and the majority of his novels have been filmed, though with mixed degrees of success. An original screenplay (that Leonard later novelized) was the violent 1974 Charles Bronson vehicle *Mr. Majestyk*, about a watermelon farmer fighting the mob. Like *3:10 to Yuma*, *52 Pick-Up*, his first Detroit thriller, was filmed twice, once in 1984 as *The Ambassador*, and again in 1986 under its own title, directed by John Frankenheimer and starring Roy Scheider.

He finally hit big in the movies with *Get Shorty*, a 1995 film by Barry Sonnenfeld starring John Travolta, from his 1990 book of the same name. Its sequel, *Be Cool* (2005), came out a decade later but didn't fare as well. *Out of Sight* (1998) was a breakout movie for both George Clooney and Jennifer Lopez, directed by Stephen Soderbergh. Leonard's biggest Hollywood success was probably the Quentin Tarantino directed version of the novel *Rum Punch* (1992). It was retitled *Jackie Brown* and released in 1997. The movie starred an ensemble cast which included Samuel Jackson, Pam Grier, Robert Forster, Bridget Fonda and Robert De Niro.

In 1984 Leonard won an Edgar award for best novel from the Mystery Writers of America for his 1983 book *LaBrava*, about an ex-Secret Service agent, a former glamour queen, and a murderous Cuban go-go dancer. The movie version was in development with Dustin Hoffman who at one point abruptly left the project. He later believed *Get Shorty* was written as a jab at him by Leonard.

*Stick* (1983), the sequel to 1976's *Swag*, was Leonard's first book to hit really big. It was filmed to moderate success with Burt Reynolds directing and starring in 1985. More importantly, it led to a *Newsweek* magazine cover and a declaration that Leonard was "possibly the best crime writer ever." *TIME* Magazine chimed in calling him "the Dickens of Detroit."

Leonard enjoyed success on the small screen as well, with several television movies and series produced, including a pilot based on his 1991 novel *Maximum Bob* and a series called *Karen Sisco* based on the Jennifer Lopez part from the film *Out of Sight*. Currently, the short story "Fire in the Hole" (2001) as well as the novels *Pronto* (1993) and *Riding the Rap* (1995) serve as the basis for the FX show *Justified* starring Timothy Olyphant as Deputy U.S. Marshal Raylan Givens. Leonard's 2012 novel *Raylan* was inspired by the continuity of the series.

In addition to the success in screen and on print, Leonard once came up with what have become known as his "Ten Rules of Writing" for a *New York Times* essay on July 16th, 2001 ("Essay on the Adverbs, Exclamation Points and Hopptedoodle"). Somewhat controversial, they were given their own book (*Elmore Leonard's Ten Rules of Writing*, 2007) and have generated endless hours of discussion. One of his messages is to leave out the boring parts that people don't want to read ("I'll bet you don't skip dialogue," he says). Another Florida writer, James W. Hall disagrees and asks, "But what if you like those parts?" Perhaps the best way to think of Leonard's rules is to consider them as rules that work for Elmore Leonard.

He writes in longhand on unruled paper, for him dialogue and pace take precedence over plot, "if proper usage gets in the way, it may have to go" (from his Ten Rules), and whatever he's doing he's been doing it very well for a very long time. In 2014 Leonard will be among the handful of living writers ever to be honored with editions of his work published by the Library of America.

**Further Reading:**
THE BOUNTY HUNTERS (1953)
THE LAW AT RANDADO (1954)
ESCAPE FROM FIVE SHADOWS (1956)
LAST STAND AT SABER RIVER (1959)
HOMBRE. NEW YORK (1961)
THE BIG BOUNCE (1969)
THE MOONSHINE WAR (1969)
VALDEZ IS COMING (1970)
FORTY LASHES LESS ONE (1972)
MR. MAJESTYK (1974)
FIFTY-TWO PICKUP (1974)
SWAG (1976)
UNKNOWN MAN NO. 89 (1977)
THE HUNTED (1977)
THE SWITCH (1978)
GUNSIGHTS (1979)
CITY PRIMEVAL (1980)
GOLD COAST (1980)
SPLIT IMAGES (1981)
CAT CHASER (1982)
STICK (1983)
LaBRAVA (1983)
GLITZ (1985)
BANDITS (1987)
TOUCH (1987)
FREAKY DEAKY (1988)
KILLSHOT (1989)
GET SHORTY (1990)
MAXIMUM BOB (1991)
RUM PUNCH (1992)

PRONTO (1993)
RIDING THE RAP (1995)
OUT OF SIGHT (1996)
CUBA LIBRE (1998)
BE COOL (1999)
PAGAN BABIES (2000)
TISHOMINGO BLUES (2002)
MR. PARADISE (2004)
A COYOTE'S IN THE HOUSE (2004)
THE HOT KID (2005)
COMFORT TO THE ENEMY (2009)
UP IN HONEY'S ROOM (2007)
ROAD DOGS (2009)
DJIBOUTI (2010)
RAYLAN (2011)

*Short story collections:*
THE COMPLETE WESTERN STORIES OF ELMORE LEONARD (2007)
FIRE IN THE HOLE (2001)

---

**If you like Elmore Leonard,** you might like: George V. Higgins, John D. MacDonald, Donald E. Westlake

# John D. MacDonald

(also wrote short stories as John Wade Farrel, Robert Henry, John Lane, Scott O'Hara, Peter Reed, Henry Reiser). Born in Sharon, Pennsylvania, 1916. Died in Milwaukee, Wisconsin, 1986.

 John D. MacDonald, in his introduction to a collection of Norbert Davis's short stories called *The Adventures of Max Latin* (1988), writes about Davis's decision to abandon the pulps in favor of the more socially acceptable slick magazines: "Pulp fiction was not some sort of whoredom. What you do, as a craftsman, is recognize the stipulations and the limits and the requirements of a specific market, and then, within those limits, you write just as damn well good as you can."

And that's as good as any an introduction to MacDonald's own life and work.

John D. MacDonald earned an MBA at Harvard. During World War II, he served in the OSS (later the basis for the CIA) from 1940-1946. After the war, MacDonald received four months of terminal leave pay, from September 1945-January 1946. During that time he "wrote 800,000 words of short stories in those four months, tried to keep 30 of them in the mail at all times, slept about six hours a night and lost 20 pounds." ("John D. Macdonald," interviewed by Ed Gorman, from *The Big Book of Noir*, pg. 209). The magazines he wrote for sound like a *Who's Who* of the pulps: *Black Mask, Dime Detective, Dime Mystery, Mammoth Mystery, Detective Story Magazine, New Detective, Astounding Science Fiction, Startling Stories, Thrilling Detective, Thrilling Wonder Stories, Argosy, Fifteen Sports Stories* and *Fifteen Western Tales*, among many others. He also wrote for the new digests like *Manhunt*, as they began to emerge during the early 1950's.

MacDonald moved to Florida in the late 1940's; most of his stories are set there. The success of his first novel, *The Brass Cupcake* (1950), made him a Gold Medal staple, and he wrote approximately 30 novels for the publisher. *The Damned* (1952) is a suspense novel about a group of people waiting to cross a dangerous river in Mexico. *The Neon Jungle* (1953) is a juvenile delinquent story. In *Soft Touch* (1958), an average suburbanite becomes involved in an old Army buddy's plot to steal a large amount of cash. *One Monday We Killed Them All* (1961) is a story about a policeman who has to protect his family from his own brother in law, a violent ex-con.

MacDonald is best known for his series character, Travis McGee. McGee is a "salvage consultant"—meaning he recovers missing or stolen goods. He lives on his houseboat, the *Busted Flush*, docked at the Fort Lauderdale marina. MacDonald has created a complex, three-dimensional character for McGee—he is well read, showing a knowledge of novelist Sinclair Lewis, the poet Rilke and the Second Law of Thermodynamics; he cares about a woman's emotional state as much as her physical appearance; and he knows how to fight, but derides machismo.

The McGee novels show a more digressive, philosophical bent than MacDonald's earlier works. McGee is an environmentalist, and bemoans the destruction of Florida's natural habitat and wildlife by developers creating shopping centers, condominiums, and industrial pollution. MacDonald wrote twenty-one novels featuring McGee, starting with *The Deep Blue Good-by* (1964) and ending with *The Lonely Silver Rain* (1984).

A number of movies and TV shows have been based on MacDonald stories. *Cape Fear* (1962, starring Robert Mitchum and Gregory Peck; remade in 1991 starring Nick Nolte and Robert DeNiro, directed by Martin Scorsese) was based the 1958 novel *The Executioners*. *Darker Than Amber* (1970, starring Rod Taylor) was based on the 1966 McGee novel of the same name. *The Girl, the Gold Watch, and Everything* (1980, starring Robert Hayes and Pam Dawber) was a TV movie based on the 1962 novel of the same name. TV shows which have adapted MacDonald stories for various episodes include *Studio One*, *Thriller*, *Alfred Hitchcock Hour*, *Tales of Tomorrow* and *Run for Your Life*.

MacDonald served as president of The Mystery Writers of America, and was elected Grand Master in 1972.

**Further Reading:**
*Travis McGee series:*
THE DEEP BLUE GOODBYE (1964)
NIGHTMARE IN PINK (1964)
A PURPLE PLACE FOR DYING (1964)
THE QUICK RED FOX (1964)
BRIGHT ORANGE FOR THE SHROUD (1965)
DARKER THAN AMBER (1966)
ONE FEARFUL YELLOW EYE (1966)
PALE GRAY FOR GUILT (1968)
THE GIRL IN THE PLAIN BROWN WRAPPER (1968)
DRESS HER IN INDIGO (1969)
THE LONG LAVENDER LOOK (1970)
A TAN AND SANDY SILENCE (1972)
THE SCARLET RUSE (1973)
THE TURQUOISE LAMENT (1973)
THE EMPTY COPPER SEA (1978)
THE GREEN RIPPER (1979)
FREE FALL IN CRIMSON (1981)
CINNAMON SKIN (1982)

THE LONELY SILVER RAIN (1985)
THE BRASS CUPCAKE (1950)
WEEP FOR ME (1951)
THE DAMNED (1952)
DEAD LOW TIDE (1953)
THE NEON JUNGLE (1953)
A BULLET FOR CINDERELLA (1955; as ON THE MAKE, 1960)
DEATH TRAP (1957)
THE EXECUTIONERS (1958; as CAPE FEAR, 1962)
SOFT TOUCH (1958)
SLAM THE BIG DOOR (1960)
ONE MONDAY WE KILLER THEM ALL (1961)
WHERE IS JANICE GANTRY? (1961)
THE GIRL, THE GOLD WATCH, AND EVERYTHING (1962)

---

**If you like John D. MacDonald,** you might like: Charles Williams, Wade Miller

# Ross Macdonald

(real name Kenneth Millar; also wrote as Ken Millar, John Macdonald, John R. Macdonald, John Ross Macdonald). Born in Los Gatos, California, 1915. Died in Santa Barbara, California, 1983.

 Many mystery critics and historians consider Ross Macdonald to stand alongside Dashiell Hammett and Raymond Chandler in stature, and the literary and intellectual bent of his Lew Archer novels gained appreciation from both mystery and mainstream critics. Though Chandler famously disparaged Macdonald's work, Macdonald became known for using his Santa Barbara settings almost like a separate character in his books, much like Chandler wrote about Los Angeles.

Kenneth Millar, although born in California, grew up in Canada. Abandoned by his father, Millar was raised by his mother and various relatives. After high school, Millar attended college at the University of Western Ontario, 1933-38, and the University of Michigan at Ann Arbor, 1941-44. In 1939, he married a former high school classmate, Margaret Sturm, who went on to have a successful career as a mystery novelist under the name Margaret Millar. During WWII, Millar served in the U.S. Naval Reserve; he and Millar moved to California and settled in Santa Barbara.

In 1944, Millar wrote his first novel, *The Dark Tunnel*, an espionage thriller about an American college professor who foils a Nazi spy ring. He went on to publish three more novels under his own name: *Trouble Follows Me* (1946), *Blue City* (1947) and *The Three Roads* (1948). In 1949, Millar wrote his first book featuring private investigator Lew Archer, *The Moving Target*; but decided to use a pseudonym in order to avoid confusion with his novelist wife. The name he took, John Macdonald, came from his father's first and middle name. (Six more books followed using this name but by then a writer called John D. MacDonald had found success as a mystery writer and to avoid confusion yet again, Millar changed his pseudonym to Ross Macdonald.)

Archer, operating out of Southern California, is 6" 2' and 190 lbs, drives a battered Ford convertible, and his gun of choice is a .38 special. Unlike many PIs, he is a light drinker, usually imbibing only on social occasions. Archer is complex, intellectual, well-read, and thoughtful. He considers gaining understanding of the people involved in his cases as important as solving the cases themselves. He probes the psychology of the people he encounters, which he believes gains him greater compassion for people as a whole and in many ways, the people involved in Archer's cases are more central to the books than Archer himself. Archer is often a neutral observer and interviewer, which allows people to more fully reveal the truths about themselves.

The psychological dimension of the novels was in part informed by Macdonald's own experience with psychoanalysis, a process he began to undergo during the 1950's. The plots of the Archer novels began to reach new heights of complexity and a number of them dealt with multigenerational families and their various dysfunctional relationships. Macdonald wrote eighteen novels featuring Archer, ending with *The Blue Hammer* in 1976. Two Lew Archer movies were made (his name changed to Lew Harper), both starring Paul Newman: *Harper* (1966) and *The Drowning Pool* (1976).

Macdonald served as the President of the Mystery Writers of America in 1965 and was voted its Grand Master award in 1973.

**Further Reading:**
*Lew Archer series:*

*As John Macdonald*
THE MOVING TARGET (1949)

*As John Ross Macdonald*
THE DROWNING POOL (1950)
THE WAY SOME PEOPLE DIE (1951)
THE IVORY GRIN (1952; as MARKED FOR MURDER, 1953)
MEET ME AT THE MORGUE (1953)
FIND A VICTIM (1954)

*As Ross Macdonald*
THE BARBAROUS COAST (1956)
THE DOOMSTERS (1958)
THE GALTON CASE (1959)
THE FERGUSON AFFAIR (1960)
THE WYCHERLY WOMAN (1961)
THE ZEBRA-STRIPED HEARSE (1962)
THE CHILL (1964)
THE FAR SIDE OF THE DOLLAR (1965)
BLACK MONEY (1966)
THE INSTANT ENEMY (1968)
THE GOODBYE LOOK (1969)
THE UNDERGROUND MAN (1971)
SLEEPING BEAUTY (1973)
THE BLUE HAMMER (1976)

*Other books:*

*As Kenneth Millar*
THE DARK TUNNEL (1944)
TROUBLE FOLLOWS ME (1946)
BLUE CITY (1947)
THE THREE ROADS (1948)

---

**If you like Ross Macdonald,** you might like: John D. MacDonald, Raymond Chandler, Wade Miller

# Daniel Mainwaring

(also wrote as Geoffrey Homes). Born in Oakland, California, 1902. Died in Los Angeles, California, 1977.

 Daniel Mainwaring wrote both the novel and screenplay for what is widely regarded as one of the top film noirs of all time, *Out of the Past*.

Mainwaring grew up in Northern California. After graduating from Fresno State College, he worked part time as an office boy, salesman and teacher. He began his writing career as a reporter for the *San Francisco Chronicle*. His first novel (the only book published under his own name) was *One Against the Earth* (1933), a proletarian-themed story somewhat akin to the novels of Mainwaring's friend and fellow writer, A. I. Bezzerides.

Mainwaring, under his Geoffrey Homes pseudonym, wrote a series of novels featuring Robin Bishop, a cynical newspaperman, beginning with *The Doctor Died At Dusk* (1936). One of the most memorable Bishop novels was *The Man Who Didn't Exist* (1937), in which Bishop investigates the apparent suicide of a writer with the odd name of Zenophen Zwick, who may or may not have ever existed.

Mainwaring introduced his second series character, Humphrey Campbell, in quite a unique way. *Then There Were Three* (1938) featured both the end of Robin Bishop's adventures and the beginning of Humphrey Campbell's. In the story, Bishop joins forces with Campbell—a milk drinking, accordion playing, blonde chasing PI—to search for an heiress who goes missing the day before her wedding. Other notable Campbell titles include *No Hands On the Clock* (1939), where a fistful of cigarette butts, a ransom note, and a dead redhead catapult Campbell into a fast murder chase; and *Forty Whacks* (1941, aka *Stiffs Don't Vote*), where Campbell investigates an axe murder which he dubs, "the second [Lizzie] Borden case." *No Hands On the Clock* was made into a movie in 1941, starring Chester Morris. *Forty Whacks* was filmed as *Crime By Night* in 1944, starring Jerome Cowan and Jane Wyman.

Mainwaring's final series character was José Manuel Madero, an Hispanic cop who also happened to knit socks and catch cigarettes in his mouth after flipping them in the air. Madero appeared in two books: *The Street of the Crying Woman* (1942, aka *The Case of the Mexican Knife*) and *The Hill of the Terrified Monk* (1943, aka *Dead as a Dummy*).

Mainwaring hit a high point when he wrote his last book, the non-series novel *Build My Gallows High* (1946). Red Bailey, a former private detective, is hiding out in a small town, having doublecrossed Whit

Sterling, a gambler who'd hired Bailey to find his mistress. Bailey, who presently runs a gas station and is engaged to a local girl, wants to maintain a low key, anonymous lifestyle, hoping Sterling will never find him. Unfortunately for Red, his past catches up with him.

*Build My Gallows High* was quickly bought by RKO studios. Mainwaring was hired to write the screenplay (under his Geoffrey Homes pseudonym), and Robert Mitchum, Kirk Douglas and Jane Greer starred in a noir classic, the title changed to *Out of the Past* (1947, directed by Jacques Tourneur).

After the success of *Out of the Past*, Mainwaring devoted himself exclusively to screenwriting, and wrote or co-wrote numerous first rate crime films, including *The Big Steal* (1949, as Homes, re-teaming Mitchum and Greer, directed by Don Siegel), *Roadblock* (1951, as Homes, co-written with Steve Fisher) and *The Phenix City Story* (1955, as Dan Mainwaring, directed by Phil Karlson). Next to *Out of the Past*, the most successful and well known movie Mainwaring wrote was *The Invasion of the Body Snatchers*, adapted (in 1956, under his own name) from Jack Finney's science fiction story, "The Body Snatchers." He also wrote teleplays for *Adventures in Paradise, The Wild Wild West* and *Mannix*.

**Further Reading:**
ONE AGAINST THE EARTH (1933)

**As Geoffrey Homes**
*Robin Bishop series (complete):*
THE DOCTOR DIED AT DUSK (1936)
THE MAN WHO MURDERED HIMSELF (1936)
THE MAN WHO DIDN'T EXIST (1937)
THE MAN WHO MURDERED GOLIATH (1938)
THEN THERE WERE THREE (1938)

*Humphrey Campbell series (complete):*
THEN THERE WERE THREE (1938)
NO HANDS ON THE CLOCK (1939)
FINDERS KEEPERS (1940)
FORTY WHACKS (1941; as STIFFS DON'T VOTE, 1947)
SIX SILVER HANDLES (1944, as THE CASE OF THE UNHAPPY ANGELS, 1950)

*Jose Manuel Madero series (complete):*
THE STREET OF THE CRYING WOMAN (1942; as
  THE CASE OF THE MEXICAN KNIFE, 1948)
THE HILL OF THE TERRIFIED MONK (1943, as DEAD AS A DUMMY, 1949)

BUILD MY GALLOWS HIGH (1946)

---

**If you like Daniel Mainwaring,** you might like: Richard Deming, A. I. Bezzerides

# Dan J. Marlowe

(also wrote as Dan Marlowe, Jaime Sandaval, Albert Avellano, Gar Wilson, Rod
Waleman, Major D. Lawn, Mande Woljar, Alma Werdon). Born in Lowell,
Massachusetts, 1914. Died in Tarzana, California, 1986.

Dan J. Marlowe wrote heist novels so realistically, and
understood the mechanics of criminous activities so
accurately, you'd think he knew a real-life thief. He
did.

More on that later.

On the surface, there was nothing in Dan Marlowe's
life to indicate he would end up writing some of Gold
Medal's most relentlessly hardboiled crime novels during the 1960's. He had earned an accounting degree from the Bentley
School of Accounting and Finance in Boston. He had worked in bookkeep-
ing, insurance and public relations. He loved crossword puzzles and the
theater. He was a member of the Rotarian Club and served on the City
Council of Harbor Beach, Michigan. He even *looked* like an accountant: he
wore a well-tailored suit, had developed a double chin and slight paunch
and had slicked back, thinning, gray-white hair.

But his wife's death in 1956 changed all that. Marlowe had toyed with
writing while his wife was still alive, but her death left him in a state of
shock. He walked out on his job and his home in Washington, DC and
moved to New York with the intention of becoming a full time writer.

His first novel was published by Avon in 1959, *Doorway to Death*. It was
the first of a five novel series featuring hotel dick and private detective
Johnny Killian. The other four are *Killer with a Key* (1959), *Doom Service*
(1960), *The Fatal Frails* (1960) and *Shake a Crooked Town* (1961). Killian was reminiscent of the hardboiled PI's of the era: buffed, rough and tough; he was
handy both with a wisecrack and with the ladies.

In 1962, Marlowe scored with his book *The Name of the Game is Death*, published by Gold Medal. The story is about Chet Arnold, who works part time
in the seemingly harmless occupation of a tree surgeon. But beneath
Arnold's nature-loving mask lies a ruthless, amoral, cold-blooded bank robber and killer. Arnold and his partner stage a bank holdup, and when
Arnold is wounded, he and his partner split up, and Arnold travels cross-
country in search of his partner and his share of the loot.

Mystery writer and historian Bill Pronzini has called *Game* a "master-
piece." Bill Crider, also a respected mystery writer and historian, wrote
that the book, "is just about as good as original paperback writing can get."
Stephen King dedicated his book *The Colorado Kid* as follows: "With admira-
tion, for Dan J. Marlowe, author of *The Name of the Game is Death*: Hardest of
the hardboiled."

Now comes the strange twist in Marlowe's life story.

Twenty-seven year old Al Nussbaum, a real life bank robber and expert at making pipe bombs, read *Game* while in hiding from the FBI. Nussbaum was so impressed with the criminous aspects of the novel, he telephoned Marlowe (using a fake name) to praise the book and to ask for advice about how he might get his own writing career started. Soon after, Nussbaum was captured but he and Marlowe continued communicating by letter (Marlowe, by this time, knew who Nussbaum was), and Marlowe even visited Nussbaum in prison.

Marlowe and Nussbaum began collaborating, with Nussbaum sharing his knowledge of weapons, ballistics, locks, safes, vaults and alarm systems. When Marlowe began using Nussbaum's information in his novels, he actually had to leave out certain details so the books wouldn't become "how to" manuals for criminals. These novels include *Strongarm* (1963), *Four for the Money* (1966), *The Vengeance Man* (1966) and *One Endless Hour* (1969, a sequel to *Game*), among others. All were published by Gold Medal. Marlowe helped Nussbaum eventually obtain his parole, and Nussbaum went on to have his own successful writing career.

In the early '70's, the "Chet Arnold" character from *Game* was turned into a series character and his name was changed to Earl Drake. The character was changed as well. Drake was now a secret agent working for the government. The titles of these books all started with the word "Operation," such as *Operation Breakthrough* (1971), *Operation Stranglehold* (1973) and *Operation Hammerlock* (1974).

Dan J. Marlowe led a life filled with twists and turns. He once wrote, in a column for the *Harbor Beach Times*, "My agent says I'm living proof that stories don't care who writes them."

Further Reading:
*Johnny Killain series (complete):*
DOORWAY TO DEATH (1959)
KILLER WITH A KEY (1959)
DOOM SERVICE (1960)
THE FATAL FRAILS (1960)
SHAKE A CROOKED TOWN (1961)

*Earl Drake series:*
THE NAME OF THE GAME IS DEATH (1962; as OPERATION OVERKILL, 1973)
ONE ENDLESS HOUR (1969; as OPERATION ENDLESS HOUR, 1975)
OPERATION FIREBALL (1969)
OPERATION BREAKTHROUGH (1971)
OPERATION CHECKMATE (1972)
OPERATION DRUMFIRE (1972)
OPERATION STRANGLEHOLD (1973)
OPERATION WHIPLASH (1973)
OPERATION OVERKILL (1963)
OPERATION HAMMERLOCK (1974)
OPERATION ENDLESS HOUR (1975)

BACKFIRE (1961)
STRONGARM (1963)
NEVER LIVE TWICE (1964)
DEATH DEEP DOWN (1965)
FOUR FOR THE MONEY (1966)
THE VENGEANCE MAN (1966)

---

**If you like Dan J. Marlowe,** you might like: Lionel White, Richard Stark (pseudonym of Donald E. Westlake

# Stephen Marlowe

(born Milton Lesser; also wrote as Andrew Frazer, Jason Ridgeway, Adam Chase, Ellery Queen, S. M. Tenneshaw, Christopher H. Thames, C. H. Thames, Darius John Granger, Steve Wilder). Born in Brooklyn, New York, 1928. Died in Williamsburg, Virginia, 2008.

 Stephen Marlowe is notable for his successful paperback series featuring private detective Chester Drum. Unlike dozens of urban-based PI's created during the 1950's and '60's, Drum's investigations take him globetrotting through international locales such as South Africa, Moscow, Rome, Spain and Iceland. In addition, the plots often involve as much espionage as they do PI work. The first Chester Drum novel was *The Second Longest Night* (1955).

Marlowe graduated from the College of William and Mary in Williamsburg, Virginia. He served in the U.S. Army from 1952-54.

Marlowe created a thorough background for Drum that established logical reasons for a private detective to be traveling through different countries and to be involved in government intelligence matters. That background included the fact that Drum, prior to becoming a PI, had worked as an FBI field man and had made valuable connections during that time. Also contributing to this background was the fact that Drum's private eye office was located in Washington, DC. The Drum novels were published by Gold Medal and had snappy, colorful titles such as *Killers Are My Meat* (1957), *Murder is My Dish* (1957), *Violence is My Business* (1958), *Jeopardy is My Job* (1962), *Terror is My Trade* (1958) and *Death is My Comrade* (1960).

A high point in the Drum series came when Marlowe and Richard S. Prather, creator of PI Shell Scott, collaborated and wrote a Chester Drum/Shell Scott crossover novel, *Double in Trouble* (1959). Marlowe and Prather communicated by mail and phone and the authors and their characters alternated chapters. Altogether, Marlowe produced twenty Chester Drum novels for Gold Medal between 1955 and 1968; sales eventually reached the millions.

During the late 1960's and throughout the '70's, Marlowe wrote straight spy and political intrigue fiction: *The Search for Bruno Heidler* (1966), *The Summit* (1970) and *The Valkyrie Encounter* (1978).

Later in life, Marlowe wrote a well-received series of historical novels: *The Memoirs of Christopher Columbus* (1987), *The Lighthouse at the End of the World* (1995, a study of Edgar Allan Poe) and *The Death and Life of Miguel de Cervantes*

(1996). He received a lifetime achievement award from the Private Eye
Writers of America in 1997.
**Further Reading:**
*Chester Drum series (complete):*
THE SECOND LONGEST NIGHT (1955)
MECCA FOR MURDER (1956)
KILLERS ARE MY MEAT (1957)
MURDER IS MY DISH (1957)
TROUBLE IS MY NAME (1957)
VIOLENCE IS MY BUSINESS (1958)
TERROR IS MY TRADE (1958)
DOUBLE IN TROUBLE (1959, with Richard S. Prather, co-featuring Shell
Scott)
HOMICIDE IS MY GAME (1959)
DANGER IS MY LINE (1960)
DEATH IS MY COMRADE (1960)
PERIL IS MY PAY (1960)
MANHUNT IS MY MISSION (1961)
JEOPARDY IS MY JOB (1962)
FRANCESCA (1963)
DRUM BEAT–BERLIN (1964)
DRUM BEAT–DOMINIQUE (1965)
DRUM BEAT–MADRID (1966)
DRUM BEAT–ERICA (1967)
DRUM BEAT–MARIANNE (1968)

CATCH THE BRASS RING (1954)
MODEL FOR MURDER (1955)
BLONDE BAIT (1959)

**As Andrew Frazer**
FIND EILEEN HARDIN—ALIVE! (1959)
THE FALL OF MARTY MOON (1960)

**As Jason Ridgeway**
WEST SIDE JUNGLE (1958)
PEOPLE IN GLASS HOUSES (1961)
HARDLY A MAN IS NOW ALIVE (1962)

**If you like Stephen Marlowe,** you might like: Richard S. Prather, Richard
Jessup, Edward S. Aarons

# *Harold Q. Masur*

(also wrote as Hal Q. Masur, Helen Traubel, Edward James, Guy Fleming). Born in New York City, New York, 1909. Died in Boca Raton, Florida, 2005.

 Most of Harold Q. Masur's novels, as well as short stories, feature lawyer/detective Scott Jordan. Perhaps the following characterization, by Masur himself, describes Jordan best: "The series character, Scott Jordan, a New York attorney, was first conceived to fall somewhere between [Erle Stanley Gardner's] Perry Mason and [Rex Stout's] Archie Goodwin. It was [my] hope to invent plots as ingenious as Gardner's, featuring a protagonist with the dash and insouciance of Rex Stout's Archie." (*Twentieth Century Crime and Mystery Writers*, pg. 725.)

Harold Q. Masur was himself a lawyer, having graduated from the New York University School of Law in 1934. He worked in private practice from 1935-1942, and served in the United States Air Force during WWII. During the early 1940's, and before entering Scott Jordan territory, he wrote short stories for *Ten Detective Aces* and *10-Story Detective Magazine*.

Masur's first novel, and the first to feature Jordan, was *Bury Me Deep* (1947). The book has a lulu of an opening: Jordan enters his apartment and finds a luscious blonde sitting on his sofa sipping brandy, wearing only a black bra and black panties. He clothes the blonde and sends her home in a taxi (silly boy), only to find out later that she died—poison was in the brandy. Jordan takes action to solve the murder, all the while having to elude her angry, giant-sized boyfriend, as well as the cops. In this book and other Jordan stories, Masur draws on his legal background to provide springboards which catapult the crimes.

*Bury Me Deep* also demonstrates how Masur's novels differ from Gardner's. Courtroom scenes exist minimally, if at all. Jordan spends most of his time as a private detective and the crime is usually solved before legal proceedings are too far underway.

As for Jordan himself, he thinks and acts fast. He has a helpful friend in the police department, homicide detective John Nola. Jordan sometimes bends the law to get the information he needs. Other notable Jordan novels include *Tall, Dark and Deadly* (1956), where Jordan faces disbarment when he is accused of having faked evidence in a divorce case; *Send Another Hearse* (1960), where Jordan investigates police corruption; and *Make A Killing* (1964), where Jordan becomes involved in a proxy battle for control of a movie studio.

Throughout the 1960's and '70's, Masur wrote for such crime digests as *Manhunt*, *Ellery Queen's Mystery Magazine* and *Alfred Hitchcock's Mystery Magazine*.

In 1973, Masur served as President of the Mystery Writers of America.

**Further Reading:**
*Scott Jordan series (complete):*
BURY ME DEAD (1947)
SUDDENLY A CORPSE (1949)
YOU CAN'T LIVE FOREVER (1950)
SO RICH, SO LOVELY, AND SO DEAD (1952)
THE BIG MONEY (1954)
TALL, DARK, AND DEADLY (1956)
THE LAST GAMBLE (1958; as MURDER ON BROADWAY, 1959)
SEND ANOTHER HEARSE (1960)
MAKE A KILLING (1964)
THE LEGACY LENDERS (1967)
THE MOURNING AFTER (1983)

THE METROPOLITAN OPERA MURDERS (1951, ghostwritten for Helen
  Traubel)

---

**If you like Harold Q. Masur,** you might like: Erle Stanley Gardner, Rex Stout, William Campbell Gault

# Richard Matheson

(also wrote as Logan Swanson, Josh Rogan). Born in Allendale, New Jersey, 1926. Currently living in California.

Richard Matheson is a science fiction/horror/fantasy writer who is equally adept at producing top-notch short stories for the pulps, noir tinged novels, teleplays and screenplays.

Matheson became interested in science fiction and fantasy at an early age. In an interview, Matheson said that the first book he borrowed from the library at age seven was a fantasy novel and that his first poems and stories were also of a fantasy nature. Matheson believes, "In essence, I was 'born' to be a writer, and probably a fantasy writer predominantly." (*The Twilight Zone Companion*, by Mark Scott Zicree, pg. 56)

After seeing combat in Germany during World War II, Matheson graduated from the University of Missouri with a degree in journalism. It wasn't an easy go, at first. Despite his journalism degree, he couldn't find a job on a newspaper or magazine. A friend suggested that Matheson get a menial night job and write during the day. Matheson took the advice, wrote short stories, and within a few months sold his first story, "Born of Man and Woman," to *The Magazine of Fantasy and Science Fiction* (Summer issue, 1950).

The plot showed the direction in which Matheson was headed: a hideous mutant child is kept chained in a basement. The story immediately catapulted Matheson into the front ranks of the science fiction field, and he published approximately sixty short stories during the next ten years in pulps such as *Amazing* and *Thrilling Wonder Stories*.

Matheson's first novel was *Someone is Bleeding* (1953). Published by Lion Books, *Bleeding* forgoes science fiction and fantasy and is a noirish tale about David Newton, a war veteran who goes to California to write novels. Newton meets and falls in love with a woman who may or may not be a psychotic killer. The front cover blurb is a classic: "MEN—THEY'RE ALL PIGS!" Matheson's next novel covers the kind of territory he is most well known for. *I Am Legend* (1954) is set in the near future world of 1976. It tells the story of Robert Neville, who has witnessed the end of the world—the population has been obliterated by a vampire virus. As Neville struggles to protect himself against the vampires who seek to destroy him, he searches for a way to discover the source of the plague and put an end to the vampires. *I Am Legend* regularly appears on critics' lists of the ten best horror novels, and has been made into a movie three times: as *The Last Man On Earth* (1964), *The Omega Man* (1971) and *I Am Legend* (2007).

Perhaps Matheson's most well known novel is *The Shrinking Man* (1956, the title changed to *The Incredible Shrinking Man* for reprints). The story is about Scott Carey, who is exposed to radioactive spray during a boat trip. When he gets home and the days and weeks pass, Carey progressively shrinks, and ordinary household animals and items—a cat, a pair of scissors, a spider—become a perilous nightmare. The movie, *The Incredible Shrinking Man* (1957), is one of the most famous films of the '50's; Matheson himself penned the screenplay. Other highly praised novels include *Hell House* (1971), *Somewhere in Time* (1975) and *What Dreams May Come* (1978).

During the early 1960's, Matheson was one of the pillars of the classic TV show *The Twilight Zone*. Matheson wrote many of the "Remember the one where...?" episodes you might bring up when talking about the show with friends. In that spirit.... Remember the one where William Shatner is on an airplane and sees a hairy monster out on the wing? ("Nightmare at 20,000 Feet"). Remember the one where the guy is a well-to-do businessman and all of a sudden he sees that his office is nothing but a Hollywood set and that he's nothing but an alcoholic, washed up actor? ("A World Of Difference"). How about the one where Shatner and his wife are at a café and Shatner becomes obsessed with a fortune telling machine with a bobbing devil's head on top? ("Nick Of Time"). Or the one where a haggard, mute woman battles two tiny space aliens? ("The Invaders"). Matheson wrote more than fifteen classic episodes during the show's run.

Among Matheson's screenplay credits are numerous movies in Roger Corman's excellent "Edgar Allen Poe" series: *House of Usher* (1960), *The Pit and the Pendulum* (1961), *The Raven* (1963) and *The Comedy of Terrors* (1963). He also wrote the screenplay for Steven Spielberg's first feature length film, the TV movie *Duel* (1971).

Stephen King sums up Matheson's stories this way: "He was the first guy that I ever read that seemed to be doing something that Lovecraft wasn't doing. It wasn't Eastern Europe—the horror could be in the Seven-Eleven store down the block, or it could be just up the street... He was putting the horror in places that I could relate to." (*The Twilight Zone Companion*, by Marc Scott Zicree, pg. 57)

**Further Reading:**
SOMEONE IS BLEEDING (1953)
I AM LEGEND (1954; aka THE OMEGA MAN)
THE SHRINKING MAN (1956, aka THE INCREDIBLE SHRINKING MAN)
A STIR OF ECHOES (1958)        RIDE THE NIGHTMARE (1959)
HELL HOUSE (1971)              THE NIGHT STRANGLER (1973)
SOMEWHERE IN TIME (1975)       WHAT DREAMS MAY COME (1978)

---

**If you like Richard Matheson,** you might like: Jack Finney, Robert Bloch

## Horace McCoy

Born in Pegram, Tennessee, 1897. Died in Hollywood, California, 1955.

Horace McCoy wrote one bona fide classic: *They Shoot Horses, Don't They?* (1935). Crossing the boundaries of crime fiction its portrayal of a segment of American society during the 1930's make it as much of a must-read as Hemingway, Fitzgerald or Steinbeck. On the surface, *They Shoot Horses, Don't They?* is a brutal and concisely written account of a woman and her partner, along with selected other couples, during the hours of a grueling dance marathon in Southern California, and of the spectators who get their kicks watching the exhausted couples drop like flies. Dig a little deeper and you'll find a book about despairing characters at the ends of their ropes, desperately grabbing at a few extra bucks in order to survive another day, their dreams of Hollywood stardom having been washed away with the California tide. A vein of madness runs through the book, only coming to fruition with the book's final stunning sentence.

Horace McCoy held many jobs during his lifetime. He was a mechanic, taxi driver, World War I fighter pilot, bodyguard, journalist, Hollywood extra and a bouncer at the dance marathon that would form the backdrop for *Horses*. He started writing short stories for *Black Mask* in 1927, and between 1929-1934 he wrote more than fifteen stories for that seminal pulp. Most featured Jerry Frost, pilot and member of a Texas Rangers outfit nicknamed "Hell's Stepsons," McCoy published action-adventure stories in *Battle Aces* and *Western Trails*.

McCoy's other novels, which were few and not quite up to the standard of *Horses*, still retained a cynical, hardboiled tone and dug deep into the souls of their characters—mostly desperate people living on the margins of society. *No Pockets in a Shroud* (1937) is about a tough journalist waging a lone war against corruption. *I Should Have Stayed Home* (1938) is about a young man who starts out in Hollywood as a movie extra and ends up as the "kept man" of an older woman. *Kiss Tomorrow Goodbye* (1948) is about an amoral, psychopathic criminal with an unusually high intellect. *Scalpel* (1952) is about a doctor who must choose between dedicating himself to treating the suffering poor or building himself a swank office and getting rich by flattering wealthy women who have imaginary ailments. *Corruption City* (1959, originally a movie treatment that was filmed in 1952 as *The Turning Point*), published posthumously, is about a young lawyer appointed by the state governor to smash a crime syndicate.

McCoy wrote more than thirty screenplays. Two of his most successful were *Gentleman Jim* (1942, starring Errol Flynn) and *The Lusty Men* (1952, starring Robert Mitchum and Susan Hayward, directed by Nicholas Ray).

*Kiss Tomorrow Goodbye* was filmed in 1950 and starred James Cagney. *They Shoot Horses, Don't They?* was filmed in 1969 and starred Jane Fonda; Gig Young won an Academy Award as the dance marathon's MC.

**Further Reading:**
THEY SHOOT HORSES, DON'T THEY? (1935)
NO POCKETS IN A SHROUD (1937)
I SHOULD HAVE STAYED HOME (1938)
KISS TOMORROW GOODBYE (1948)
SCALPEL (1952)
CORRUPTION CITY (1959)

---

**If you like Horace McCoy,** you might like: James M. Cain, Nathanael West

# William P. McGivern

(also wrote as Bill Peters, P. F. Costello, Gerald Vance). Born in Chicago, Illinois, 1922. Died in Palm Desert, California 1982.

William P. McGivern wrote about cops. Good cops, bad cops, young cops, old cops, corrupt cops, honest cops, vengeful cops, cowardly cops, remorseful cops, ex-cops and dead cops. As McGivern's narratives weave their way through various levels of law enforcement, they bring to light wide ranging corruption within both city and state government agencies.

McGivern was born in Chicago but grew up in Mobile, Alabama. After high school he developed an interest in writing and broadened his literary horizons by reading Hawthorne, Hemingway and Fitzgerald. He entered the U.S. Army in 1943 and was promoted to line sergeant, winning the Soldier's Medal for saving the crew aboard a bombed tanker. He was honorably discharged in 1946. McGivern then sharpened his writing skills working as a police reporter on *The Philadelphia Evening Bulletin*.

The first cop book McGivern is well known for is *The Big Heat* (1953). The story is about Police Sergeant Dave Bannion, who is warned by gangsters and law enforcement officials alike not to investigate the recent "suicide" of a colleague. Bannion ignores the warnings, and as a result his wife is murdered. As Bannion obsessively pursues his investigation, he receives pressure both from law enforcement members, who cherish their career more than justice, and from thugs of the city's crime boss. Bannion eventually untangles a thread of corruption involving a number of government officials—but in the process his soul is scarred, leaving him cynical and pessimistic.

*The Big Heat* was made into a classic film noir in 1953, starring Glenn Ford, Gloria Grahame and Lee Marvin, and directed by Fritz Lang. The character of Bannion serves as a precursor to vigilante cops-on-the-rampage movies like *Dirty Harry*.

Another McGivern book about cops and their environs is *Rogue Cop* (1954). It tells the story of detective Mike Carmody, a cop on the payroll of a local gangland boss, and Mike's younger brother, Eddie, a bright eyed and bushy tailed young cop on the force. When Eddie is killed as a result of his investigation into the mob, Mike is forced to make a decision that will cost him either his conscience or his life. *Rogue Cop* was made into an excellent film noir starring Robert Taylor as Mike, with George Raft as the crime boss.

Another strong McGivern showing, along the lines of a caper novel, is *Odds Against Tomorrow* (1957). There are four main characters: an ex-cop trying to score a big heist so he can live out his days in luxury; a white racist veteran named Earl Slater, who has found little success readjusting to civilian life upon returning from the war; a young black gambler named Johhny Ingrahm, in heavy debt to gangsters; and an on-the-square observant local lawman. Also made into a classic film noir, *Odds Against Tomorrow* (1959) was directed by Robert Wise, and starred Ed Begley, Sr. as the ex-cop, Robert Ryan as Earl Slater, and Harry Belafonte as Johnny Ingrahm. The character of the local law officer was dropped.

Other novels McGivern wrote about police and police work include *Shield for Murder* (1951, made into a movie starring and directed by Edmond O'Brien) and *The Darkest Hours* (1954, *aka Waterfront Cop*). He also wrote PI novels (as Bill Peters), as well as stories about espionage, newspaper reporters, paid assassins and out and out psychopaths.

McGivern wrote screenplays for frightmeister William Castle's *I Saw What You Did* (1965), for the Matt Helm-Dean Martin movie *The Wrecking Crew* (1969) and for John Wayne in *Brannigan*. He wrote teleplays for *Kojack*, *Ben Casey* and *Adam-12*.

**Further Reading:**
BUT DEATH RUNS FATER (1948; as THE WHISPERING CORPSE, 1950)
HEAVEN RAN LAST (1949)
VERY COLD FOR MAY (1950)
SHIELD FOR MURDER (1951)
THE CROOKED FRAME (1952)
THE BIG HEAT (1953)
MARGIN OF TERROR (1953)
ROGUE COP (1954)
THE DARKEST HOUR (1955; as WATERFRONT COP, 1956)
THE SEVEN FILE (1956)
NIGHT EXTRA (1957)
ODDS AGAINST TOMORROW (1957)
SAVAGE STREETS (1959)
SEVEN LIES SOUTH (1960)
KILLER ON THE TURNPIKE (1961, short stories)
THE ROAD TO THE SNAIL (1961)
A PRIDE OF PLACE (1962)
A CHOICE OF ASSASSINS (1963)
THE CAPER OF THE GOLDEN BULLS (1966)
LIE DOWN, I WANT TO TALK TO YOU (1967)
NIGHT OF THE JUGGLER (1975)

-------------------------------------------------------------

**If you like William P. McGivern,** you might like: Evan Hunter/Ed McBain, Lionel White

## James McKimmey

(also wrote as John Peter Drummond, Turkel Jones, Benjamin Swift). Born in Holdredge, Nebraska, 1923. Died in 2011.

During the late 1950's-'60's, James McKimmey wrote more than fifteen noir tinged PBOs, most notably for Dell. Mystery historian Allan Guthrie characterizes McKimmey's stories as offering "fast-paced plots, snappy dialogue, fleshed-out characters [and] enough tension to snap a bungee cord." (www.Allan Guthrie.co.uk)

McKimmey grew up in Nebraska. He served in the Army during WWII, receiving two campaign battle stars—the Combat Infantryman Badge and the Bronze Star. After attending the University of San Francisco, majoring in American Literature, he wrote a column for the *San Mateo Times*. As John Peter Drummond, he wrote Ki-Gor stories (a Tarzan spin-off) for the pulp magazine *Jungle Stories*. In 1953, he wrote a few sci-fi novelettes for *Planet Stories*.

McKimmey's first novel, and his favorite among his own books, was *The Perfect Victim* (1958), a story about a traveling salesman who, during a stopover in a small town, is accused of the murder of a local waitress. Writer John D. MacDonald praised the book thusly: "This man [McKimmey] can manipulate tension and character in ways that are beginning to alarm me."

In *Cornered* (1960), a pair of hit men come to a small town to snuff out a woman who's a potential witness against their boss. *Squeeze Play* (1962) is about an amnesiac who searches for the truth after learning he's suspected of his wife's murder. Other notable books include *Winner Take All* (1959), *The Long Ride* (1961) and *Run for Cover* (1963, McKimmey's first hardcover).

McKimmey did not write about PI's; he often focused on the viewpoint of the victim or the criminal. Writer Bill Crider sums up the appeal of McKimmey's best work: "McKimmey's interest is as much in character as in action. It's not that there's a shortage of the latter; it's just that the interplay of the characters is what raises the books above the ordinary and makes them engrossing reading even today." (Allan Guthrie.co.uk)

All of McKimmey's PBOs were optioned for the movies, but, as so often happens with stories "in development," none actually made it to the screen. A short story did manage to be adapted for an episode of TV's *G.E Theater*: "Last Reunion," which starred the great Lee Marvin. During the 1970's, McKimmey wrote scores of short stories for *Alfred Hitchcock's Mystery Magazine* and *Mike Shayne Mystery Magazine*.

Further Reading:
THE PERFECT VICTIM (1958)
WINNER TAKE ALL (1959)
CORNERED (1960)
THE LONG RIDE (1961)
THE WRONG ONES (1961)
24 HOURS TO KILL (1962)
SQUEEZE PLAY (1962)
RUN IF YOU'RE GUILTY (1963)
BLUE MASCARA TEARS (1965)
A CIRCLE IN THE WATER (1965)
THE HOT FIRE (1969)
THE MAN WITH THE GLOVED HAND (1972)

---

**If you like James McKimmey,** you might like: Helen Nielsen, Charles Williams

# Bob McKnight
Born in Ohio, 1906. Died in 1981.

Bob McKnight wrote eleven noirish PBOs during the late 1950's-'60's, most dealing with high-stakes gambling in the world of horse racing. McKnight's series character, Nathan Hawk, in books like *Murder Mutual* (1958) and *A Stone Around Her Neck* (1962), investigates bookie joints and horse betting scams. McKnight's non-series protagonists—appearing in books such as *Swamp Sanctuary* (1959), *A Slice of Death* (1960) and *Drop Dead, Please* (1961)—are mostly amateur sleuths, including a horse trainer, a track security consultant and a handicapper. Most of the books are set in South Florida, where McKnight lived for many years. The stories have the lickety split pacing of Seabiscuit—the majority are only 100-115 pages long.

McKnight studied mining engineering in New Mexico before switching gears (literally) and deciding to become a pilot, obtaining a commercial transport license. During the early 1950's, he developed an interest in horse racing, and began publishing racing related short stories and articles in magazines such as *Turf and Sports Digest, American Turf Monthly, Man to Man, Mr.,* and *Sir!* He also wrote successful non-fiction books about playing the ponies, including *How to Pick Winning Horses* (1963) and *Eliminate the Loser\$, Pick the Winner\$*(1965).

**Further Reading:**
DOWNWIND (1957)
MURDER MUTUEL (1958)
SWAMP SANCTUARY (1959)
THE BIKINI BOMBSHELL (1959)
A SLICE OF DEATH (1960)
RUNNING SCARED (1960)
KISS THE BABE GOODBYE (1960)
DROP DEAD, PLEASE (1961)
THE FLYING EYE (1961)
A STONE AROUND HER NECK (1962)
HOMICIDE HANDICAP (1963)
HOW TO PICK WINNING HORSES (1963)
ELIMINATE THE LOSER\$, PICK THE WINNER\$ (1965)

---

**If you like Bob McKnight,** you might like: William Campbell Gault, Louis Trimble

# John McPartland

Born in Illinois, 1911. Died in Monterey, California, 1958.

Gold Medal books set the bar for hardboiled paperback fiction throughout the 1950's and '60's, but they published so many excellent authors some were inevitably bound to fall through the cracks, though not through lack of merit. John McPartland was one such author. Eleven of his twelve novels were published by Gold Medal.

Not much is known about McPartland's life. According to his obituary in *Time* magazine, on September 29, 1958, McPartland was a 47 year-old, "husky, bushy-haired chronicler of suburban sex foibles (*No Down Payment*), successful freelance journalist; [died] of a heart attack in Monterey, Calif."

McPartland published his first novel, *Love Me Now*, in 1952. The story is about a man who becomes ensnared in the web of a femme fatale. In *Tokyo Doll* (1953), Mate Buchanan, an ex-Army captain, is visited by mysterious men claiming to work for the U.S. government on a mission to retrieve a miracle cure for atomic radiation poisoning. But all is not what is seems when the "Tokyo Doll," a beautiful blonde singer, steps into the picture. Suddenly Mate is being chased by both the U.S. military and communist spies.

In 1957, McPartland found mainstream success with his novel *No Down Payment* (his only non-Gold Medal book, first published in hardcover by Simon & Schuster). The story is about the emotional turmoil of four young couples living in a new suburban housing development. McPartland writes the book using multiple points of view, allowing us into the mind of each character, and showing the restless lives lurking beneath the quaintly constructed tract housing neighborhood. *No Down Payment* was made into a major motion picture the same year and starred Tony Randall, Joanne Woodward, Jeffrey Hunter and Barbara Rush.

McPartland's last novel was *The Kingdom of Johnny Cool* (1959). The book is one of the earliest to feature the Mafia, and tells of the rise and fall of a young criminal from Italy named Giuliano. Rigorously trained in the ways and means of organized crime, Giuliano is sent to America to help rule a crime empire. But Giuliano, known as "Johnny Cool" in America, lets his power go to his head, and loses both his cool and his throne. The book was made into a movie in 1963, with quite an offbeat cast: Henry Silva, Elizabeth (*Bewitched*) Montgomery, comedians Joey Bishop and Mort Sahl, Telly Savalas, Sammy Davis, Jr. and a number of other familiar faces.

McPartland found some solid work experiences in Hollywood. He wrote the screenplays for *The Wild Party* (1956, starring Anthony Quinn), *No Time to Be Young* (1957, starring Robert Vaughn) and a sci-fi movie, *The Lost Missile* (1958, starring Robert Loggia).

As his career was just beginning to take off, he died of a heart attack at forty-seven years old.

**Further Reading:**
LOVE ME NOW (1952)
TOKYO DOLL (1953)
BIG RED'S DAUGHTER (1953)
AFFAIR IN TOKYO (1954)
FACE OF EVIL (1954)
I'LL SEE YOU IN HELL (1956)
DANGER FOR BREAKFAST (1956)
THE WILD PARTY (1956)
NO DOWN PAYMENT (1957)
RIPE FRUIT (1958)
THE LAST NIGHT (1959)
THE KINGDOM OF JOHNNY COOL (1959)

---

**If you like John McPartland,** you might like: Frank Gruber, Dan J. Marlowe

# *Margaret Millar*

(née Sturm). Born in Kitchener, Ontario, Canada, 1915. Died in Montecito, California, 1994.

 Margaret Millar attended the Kitchener-Waterloo Collegiate Institute, Ontario, and the University of Toronto (1933-36), majoring in classic literature. In 1939 she married former classmate Kenneth Millar, who later became one of the most celebrated mystery novelists of the 20th century under the name Ross Macdonald. For the first twenty years of their marriage, though, Margaret was the more successful author. Things were reversed during the later years after her husband's Lew Archer series became the classic we know it as today. Throughout their lives, each of them claimed the other was the better writer. Ken was the first to sell professionally with a short story but Maggie was the first to sell a novel.

Millar started out writing lightly comic mysteries but later moved on to standalone novels of psychological suspense. Her first novel was *The Invisible Worm* (1941), which featured a psychiatrist detective named Paul Prye, characterized as "dressed in immaculate white flannels topped with a navy blue blazer, [who] looked like a man of the world, and the rather quizzical smile in his blue eyes suggested that he was also a man amused at the world." She wrote two more books featuring Prye, *The Weak-Eyed Bat* (1942) and *The Devil Loves Me* (1942), before taking a supporting character from the Prye series, Inspector Sands of the Toronto Police Department, and featuring him in his own two-book series, *Wall of Eyes* (1943) and *The Iron Gates* (1945).

Beginning in 1950, most of Millar's books were set in California; she and her husband had moved to Santa Barbara–fictionalized as San Felice or Santa Felicia in her novels–during the late '40's. In 1955, she won an Edgar award from the Mystery Writers of America for her novel, *The Beast In View* (1955). Anthony Boucher wrote that the book was "so detailedly convincing a study in abnormal psychology, so admirably written with such complete realization of every character, that the most bitter antagonist of mystery fiction may be forced to acknowledge it as a work of art." In a discussion of contemporary detective fiction, no less a name than Agatha Christie praised Miller as "very original."

Though her books are not generally considered detective mysteries, Millar was particularly noted for her surprise endings, foreshadowed but never spelled out for the reader until the final page. In the area of film, her novel *The Iron Gates* was optioned by Warner Brothers for Bette Davis, but the movie was never produced. However, in the early '60s, two of her novels—*Beast in View* and *Rose's Last Summer* (1965)—were adapted for the TV anthology series *Alfred Hitchcock Presents* and *Thriller*. Over her nearly fifty year career Millar was nominated for Edgar Awards twice, and in recognition of her overall achievements in the mystery field was awarded the Grand Master Award by the Mystery Writers of America in 1983.

Millar was also active in the conservation movement in California. She and her husband helped found a chapter of the National Audubon Society and her observations on the wildlife near her home were collected in her autobiography, *The Birds and the Beasts Were There* (1968). In 1965 she was named a Woman of the Year by the *Los Angeles Times*.

Other notable novels include *A Stranger in My Grave* (1960), the story of a woman who has a recurring nightmare in which she sees her own grave; *The Fiend* (1964), about a man who is friendly with children but who finds himself the main suspect when a little girl disappears; *How Like an Angel* (1962), featuring Joe Quinn, a former private eye who searches for a missing man inside a religious cult called The True Believers. Though she only wrote a handful of short pieces in her long career, oddly enough both her first and last sales were shorts.

**Further Reading:**
THE INVISIBLE WORM (1941)
THE WEAK-EYED BAT (1942)
WALL OF EYES (1943)
FIRE WILL FREEZE (1944)
DO EVIL IN RETURN (1950)
VANISH IN AN INSTANT (1952)
BEAST IN VIEW (1955)
AN AIR THAT KILLS (1957)
THE LISTENING WALLS (1959)
A STRANGER IN MY GRAVE (1960)
HOW LIKE AN ANGEL (1962)
THE FIEND (1964)
BEYOND THIS POINT ARE MONSTERS (1970)
ASK FOR ME TOMORROW (1976)
MERMAID (1982)
BANSHEE (1983)

---

**If you like Margaret Millar,** you might like: Helen Nielsen, Dorothy B. Hughes

# *Wade Miller*

(pseudonym of Robert Wade and Bill Miller; they also wrote as Whit Masterson, Dale Wilmer, Will Daemer). Robert Wade—born in San Diego, California, 1920. Died in San Carlos, California, 2012. Bill Miller—born in Garrett, Indiana, 1920. Died in San Diego, California, 1961.

  The team of Robert Wade and Bill Miller achieved several notable distinctions throughout their career: They successfully created their own private eye (Max Thursday); they wrote a book (*Badge of Evil*) that served as the basis for one of the best film noirs (*Touch of Evil*); and wrote another book (*Kitten with a Whip*) that was the basis for one of the most entertaining "so-bad-it's-good" films.

Wade and Miller started their partnership early. They were twelve years old and both attending Woodrow Wilson Junior High when they met for the first time at a music lesson. They began writing together while teenagers—plays, sketches and radio scripts. They both attended San Diego State College and edited the college newspaper. When WWII came along, they enlisted in the air force.

After WWII, Wade and Miller combined their surnames and wrote their first novel, *Deadly Weapon* (1946). It was a fine debut from the team and features PI Walter James, who is in San Diego investigating the shooting of his partner. Their next effort, *Guilty Bystander* (1947), features private detective Max Thursday, an unkempt alcoholic with an unpredictable temper who lives in a fleabag hotel. In the story, Thursday's ex-wife shows up to tell him their son has been kidnapped and, along with battling to stay sober, he has to battle assorted cops, thugs and doublecrossing hookers.

Reviewers compared *Guilty Bystander* favorably with the work of Hammett and Chandler. It was made into a movie in 1950, starring Zachary Scott. The other Thursday novels are *Fatal Step* (1948), *Uneasy Street* (1948), *Calamity Fair* (1950), *Murder Charge* (1950) and *Shoot To Kill* (1951).

Wade and Miller wrote numerous standalone novels. *Kitten with a Whip* (1959) is the story of a seductive juvenile delinquent who blackmails a happily married man. It was made into an over-the-top, camp classic starring Ann-Margret and John Forsythe. Other notable standalone efforts are *Devil May Care* (1950), the story of an ex-soldier of fortune (with the classic tough guy name of Biggo Venn) who is hired to go to Mexico and obtain a deathbed confession that will exonerate a deported mobster and allow him back into the U.S. to start new rackets; *The Killer* (1951), where a big game hunter is hired by a father to track down a man who killed his son; and *Branded Woman* (1952), about a woman who goes to Acapulco to get revenge against the man who branded an "X" into her forehead.

Wade and Miller wrote several novels under the name Whit Masterson. They used the Masterson name on their novel *Badge of Evil* (1956)—the basis for the classic film noir *Touch of Evil* (1959), directed by Orson Welles and starring Welles, Charlton Heston and Janet Leigh. Other excellent Masterson novels are *A Cry in the Night* (1955), which deals with a kidnapping, and *A Hammer in His Hand* (1960), which features a police-woman as the protagonist.

Bill Miller died of a heart attack in 1961. He was only 41 years old. Robert Wade continued his career as a successful writer, penning novels both under his own name and as by Whit Masterson, as well as writing a regular column for the *San Diego Union*. In 1988, Wade was awarded a Lifetime Achievement Award by the Private Eye Writers of America.

Further Reading:
*Max Thursday series (complete):*
GUILTY BYSTANDER (1947)
FATAL STEP (1948)
UNEASY STREET (1948)
CALAMITY FAIR (1950)
MURDER CHARGE (1950)
SHOOT TO KILL (1951)

DEADLY WEAPON (1946)
POP GOES THE QUEEN (1947, as MURDER–QUEEN HIGH, 1958)
DEVIL ON TWO STICKS (1949, as KILLER'S CHOICE, 1950)
DEVIL MAY CARE (1950)
STOLEN WOMAN (1950)
THE KILLER (1951)
BRANDED WOMAN (1952)
SOUTH OF THE SUN (1953)
KISS HER GOODBYE (1956)
KITTEN WITH A WHIP (1959)
SINNER TAKE ALL (1960)
NIGHTMARE CRUISE (1961)
THE GIRL FROM MIDNIGHT (1962)

**As Whit Masterson**
ALL THROUGH THE NIGHT (1955, as A CRY IN THE NIGHT, 1956)
DEAD, SHE WAS BEAUTIFUL (1955)
BADGE OF EVIL (1956, as TOUCH OF EVIL, 1958)
THE DARK FANTASTIC (1959)
A HAMMER IN HIS HAND (1960)
EVIL COME, EVIL GO (1961)
711–OFFICER NEEDS HELP (1965; as WARNING SHOT, 1967)

**As Dale Wilmer**
MEMO FOR MURDER (1951)
DEAD FALL (1954)
JUNGLE HEAT (1954)

---

**If you like Wade Miller,** you might like: Stephen Marlowe, A. S. Fleischman

# *Frederick Nebel*

(also wrote as Grimes Hill, Eric Lewis, Lewis Nebel). Born in Staten Island, New York, 1903. Died in Laguna Beach, California, 1967.

 The assessments of two pulp historians nicely sum up Frederick Nebel's contribution to pulp fiction. From Ron Goulart: "Two of the writers who did the most toward developing the hardboiled private eye after Hammett were Nebel and [Raoul] Whitfield." (*The Dime Detectives*, p.41) From Lee Server: "During [*Black Mask's*] greatest era, Nebel was among those instrumental in creating a new form of popular literature." (*Encyclopedia of Pulp Fiction Writers*, p. 197)

Early in life, Nebel was something of a drifter. He worked on the New York docks and on tramp steamers, and traveled throughout Europe. Nebel's attraction to an unfettered lifestyle was well expressed by his character, Tough Dick Donahue: "it [a job as a detective] keeps me in butts and I see the country and I don't have to slave over a desk."

Nebel started writing for the pulps in 1925; his earliest stories were adventure tales of the Northwest Mounties (he'd lived with his grandfather in Canada when a child), published in *Northwest Stories*. In 1926, he cracked the ranks of *Black Mask* with his story, "The Breaks of the Game." It was the beginning of a run that would last for sixty-seven stories, topped only by Erle Stanley Gardner.

Nebel created his first series characters for *Black Mask* in September, 1928. "Raw Justice" featured the crime fighting team of Kennedy of *The Free Press* and Captain Steve MacBride. MacBride was a tough, old school police captain and devoted family man. Kennedy was his sidekick, a smart-alecky, heavy drinking newspaper reporter. Together they appeared in thirty-seven stories over a period of eight years. The Kennedy and MacBride tales served as the basis for a series of zippy Warner Brothers B-movies during the late 1930's, the character of Kennedy changed to a wise-cracking dame named Torchy Blane, played by Glenda Farrell.

Nebel's final series character for *Black Mask*, Tough Dick Donahue, appeared in fifteen stories, from 1930-35. According to Ron Goulart's *The Dime Detectives*, the character of Donahue came about because Black Mask editor Joseph T. Shaw asked Nebel to come up with a new private eye directly in the Sam Spade mode, since Dashiell Hammett was earning big money in Hollywood and would not provide more stories to the pulps. Donahue is an operative for the Inter-State Detective Agency in New York; his approach to his profession is that detective work is "not a polite business of question-and-answer bunk. You work against crooks and you've got to beat them at their own game."

For *Dime Detective*, Nebel created what is likely his most popular character, Cosmos Detective Agency PI, Jack Cardigan. Cardigan appeared in forty-four pulp stories from 1931-37. Ron Goulart, in *The Dime Detectives*, characterizes Cardigan as "rude, restless, streetwise, and shrewd." Though the Cosmos Agency is centrally located in St. Louis, Cardigan appears transnationally, in New York City, San Francisco and cities in the Midwest and New England.

Nebel published few novels. *Sleepers East* (1933) is a Grand Hotel-type story set on a train, depicting the intersecting lives of disparate characters. *But Not the End* (1934) is a mainstream novel of Depression-era New York. *Fifty Roads to Town* (1936) is a mystery story about a group of strangers who are stranded in a snowbound Maine town.

In 1937, Nebel quit writing hardboiled crime stories for the pulps in favor of higher paying slick magazines such as *The Saturday Evening Post*, *Collier's* and *Cosmopolitan*. He returned to crime writing only for a handful of short stories published in *Ellery Queen's Mystery Magazine* during the late 1950's.

**Further Reading:**
SLEEPERS EAST (1934)
BUT NOT THE END (1943
FIFTY ROADS TO TOWN (1936)
THE COMPLETE CASEBOOK OF CARDIGAN, VOLUMES 1-4 (2012)
TOUGH AS NAILS: THE COMPLETE CASES OF DONAHUE (2012)

---

**If you like Frederick Nebel,** you might like: Dashiell Hammett, Raoul Whitfield, Paul Cain

# *Helen Nielsen*

(also wrote as Kris Giles). Born in Roseville, Illinois, 1918. Died in Prescott, Arizona 2002.

Helen Nielsen wrote mystery and suspense novels that were noted for vividly capturing the atmosphere of Southern California (she lived in Laguna Beach and Oceanside for many years). She was one of the few female writers published in the male oriented digest *Manhunt*, and also had numerous short stories published in *Alfred Hitchcock's Mystery Magazine* and *Ellery Queen's Mystery Magazine*. She wrote teleplays for *Alfred Hitchcock Presents* and *Perry Mason*, as well.

Before turning to writing, Nielsen had a varied and colorful career. After graduating from the Chicago Art Institute, she worked as a freelance commercial artist from 1938-1942. In 1942, she was an aeronautical engineer for the United States Defense Engineering Program. She worked as a draftsman in Los Angeles from 1942-46.

Mystery reviewers have noted several novels in particular as exemplary of Nielsen's work. *The Woman On the Roof* (1954) is about an emotionally disturbed woman who becomes involved in a murder that occurs in a bungalow court owned by her rich brother. In *A Killer in the Street* (1967), a man who witnesses the murder of a garage attendant is forced to flee across the country to save his own life. *Sing Me a Murder* (1960) is about a widower who becomes involved in the murder of a waitress who happens to be a look-alike for his dead wife. *Detour* (1953, aka *Detour to Danger*) is a story about eighteen-year old Danny Ross, a drifter who the people of Cooperton believe is responsible for the murder of one of their prominent local citizens.

Nielsen wrote teleplays for *Alfred Hitchcock Presents* and *Perry Mason* throughout the 1960's. During the 1980's, her work saw a resurgence when *Detour* and *Sing Me a Murder* were included in the well known Black Lizard series of crime novels.

Further Reading:
THE KIND MAN (1951)
GOLD COAST NOCTURNE (1951; as DEAD ON THE LEVEL, 1954)
OBIT DELAYED (1952)
DETOUR (1953; as DETOUR TO DEATH, 1955)
THE WOMAN ON THE ROOF (1954)
STRANGER IN THE DARK (1955)
THE CRIME IS MURDER (1956)
BORROW THE NIGHT (1957; as SEVEN DAYS BEFORE DYING, 1958)
THE FIFTH CALLER (1959)
FALSE WITNESS (1959)
SING ME A MURDER (1960)
WOMAN MISSING AND OTHER STORIES (1961, short stories)
VERDICT SUSPENDED (1964)
AFTER MIDNIGHT (1966)
A KILLER IN THE STREET (1967)
DARKEST HOUR (1969)
SHOT ON LOCATION (1971)
THE SEVERED KEY (1973)
THE BRINK OF MURDER (1976)

---

If you like Helen Nielsen, you might like: James McKimmey, Bill S. Ballinger

# Earl Norman

(born Norman Thomson). Born in Springfield, Massachusetts, 1915. Died in Pasadena, California, 2000.

Earl Norman wrote a ten book paperback series from 1958-1976 that was somewhat akin to the "Assignment" novels written by Edward Aarons, as well as being a precursor to the men's adventure series during the 1970's which featured such characters as the Executioner and the Destroyer. Norman's series features Tokyo-based private eye, Burns Bannion and all the titles start with the phrase, "Kill Me in", and then follow with the name of a Japanese location, e.g. *Kill Me in Hong Kong, Kill Me in Shimbashi, Kill Me in Atami.*

Before writing the "Kill Me" series, Norman (under his real name) had a fairly extensive acting career. He appeared in a number of Broadway plays and was one of the founding members of the Orson Welles Mercury Theatre. He acted as stand-in for John Wayne, often boozing it up with the Duke during their thirty-five year friendship. Norman served in the Armed Forces during WWII and was recruited as an Entertainment Supervisor for all the U.S. bases in the Far East. After the war, he remained in Tokyo and became an expert in karate.

Norman's first book featuring Burns Bannion was *Kill Me in Tokyo* (1958). Like Norman, Bannion is an ex-GI who stayed in Tokyo after the war. Bannion is a martial arts expert who becomes a private detective after being mistaken for one. Some of the cover blurbs for the Bannion books compare him to Mike Hammer, and like Hammer, Bannion is a hard-boiled, kick-ass kind of guy. What distinguishes the Bannion series from Spillane's are a number of items. Bannion is one of the earliest action heroes (most likely *the* earliest) to engage in the bone-crunching sport of karate. Also, because of Norman's extensive experience in Japan, the exotic Asian settings are detailed and have a ring of authenticity. Stylistically, Norman wrote over the top prose in what might be called the "ultra kick-ass" mode.

A few notable Bannion titles are Bannion's debut, *Kill Me in Tokyo* (1958); *Kill Me in Yoshiwara* (1961), where Bannion storms through the red light district of Tokyo to find the slayer of a prostitute; and *Kill Me in Roppongi* (1967), where Bannion tangles with a Nazi abortionist.

Earl Norman settled back in the United States during the last years of his life.

Further Reading:
KILL ME IN TOKYO (1958)
KILL ME IN SHIMBASHI (1959)
KILL ME IN YOKOHAMA (1960)
KILL ME IN SHINJUNKU (1961)
KILL ME IN ATAMI (1962)
KILL ME ON THE GINZA (1962)
KILL ME IN YOSUKA (1966)
KILL ME IN ROPPONGI (1967)
KILL ME IN HONG KONG (1976)

---

**If you like Earl Norman,** you might like: Edward S.Aarons, Mickey Spillane, John McPartland

# Milton K. Ozaki

(also wrote as Robert O. Saber, Mark Shane). Born in Racine, Wisconsin, 1913. Died in Sparks, Nevada, 1989.

Milton K. Ozaki, of Japanese descent, was one of the first mystery writers with his heritage writing with English as his primary language. He wrote nearly two dozen crime related books between 1946 and 1960; all but two were PBO's, half written under his own name and half under the name Robert O. Saber.

Ozaki's mother was American; his father, Japanese. Before starting his novel writing career, he worked as a newspaper reporter, artist and as the operator of a beauty parlor.

Ozaki created numerous detectives, both amateur and professional. His first three books–*The Cuckoo Clock* (1946), *A Fiend in Need* (1950), and *The Dummy Murder Case* (1951)–feature amateur detectives Professor Androcles Caldwell, head of the psychology department at a Chicago university, and Bendy Brinks, his Watson/assistant. *The Cuckoo Clock* (1946) takes place in a beauty parlor similar to the one Ozaki operated. In a unique move, forty-three years later it was rewritten and updated by Ozaki's daughter as *Ticked Off!* (1989). Ozaki also created PIs Rusty Forbes (*Dressed To Kill*, 1954), Carl Guard (*Maid for Murder*, 1955) and Bob Wherry (*Never Say Die*, 1956). Under the name Robert O. Saber, Ozaki created PIs Max Keene, Phil Keene, Carl Good, Pete Mallary and Bob Stille.

Ozaki's best works are considered his non-PI PBO's, characterized by snappy dialogue, convoluted plots, double crosses, secret identities and unconventional motives. A unique aspect of Ozaki's work was his ability to create cock-eyed, crackpot similes and metaphors:

"The back of my head jumped spastically like a caterpillar on a hot stove and my cranial cavity seethed with thick volatile chili juice." –*The Deadly Pick-Up* (1952)

"Then her cool arms were around my neck and her warm breasts were digging into my chest and she was kissing me like a French horn in reverse." –*Sucker Bait* (1955), as Robert O. Saber

"With a face like that, Frank Laughton had about as much chance of avoiding recognition as a one-legged midget on crutches." –*The Affair of the Frigid Blonde* (1950), as Robert O. Saber

Ozaki had other achievements outside crime fiction. He designed a dice game, *Murder Dice*, which was similar to *Yahtzee* and was based upon the events in a murder trial. He was a well regarded stamp expert and wrote *How to Play the Stamp Market* (1969), which featured stamp collecting as an investment. He was also President of the Chicago chapter of the Mystery Writers of America.

Ozaki was something of an eccentric wag. During the early 1970's, he received a slap on the wrists from the authorities in Colorado for peddling phony honorary college degrees. He also ran a mail order school teaching ESP and hypnotism. And in a newspaper interview, when asked if the characters in his novels were anything like Agatha Christie's, he stated the negative, citing that Ms. Christie's characters were "more sexy."

**Further Reading:**
*Professor Caldwell and Bendy Brinks series (complete):*
THE CUCKOO CLOCK (1946; as TOO MANY WOMEN, 1950)
A FIEND IN NEED (1947)
THE DUMMY MURDER CASE (1951)

THE DEADLY PICK-UP (1952)
DRESSED TO KILL (1954)
MAID FOR MURDER (1955)
NEVER SAY DIE (1956)
CASE OF THE DEADLY KISS (1957)
CASE OF THE COP'S WIFE (1958)
WAKE UP AND SCREAM (1959)
INQUEST (1960)

**As Robert O. Saber**
THE BLACK DARK MURDERS (1949)
THE AFFAIR OF THE FRIGID BLONDE (1950)
THE DOVE (1951; as CHICAGO WOMAN, 1953)
THE DEADLY LOVER (1951)
THE SCENTED FLESH (1951)
NO WAY OUT (1952)
CITY OF SIN (1952; as by Milton K. Ozaki, 1962)
MURDER DOLL (1952; as by Milton K. Ozaki, 1959)
TOO YOUNG TO DIE (1954)
SUCKER BAIT (1955)
A DAME CALLED MURDER (1955)
A TIME FOR MURDER (1956)

---

**If you like Milton K. Ozaki,** you might like: Michael Avallone, Douglas Sanderson

# *Vin Packer*

(real name Marijane Meaker; also wrote as Ann Aldrich, M. E. Kerr, Mary James, M. J. Meaker, Larura Winston). Born in Auburn, New York, 1927. Presently living in East Hampton, New York.

Marijane Meaker was a pioneer in lesbian themed fiction and non-fiction PBOs during the 1950's.

Meaker graduated from the University of Missouri in 1949. Shortly thereafter, she was hired as a reader at paperback house Gold Medal Books. In 1950, one of Gold Medal's biggest sellers had been the reprinting of a book called *Women's Barracks*, by Tereska Torres, a wartime story with a lesbian subtext. Eager to continue their financial success, editor Dick Carroll asked Meaker to write a book with a lesbian theme. "The only restriction he gave me," said Meaker, "was that it couldn't have a happy ending and he suggested it end with the lesbian going crazy. Otherwise, the post office might seize the books as obscene." (*Encyclopedia of Pulp Fiction Writers*, by Lee Server, p.205)

Meaker's book (titled *Spring Fire* by Carroll and written under the pseudonym, Vin Packer) about two university sorority sisters—naïve, earnest Mitch and worldly, predatory Leda—was a financial blockbuster, and started a revolution in the paperback field. Within a few years, lesbian themed novels were a staple at every paperback publisher.

Perhaps *Spring Fire*'s biggest surprise was that it wasn't a titillating, exploitative story that appealed to men, but a realistically written tale that caught the attention of women. "I think Dick Carroll figured the story would have prurient appeal to men," Meaker said, "but when it came out I got just hundreds of letters, boxes of them, all from women, gay women. It took them all by surprise, this big audience out there."

Under the name Ann Aldrich, Meaker continued writing about lesbian culture in non-fiction works—using her own observations of lesbians and the lives of lesbians—that included *We Walk Alone* 1955); *We, Too, Must Love* (1958) and *Carol in a Thousand Cities* (1960).

Ms. Meaker was a writer of wide and varied talents, and as Vin Packer, she continued to write novels about crime (*Something in the Shadows* and *Intimate Victims*), emotionally disturbed youth (*The Thrill Kids* and *The Evil Friendship*) and race relations in the South (*3 Day Terror* and *Dark Don't Catch Me*).

In the 1970's Meaker dropped the Packer and Aldrich pseudonyms, and adopted the pen name M. E. Kerr, under which she wrote young adult fiction.

Meaker was involved romantically with *Strangers On a Train* author

Patricia Highsmith for two years. She wrote about this relationship in the 2003 non-fiction memoir *Highsmith: A Romance of the 1950's.*

**Further Reading:**
SPRING FIRE (1952)
DARK INTRUDER (1952)
LOOK BACK TO LOVE (1953)
COME DESTROY ME (1954)
WHISPER HIS SIN (1954)
THE THRILL KIDS (1955)
THE YOUNG AND VIOLENT (1956)
DARK DON'T CATCH ME (1956)
3-DAY TERROR (1957)
5:45 TO SUBURBIA (1958)
THE EVIL FRIENDSHIP (1958)
THE TWISTED ONES (1959)
THE DAMNATION OF ADAM BLESSING (1961)
THE GIRL ON THE BESTSELLER LIST (1960)
SOMETHING IN THE SHADOWS (1961)
INTIMATE VICTIMS (1962)
ALONE AT NIGHT (1963)
THE HARE IN MARCH (1966)

**As Ann Aldrich**
WE WALK ALONE (1955)
WE, TOO, MUST LOVE (1958)
CAROL IN A THOUSAND CITIES (1960)
WE TWO WON'T LAST (1963)
TAKE A LESBIAN TO LUNCH (1972)

**As M. E. Kerr**
DINKY HOCKER SHOOTS SMACK (1972)
THE SON OF SOMEONE FAMOUS (1974)
IS THAT YOU, MISS BLUE? (1975)
I'LL LOVE YOU WHEN YOU'RE MORE LIKE ME (1977)
WHAT I REALLY THINK OF YOU (1982)

---

**If you like Vin Packer,** you might like: John O'Hara, Ann Bannon, Fletcher Flora

# Stuart Palmer

(born Charles Stuart Hunter Palmer, also wrote as Jay Stewart, Theodore Orchards). Born in Baraboo, Wisconsin, 1905. Died in 1968.

Stuart Palmer was famous for creating Hildegarde Withers, the epitome of the crotchety old schoolmarm turned amateur detective. Withers was popular in both books and movies. Palmer also wrote screenplays during the 1930's and '40's for movies featuring numerous other sleuths, including the Falcon, Bulldog Drummond and the Lone Wolf. Oddly enough, Palmer didn't write the screenplays for any of the Withers films.

Palmer grew up in the Midwest and was well educated. He attended the Chicago Art Institute from 1922-24 and the University of Wisconsin at Madison from 1924-1926. He served in the Army from 1943-48, working as a liaison chief for official Army film making, and emerged with the rank of major.

His first Hildegarde Withers novel, *The Penguin Pool Murder* (1931), was his second book overall. In the story, school teacher Withers takes her class to the New York Aquarium, where they discover a dead body floating in the penguin pool. When the police arrive to investigate, Withers believes they are barely above the level of class dunces, and that she can do a much better job of solving the murder. Withers' character is very distinct: she is sharp-tongued, stern and austere. She is a domineering busybody, and treats both the police and suspects as though they were backwards children in her class. She also wears eccentric and grotesque hats. Yet, for all these qualities, Palmer keeps Withers from becoming a repellent character, and beneath the austere mask he endows her with a great deal of kindness and humor. Her comic foil in the stories is homicide inspector Oscar Piper: tough talking, cigar chomping and perennially frustrated with the snoopy Withers, he would have spent much time standing in the corner were he a student in Miss Withers' class. Withers' interplay with Piper, and her interference in his cases, is a great deal of fun, and at the end of each adventure, Piper is forced to admit that the shrewd Withers is more help than hindrance.

Both *The Penguin Pool Murder* and Hildegarde Withers were a success. *Penguin Pool* was made into a movie the year after it was published. The horse-faced Withers was played to perfection by horse-faced character actress Edna May Oliver, and Oliver played the character in two more movies. Helen Broderick and ZaSu Pitts played the spinster in later films. Altogether, there were fourteen Withers' novels and short story collections, and six movies. In addition to the debut Withers novel, critics have singled out *The Puzzle of the Red Stallion* (1936), *Miss Withers Regrets* (1937), *The Green Ace* (1950) and *Cold Poison* (1954) as excellent entries in the series.

**Further Reading:**
*Hildegarde Withers series:*
THE PENGUIN POOL MURDER (1931)
MURDER ON WHEELS (1932)
MURDER ON THE BLACKBOARD (1934)
THE PUZZLE OF THE PEPPER TREE (1933)
THE PUZZLE OF THE SILVER PERSIAN (1934)
THE PUZZLE OF THE RED STALLION (1936)
THE PUZZLE OF THE BLUE BANDARILLA (1937)
THE PUZZLE OF THE HAPPY HOOLIGAN (1941)
MISS WITHERS REGRETS (1947)
FOUR LOST LADIES (1949)
THE GREEN ACE (1950)
COLD POISON (1954)

---

**If you like Stuart Palmer,** you might like: Dolores Hitchens, Fletcher Flora

# Richard Powell

(also wrote as Jeremy Kirk). Born in Philadelphia, Pennsylvania, 1908. Died in Fort Myers, Florida, 1999.

Besides scoring success with mainstream novels such as *The Philadelphian* (1957), Richard Powell wrote a series of mysteries featuring PIs Arab and Andy Blake, as well as a number of witty standalone crime novels.

Powell graduated from Princeton University and began work as a police reporter, writing fiction in his spare time. After selling a few stories, he joined an ad agency before turning to writing mysteries, beginning with the successful Arab and Andy Blake series.

Andy Blake is a laid back antique dealer and army reservist. His wife Arabella is a free-spirited blonde, an ex-debutante and a sharpshooter. The Blake series has a whimsical, lighthearted tone–Arab and Andy could be compared to Hammett's Nick and Nora Charles, albeit with less drinking involved. The first in the series was *Dark Don't Catch Me* (1944), in which newlyweds Arab and Andy find a fake Chippendale chair on a Sunday outing through Pennsylvania Dutch country. This leads the couple to stumble across a shooting spree, and to housebreaking into a castle, arson, and foiling the plans of Nazi agents trying extort a million dollars.

Nazis also appear in *All Over but the Shooting* (1946), where Arab and Andy struggle to uncover a nest of Axis agents who are about to reveal Allied D-Day plans to the enemy. The other books in the series are *Lay That Pistol Down* (1945), *Shoot if You Must* (1946) and *And Hope to Die* (1947).

After serving in WWII on General Douglas MacArthur's staff, Powell moved his family–wife Marian and two children–to Florida, where he produced more mysteries. *Shell Game* (1951) is about a tourist on vacation in Florida who gets involved with a beautiful murder suspect. In *A Shot in the Dark* (1952, no relation to the Blake Edwards Pink Panther movie), a lazy playboy goes on a mission to avenge the death of a friend. *Say It with Bullets* (1953) tells the story of Bill Wayne, who takes a bus tour of the U.S. to track down a fellow serviceman who shot him in the back and left him for dead during the war. These stand alone mysteries of Powell's feature an excellent blend of humor and tension.

Powell's mainstream novel *The Philadelphian* (1957) was made into a successful movie starring Paul Newman, and *Pioneer, Go Home!* (1959) was filmed as *Follow That Dream* (1962), starring Elvis Presley. His *Don Quixote, U.S.A.* (1957) was a popular *Reader's Digest* Condensed Book and served as the basis for the 1971 Woody Allen movie, *Bananas* (with Allen and Louise Lasser).

**Further Reading:**
*Crime fiction:*
DON'T CATCH ME (1944)
LAY THAT PISTOL DOWN (1945)
ALL OVER BUT THE SHOOTING (1946)
SHOOT IF YOU MUST (1946)
AND HOPE TO DIE (1947)
SHARK RIVER (1950)
SHELL GAME (1951)
SHOT IN THE DARK (1952)
SAY IT WITH BULLETS (1953)
FALSE COLORS (1955)

*Mainstream novels:*
THE BUILD-UP BOYS (as by Jeremy Kirk, 1956)
THE PHILADELPHIAN (1957)
PIONEER, GO HOME (1959)
THE SOLDIER (1960)
I TAKE THIS LAND (1962)
DAILY AND SUNDAY (1964)
DON QUIXOTE, U.S.A. (1966)
TICKETS TO THE DEVIL (1968)
WHOM THE GODS WOULD DESTROY (1970)

------------------------------------------------------------

**If you like Richard Powell,** you might like: David Dodge, Richard Sale

## *Talmage Powell*

(also wrote as Robert Hart Davis, Robert Henry, Milton T. Lamb, Milton Land, Jack McCready, Anne Talmage, Dave Sands; ghosted a number of Ellery Queen novels). Born in Henderson, North Carolina, 1920. Died in Asheville, North Carolina, 2000.

 Talmage Powell was a prolific crime writer who wrote nearly 500 short stories as well as 20 novels, five of which feature private detective Ed Rivers.

Powell sold his first short story to the pulps in 1943. He wrote for a variety of genres—detective, hero, weird menace, western, and western romance. Some of the many pulps he wrote for included *Dime Detective, The Shadow, Dime Mystery, Fifteen Western Tales* and *Ranch Romances.* He wrote more than 200 stories for the pulps throughout the 1940's and early 1950's. When the pulps died out in the early '50's, Powell wrote more than 300 stories for crime digests such as *Manhunt, Guilty, Trapped, Alfred Hitchcock's Mystery Magazine, Mike Shayne Mystery Magazine* and *Ellery Queen's Mystery Magazine.*

In 1959, Powell wrote *The Killer is Mine,* his first novel featuring Tampa based private detective Ed Rivers. Rivers is in his early forties, is 6 feet tall and weighs 190 pounds. As for his face, he admits he doesn't have the prettiest puss in the business:

"Women either get a charge from the face or want to run from it. Men fear it or trust it to the hilt."

Rivers carries a .38, as well as a knife in a sheath at the nape of his neck. He has a friend and ally in the police department named Steve Ivey. Ed is tough but human and starting with the third novel, *With a Madman Behind Me* (1961), Rivers begins taking on some of the knightly traits of Raymond Chandler's Philip Marlowe. In that story, Rivers tracks down the killer of a strangled girl and breaks up a porno ring. In *Start Screaming Murder* (1962), Rivers befriends midget singer Tina La Flor, and investigates the murder of a brute named Bucks Jordan. *Corpus Delectable* (1964) takes place during the annual Gasparilla Festival—Tampa's version of the Mardi Gras. Throughout the series, Powell does an excellent job evoking the seedy atmosphere of slum-like areas in Tampa.

Powell wrote four books for the long-running Ellery Queen series: *Murder with a Past* (1963), *Beware the Young Stranger* (1965), *Where is Bianca?* (1966) and *Who Spies, Who Kills?* (1967). He wrote novelizations for TV's *Mission: Impossible* as well, and nearly ten standalone novels.

Further Reading:
*Ed Rivers series (complete):*
THE KILLER IS MINE (1959)
THE GIRL'S NUMBER DOESN'T ANSWER (1960)
WITH A MADMAN BEHIND ME (1962)
START SCREAMING MURDER (1962)
CORPUS DELECTABLE (1965)

THE SMASHER (1959)
MAN-KILLER (1960)
THE GIRL WHO KILLED THINGS (1960)
THE RAPER (1962, as Jack McCready)

As Ellery Queen
MURDER WITH A PAST (1963)
BEWARE THE YOUNG STRANGER (1965)
WHERE IS BIANCA? (1966)
WHO SPIES, WHO KILLS? (1966)

---

If you like Talmage Powell, you might like: Thomas B. Dewey, William Campbell Gault

# Richard S. Prather

(also wrote as David Knight, Douglas Ring). Born in Santa Ana, California, 1921. Died in Sedona, Arizona, 2007.

During the 1950's, Richard S. Prather put a fresh spin on the character of the hardboiled detective when he created Shell Scott, a jaunty, wisecracking, happy-go-lucky private eye who often found himself in out-landishly comic situations.

Prather grew up in Santa Ana, California, and attended Riverside Junior College. When WWII broke out, he joined the Merchant Marines, serving as a fire-man and engineer from 1941-45. After the war, he worked as a clerk at March Air Force Base in Riverside.

Prather's first book featuring Shell Scott was *The Case of the Vanishing Beauty* (1950). Scott is thirty years-old, 6'2", 200-lbs., sports a bleached-looking buzz cut and equally white eyebrows, and is missing a small chunk from the tip of his left ear. He lives and works in Hollywood, is well tanned and a snappy dresser. His regular drink is bourbon and water, but he is also partial to martinis. In other words, he is a "swinger."

Scott started out in the series in the typical Mike Hammer mode, indistinguishable from dozens of tough-guy paperback PI's during the 1950's. As the series progressed, Prather blazed a trail in a different direction, and Scott's adventures became increasingly screwball in nature. In *Strip for Murder* (1955), Scott not only gallivants through a nudist camp, but flies naked in a hot air balloon, as well. In *The Cockeyed Corpse* (1964), he is tracking down leads on the set of a softcore western "nudie" movie; at one point he is forced to take refuge in a giant movie prop boulder. In *The Trojan Hearse* (1964), he rides a demolition ball through the wall of a building while in pursuit of a suspect.

Besides situationally, Prather created humor by virtue of Scott's breezy, wisecracking narration. Rather than a fist, Scott often cuts his antagonists down to size with a witty remark:

> "This was a party that Cholly Knickerbocker, in tomorrow's *Los Angeles Examiner*, would describe as 'a gathering of the Smart Set,' and if this was the Smart Set, I was glad I belonged to the Stupid Set." –*Strip for Murder* (1955)

> "Mr. Cheim, I do not ordinarily hit weak old men lying on their deathbeds, but you will have a better chance of living to an even riper state of cantankerous senility if you will kindly quit swearing at me." –*The Cheim Manuscript* (1969)

Prather's Shell Scott series was enormously successful. Over a thirty year period, the series sold more than 40 million copies, numbering nearly 35 titles. During the mid-sixties, Shell Scott had his own digest, *Shell Scott's Mystery Magazine*.

All but a handful of entries in the series were paperback originals, first for Gold Medal and later for Pocket Books. Astonishingly, Shell Scott never made it to the big or small screen, which is a shame; he would have fit in perfectly with "swinging '60's" PI and cop shows such as *Peter Gunn* or *Burke's Law*. According to Prather, options were taken but all deals ultimately fell through.

**Further Reading:**
CASE OF THE VANISHING BEAUTY (1950)
BODIES IN BEDLAM (1951)
EVERYBODY HAD A GUN (1951)          WAY OF A WANTON (1952)
LIE DOWN, KILLER (1952)                  DARLING, IT'S DEATH (1952)
RIDE A HIGH HORSE (1953; as TOO MANY CROOKS, 1956)
ALWAYS LEAVE 'EM DYING (1954)     STRIP FOR MURDER (1955)
THE WAILING FRAIL (1956)                SLAB HAPPY (1958)
TAKE A MURDER, DARLING (1958)     OVER HER DEAD BODY (1959)
DOUBLE IN TROUBLE (1959, with Stephen Marlowe)
DANCE WITH THE DEAD (1960)
DIG THAT CRAZY GRAVE (1961)
KILL THE CLOWN (1962)
DEAD HEAT (1963)
JOKER IN THE DECK (1964)
THE COCKEYED CORPSE (1964)
THE TROJAN HEARSE (1964)
KILL HIM TWICE (1965)
DEAD MAN'S WALK (1965)
THE MEANDERING CORPSE (1965)
THE KUBLA KHAN CAPER (1966)
GAT HEAT (1967)
THE CHEIM MANUSCRIPT (1969)
DEAD BANG (1971)
THE SWEET RIDE (1972)
THE SURE THING (1965)
THE AMBER EFFECT (1986)
SHELLSHOCK (1987)

------------------------------------------------------------

**If you like Richard S. Prather,** you might like: Stephen Marlowe, Robert Leslie Bellem

# Ellery Queen

(pseudonym of Manfred B. Lee and Frederic Dannay, original names Manfred Lepofsky and Daniel Nathan, respectively; also wrote as Barnaby Ross, Daniel Nathan (Dannay only). Manfred B. Lee, born 1905, Brooklyn, New York. Died Roxbury, Connecticut, 1971. Frederic Dannay born 1905, Brooklyn, New York. Died White Plains, New York, 1982.

  First cousins Manfred B. Lee and Frederic Dannay took on the name of "Ellery Queen" in order to write a novel and submit it to a contest sponsored by *McClure's* magazine. Told initially they'd won the $7500 prize, the magazine changed hands and the prize was awarded to someone else. But the careers of the most successful collaborating mystery writing team were born.

Proponents of the "fair play" mystery, where all the clues necessary to solve the crime were present in the story, they named their protagonist the same as their pseudonym, "Ellery Queen," and made him a writer as well as an amateur detective. Ellery frequently helped his father on cases, who was a "real life" police inspector.

Frequently stopping the action to query the reader and ask if they could solve the puzzle, the cousins took this technique into their radio series, as well, usually stumping the celebrity guest. The radio show began in 1939 and ran for nine years, appearing after the first two Queen films were released in 1935 (*The Spanish Cape Mystery* with Donald Cook starring) and 1937 (*The Mandarin Mystery* with Eddie Quillan). Beginning with 1941's *Ellery Queen, Master Detective*, Ralph Bellamy took over the role of Ellery and continued for three more films, before William Gargan took over for the next trio. In 1972, Orson Welles starred in *Ten Days' Wonder*, based on a Queen novel but not featuring Ellery himself.

There were a number of television adaptations as well, culminating in perhaps the best onscreen presentation of Ellery Queen, a show that ran for one season in 1975 starring Jim Hutton as Ellery and veteran actor David Wayne as his father, Inspector Queen. The first episode was based on one of the novels but the rest were based mostly on stories from the radio series, even going so far as reviving the "challenge to the reader," where the action is paused as Ellery gives the audience an opportunity to figure out the solution before he reveals his own.

The character of Queen changed somewhat over the years, starting with Ellery being portrayed as more of an effete sophisticate, an upgraded version of S. S. Van Dine's popular "Philo Vance" character. Later Ellery became more accessible as the books were tailored somewhat to the cousins' perceptions of the wants of the slick magazines, as well as those of the Hollywood studios. Still later, the books contained more allegory and peered deeper into the characters' personalities. The last books were lighter and re-used some of the themes and motifs of the earlier stories.

In addition to the "Ellery Queen" series, Lee and Dannay adopted the name "Barnaby Ross" and wrote four books about an actor/detective called "Drury Lane." Under his own name, Daniel Nathan, Fred Dannay wrote the autobiographical novel *The Golden Summer* (1953).

In 1933 Dannay and Lee started a mystery magazine called *Mystery League* that lasted only four issues before the publisher went under. After a long convalescence from a car accident that nearly killed Dannay, the cousins tried again in 1941 with *Ellery Queen's Mystery Magazine*. While Manny Lee stayed out west to concentrate on the radio program, Dannay moved east to edit the magazine, which he did until shortly before his death in 1982.

Eventually Lee moved back east as well, partially to try to improve the cousins' working relationship. As successful and prosperous as they were publicly, privately the two men were constantly at odds, often viciously so. Neither Dannay nor Lee could work well without the other and their relationship was marred with constant fighting and misunderstandings. The only exceptions were the one autobiographical novel by Dannay (*The Golden Summer*) and a short story by Manny Lee from 1948, "The Dauphin's Doll." Each cousin seemed to resent their dependence on the other, but neither had an answer for it, making them competitors as much as collaborators, according to Dannay. This lasted all the way up to the time of Lee's premature death from heart attack in 1971.

Their usual way of working was that Dannay would create detailed outlines of many thousands of words and ship them off to Lee. Manny would then take these blueprints and try to realize Fred's vision in novel form, but often finding technical issues or other points he wanted to address. This is what led to much of the conflict between the cousins. For a period, Lee became unable to write, afflicted with a terrible case of writer's block, and Dannay farmed his outlines out to a number of other authors for completion, among them Theodore Sturgeon, Avram Davidson and Fletcher Flora.

The influence the two men exerted on the crime and mystery field is still felt to this day. From the excellence of many of their books, to the establishment of their pseudonym and protagonist in Hollywood, radio and TV, to their accomplishments helping to found the Mystery Writers of America and championing the works and careers of many new writers,

Lee and Dannay had as great an impact on the genre as any one, or any two, people. As scholars, editors, anthologists, collectors and proponents of the literature they loved so much, both men deserve to live on in the annals of literary history.

**Further Reading:**
*Ellery Queen series:*
THE ROMAN HAT MYSTERY (1929)
THE GREEK COFFIN MYSTERY (1932)
THE EGYPTIAN CROSS MYSTERY (1933)
THE CHINESE ORANGE MYSTERY (1934)
THE SPANISH CAPE MYSTERY (1935)
THE FOUR OF HEARTS (1938)
CALAMITY TOWN (1942)
TEN DAYS' WONDER (1948)
CAT OF MANY TAILS (1949)
DOUBLE, DOUBLE (1958)
THE ORIGIN OF EVIL (1951)
THE FINISHING STROKE (1958)
AND ON THE EIGHT DAY (1964)
A FINE AND PRIVATE PLACE (1971)

*Drury Lane series (complete):*
THE TRAGEDY OF X (1932)
THE TRAGEDY OF Y (1932)
THE TRAGEDY OF Z (1933)
DRURY LANE'S LAST CASE (1933)

*Non-series novels:*
THE GLASS VILLAGE (1954)
COP OUT (1969)

**As Daniel Nathan (Fredric Dannay only)**
THE GOLDEN SUMMER (1953)

---

**If you like Ellery Queen,** you might like: S. S. Van Dine, Anthony Boucher

# Peter Rabe

(also wrote as Marco Malaponte, J. T. MacCargo). Born Peter Rabinowitsch in
Halle, Germany, 1921. Immigrated to America in 1938. Died in Atascadero,
California, 1990.

What do the Gold Medal crime novel *Kill The Boss Good-by*
and the textbook *Psychotherapy from the Center: A
Humanistic View of Change and of Growth* have in common?
They were both written by the same man, Peter
Rabe.
Rabe was a full fledged PhD, earning his doctorate
in psychology in Cleveland, Ohio. He became interested
in crime novels and, amazingly, his first three books in
the genre were all snatched up by Gold Medal and published the same
year, 1955. They were *Stop This Man!*, *Benny Muscles In* and *A Shroud for Jesso*.
Rabe became a Gold Medal favorite, penning twenty-two novels for the
paperback publisher.

For a good chunk of his career, Rabe wrote about gangsters in organized crime syndicates. His writing about these kinds of men had a certain
level of authenticity, as Rabe had spent a substantial amount of time in
Europe soon after WWII, observing the kind of black market activities
shown in movies such as *The Third Man*. One of his two series characters,
Daniel Port, who first appears in *Dig My Grave Deep* (1956), is a gangster who
uses both his guts and his brains to maneuver his way out of the syndicate
and survive. The remaining Port novels are *The Out is Death* (1957), *It's My
Funeral* (1957), *The Cut Of The Whip* (1958), *Bring Me Another Corpse* (1958) and
*Time Enough to Die* (1959). Rabe's prose style is hardboiled but understated,
somewhat akin to the work of Dashiell Hammett and W. R. Burnett, and
his work in psychology undoubtedly helped him delve into the minds of
his brutal, warped characters.

Rabe also wrote a series featuring Manny DeWitt, a lawyer for a multi-
national industrial firm whose job leads him into espionage adventures
and exotic locales. The DeWitt novels are *Girl in a Brass Bed* (1965), *The Spy
Who was Three Feet Tall* (1966), and *Code Name Gadget* (1967). Rabe wrote the
DeWitt novels with a more humorous approach than that of his other novels. The DeWitt novels aren't quite parodies of James Bond, but Rabe is certainly having fun with the spy genre.

Rabe wrote several standalone novels. Notable examples include *A
House in Naples* (1956), *Anatomy of a Killer* (1960, not to be confused with
*Anatomy of a Murder*) and *The Box* (1962). *A House in Naples* was filmed in 1970,
co-starring Jake "The Raging Bull" LaMotta.

During the early 1960's Rabe experienced health problems and needed quick cash, so he wrote two books for Beacon, an "adults only" publisher, using the pseudonym Marco Malaponte—*Her High School Lover* (1962) and *New Man in the House* (1962).

He wrote two novelizations of the *Mannix* TV series under the house name "J. T. MacCargo."

If having a doctorate in psychology and writing hardboiled gangster novels wasn't incongruous enough, Rabe also received story credit for two episodes of the campy 1960's *Batman* TV show—episode #81, "The Joker's Last Laugh," and #82, "The Joker's Epitaph." (Rabe was friends with the show's head writer, Lorenzo Semple, Jr.)

**Further Reading:**
*Daniel Port series (complete):*
DIG MY GRAVE DEEP (1956)          IT'S MY FUNERAL (1957)
THE CUT OF THE WHIP (1958)        THE OUT IS DEATH (1957)
BRING ME ANOTHER CORPSE (1959)
TIME ENOUGH TO DIE (1959)

*Manny DeWitt series (complete):*
GIRL IN A BIG BRASS BED (1965)
THE SPY WHO WAS THREE FEET TALL (1966)
CODE NAME GADGET (1967)

BENNY MUSCLES IN (1955)
A SHROUD FOR JESSO (1955)
STOP THIS MAN! (1955)
A HOUSE IN NAPLES (1956)
KILL THE BOSS GOOD-BY (1956)
JOURNEY INTO TERROR (1957)
ANATOMY OF A KILLER (1960)
MURDER ME FOR NICKELS (1960)
MY LOVELY EXECUTIONER (1960)
THE BOX (1962)
PSYCHOTHERAPY FROM THE CENTER: A HUMANISTIC VIEW OF CHANGE AND OF GROWTH (1969, non-fiction)

**As Marco Malaponte**
HER HIGH SCHOOL LOVER (1962)
NEW MAN IN THE HOUSE (1962)

---

**If you like Peter Rabe,** you might like: W. R. Burnett, Dashiell Hammett, Patricia Highsmith

# Helen Reilly

(born Helen Kieran; also wrote as Kieran Abbey). Born in New York, New York, 1891. Died in 1962.

 Helen Reilly joins Ed McBain and Jonathan Craig in writing an acclaimed series of police procedurals. Of her thirty year series featuring Inspector Christopher McKee, critic Howard Haycraft said "they were among the most convincing that have been composed on the premise of actual police procedure."

Reilly grew up in New York City. She came from a well educated family: her father, Dr. James Kieran, was president of Hunter College, and her brother, John, was a panelist on the radio quiz show, *Information Please*.

Her series character, Lieutenant Christopher McKee, head of the Manhattan Homicide Squad, is a short, thick Scotsman who wears tweeds and eyeglasses. He combines seasoned hunches with rigorous investigatory work. The series has a continuing cast of characters: ambitious District Attorney Dwyer; Dr. Fernandez, the assistant medical examiner; Lucy Sturm, a nurse and undercover agent; and Inspector Todhunter, an unobtrusive, seemingly innocuous, but clever detective.

The series began in 1930 with *The Diamond Feather* (1930), and lasted for thirty-one titles, until 1962's *The Day She Died*.

**Further Reading:**
THE THIRTY-FIRST BULLFINCH (1930)
MAN WITH THE PAINTED HEAD (1931)
MURDER IN THE MEWS (1931)
THE DOLL'S TRUNK MURDER (1932)
THE LINE-UP (1934)
McKEE OF CENTER STREET (1934)
DEAD MAN CONTROL (1936)
MR. SMITH'S HAT (1936)
THE FILE ON RUFUS RAY (1937)
ALL CONCERNED NOTIFIED (1939)
DEAD FOR A DUCAT (1939)
DEATH DEMANDS AN AUDIENCE (1940)
MURDER IN SHINBONE ALLEY (1940)
THE DEAD CAN TELL (1940)
MOURNED ON SUNDAY (1941)
THREE WOMEN IN BLACK (1941)
NAME YOUR POISON (1942)

THE OPENING DOOR (1944)
MURDER ON ANGLER'S ISLAND (1945)
THE SILVER LEOPARD (1946)
THE FARMHOUSE (1947)
STAIRCASE 4 (1949)
MURDER AT ARROWAYS (1950)
LAMENT FOR THE BRIDE (1951)
THE DOUBLE MAN (1952)
THE VELVET HAND (1953)
TELL HER IT'S MURDER (1954)
COMPARTMENT K (1955)
THE CANVAS DAGGER (1956)
DING DONG BELL (1958)
NOT ME, INSPECTOR (1959)
FOLLOW ME (1960)
CERTAIN SLEEP (1961)
THE DAY SHE DIED (1962)

---

**If you like Helen Reilly,** you might like: Jonathan Craig, Ed McBain

# Craig Rice

(pseudonym for Georgiana Ann Randolph Walker Craig; also wrote as Ruth Malone, Daphne Sanders, Michael Venning; ghost wrote for George Sanders and Gypsy Rose Lee). Born in Chicago, Illinois, 1908. Died in Los Angeles County, California, 1957.

Georgiana Ann Randolph, under her Craig Rice pseudonym, wrote in the "screwball noir" school of mystery fiction, à la Jonathan Latimer's Bill Crane and company, and Dashiell Hammett's Nick and Nora Charles. Her books blended zany characters, wacky plots, macabre humor and elements of surrealism.

Rice's debut novel, *8 Faces at 3* (1939), was the first of her 12 novel series featuring the crew of John J. Malone and Jake and Helene Justus. John J. Malone, technically, is "Chicago's noisiest and most noted criminal lawyer." But in actuality, he is much more interested (when not chasing booze or broads) in amateur sleuthing, along with friends and helpmates Jake and Helene Justus. Appearance wise, Malone is short and pudgy; he has a reddish face and unkempt hair. He generally wears a suit which looks like he slept in it and his vest is smudged with cigar ashes. He inventively keeps the bottles of liquor in his office stashed away in filing cabinets labeled "Confidential," "Unanswered Correspondence" and "Emergency." His favorite drink is rye, although he doesn't mind an occasional shot of gin with a beer chaser. Malone can be found far more easily in Joe The Angel's City Hall Bar than in any courtroom. Jake Justus works as a press agent, but is often unemployed. Luckily, he is married to Helene, a beautiful blonde heiress.

Some of the wackier plot elements can be found in *The Big Midget Murders* (1942), where a night club mimic is strangled with a noose made from eleven unmatched silk stockings, and Jake Justus has to hide the oversized corpse in a bass fiddle case; *Having Wonderful Crime* (1943), where the head of a corpse doesn't match the body; *Trial By Fury* (1941), where an ex-senator is assassinated right in the middle of a large crowd; and *The Fourth Postman* (1948), where three postmen are murdered in the same Chicago alleyway.

Rice also wrote short stories featuring Malone. Many of these were collected in *The Name is Malone* (1958) and *People vs. Withers and Malone* (1963, co-written with "Hildegarde Withers" creator and fellow mystery writer, Stuart Palmer).

Rice also wrote 2½ books (the "half" to be explained shortly), featuring the team of Bingo Riggs and Handsome Kusak. These stories took the tone of farce and frenzy to even greater heights of comic insanity. Riggs and

Kusak are a pair of con men who, in their masquerade as traveling photographers, are interested in bilking their customers for big bucks. The problem for Riggs and Kusak is that they either end up liking their marks or getting scammed themselves. Even more problematic, corpses start piling up in the most unusual places. The three Riggs-Kusak books are *The Sunday Pigeon Murders* (1942), *The Thursday Turkey Murders* (1943) and *The April Robin Murders* (1958, the second half of this book was written by crime writer Ed McBain after Rice's relatively early death).

Rice also wrote an excellent standalone novel that was loosely based on herself and her three children, titled *Home Sweet Homicide* (1944), about a mystery writer whose children try to solve a murder. It was made into a movie in 1946, featuring stand out performances by ten year-old Dean Stockwell as the son, and fifteen year-old Peggy Ann Garner as the oldest daughter. Rice wrote non-fiction, as well: a series of true crime articles were collected in *45 Murders: A Collection of True Crime Stories* (1953).

Under the name Daphne Sanders she wrote *To Catch a Thief* (1943, no relation to the Hitchcock film, which was based on a novel by David Dodge). As Michael Venning, she write three books about a grim, moody, "gray little" private detective named Melville Fairr: *The Man Who Slept All Day* (1942), *Murder Through the Looking Glass* (1943) and *Jethro Hammer* (1944). As Ruth Malone, she wrote a few stories for *Mike Shayne Mystery Magazine*.

As a ghostwriter, Rice wrote two books for "ecdysiast" (aka, stripper) Gypsy Rose Lee: *The G-String Murders* (1941, aka *Lady of Burlesque*) and *Mother Finds a Body* (1942). She also co-ghosted a book for actor George Sanders: *Crime On My Hands* (1944).

Further Reading:
*John J. Malone series:*
8 FACES AT 3 (1939)
THE CORPSE STEPS OUT (1940)
THE RIGHT MURDER (1941)
TRIAL BY FURY (1941)
THE BIG MIDGET MURDERS (1942)
HAVING WONDERFUL CRIME (1944)
THE LUCKY STIFF (1945)
THE FOURTH POSTMAN (1948)
KNOCKED FOR A LOOP (1957)
MY KINGDOM FOR A HEARSE (1957)
THE NAME IS MALONE (1958, short stories)

*Bingo Riggs and Handsome Kusak series:*
THE SUNDAY PIGEON MURDERS (1942)
THE THURSDAY TURKEY URDERS (1943)
THE APRIL ROBIN MURDERS (1958, completed by Ed McBain)

THE G-STRING MURDERS (1941, ghostwritten for Gypsy Rose Lee)
CRIME ON MY HANDS (1944, ghostwritten for George Sanders)
HOME SWEET HOMICIDE (1944)
45 MURDERS: A COLLECTION OF TRUE CRIME STORIES (1952, non-fiction)
PEOPLE VS. WITHERS AND MALONE (1963, short stories, with Stuart Palmer)

---

**If you like Craig Rice,** you might like: Jonathan Latimer, Richard Powell, Donald E. Westlake, Gregory Mcdonald

# *Mike Roscoe*

(a team of two writers, John Roscoe and Mike Ruso). Birth and death dates unknown.

John Roscoe and Mike Ruso were a pair of writers who jumped on the Mike Hammer express during the 1950's—with one significant difference. They both actually *were* private detectives, who met while working at the Hargrave Detective Agency in Kansas City.

Between 1952 and 1958, Roscoe and Ruso wrote five paperback originals featuring rough and tumble PI, Johnny April. The books were notable for their terse prose. In this snippet from *Riddle Me This* (1952), Johnny and his secretary, Sandy, discuss the death of Johnny's friend, Paul:

> Sandy came in.
> "How badly—"
> "Dead."
> "Oh. Oh, Johnny, I'm sorry— I'm—"
> "Forget it. A man is born. He lives. He dies. Today they wanted Paul. Tomorrow some other guy will get his retirement papers."

An unusual aspect of the Roscoe PI novels is their attempt to be socially conscious. In *Riddle Me This*, Paul Benson is a young, black private detective who Johnny April had trained and helped get started in the PI business. When Benson is murdered, Johnny sets out to avenge his death, and his quest leads him down various segregated avenues in contemporary Kansas City. Johnny delivers a swift punch in the nose to anyone who refers to Benson using racially derogatory terms.

Johnny April's other tough, fast paced adventures are: *Death is a Round Black Ball* (1952), *Slice of Hell* (1954), *One Tear for My Grave* (1955) and *The Midnight Eye* (1958).

Author and critic Anthony Boucher called Johnny April "the only genuine private eye I know."

**Further Reading:**
*Johnny April series (complete):*
DEATH IS A ROUND BLACK BALL (1952)
RIDDLE ME THIS (1952)
SLICE OF HELL (1954)
ONE TEAR FOR MY GRAVE (1955)
THE MIDNIGHT EYE (1958)

---

**If you like Mike Roscoe,** you might like: Mickey Spillane, Ed Lacy

# Sax Rohmer

(born Arthur Henry Sarsfield Ward). Born in Birmingham, England, 1883. Died in White Plains, New York, 1959.

During the 1930's and '40's there was a type of story, very popular in the pulp magazines, known as the "yellow menace" or "yellow peril" story. These were tales where a ruthless and cunning Asian tried to invade the Western world and work his malevolent machinations within America's numerous Chinatown districts. The stories had titles such as, "Tong Torture," "Corpses in Chinatown" and "Blood on the Buddha."

There were even two pulps devoted exclusively to the yellow menace: *The Mysterious Wu Fang* and *Dr. Yen Sin*. The popularity of yellow menace stories can almost exclusively be attributed to one man and to one creation: an Englishman named Arthur Henry Ward, aka Sax Rohmer, and his super-villain supreme, the insidious Dr. Fu Manchu. And while Rohmer wasn't the first to pen a yellow menace story, judging by sales accounts, he was certainly the best.

Rohmer began his career when he was twenty years old, moving to London and writing newspaper articles and short stories. From the beginning, Rohmer's interests centered around the foreign, the occult, the outré. As a newspaper reporter, Rohmer also learned about London's Chinatown district.

Rohmer's first Fu Manchu novel was *The Mystery of Dr. Fu Manchu* (1913, U.S. title *The Insidious Dr. Fu Manchu*). Rohmer described Fu Manchu thusly: "Imagine a person, tall, lean and feline, high-shouldered, with a brow like Shakespeare and a face like Satan...one giant intellect, with all the resources of science past and present...Imagine that awful being, and you have a mental picture of Dr. Fu Manchu, the yellow peril incarnate in one man."

Fu Manchu, rather than using guns or other conventional weapons to achieve and maintain his power, preferred such exotic items as pythons, deadly spiders and ancient viruses and poisons. Fu Manchu's arch-enemies were Sir Denis Nayland Smith (a commissioner in the British government) and Dr. Petrie, who were in the Sherlock Holmes and Dr. Watson tradition, with Dr. Petrie serving as narrator of the stories. Much like Dashiell Hammett, Paul Cain and other American pulp writers, the Fu Manchu books were first serialized in pulp-style magazines, and only afterward assembled as novels.

Rohmer killed off Fu Manchu at the end of the third Fu Manchu novel, *The Si-Fan Mysteries* (1917, U.S. title *The Hand of Fu Manchu*), but the character was so popular that he was resurrected in *Daughter of Fu Manchu* (1931). The Fu Manchu stories reached the height of their popularity during the 1930's and '40's and made Rohmer wealthy and internationally famous. Radio adaptations, movies and a television series insured that the character of Fu Manchu would successfully invade American pop culture. Notable titles from this period include *President Fu Manchu* (1936), where Fu Manchu is the power behind a U.S. presidential candidate (shades of *The Manchurian Candidate*); *The Drums of Fu Manchu* (1939), where Fu Manchu fights a fascist dictator with the Hitleresque name "Rudolph Adlon"; and *The Island of Fu Manchu* (1941). Some of these later adventures were narrated in the third person, rather than by Dr. Petrie.

Incredibly prolific, Rohmer also wrote light-hearted songs and comedy sketches for British music hall performers, an early book with a drug trafficking theme (*Dope*, 1919), a series of stories about a "psychic detective" named Morris Klaw and a female version of Fu Manchu named Sumuru.

On the silver screen Fu Manchu has appeared, most famously, in his own serial, *The Drums of Fu Manchu* (1940); a movie, *The Mask of Fu Manchu* (1932), with Boris Karloff playing the wicked Doctor; a series of five movies starring Christopher Lee, *The Face of Fu Manchu* (1965), *The Brides of Fu Manchu* (1966), *The Vengeance of Fu Manchu* (1967), *The Blood of Fu Manchu* (1968) and *The Castle of Fu Manchu* (1969); and in Peter Sellers' last film, the spoof *The Fiendish Plot of Dr. Fu Manchu* (1980).

The Fu Manchu stories have never been out of print and continue to attract readers to this day, although they are controversial and have been charged with promoting negative racial stereotypes.

Further Reading:
*Fu Manchu series:*
THE MYSTERY OF DR. FU-MANCHU (1913, U.S. title,
  THE INSIDIOUS DR. FU-MANCHU)
THE DEVIL DOCTOR (1916, U.S. title, THE RETURN OF DR. FU-MANCHU)
THE SI-FAN MYSTERIES (1917, U.S. title, THE HAND OF FU-MANCHU)
THE DAUGHTER OF FU-MANCHU (1931)
THE MASK OF FU-MANCHU (1932)
THE BRIDE OF FU-MANCHU (1933)
THE TRAIL OF FU-MANCHU (1934)
PRESIDENT FU-MANCHU (1936)
THE DRUMS OF FU-MANCHU (1939)
THE ISLAND OF FU-MANCHU (1941)
THE SHADOW OF FU-MANCHU (1948)
RE-ENTER: FU-MANCHU (1957)
EMPORER FU-MANCHU (1959)

THE YELLOW CLAW (1915)
DOPE (1919)
TALES OF CHINATOWN (1922)
THE EMPEROR OF AMERICA (1929)
THE SINS OF SUMURU (1950, U.S. title, NUDE IN MINK)
THE SLAVES OF SUMURU (1951, U.S. title, SUMURU)
VIRGIN IN FLAMES (1952, U.S. title, THE FIRE GODDESS)
SAND AND SATIN (1954, U.S. title, RETURN OF SUMURU)

---

**If you like Sax Rohmer,** you might like: Dan Cushman, Kendell Foster
Crossen

## Charles Runyon

(born Charles West Runyon; also wrote as Ellery Queen, Charles Runyon Jr., Charles W. Runyon, Mark West, Mark Starr). Born June 9, 1928, in Sheridan, Missouri.

 Charles Runyon wrote both crime novels and science fiction, plus at least one mainstream novel, *Gypsy King* (1979). He is best known for *The Prettiest Girl I Ever Killed* (1965), which is often compared to the works of Jim Thompson, and *Power Kill* (1972), which was nominated for the Edgar Allan Poe Award from the Mystery Writers of America.

Runyon, the son of two school teachers, was educated at the University of Missouri, Indiana University and University of Munich. He ran away from home at age 16 and worked on a ranch in West Texas. He served in the military twice during the Korean War, in 1948-50 and 1951-53, then worked as a newspaper reporter in Columbus, Missouri, and an industrial editor for Standard Oil Company from 1957 to 1960.

His first published novel was *Anatomy of Violence* (1960), published as a paperback original by Ace Books. This established Runyon as an up and coming writer of psychological suspense with his tale of a violated beauty queen who seeks vengeance on her perpetrator. This novel was quickly followed by three pseudonymous works by "Mark West" for Beacon Books and the adult softcore sex market—*Office Affair* (1961), *His Boss's Wife* (1962) and *Object of Lust* (1962)—before Runyon continued with more crime novels under his own name for Fawcett's Gold Medal line. These were books like *Color Him Dead* (1963), *The Black Moth* (1967), *No Place to Hide* (1970) and *To Kill a Dead Man* (1976).

Adding his middle initial "W" to his name, Runyon began to vary his output in 1966 with a war novel for Ace (*The Bloody Jungle*, 1966); SF novels for Doubleday (*Pigworld*, 1971, and *I, Weapon*, 1974) and Curtis Books (*Ames Holbrook, Deity*, 1972). He wrote a horror novel for Avon (*Soulmate*, 1974) and another psycho thriller for Pyramid (*Kiss the Girls and Make Them Die*, 1977). In addition he penned three Ellery Queen mysteries—*The Last Score* (1964), *The Killer Touch* (1965) and *Kiss and Kill* (1969). He also wrote short stories, contributing to magazines like *Manhunt*, *Mike Shayne Mystery Magazine*, *Alfred Hitchcock's Mystery Magazine*, *Super-Science Fiction*, *Fantastic*, *Worlds of If* and *The Magazine of Fantasy & Science Fiction*.

Runyon preferred his science fiction novels over his crime thrillers since SF gave him a chance to expand his ideas on the future of the human race at a time when the New Wave and the drug culture were predominant. *I, Weapon* remains a favorite of many 1970's SF fans.

Interestingly enough, only his science fiction was published in hardback. Otherwise, Runyon primarily remained a paperback author. As a crime fiction writer, he specialized in stories about psychopaths and killers next door. In 1967 his own brother was murdered, and after that Runyon began to write fewer crime novels, concentrating instead on his SF output, at times achieving a pre-cyberpunk sensibility.

In 1979, Jove published what the author thought would be his breakout book, *Gypsy King* (1979), about a handsome young gypsy who creates a drug empire that raises him to the heights of wealth and power. That success did not come, and instead of breaking out Runyon, this book became his last published work. After that, rumors that he had died in 1987 began to circulate. One of his previous novels had the distinction of being bought ˙ by Lancer Books (as *Dorian-7*, retitled by the publisher as *Something Wicked*) right before the publisher went out of business, never to be published at all. Discouraged by the vagaries of the marketplace, he took a break from writing, and earned a Master's degree in Creative Writing from the University of Missouri. There then followed a three year stint working in workshops. Runyon later returned to Texas with his wife, Ruth, and began teaching writing and English.

Runyon has the distinction of having two of his Gold Medal thrillers—*The Death Cycle* (1963) and *The Prettiest Girl I Ever Killed*—optioned for films. Stark House Press reprinted *The Prettiest Girl* in 2007. The author, now retired, continues to live in Lampasas, Texas.

**Further Reading:**
THE ANATOMY OF VIOLENCE (1960)
COLOR HIM DEAD (1963)
THE DEATH CYCLE (1963)
THE PRETTIEST GIRL I EVER KILLED (1965)
THE BLACK MOTH (1967)
NO PLACE TO HIDE (1970)
POWER KILL (1972)

---

**If you like Charles Runyon,** you might like: Dan J. Marlowe, Donald Hamilton, Wade Miller

## *Richard Sale*

(also wrote as Bernard Elas, John St. John). Born in New York City, New York, 1903. Died in Los Angeles, California, 1993.

Although many pulp writers from the 1930's and '40's went to Hollywood to become screenwriters, Richard Sale is the only such writer who also became a movie director, helming (among other movies) no less a popular success than *Gentleman Marry Brunettes*, starring Jane Russell.

Sale's interest in writing developed early. As a teenager, he sold poems to the *New York Herald-Tribune*, and while still a journalism student at Washington and Lee University in Virginia during the early 1930's, he started sending stories to magazines, selling his first to *College Stories* for $100, excellent money during those depression-era days. Sale left college before graduating and worked for New York newspapers by day, and wrote fiction by night. He quickly caught on to the frenetic pace it took to write pulp stories—both in terms of the amount of words he'd need to pound out to make a decent living, and in terms of the stories' fast paced action. Between 1933-44, he wrote approximately 200 stories for such pulps as *Detective Fiction Weekly, Argosy, Thrilling Detective, Secret Agent "X," The Shadow, Public Enemy, All American Fiction, Thrilling Detective* and *Double Detective*, among others.

Sale's novels showed a penchant for the bizarre. His first book, *Not Too Narrow, Not Too Deep* (1936), combined hardboiled characters, an adventure style plot and religious evangelism. The story is about a ragtag group of convicts attempting to escape a Devil's Island-type penal colony—among their lot are rapists, psychopaths, and a mysterious, enigmatic religious figure. In 1940, the book was made into an "A" production, the title changed to *Strange Cargo*, starring Clark Gable, Joan Crawford and Peter Lorre. The film was a powerful drama, successful both with the critics and at the box office.

Sale's other novels continued his trend to introduce bizarre elements into a mystery story. *Lazarus #7* (1942), set in Hollywood, includes leprosy, a doctor who's trying to raise animals from the dead and a group of "industry" people trying to cover up a murder in order to avoid bad publicity. *Passing Strange* (1942) is the story of a surgeon who's fatally shot while performing a Cesarean section on an Oscar winner, and the attendant hoopla created by Hollywood columnists and newspaper reporters. *Benefit Performance* (1946) is another Hollywood murder mystery, this time revolving around tinseltown's glamorous nightlife.

Sale went to Hollywood in 1946 and wrote westerns (*A Ticket to Tomahawk*, 1950), comedies (*Mr. Belvedere Goes To College*, 1949) and western-comedies (*The Dude Goes West*, 1948). He also wrote the tightly plotted film noir *Suddenly* (1954, starring Frank Sinatra and Sterling Hayden), one of the earliest movies about an assassin on a mission to kill the President.

As mentioned previously, besides writing screenplays for Hollywood, Sale was also a director, helming twelve movies, beginning with *Spoilers of the North* (1947) and ending with *Abandon Ship* (1957). He also directed TV episodes of *Yancy Derringer* and *The High Chaparral* during the 1950's and '60's.

In later years, Sale intermittently returned to novels: *The Oscar* (1963), an insider's exposé of the sleazy side of Hollywood, was later made into an over the top, *Valley Of The Dolls*-type movie starring Elke Summer; *For The President's Eyes Only* (1971) was a well-received spy story.

**Further Reading:**
NOT TOO NARROW, NOT TOO DEEP (1936)
LAZARUS NO. 7 (1942; as LAZARUS MURDER SEVEN, 1943)
PASSING STRANGE (1942)
SAILOR, TAKE WARNING (1942)
BENEFIT PERFORMANCE (1946)
THE OSCAR (1963)
FOR THE PRESIDENT'S EYES ONLY (1971)

---

**If you like Richard Sale,** you might like: John D. MacDonald, Kendell Foster Crossen, Lester Dent

# Douglas Sanderson

(born Ronald Douglas Sanderson; also wrote as Martin Brett, Malcolm Douglas).
Born in Kent, England, 1920. Died in Spain, 2002.

 Ronald Douglas Sanderson wrote nearly two dozen hardboiled crime paperbacks during the '50's and '60's for Gold Medal, Avon and Dodd, Mead. According to Kevin Burton Smith, Thrilling Detective.com webmaster:

"Sanderson's specialty was a sort of baroque noir. His books were twitchy, neurotic pulp fiction; jacked-up kaleidoscopic whirls of desperate, gloriously flawed characters, audacious coincidence and almost impressionistic action scenes punctuated by jarring explosions of violence and sex that would only finally make sense at the very end. And sometimes not even then." (Introduction to *Pure Sweet Hell* and *Catch A Fallen Starlet*, Stark House Press, 2004)

Sanderson grew up in England and joined the RAF during WWII. He wrote, performed and directed short theatrical comedies for his fellow servicemen, and also wrote scientific articles for an RAF magazine which was edited by none other than *No Orchids for Miss Blandish* author, James Hadley Chase. After the war, Sanderson immigrated to Canada, where he worked as a jewelry salesman, in a factory and as a cabaret singer. His first book was *Dark Passions Subdue* (1953), a literary novel dealing with homosexuality, criticizing the hypocrisy and Puritanism within Montreal high society.

Sanderson's first crime novel was *Exit in Green* (1953), also set in Canada, and is not as hardboiled as his forthcoming "Garfin" books, nor as feverish as *Dark Passions Subdued* but is worth mentioning as a transitional novel. Sanderson's second crime novel, *Hot Freeze* (1954, written as by Martin Brett), featured Mike Garfin, an obsessive, driven, angry, Montreal-based private eye who also appeared in *The Darker Traffic* (1954) and *A Dum-Dum for the President* (1961). *Pure Sweet Hell* (1957, written as by Malcolm Douglas) is a non-series book about an undercover agent's attempt to break up a drug network in Spain. In *Catch a Fallen Starlet* (1960), an alcoholic Hollywood screenwriter, Al Dufferin, tries to get back on track by accepting a writing assignment with a hack director attempting his own comeback. But the director ends up dead, and Dufferin makes a convenient fall guy.

Sanderson's work has been particularly lauded in France; his stories have been embraced for their bleak, existential outlook. Fifteen of his novels were published as part of the prestigious Serie Noire series by Gallimard in France.

Later in life, Sanderson moved his family to the city of Alicante in Spain, where his son John still lives and works.

**Further Reading:**
DARK PASSIONS SUBDUE (US,1952)
FINAL RUN (UK,1956) aka FLEE FROM TERROR (US,1957) and UN BOUQUET DE CHARDONS (Fr,1957) both as by Martin Brett
NIGHT OF THE HORNS (UK,1958) aka MURDER COMES CALLING (US,1958) as by Malcolm Douglas
CRY WOLFRAM (UK,1959) aka MARK IT FOR MURDER (US,1959) and LA SEMAINE DE BONTE (Fr,1958) as by Martin Brett
CATCH A FALLEN STARLET (US,1960) aka THE STUBBORN UNLAID and CINEMALEFICES (Fr,1960) as by Martin Brett
LAM TO SLAUGHTER (UK,1964) aka AS-TI VU CARCASSONE? (Fr,1963) as by Martin Brett
BLACK REPRIEVE (UK,1965) aka WHITE MAN DEAD and COUPER CABECHE (Fr,1964) as by Martin Brett
NO CHARGE FOR FRAMING (UK,1969)
A DEAD BULLFIGHTER (UK,1975)

**As Martin Brett**
EXIT IN GREEN (US,1953) re-written as MURDER CAME TUMBLING (UK,1959)
HOT FREEZE (US,1953) aka MON CADAVER AU CANADA (Fr,1955) and HEISSER SCHNEE (Germany, 1975) as by Malcolm Douglas
DARKER TRAFFIC (US,1954) aka BLONDES ARE MY TROUBLE (US,1955) and SALMIGONZESSES (Fr,1956)
FLEE FROM TERROR (US,1957) aka FINAL RUN (UK,1956) and UN BOUQUET DE CHARDONS (Fr, 1957).
THE SHREDS published as SABLES-D'OR-LES-PAINS! (Fr,1958)
THE DEAD CONNECTION published as LA CAME A PAPA (Fr,1961)
A DUM-DUM FOR THE PRESIDENT (UK,1961) aka ESTOCADE AU CANADA (Fr,1961)
SHOUT FOR A KILLER published as CHABANAIS CHEZ LES PACHAS (Fr,1963)
SCORE FOR TWO DEAD published as LE MOINE CONNAIT LA MUSIQUE (Fr,1964)

**As Malcolm Douglas**
PREY BY NIGHT (US,1955) aka A BOULETS ROUGES (Fr,1956) as by Martin Brett
RAIN OF TERROR (US,1955) aka AND ALL FLESH DIED and LE FETE A LA

GRENOUILLE (Fr,1956) as by Martin Brett; and ALPTRAUM AUF ITAL-
IENISCH (Germany, 1975) as by Malcolm Douglas
THE DEADLY DAMES (US,1956) aka DU REBECCA CHEZ LES FEMMES
(Fr,1956) as by Martin Brett
PURE SWEET HELL (US,1957) aka ZUM STERBEN HAT JEDER MAL ZEIT
(Germany, 1975)
MURDER COMES CALLING (US,1958) aka NIGHT OF THE HORNS (UK,1958)
as by Douglas Sanderson; and RUH IN FRIEDEN, LIEBER SCHATZ
(Germany, 1974) as by Malcolm Douglas

-------------------------------------------------------------

If you like Douglas Sanderson, you might like: Mickey Spillane, Cornell
Woolrich, David Goodis, Dan J. Marlowe

# Irving Shulman
Born in Brooklyn, New York, 1913. Died in Sherman Oaks, California, 1995.

Irving Shulman's first novel, *The Amboy Dukes*, was such a sensation it created a whole new genre of paperback fiction, sometimes referred to as "JD lit."

Shulman grew up in a lower class section of Brooklyn, New York. His parents taught him to value education, and he earned a BA at Ohio University and a master's degree at Columbia. He had planned on getting a PhD, but the onset of World War II changed his plans, and he started working for the War Department's troop education program.

During that time, Shulman began to notice a significant change in the American family: while Daddy was on the front lines fighting the Axis and Mommy was in the workplace doing her Rosie the Riveter bit, Junior was hitting the streets and learning how to use a set of brass knuckles and a zip gun.

It was from these observations that Shulman wrote *The Amboy Dukes* (1947).

*The Amboy Dukes* is about a teenage gang called the Dukes, whose turf is Amboy Street. The Dukes hang around on street corners and down in cellars—drinking, robbing, molesting, smoking pot, fighting other gangs and having gangbangs with "debs" (girl members).

Though *The Amboy Dukes* sold over four million copies, the specifics of the book's plot and characters became dwarfed in the groundswell of concern and controversy over "juvenile delinquents," "troubled youth," "youth running wild." It was difficult for adults to believe that children, *their* children, were not only capable of assault, rape and murder, but may even enjoy these pursuits and wear them as a badge of honor. *The Amboy Dukes* was condemned as obscene by the House of Representatives, the mayor of Brooklyn and public school officials.

*The Amboy Dukes* spawned a movie, *City Across the River* (1949), which was financially successful but was a heavily sanitized version of the book. Shulman was hired by Warner Bros. to contribute to the ultimate juvenile delinquent movie, *Rebel Without a Cause* (though he received no screen credit). In a unique hybrid—more than a novelization, yet not quite an original story—he wrote a novel, *Children of the Dark* (1955), based on *Rebel Without A Cause*, making minor changes to the story.

The success of *The Amboy Dukes* was a boon to the burgeoning paperback industry and it spawned a sub-genre of juvenile delinquent-related books with flashy, sensationalistic titles like *D for Delinquent; Teen-Age Terror; The Young Punks; The Little Caesars; Juvenile Jungle; Reefer Girl; Zip-Gun Angels; Go, Man, Go!; Play It Cool* and *1,000,000 Delinquents.*

Shulman wrote two successful sequels to *The Amboy Dukes: Cry Tough* (1949) and *The Big Brokers* (1961), which followed the surviving members of the Dukes into their adult lives.

During the 1960's, Shulman fell several rungs down the literary ladder, and worked on novelizations of Grade Z films like *Platinum High School* and *College Confidential*. His last books were non-fiction (although lacking much accurracy) biographies of Jean Harlow and Rudolph Valentino, written in the popular but melodramatic style of Harold Robbins and Jacqueline Susann.

**Further Reading:**
THE AMBOY DUKES (1947)
CRY TOUGH (1949)
THE BIG BROKERS (1951)
THE SQUARE TRAP (1953)
CHILDREN OF THE DARK (1955)
GOOD DEEDS MUST BE PUNISHED (1955)
CALIBRE (1956)
THE VELVET KNIFE (1959)
THE SHORT END OF THE STICK (1960)
COLLEGE CONFIDENTIAL (1960, movie novelization)
PLATINUM HIGH SCHOOL (1960, movie novelization)
WEST SIDE STORY (1961, movie novelization)
HARLOW (1964, biography)
VALENTINO (1967, biography)

---

**If you like Irving Shulman,** you might like: Hal Ellson, Wenzell Brown

# Bart Spicer

(also wrote as Jay Barbette). Born in Richmond, Virginia, 1918. Died in Tucson, Arizona, 1978.

Bart Spicer is the creator of Carney Wilde, a realistic private eye who is neither hardboiled to the point of caricature, nor soft and sentimental.

Spicer enlisted in the Army during World War II, and when released had achieved the rank of captain. After the war he worked as a journalist and a radio newswriter. He also worked in public relations for Universal Military Training and for the World Affairs Council.

Spicer began the Carney Wilde series with *The Dark Light* (1949). Wilde is a Philadelphia-based PI who occasionally operates in other locations. Throughout the seven novel series, a story arc is presented, covering Wilde's personal and professional evolution: he starts out as a bachelor living in run down surroundings; by the last novel, he is married and owns a successful, well run detective agency. In *The Dark Light*, Wilde is hired by a church deacon to find a missing minister. When the deacon is murdered, Wilde has to deal with the church's wealthy sponsor, investigating a matter they would rather he not investigate. *The Dark Light* was nominated for the Edgar award for Best First Novel.

In *Blues for the Prince* (1950), Spicer exhibits his extensive knowledge of jazz by writing about Wilde's involvement with a group of musicians. In *The Golden Door* (1951), Carney deals with perfume smugglers, illegal immigrants and a seven million dollar inheritance. In *The Long Green* (1952), Wilde travels to Arizona to find a friend's kidnapped daughter. Mystery critic Art Scott writes: "Spicer's Wilde tales are among the very best private-eye novels [of the 1950's] or any decade." (*Twentieth-Century Crime & Mystery Writers*, pg. 976)

Spicer wrote some excellent non-series suspense novels. *The Day of the Dead* (1955) is a spy novel set in Mexico. *Act of Anger* (1963) and *The Adversary* (1974) are powerfully written courtroom dramas. *Kellogg Junction* (1969) is about the attempt of a group of rich and powerful men to legalize gambling in their corrupt small town. *Festival* (1970) is a Hollywood roman a clef set in Cannes, featuring an Italian nymphomaniac movie star and characters based on John Ford and John Huston.

**Further Reading:**
*Carney Wilde series (complete):*
THE DARK LIGHT (1949)
BLUES FOR THE PRINCE (1950)
THE GOLDEN DOOR (1951)
BLACK SHEEP, RUN (1951)
THE LONG GREEN (1952)
THE TAMING OF CARNEY WILDE (1954)

THE DAY OF THE DEAD (1955)
EXIT, RUNNING (1959)
ACT OF ANGER (1962)
THE BURNED MAN (1966)

**As Jay Barbette**
FINAL COPY (1950)
DEAR DEAD DAYS (1953; as DEATH'S LONG SHADOW, 1955)
THE DEADLY DOLL (1958)
LOOK BEHIND YOU (1960)

---

**If you like Bart Spicer,** you might like: Talmage Powell, Douglas Sanderson

# Mickey Spillane

(born Frank Morrison Spillane). Born in Brooklyn, New York, 1918. Died in Murrells Inlet, South Carolina, 2006.

Let's get one thing straight. The Mick was no goddamn "author." He was a writer. Authors are snooty guys or dames with three-word names. Authors go to cocktail parties. Authors think they're something special if they live in a rat hole and starve, then can't pay the rent for their rat hole so they get evicted and die in the gutter from an overdose of absinthe. All without getting a word published.

Where do I get balls big enough to say all this? I oughta know. I'm Mike Hammer.

The Mick was born in Brooklyn, but grew up in New Jersey. In 1940 he started writing for comic books ("graphic novels" to you "authors" out there). He wrote stories for Timely Comics, which later changed its name to Marvel. He wrote stories for Captain America, the Human Torch and Sub-mariner. He also wrote two-page text stories. 'Nuff said!

The Mick's writing career was interrupted when he signed up for the Army Air Corps on December 8, 1941. The day after Pearl Harbor.

The Mick got married during the war, and after it ended he needed to make some bucks and make 'em fast. So he took a character he created for the comics (but didn't use) called Mike Danger, changed the character's name to that of yours truly, Mike Hammer, and wrote his first book in 19 days. He called it, *I, The Jury* (1947).

If there's one thing the Mick taught me, it's honesty, so let me tell it to you straight. When *I, The Jury* was first published in hardcover, it only sold seven thousand copies. (Almost makes the Mick sound like some of you "authors"!) But when it was reprinted in paperback by Signet Books in 1948, it sold two million copies within two years. And from then on—oh, baby, what a ride!

The Mick wrote his books quickly. He wrote six of 'em in five years. *My Gun is Quick* (1950), *Vengeance is Mine!* (1950), *The Big Kill* (1951), *The Long Wait* (1951, the only book the Mick wrote during the 1950's without me in it), *One Lonely Night* (1951) and *Kiss Me, Deadly* (1952). They were all bestsellers. Big bestsellers. So big that, by 1968, seven of the twenty-five best sellers of all time were the Mick's.

Naw, you ain't got chewing gum stuck in your ear. I said of *all time*.

But let's continue with that ride I was talking about. Besides the books, there was a Mike Hammer radio show, two Mike Hammer television series and seven movies made from the Mick's books. Hell, the Mick even got into the act himself. He co-starred in the movie *Ring of Fear* (1954), and he played me, Mike Hammer, in *The Girl Hunters* (1963). He even made beer commercials during the '70's and '80's. I'm tellin' ya, baby, that boy could sell!

Now, about those Hammer books. The way the Mick wrote 'em was kinda like me—fast, sexy and violent. Besides being entertaining as hell. And did that bring the goddamn house down! U.S. Senators, churches, highfalutin' literary critics, and even the Mick's fellow writers all picked up a bat and took a swing at the Mick. Hell, with all the bitching and moaning about the Mick's books, you'd think they were responsible for every evil from the fall of Adam to the A-bomb.

You think any of this bothered the Mick? Hell, no! He lived a quiet and contented life and laughed all the way to the bank.

In 1952, the Mick joined the Jehovah's Witnesses, and he didn't write any books for almost ten years. The only thing I got to say (aside from grunting a few four letter words that ain't exactly printable) is that the Mick never consulted *me* about it.

After the Mick's writing hiatus, he came back with more books about me, as well as books about some new characters. He wrote about a spy called Tiger Mann during the '60's, in books including *Day of the Guns* (1964), *Bloody Sunrise* (1965) and *The Death Dealers* (1965). He wrote one about a family's black sheep named Dogeron "Dog" Kelly coming home to collect his inheritance in *The Erection Set* (1972). His later books about me included *The Girl Hunters* (1962), *The Twisted Thing* (1966), *The Body Lovers* (1967) and *The Killing Man* (1989).

Maybe today certain "authors" make fun of the Mick and call him a "Joe Six-Pack" type. Maybe they'd call the Mick's readers that, too. But the Mick knew what he liked, and his readers knew what they liked—all 160 million of 'em. And they liked the Mick. And, of course, they liked me, as well.

Further Reading:
*Mike Hammer series:*
I, THE JURY (1947)
MY GUN IS QUICK (1950)
VENGEANCE IS MINE (1950)
ONE LONELY NIGHT (1951)
THE BIG KILL (1951)
KISS ME, DEADLY (1952)
THE GIRL HUNTERS (1962)
THE SNAKE (1964)
THE TWISTED THING (1966)
THE BODY LOVERS (1967)
SURVIVAL...ZERO (1970)
MIKE HAMMER: THE COMIC STRIP (1982-84, two volumes, edited by Max Allan Collins)
THE KILLING MAN (1989)
THE GOLIATH BONE (2008, completed by Max Allan Collins)
THE BIG BANG (2010, completed by Max Allan Collins)

*Tiger Mann series:*
DAY OF THE GUNS (1964)
BLOODY SUNRISE (1965)
THE DEATH DEALERS (1965)
THE BY-PASS CONTROL (1966)

THE LONG WAIT (1951)
THE DEEP (1961)
THE DELTA FACTOR (1967)
THE ERECTION SET (1972)
THE SHIP THAT NEVER WAS (1982, children's book)

---

**If you like Mickey Spillane,** you might like: David J. Gerrity, John B. West

## *Stewart Sterling*

(pseudonym of Prentice Winchell; also wrote as Spencer Dean, Jay De Bekker, Dexter St. Clair, Dexter St. Clare). Born in Evanston, Illinois, 1895. Died in Tallahassee, Florida, 1976.

Prentice Winchell specialized in writing about PIs who worked for businesses other than detective agencies: a fire chief, a hotel detective, a department store detective. Throughout his career, he successfully adapted his pulpish style to short stories, novels, radio, movies and TV. According to Art Scott, in *20th Century Crime and Mystery Writers*, Winchell's stories are characterized by their "headlong pace, complex plots, and snappy dialogue."

Winchell had an extensive history with the pulps. For *Black Mask*, during the late 1930's-'40's, he wrote nine novelettes featuring the "Special Squad," which highlighted the adventures of crime fighting organizations such as the Bomb and Forgery Squad, the Pickpocket and Confidence Bureau, and the uniquely named Air Police. He also wrote stories for pulp heroes the Black Bat, the Spider and the Phantom Detective. From the late 1930's-1950's he wrote scores of detective stories for pulps such as *Five-Novels Monthly*, *Dime Mystery*, *Thrilling Detective* and *Popular Detective*, and wrote sports-oriented stories for *Thrilling Sports*, *Football Action*, *Baseball Stories* and *Exciting Sports*.

From the 1940's-1960's, Winchell wrote forty short stories and nine novels about Fire Marshall Ben Pedley. According to Art Scott, "Ben Pedley is a humorless, hardbitten, veteran smoke-eater driven by an almost pathological hatred of arsonists." Pedley's first appearance was in *Five Alarm Funeral* (1942). Gil Vine, a hotel dick for the Plaza Royale in New York, was featured in eight novels, beginning with *Dead Wrong* (1947). The Vine books are in line with the typical hardboiled PI novels of the era—narrated in the first person, slangy, with plenty of dames and wisecracks.

Don Cadee, a department store detective, appears in nine novels, beginning with *The Scent of Fear* (1954, aka *The Smell of Fear*; all Cadee novels as by Spencer Dean). A number of Winchell's books (*Dead Right*, *Credit for Murder*, *Kick of the Wheel*) are set in Ft. Lauderdale and Palm Beach, Florida, where he lived for many years.

Winchell's pulp adventures had an element of realism, based on research he had done: "In his search for authentic background material, Winchell once worked in one of the largest department stores on the east coast in the security department just to learn how store detectives work." (The Palm Beach Post, July 16, 1961). Besides his fictional detectives,

Winchell put information gleaned from these experiences to good use in non-fiction books like *I Was a Hotel Detective* (1954, with Dev Collans).

Under the name Jay de Bekker, he wrote two iconic sleaze books for Beacon: *Gutter Gang* (1954) and *Keyhole Peeper* (1952).

As Dexter St. Claire, he wrote *The Lady's Not for Living* (1963) for Gold Medal. As Dexter St. Clare, also for GM, he wrote *Saratoga Mantrap* (1951).

Sterling lived in the Daytona Beach area of Florida starting in 1955. He was skipper of his own houseboat, the *Elgee*, where boating companions included colorful characters like ex-president Herbert Hoover, Princess Dona Marguerita de Condresonos and a local eccentric who called himself Mr. Red Beard. In later years he wrote a bridge column, "The Cardboard Jungle," and gave lectures on literature and poetry at women's clubs and teacher's associations.

**Further Reading:**
*Fire Marshall Ben Pedley series (complete):*
FIVE ALARM FUNERAL (1942)
WHERE THERE'S SMOKE (1946)
ALARM IN THE NIGHT (1949)
NIGHTMARE AT NOON (1951)
THE HINGES OF HELL (1955)
CANDLE FOR A CORPSE (1957; as TOO HOT TO KILL, 1958)
FIRE ON FEAR STREET (1958)
DYING ROOM ONLY (1960)
TOO HOT TO HANDLE (1961)

*Gil Vine series (complete):*
DEAD WRONG (1947)
DEAD SURE (1949)
DEAD OF NIGHT (1950)
ALIBI BABY (1955)
DEAD RIGHT (1956; as THE HOTEL MURDERS, 1957)
DEAD TO THE WORLD (1958; as THE BLONDE IN SUITE 14, 1959)
THE BODY IN THE BED (1959)
DEAD CERTAIN (1960)

I WAS A HOUSE DETECTIVE (1954, non-fiction, with Dev Collans)
BLAZE BATTLERS (1955, children's book)
DANGER! DETECTIVES WORKING (1955, non-fiction, as Prentice Winchell)

**As Spencer Dean**
*Don Cadee series:*
THE FRIGHTENED FINGERS (1954)
MARKED DOWN FOR MURDER (1956)
DISHONOR AMONG THIEVES (1958)

**As Jay de Bekker**
GUTTER GANG (1954)
KEYHOLE PEEPER (1955)

---

**If you like Stewart Sterling,** you might like: George Harmon Coxe, W. T. Ballard

# Rex Stout

(also wrote as Evans Day). Born in Noblesville, Indiana, 1886. Died in Danbury, Connecticut, 1975.

Rex Stout's Nero Wolfe and his partner Archie Goodwin are two of the most popular characters in mystery fiction, taking their place alongside such giants of the genre as Sherlock Holmes and Dr. Watson, Charlie Chan and Hercule Poirot. Wolfe's and Goodwin's adventures lasted for forty-one years and forty-two books, from *Fer-de-Lance* (1934) to *A Family Affair* (1975). Their life extended beyond the novels and they appeared in movies, radio, television and a comic strip. Wolfe and Goodwin offer a unique experience for the mystery fan: Wolfe uses his powers of deductive reasoning to solve his cases, which appeals to fans of the cerebral, while Archie is a man of action, appealing to fans of the hardboiled. Archie is also the narrator of the stories.

Stout was a child prodigy. He read the 1200 books in his father's library by the age of ten, and was Kansas's state spelling champion at thirteen. When he was eighteen he joined the Navy, and his abilities earned him a spot as a crewman on the yacht of President Theodore Roosevelt. He invented a banking system that was used in four hundred cities across the U.S., which made him independently wealthy enough to start a full time writing career.

Nero and Archie's first adventure was published as the aforementioned *Fer-de-Lance* in 1934. Stout endowed both characters with distinct characteristics. Nero Wolfe is in his fifties, is 5'11", and weighs somewhere "between 250 [lbs.] and a ton." It should come as no surprise then, that he is a connoisseur of fine and exotic foods. He might very well be the first private detective to have a beer belly—he guzzles a minimum of 5 quarts per day. He is also a connoisseur and cultivator of orchids—a greenhouse on his rooftop holds 10,000 plants. He dresses and grooms himself fastidiously, usually in a three piece suit, complete with vest pocket platinum watch.

He is what we might today call an "agoraphobic," leaving his brownstone in New York only when absolutely necessary. When he does venture beyond his abode, he is quick to voice his contempt for flies, cinnamon rolls, gin drinkers, paper cups and more than six diners at a table. But, of course, Wolfe's most entertaining quality is his personality: prickly, cantankerous, curmudgeonly, and egotistical, with a wit as rapier-sharp as a character in an Oscar Wilde play. Here are a few tasty morsels of the wisdom of Wolfe:

"That is of course the advantage of being a pessimist; a pessimist gets nothing but pleasant surprises, an optimist nothing but unpleasant." (*Fer-de-Lance*, 1934)

"Not that I disapprove of [women], except when they attempt to function as domestic animals. When they stick to the vocations for which they are best adapted, such as chicanery, sophistry, self-adornment, cajolery, mystification and incubation, they are sometimes splendid creatures." (*The Rubber Band*, aka *To Kill Again*, 1936)

"I tell only useful lies, and only those not easily exposed." (*Over My Dead Body*, 1940)

Archie Goodwin, Wolfe's partner in investigations and all around man-Friday, is essential, not only to the stories, but also to the readership. He is a "working man," and as readers, we are more easily able to identify with his point of view then the sometimes highfalutin' perspective of Wolfe. Physically, Archie is handsome and athletic, and does quite well with the ladies. He's been told he looks like Clark Gable, but he believes a comparison with Gary Cooper is more apt. Archie is sometimes able to use his charm with women to help elicit clues. As for his most useful investigative skills, Archie is not only a first rate burglar, but a master impersonator, and throughout the series has gathered data by successfully impersonating a photographer, policeman, florist, financial secretary and crook. Archie is an independent and proud-minded man, who will be pushed around by no one, not even Wolfe. More than once, he has had occasion to tell his boss to go to hell and to walk off the job, but he always returns to the fold.

There are so many books in the Wolfe series, and so many of high quality, it is difficult to pick out a few which stand head and shoulders above the rest. But mystery critics and Wolfe aficionados have noted the excellence of *Fer-de-Lance* (1934), *Too Many Cooks* (1938), *Some Buried Caesar* (1939), *And Be a Villain* (1948, which introduced Arnold Zeck, who appeared in three books as Wolfe's arch-enemy), *The Black Mountain* (1954), *Might as Well Be Dead* (1956) and *The Doorbell Rang* (1965).

Besides Nero Wolfe, Stout created other PI's: Tecumseh Fox (Stout called his Fox novel, *Double for Death*, the best detective story he'd ever written), Theolinda "Dol" Bonner (one of the earliest female PI's) and Alphabet Hicks (whose business card reads that he is an "M.S.O.T.P.B.O.M", which stands for "Melancholy Spectator of the Psychic Bellyache of Mankind."

Further Reading:
*Nero Wolfe series:*
FER-DE-LANCE (1934)
THE LEAGUE OF FRIGHTENED MEN (1935)
THE RUBBER BAND (1936)
TOO MANY COOKS (1938)
OVER MY DEAD BODY (1940)
WHERE THERE'S A WILL (1940)
THE SILENT SPEAKER (1946)
TOO MANY WOMEN (1947)
AND BE A VILLAIN (1948)
THE SECOND CONFESSION (1949)
IN THE BEST FAMILIES (1950)
MURDER BY THE BOOK (1951)
PRISONER'S BASE (1952)
THE GOLDEN SPIDERS (1953)
MIGHT AS WELL BE DEAD (1956)
IF DEATH EVER SLEPT (1957)
CHAMPAGNE FOR ONE (1958)
TOO MANY CLIENTS (1960)
GAMBIT (1962)
A RIGHT TO DIE (1964)
DEATH OF A DUDE (1969)
PLEASE PASS THE GUILT (1970)

*Tecumseh Fox series:*
DOUBLE FOR DEATH (1939)
BAD FOR BUSINESS (1940)
THE BROKEN VASE (1941)

THE PRESIDENT VANISHES (1934)
THE HAND IN THE GLOVE (1937)
ALPHABET HICKS (1941)

---

If you like **Rex Stout,** you might like: Erle Stanley Gardner, Ellery Queen

# Tedd Thomey

(real name Harold John Thomey). Born in Butte, Montana, 1920. Died in California, 2008.

Tedd Thomey's claim to fame came about almost by accident. In 1961, having already written a number of successful novels, he got a call from his agent at the Scott Meredith Literary Agency. Thomey's agent asked him to write an "as told to" biography with Mrs. Florence Aadland about her daughter, Beverly, and her experience as the underage mistress of Errol Flynn during the last years of Flynn's life. (Flynn, who had died in 1959 at the age of fifty, had been seeing Beverly since she was fifteen.)

Thomey most likely figured it was just another assignment—just a cheap, lurid, Confidential-style saga about innocence defiled; something that would probably be on the racks one month and gone the next. And he had good reason. The book cover's blurb read: "Teen-ager Beverly Aadland's Scorching Romance with Errol Flynn — Told for the First Time by the One Person Who Shared All of Their Intimate Secrets!"

But what Thomey found was something altogether different. According to Lee Server, "Thomey found that Aadland's stories about Flynn were gold and her offbeat perspective on life was priceless." (Encyclopedia of Pulp Fiction Writers, by Lee Server, pg. 250)

What Thomey found was a woman who was at times campy, pushy, and self-pitying, and who was at all times self-deluded. The book was titled The Big Love, published by the low budget outfit, Lancer Books. Published with little fanfare, its modest goal was just to exploit the tail end of the Flynn-Aadland scandal. But then things started happening.

Author William Styron (a literary heavyweight at the time, ranked alongside writers like Norman Mailer and Philip Roth) gave the book a rave review in Esquire magazine, calling it "a work of wild comic genius." Movie director Robert Aldrich bought the film rights and planned to star Bette Davis as Florence (the film was never made). The book gained a solid cult following and, as the years passed, copies started selling for multiples of the original cover price. (Today a copy will set you back anywhere from $50-$150, depending on condition.) In 1991, the book was made into a Broadway play, starring Tracey Ullman as Florence.

Besides his piece de resistance, Thomey had other notable achievements. During World War II, he was part of the Marine forces at the battle of Iwo Jima, earning a Purple Heart and a Presidential Unit Citation for his service; years later he published a related book, Immortal Images: A Personal History of Two Photographers and the Flag-raising On Iwo Jima (1996). After the war, Thomey settled in California and became the crime beat reporter for the San Francisco Chronicle. He began selling short stories to the pulps during

their dying days in the late 1940's, and then began selling to the burgeoning digest market.

Thomey's first crime novel was *And Dream of Evil* (1954). The plot is the
often used "man framed for a murder he didn't commit." Thomey
describes the book's killer opening: "I've got a hero on a roof and he's
handcuffed to a slot machine. He's going down a fire escape lugging this
thing...and then he makes love to a beautiful girl while still handcuffed
to the slot machine. All in the first chapter!" (Server, pg. 250) Thomey's
book *Killer in White* (1956), about a phony chiropractor, has been called a Jim
Thompson-like story about a sociopath in a hospital milieu. *The Sadist*
(1960) is about the kidnapping of a man's three-day bride and the trauma
she endures.

Thomey also wrote several fiction and non-fiction military and spy
related books, including *Jet Ace* (1958), *Flight to Takla-Ma* (1961) and *The Prodigy
Plot* (1967).

During Thomey's last years, he wrote popular restaurant reviews for
the *Long Beach Press-Telegram*.

**Further Reading:**
AND DREAM OF EVIL (1954)
JET PILOT (1955)
KILLER IN WHITE (1956)
JET ACE (1958)
I WANT OUT (1959)
THE SADIST (1961)
THE BIG LOVE (1961)
FLIGHT TO TAKLA-MA (1961)
ALL THE WAY (1964)
THE GLORIOUS DECADE (1971)

---

**If you like Ted Thomey,** you might like: Day Keene, Edward S. Aarons

# Jim Thompson

(real name James Myers Thompson; also wrote as James Dillon, Dillon Roberts).
Born in Anadarko, Oklahoma, 1906. Died in Los Angeles, California, 1977.

Today, Jim Thompson's bleak, nihilistic novels of psychopaths, grifters and lowlifes are celebrated by readers, critics, and his peers, including such high profile writers as Stephen King, who wrote, "My favorite crime novelist–often imitated but never duplicated–is Jim Thompson." Thompson's work has been adapted for such major motion pictures as *The Grifters* (1990, starring John Cusack and Angelica Huston, directed by Stephen Frears, produced by Martin Scorsese, screenplay by Donald E. Westlake), which was nominated for four Academy Awards. And Thompson is the subject of two biographies, one of which, *Savage Art* (by Robert Polito, 1995), won the National Book Critics Circle Award and an Edgar award.

Yes, today, the work of Jim Thompson is an unmitigated success. Huzzah!

Too little, too late, it turns out.

James Myers Thompson was born in Anadarko, Oklahoma. His father, James Sr., was a one-time sheriff who spent most of his time drinking and playing cards. After embezzling $5,000 from the county, Sheriff James went on the run, taking his family with him, involving them in a transient lifestyle.

Throughout his twenties, Jim worked many jobs during the day while toiling at his fiction writing at night. At the Hotel Texas, he worked as a bellboy, where he observed and interacted with a motley crew of downtrodden characters, sometimes procuring bootleg hooch and marijuana for hotel patrons who might flip him an extra two-bits (an experience which figured into Thompson's novel, *A Swell-Looking Babe*, 1954). He also performed grueling physical labor working the oil fields of Texas, and as an aircraft factory worker. Thompson first wrote two unsuccessful hardcovers, *Now and On Earth* (1942) and *Heed the Thunder* (1946), both of which were loosely autobiographical, before catching on with his first crime-related book, *Nothing More Than Murder* (1949), a tale of a murder plot concocted by a small-town movie theater owner.

Thompson began his "golden age" in 1952, penning twelve paperback classics during an eighteen month period. He first wrote what director Stanley Kubrick called "the most chilling and believable first-person story of a criminally warped mind I have ever encountered." Titled *The Killer Inside Me* (1952), the story is about Deputy Lou Ford, who feigns a folksy, aw-shucks type of attitude to hide both his stunning intellect and his propensity for sadistic violence. Lou plays it dumb so no one will suspect the heinous crimes he has committed, all due to "the sickness," a psychiatric condition which he's been hiding since childhood and which causes him to intermittently erupt in murderous violence.

Although *The Killer Inside Me* was critically well-received by a few perceptive critics like Anthony Boucher and R. V. Cassill, it was still considered just another "cheap paperback" and failed to make a big splash with the reading public. *The Killer Inside Me* was filmed in 1976 starring Stacy Keach, and in 2010 starring Casey Affleck; neither version successfully managed to capture Thompson's warped and twisted vision. In *Pop. 1280* (1964), Thompson emphasized the comic side of a Lou Ford-like afflicted deputy. Early chapters read almost like farce, as apparently-bumbling Sheriff Nick Corey struggles to manage his nagging wife and her "idiot" brother-in-law amidst a series of affairs. But as the book progresses and Corey attempts to maintain his lifestyle, including the continuation of his position as sheriff, his delusions break through his placid surface in stunning displays of violence. *Pop. 1280* was adapted as the French film *Coup de Torchon* (1981), directed by Bertrand Tavernier. *Savage Night* (1953) was about a 5 foot-tall hit man named Charlie "Little" Bigger. The book ends in a surreal and violent frenzy featuring Bigger and a woman with an ax.

Besides exploring abnormal psychology, Thompson was notable for experimenting with narrative, and for breaking the boundaries of genre crime fiction. In *A Hell of a Woman* (1954), Thompson's narrative technique owes a tip of the hat to Fyodor Dostoevsky. In *The Getaway* (1958), the story concludes in an abstract, Alice-In-Wonderland, Wizard of Oz version of hell.

Thompson's books were moderately successful but because of their offbeat nature came nowhere near to making him rich. As well as the fact that as an alcoholic Thompson drank up the money he did make. But in 1955, he scored a break when a young Stanley Kubrick asked Thompson to work on his upcoming film, *The Killing* (based on Lionel White's novel, *Clean Break*). Thompson's screenplay for *The Killing* was a fine piece of work but when he viewed the completed movie he was shocked to see the credits, which read "Screenplay by Stanley Kubrick. Additional Dialogue by Jim Thompson." Kubrick, who was heavily influenced by the newly-minted notion of "the auteur," was at the beginning of his habit of taking credit for every aspect of production. Nevertheless, Thompson went to work for Kubrick on his very next picture, *Paths of Glory* (1957). Needing any work he could get, Thompson also wrote scripts for the TV shows *Dr. Kildare*, *Mackenzie's Raiders* and *Convoy*. He even acted in a remake of Raymond Chandler's *Farewell, My Lovely*, playing the supporting role of Velma's rich old husband, Grayle. Thompson shared the screen with another noir icon, Robert Mitchum, who played Marlowe.

Near the end of his life, neither rich nor famous, his body having been debilitated by chronic alcoholism and a series of strokes, and with all of his books out of print in the United States, Jim Thompson predicted that ten years after his death the quality of his work would finally be recognized and he'd be a celebrated author. He was right.

**Further Reading:**
NOW AND ON EARTH (1942)
HEED THE THUNDER (1946)
NOTHING MORE THAN MURDER (1949)
CROPPER'S CABIN (1952)
THE KILLER INSIDE ME (1952)
THE ALCOHOLICS (1953)
BAD BOY (1953)
THE CRIMINAL (1953)
RECOIL (1953)
SAVAGE NIGHT (1953)
A SWELL-LOOKING BABE (1954)
THE GOLDEN GIZMO (1954)
A HELL OF A WOMAN (1954)
THE NOTHING MAN (1954)
ROUGHNECK (1954)
AFTER DARK, MY SWEET (1955)
THE KILL-OFF (1957)
WILD TOWN (1957, Lou Ford appearance)
THE GETAWAY (1959)
THE TRANSGRESSORS (1961)
THE GRIFTERS (1963)
POP. 1280 (1964)
TEXAS BY THE TAIL (1965)
IRONSIDE (1967, TV novelization)
SOUTH OF HEAVEN (1967)
THE UNDEFEATED (1969, movie novelization)
NOTHING BUT A MAN (1970, movie novelization)
CHILD OF RAGE (1972)
KING BLOOD (1973)

---

If you like Jim Thompson, you might like: Dashiell Hammett, James M. Cain, John D. MacDonald

# Don Tracy

(also wrote as Roger Fuller, Barnaby Ross, Van Wyck Mason, Jeanne Leggitt, Tracy Mason, Tom Tucker, C. K. M. Scanlon). Born in New Britain, Connecticut, 1905. Died in Florida in 1976.

Don Tracy started his writing career as a journalist for the *New Britain Herald*, in Connecticut, and later for Maryland's *Baltimore Post*. His first novel was *Round Trip* (1934). The story is about an alcoholic news reporter on the skids. A love affair begins to help the reporter salvage his life, but tragedy sends him spiraling irrevocably downward. A reviewer for *Books* magazine wrote that *Round Trip* was "strong stuff and straight stuff...there is so much vigor in its style and such honesty in its portrait of the 'prize bum' that it cannot be dismissed as merely another routine product of the hardboiled school."

In 1934, Tracy wrote *Criss-Cross*. The story is about has-been ex-boxer Johnny Thompson. Johnny's femme fatale, Anna, doesn't love him, and she marries Slim, a local gangster and heist man. Anna and Johnny have an affair on the side. Slim finds out and hires Johnny, who works as a guard for an armored car company, to help Slim and his gang rob the car's loot, planning to kill Johnny at the end of the heist. *Criss-Cross* was filmed in 1949, directed by noir specialist, Robert Siodmak, and starred Burt Lancaster, Yvonne De Carlo and Dan Duryea. Remade in 1995, it was titled *The Underneath*, directed by Stephen Soderbergh. Other noirish Tracy titles include *Strumpet City* (1951, aka *Streets of Askelon*) and *The Big Blackout* (1959).

Tracy wrote a number of novels which took a progressive stance on interracial relationships. *How Sleeps the Beast* (1938) is a story about the heated love affair between a black man and a white woman, and the black man's subsequent lynching by a mob of local citizens. Because of the book's progressive attitude toward race relations, as well as its graphic portrayal of the lynching, no U.S. publisher would touch the book, and it was first published only in England. It was finally reprinted by paperback icon Lion Books in 1950.

Tracy returned to this theme in *The Hated One* (1964), a story about an alcoholic white lawyer struggling to defend a young black girl accused of murder. *Cherokee* (1957) is a historical novel which explores an interracial romance between a Native American man and a white girl.

Beginning in 1960 with *Deadly to Bed* (1960), Tracy wrote a series of nine books featuring Giff Speer, an MP who in reality is working undercover to investigate crimes within the ranks of the U.S. Army. Other notable Speer titles include *Naked She Died* (1962), *Look Down On Her Dying* (1968) and *The Big X* (1976).

Later in his career, Tracy forged a steady career writing under the name Roger Fuller. He wrote TV tie-in books for shows like *Burke's Law* and *The Defenders*, as well as a series of nearly ten novels that were sequels to Grace Metallious's *Peyton Place*.

The theme of alcoholism is prevalent throughout Tracy's books. This is neither coincidence nor the fact that bar hopping was such a staple of mystery and crime fiction. Tracy himself battled with the bottle and wrote a self-help book titled, *What You Should Know About Alcoholism* (1975). During the 1970's, he worked as a volunteer for an AA-type organization.

**Further Reading:**
*Giff Speer series:*

DEADLY TO BED (1960)                    NAKED SHE DIED (1962)
FUN AND DEADLY GAMES (1968)      LOOK DOWN ON HER DYING (1968)
POT OF TROUBLE (1971)
FLATS FIXED–AMONG OTHER THINGS (1971)
THE BIG X (1976)


ROUND TRIP (1934)
CRISS CROSS (1935, aka THE CHEAT)
HOW SLEEPS THE BEAST? (1938)
STREETS OF ASKELON (1951)
THE BIG BLACKOUT (1959)
NO TRESPASSING (1961)
THE BIG BRASS RING (1963)
THE HATED ONE (1963)
THE BLACK AMULET (1968)
A CORPSE CAN SURE LOUSE UP A WEEKEND (1973)
WHAT YOU SHOULD KNOW ABOUT ALCOHOLISM (1975, non-fiction)


**As Roger Fuller**
BURKE'S LAW: WHO KILLED BEAU SPARROW? (1963, tv novelization)
BURKE'S LAW: WHO KILLED MADCAP MILLICENT? (1964, TV novelization)
FEAR IN A DESERT TOWN (1964)
BURKE'S LAW: WHO KILLED SWEET BETSY? (1965, TV novelization)
EVE OF JUDGEMENT (1965)
SECRETS OF PEYTON PLACE (1968)
EVILS OF PEYTON PLACE (1969)
HERO IN PEYTON PLACE (1969)
THRILLS OF PEYTON PLACE (1969)
THE NICE GIRL FROM PEYTON PLACE (1970)
TEMPATIONS OF PEYTON PLACE (1970)

---

**If you like Don Tracy,** you might like: Charles Willeford, James Hadley Chase

# John Trinian

(real name Marvin Leroy Schmoker; also wrote as Zekial Marko). Born in
Monterey, California, 1933. Died in Centralia, Washington, 2008.

Marvin Leroy Schmoker (under the name John Trinian)
wrote noirish tales populated by ex-cons, beatniks, gigo-
los, lesbians, sex cult leaders and carny barkers.

Schmoker's early life is shrouded in mystery.
Rumors have abounded about his past as an ex-con
(although what crime he committed has never been
mentioned). Writer Ed Gorman, in *The Big Book of Noir*,
wrote that Schmoker's stories were "mostly about ex-
cons (because, it was said, he was one himself)." An article in the *Los
Angeles Times* on October 17, 1965, in reviewing the movie *Once a Thief* (a story
about an ex-con based on a novel of Schmoker's), reported that the movie
is "largely drawn from the personal experiences of the author." The
Turner Classic Movies website claims Schmoker "had begun writing fiction
upon his release from a prison stretch for a non-violent crime." But a reader of Ed Gorman's website, Ki Longfellow, in a post dated December 3, 2011,
wrote that Schmoker, "was one of the best friends I ever had. We ran
together in Marin County and Sausalito in the early to late Sixties. He was
never a criminal, much less convicted of anything. This is all myth-mak-
ing, maybe even by Marko himself." There's also an odd element as to the
shuffling of names: "Schmoker" was never used publicly or on any of his
work; "Trinian" was for novels, "Zekial Marko" for screenplays.

Schmoker's first book was *A Game of Flesh* (1959), a story about a gold-digging gigolo. *North Beach Girl* (1960, reprinted as *Strange Lovers*, 1967) features a
lesbian quartet and an eccentric cast of beatnik characters in the bohemi-
an-styled North Beach area of San Francisco. The irresistibly titled *The
Savage Breast* (1961) is another tale about a gigolo-type—a gold-digging
slimeball who takes advantage of a wayward heiress. *Scratch a Thief* (1961,
also published as *Once a Thief*, 1965, as by Marko; and in 1973, back to
Trinian, as *Once a Thief*) is about a reformed thief who is hounded by a sus-
picious police detective and by his own brother, who wants him for a
heist. *House of Evil* (1962) features a former con man, now the leader of a sex
cult, who blackmails rich Hollywoodites with "compromising movies."

Schmoker had a successful career in film and television. His book, *The
Big Grab* (1960) was filmed as *Any Number Can Play* (1963, a French-English
production, starring Jean Gabin and Alain Delon). *Scratch a Thief* was filmed
as *Once a Thief* (1965, starring Alain Delon, Ann-Margret and Jack Palance).
Schmoker wrote the screenplay (as Marko) and had a small supporting
role as a drug addict, although his voice was dubbed by voiceover artist

Paul Frees. In the mid-'70's, he wrote episodes of *The Rockford Files* (he had a bit part in the episode "Charlie Harris at Large") and *Kolchak: The Night Stalker.*

**Further Reading:**
A GAME OF FLESH (1959)
NORTH BEACH GIRL (1960; as STRANGE LOVERS, 1967)
THE SAVAGE BREAST (1961)
SCRATCH A THIEF (1961; as ONCE A THIEF, as by Zekial Marko, 1965; as ONCE A THIEF, as by John Trinian, 1973)
HOUSE OF EVIL (1962)
THE BIG GRAB (1963)
SCANDAL ON THE SAND (1964)

If you like John Trinian, you might like: H. Vernor Dixon, Malcolm Braly

# Jack Webb

(born John Alfred Webb, also wrote as John Farr; not to be confused with Jack "*Dragnet*"Webb). Born in California, 1916. Died in Coronado, California, 2008.

Jack Webb (not the "Dum-dah-dum-dum" Jack Webb, although the fact that both men created detective teams is an amazing coincidence) wrote a series of novels featuring an innovative detective duo—Jewish LAPD Detective Sammy Golden, and a Catholic priest named Father Joseph Shanley.

Webb's first published novel, as well as the novel that introduced the Golden-Shanley team, was *The Big Sin* (1952). Sammy Golden is in his mid-30's, served in WWII, and "still seems to happily turn to violence." Father Shanley, also in his mid-30's, ministers at St. Anne's Church, tends to both his rose garden and to souls, and is "a fighter by instinct, a man of the cloth by devotion and inspiration."

In spite of the presence of a Catholic priest, Webb's books are not "cozy" mysteries. Webb writes tough, clipped, hardboiled prose reflecting the violence and corruption of Los Angeles and its environs. Webb describes one of Sammy Golden's fellow officers thusly:

> "Schwartz was a harness bull of the old school, the only man left on the force who had walked the South Central beat alone. There was talk of a confession he had got out of a naked stumblebum with a thick closed door between him and his wire coat hanger." (*The Deadly Sex*, 1959)

And Webb describes Sammy Golden and a fellow officer named "Red" Adams as being, "Two personable young men well on their way to becoming experts in violent death." (*The Broken Doll*, 1955)

Throughout the Golden-Shanley novels, it is usually coincidence that brings the two old friends together. Golden is a bachelor and something of a loose cannon; he often breaks with police procedure and gets demoted and put back in uniform. Shanley frequently has to pull Golden's fat from the fire.

Webb published 10 books featuring the Golden-Shanley team, including *The Naked Angel* (1953), which concerns a missing stripper; *The Bad Blonde* (1956), which revolves around a robbery at a chemical company; and *The Delicate Darling* (1959), which includes a raging fire, a half strangled girl and a triple homicide. A number of the Golden-Shanley paperbacks sport classic covers illustrated by artist extraordinaire, Robert McGuire.

Webb published four non-series mystery novels under the name John Farr—*Don't Feed the Animals* (1955), a murder mystery with a zoo background; *She Shark* (1956), a story about modern piracy, mutiny and the femme fatale of the title; *The Lady and the Snake* (1957), another story with a zoo background; and *The Deadly Combo* (1958), a story of blackmail set in the world of jazz musicians.

Webb contributed short stories to *Manhunt, Alfred Hitchcock's Mystery Magazine* and *Mike Shayne Mystery Magazine* between 1954-1973.

**Further Reading:**
*Father Shanley and Sammy Golden series (complete):*
THE BIG SIN (1952)
THE NAKED ANGEL (1953)
THE DAMNED LOVELY (1954)
THE BROKEN DOLL (1955)
THE BAD BLONDE (1956)
THE BRASS HALO (1957)
THE DEADLY SEX (1959)
THE DELICATE DARLING (1959)
THE GILDED WITCH (1963)

ONE FOR MY DAME (1961)
MAKE MY BED SOON (1963)

**As John Farr**
DON'T FEED THE ANIMALS (1955; as NAKED FEAR, 1955)
SHE SHARK (1956)
THE LADY AND THE SNAKE (1957)
THE DEADLY COMBO (1958)

---

**If you like Jack Webb,** you might like: W. R. Burnett, Jim Thompson, Frank Gruber

# John B. West
Born-? Died-1960

John B. West was unique among the many writers who imitated Mickey Spillane throughout the 1950's and early '60's. At first glance, this may not appear to be the case. Like Spillane's Mike Hammer, West writes about a New York-based private eye, with the tough guy name of Aloysius Algernon "Rocky" Steele. Like Hammer, Rocky Steele's close friend is a high ranking member of the police department. Like Hammer, Steele has a sexy secretary he won't fool around with because she is WOMAN, while other females are merely two-bit whores. Like Hammer, Steele smokes Lucky Strikes, is an ex-commando and is handy with a .45 (nicknamed "Betsy").

West's six Rocky Steele books—*An Eye for an Eye, Cobra Venom, A Taste for Blood, Bullets are My Business, Never Kill a Cop* and *Death On the Rocks*—were all published (between 1959-1961) by Spillane's paperback publisher, Signet Books. Last, but certainly not least, West writes his own approximation of Spillane's tough-guy style:

"I still couldn't see a goddamn thing..." (*A Taste for Blood*, pg. 5)
"...thinking that was goddamn funny..." (Ibid, pg. 5)
"And...goddammitt!" (Ibid, pg. 5)
"...the son of a bitch..." (Ibid, pg. 5)
"Stop, you lousy bastard!" (Ibid., pg. 5)
"And I wasn't getting any goddamn place." (Ibid, pg. 5)
"Goddammitt!" (Ibid, pg. 5)

So just who was John B. West?
Could "John B. West" be a pseudonym for one of Spillane's buddies—like Earle Basinsky or Dave Garrity—whom the Mick helped break into print?
Not quite.
Scratch that.
*Not even close.*
West was black, and according to the back cover of West's *An Eye for an Eye*, he was "educated at Howard University and Harvard University. He holds five academic degrees. Dr. West is a specialist in the prevention and treatment of tropical diseases, and he has a general practice in Liberia, Africa. He also owns and operates the Liberian Broadcasting Company, is President of the National Manufacturing Company and President of the Liberian Hotel and Restaurant Corporation."
So there.

**Further Reading:**
*Rocky Steele series (complete):*
AN EYE FOR AN EYE (1959)
COBRA VENOM (1959)
BULLETS ARE MY BUSINESS (1960)
A TASTE FOR BLOOD (1960)
NEVER KILL A COP (1961)
DEATH ON THE ROCKS (1961)

-------------------------------------------------------------

**If you like John B. West,** you might like: Mickey Spillane, Mike Roscoe

# Donald E. Westlake

(also wrote as Richard Stark, Tucker Coe, Curt Clark, Samuel Holt, Timothy J. Culver, J. Morgan Cunningham, Judson Jack Carmichael, Edwin West, John B. Allan, Alan Marshall, John Dexter, Andrew Shaw, Barbara Wilson, P. N. Castor, Don Holliday, James Blue, Edwina West, Edwin Wood, Ben Christopher, Grace Salacious, Alan Marsh). Born Brooklyn, New York, 1933. Died Mexico, 2008.

 Donald E. Westlake was the prolific author and genius plotter of multiple series' and standalone books. Much like his friend Lawrence Block, Westlake wrote different kinds of fiction throughout his long career. Their short stories appeared in the digest magazines more than the pulps, both men were writers for the "sleaze" market, and later, were trailblazing pioneers in certain sub-genres of crime fiction. Where Block had his Matt Scudder PI series, Westlake had his Parker character, defining for many the ultimate tough guy crime novel.

Parker. No first name needed. His first appearance, in *The Hunter* (1962), was intended as a one-off, with Parker in custody at the end and on his way to prison. An editor at Pocket asked Westlake if there was any way Parker could remain free at the end of the book and therefore be available for more books. Westlake said yes, and agreed to write a series with his new creation.

At the time, Westlake was writing more than a book a year and thought he needed a pseudonym because he wanted to keep *The Hunter* separate from the books he was writing under his own name. The name itself was chosen for the essence of the books themselves and came out of the language Westlake wanted to use. From a video interview on his website, he said: [It was] "very stripped down and bleak and no adverbs ... I want it stark. ... The name is going to be 'Stark' just to remind me what we're doing here." The first name was inspired by the actor Richard Widmark and thus the persona of "Richard Stark" was born.

The series started in 1962 with *The Hunter*, where we first meet Parker crossing a bridge into New York, carving a place for himself in the grit of the city. Five minutes with this guy would convince most people that the last thing they'd ever want to do is cross him, but when your crowd is made up of professional criminals, that kind of judgment is altogether too rare. And double-crosses and hidden agendas feature often in these books.

*The Hunter* sets the pattern for the whole twenty-four book series: someone needs to put together a crew for a job, whether it be ripping off a stadium, a gambling ship, or even an entire town, and reaches out to the loose network of such men across the country. To be part of this group means someone else knows you and can vouch for you. The penalty for not being kosher is—what else?—a sudden death. Plans are made, the heist goes down, then something goes wrong, often after the initial success. Sometimes that means betrayal—and as we quickly learn, nobody rips off Parker and gets away with it. Not for long, anyway.

We see this clearly in *The Hunter* where Parker relentlessly takes on his ex-partner and the Outfit, the New York mob, in order to recover his share of money taken from him after a robbery. How nothing stops Parker, or even slows him down much, is as fascinating as the odds are long, and no amount of cocked and pointed guns are too many to keep Parker from reclaiming his share of the loot.

*The Hunter* has been filmed several times, first in 1967 as *Point Blank*, directed by John Boorman and starring Lee Marvin and Angie Dickinson; Parker was renamed "Walker." In 1999 Brian Helgeland directed Mel Gibson in a version called *Payback* (Parker was called "Porter"), and 2013 saw the release of *Parker* (based on the 2000 novel, *Flashfire*), the first version where the actual name "Parker" was used, starring Jason Statham. Other books in the series have been filmed as well, most notably *The Outfit* (1973) with Robert Duvall and Karen Black.

Under his own name, Westlake created a new series featuring another thief, John Dortmunder. The first book in that series, *The Hot Rock* (1970), was originally supposed to be a Parker novel but the premise of a heist seeming to bounce back and forth between success and failure (and back again and again) seemed suited more to a comical story than the ultra-tough kind of books that came from Richard Stark.

Despite their similarities, where Parker's crimes are usually initially successful, Dortmunder's adventures are more of a bumbling "what next?" character, often eventually working but with very little gain actually coming to Dortmunder and his cohorts. *The Hot Rock* was filmed in 1972 by Peter Yates with a screenplay by William Goldman and starring Robert Redford and George Segal. There are a total of fourteen novels in the Dortmunder series, including *Jimmy the Kid* (1974), which features a guest appearance by none other than Parker himself.

In the mid-1960's, Westlake claimed he "produced far too much." In 1966 alone he wrote a Parker novel as Richard Stark (*The Rare Coin Score*), a standalone "comic caper" novel (*God Save the Mark*) and the first of five novels featuring Mitch Tobin, *Kinds of Love, Kinds of Death*. Tobin is an ex-cop who was dismissed from the force after his partner was shot to death while Tobin was carrying on an affair with the wife of a crook he'd put behind bars. Written in a vastly different tone than the hard and violent Parkers, or the comic ingenuity of the Dortmunder books, the Tucker Coe books show a man in pain, so addled by guilt that he simply cannot function. Rather than face the disaster he's made of his life, Tobin begins the meaningless quest of building a wall around his house. When finished it would be ten feet tall on footings that extend below the frost line, and it will have no gate or entrance–the only way into the yard would be through the house. To get by in the winter months, Tobin begins digging a sub-basement by hand, "for storage" he says, but that's not it. The real reason is to keep moving, mindlessly, while feeling every ounce of guilt and remorse he feels he has coming.

In the five books about Tobin, he helps people the cops won't, only doing so reluctantly and under the unspoken pressure from his wife, the woman who has forgiven him and wants desperately for her husband to rejoin the living. By helping these people, Kate hopes Mitch will get out of the house, maybe even begin to care about something again, and restart his life.

When the Tucker Coe books came out, it was no secret that an established author was using the name as a pseudonym. But who was it? In the fourth novel by Coe, *A Jade in Aries* (1970), Mitch Tobin calls a friend of his still on the police force:

> "Don!" he said. "Good to hear from you!"
> I said, "This is Mitch. Mitch Tobin."
> "For God's sake," he said. "Hiya, Mitch. You sound just like Don Stark. You don't know him, do you?"
> "No, I don't."

Westlake could be one of the hardest, leanest writers working (the Stark books) but he could also be among the funniest with books like *The Fugitive Pigeon* (1965) and *Dancing Aztecs* (1976). Some of his funniest works are entries in the Dortmunder series. His standalones could be either serious or comic in nature.

Some of his more notable serious standalones are *The Ax* (1997), a story about the lengths an unemployed man will go to increase his odds for a new position; *The Hook* (2000), about two writers at opposite ends of their careers and what each is willing to do to get what the other has; and *Adios Scheherezade* (1970), the semi-autobiographical story of the paperback industry and how writing erotic soft-core novels can actually drive you crazy.

In addition to novel and short story writing, Westlake wrote screenplays for both the small and the big screen, often adapting other authors' works to the movies, like Patricia Highsmith, Ed McBain and Jim Thompson. The Thompson book was *The Grifters*, made into a movie of the same name in 1990, starring John Cusack and Anjelica Huston, and for which Westlake was nominated for an Oscar for best screenplay based on another medium.

Beyond his ability to write compulsively readable prose as Richard Stark, as well as his sense of humor in the Dortmunder series (and other comic novels), Westlake was an absolute genius at plotting. With over a hundred and ten novels to his credit, there's no shortage of proof, or of readers, that would agree. Unfortunately for all of us, Westlake died of a heart attack on his way to dinner on a New Year's Eve in Mexico.

**Further reading:**
*Parker series (complete):*
THE HUNTER (aka PAYBACK) (1962)
THE MAN WITH THE GETAWAY FACE (1963)
THE OUTFIT (1963)
THE MOURNER (1963
THE SCORE (1964)
THE JUGGER (1965)
THE SEVENTH (aka THE SPLIT) (1966)
THE HANDLE (1966)
THE DAMSEL (1967)
THE RARE COIN SCORE (1967)
THE GREEN EAGLE SCORE (1967)
THE DAME (1968)
THE BLACK ICE SCORE (1969)
THE SOUR LEMON SCORE (1969)
DEADLY EDGE (1969)
THE BLACKBIRD (1971)
SLAYGROUND (1971)
LEMONS NEVER LIE (1971)
PLUNDER SQUAD (1972)
BUTCHER'S MOON (1974)
COMEBACK (1997)
BACKFLASH (1998)
FLASHFIRE (2000)
FIREBREAK (2001)
BREAKOUT (2001)
NOBODY RUNS FOREVER (2004)
ASK THE PARROT (2006)
DIRTY MONEY (2008)

*Dortmunder series (complete):*
THE HOT ROCK (1970)
BANK SHOT (1972)
JIMMY THE KID (1974)

NOBODY'S PERFECT (1977)
WHY ME? (1983)
GOOD BEHAVIOR (1985)
DROWNED HOPES (1990)
DON'T ASK (1993)
WHAT'S THE WORST THAT COULD HAPPEN? (1996)
BAD NEWS (2001)
THE ROAD TO RUIN (2004)
WATCH YOUR BACK! (2005)
WHAT'S SO FUNNY? (2007)
GET REAL (2009)

*Mitch Tobin series (complete):*
KINDS OF LOVE, KINDS OF DEATH (1966)
MURDER AMONG CHILDREN (1967)
WAX APPLE (1970)
A JADE IN ARIES (1970)
DON'T LIE TO ME (1972)

THE MERCENARIES (aka THE SMASHERS, THE CUTIE) (1960)
361 (1962)
PITY HIM AFTERWARDS (1964)
THE FUGITIVE PIGEON (1965)
THE SPY IN THE OINTMENT (1966)
GOD SAVE THE MARK (1967)
SOMEBODY OWES ME MONEY (1969)
ADIOS SCHEHEREZADE (1970)
COPS AND ROBBERS (1972)
DANCING AZTECS (1976)
KAHAWA (1981)
A LIKELY STORY (1984)
HIGH ADVENTURE (1985)
TRUST ME ON THIS (1988)
SMOKE (1995)
THE AX (1997)
THE HOOK (2000)
PUT A LID ON IT (2002)
MONEY FOR NOTHING (2003)

---

**If you like Donald E. Westlake,** you might like: Lawrence Block, Peter Rabe, Lionel White, Jim Thompson, Evan Hunter/Ed McBain, Craig Rice

# Lionel White

(also wrote as L. W. Blanco). Born in Buffalo, New York, 1905. Died Asheville, North Carolina, 1985.

 Lionel White, "The King of the Caper Novels," knew of what he wrote: he was a police reporter both in Ohio (1923-1925) and New York (1925-1933), and he edited true crime magazines such as *True Detective*, *American Detective* and *Homicide Detective* (1933-1951). By the end of his tenure at the true crime mags, White was thoroughly educated in the ways and means of crime and criminals, and in 1953 he published his first book, *The Snatchers*. It is the story of a criminal gang, each member having their own specialized and specific role to play in the kidnapping and ransoming of a young girl. Because of a combination of supposedly trivial mishaps, escalating tensions among the characters and plain old bad luck, the caper comes apart at the seams.

The core of White's caper novels is that the criminals treat the heist as a business, with division of labor being the driving force. In *Clean Break/The Killing* Johnny Clay is an ex-con who plans the caper—a race track heist. Unger is a court stenographer who finances the caper. Mike is a bartender at the race track who will cause a diversion so Johnny can slip into the back room where the money is. George is a cashier at the track who will open the back room door for Johnny. Keenan is a crooked cop who will pick up and drive away with the bags of money Johnny tosses out a window. In *The Big Caper* (1955), the caper is a bank robbery, and the division of labor is as follows: safecracker, arsonist, driver, hooligan.

White's other caper novels include *Operation-Murder* (1958), a train robbery caper; *Death Takes the Bus* (1957), a hijacking caper; and *Too Young to Die* (1958), a diamond robbery caper.

White wrote successful non-caper crime books as well, including *The Money Trap* (1964), which mystery writer Ed Gorman called, "one dazzling sumbitch of a book."

A healthy portion of White's books have been made into movies. *The Snatchers*—filmed as *The Night of the Following Day* (1968, starring Marlon Brando and Richard Boone). *Clean Break*—filmed as *The Killing* (1956, starring Sterling Hayden, Elisha Cook, Jr. and Marie Windsor, directed by Stanley Kubrick, screenplay by Kubrick and Jim Thompson). *The Big Caper* (1957, starring Rory Calhoun). *The Money Trap* (1965, starring Glenn Ford, Elke Sommer and Rita Hayworth).

As an interesting side note, and as an unfortunate testament to the authenticity of White's understanding of the mechanics of a caper, in

1960, two criminals in France used *The Snatchers* as the blueprint for their own real life kidnapping caper, their victim being Peugeot auto-dynasty heir, four year-old Eric Peugeot.

**Further Reading:**
THE SNATCHERS (1953)
TO FIND A KILLER (1954; as BEFORE I DIE, 1964)
LOVE TRAP (1955)
THE BIG CAPER (1955)
CLEAN BREAK (1955; as THE KILLING, 1956)
FLIGHT INTO TERROR (1955)
OPERATION–MURDER (1956)
THE HOUSE NEXT DOOR (1956)
RIGHT FOR MURDER (1957)
DEATH TAKES THE BUS (1957)
HOSTAGE FOR A HOOD (1957)
COFFIN FOR A HOOD (1958)
TOO YOUNG TO DIE (1958)
INVITATION TO VIOLENCE (1958)
THE MERRIWEATHER FILE (1959)
RAFFERTY (1959)
RUN, KILLER, RUN (1959)
LAMENT FOR A VIRGIN (1960)
STEAL BIG (1960)
MARILYN K (1960)
THE TIME OF TERROR (1960)
A GRAVE UNDERTAKING (1961)
A DEATH AT SEA (1961)
OBSESSION (1962)
THE MONEY TRAP (1963)
THE RANSOMED MADONNA (1964)
THE HOUSE ON K STREET (1965)
A PARTY TO MURDER (1966)
THE CRIMSHAW MEMORANDUM (1967)
HIJACK (1969)
DEATH OF A CITY (1970)
THE MEXICO RUN (1974)
PROTECT YOURSELF, YOUR FAMILY, AND YOUR PROPERTY IN AN UNSAFE
WORLD (1974, non-fiction)

---

**If you like Lionel White,** you might like: Milton K. Ozaki, Gil Brewer

# Raoul Whitfield

(also wrote as Ramon Decolta, Temple Field). Born in New York City, New York, 1898. Died in Los Angeles, California, 1945.

Along with Dashiell Hammett, Raoul Whitfield was an early shaper and molder of the "Black Mask style," characterized by a tough, steely-eyed objectivity and understated realism.

Whitfield came from an upper class background, and throughout his life his personal character reflected this—suave looking, he was a natty dresser and something of a bon vivant. He wanted to be in the movies and found work as an extra in 1916, but his acting career was curtailed by the U.S. entry into WWI. He served in United States Army Air Corps and saw action in France, which lent realism to his stories written for pulps such as *Air Trails* and *Battle Stories*. After the war he worked as a reporter for the *Pittsburgh Post*.

Whitfield started writing short stories for the pulps in 1924. His earliest tales were published in *Sports Story Magazine*, *Breezy Stories* and *Droll Stories*. In April, 1926, he broke into the ranks of *Black Mask* with his story, "Scotty Scouts Around." His most popular character for *BM* was Filipino private eye Jo Gar, published under the pseudonym Ramon Decolta. Whitfield had spent much of his youth in Manila, and his experiences lent authenticity to the Gar stories. *Black Mask* published twenty-five Gar stories from February 1930 to July 1933. Mystery writer Ellery Queen wrote that the Jo Gar tales contained "the best features of the hardboiled manner; the aura of authenticity, the staccato speech, the restrained realism. The tales are lean and hard—and unforgettable." (*The Dime Detectives*, by Ron Goulart, page 43.) Whitfield wrote a total of ninety stories for *Black Mask*, from 1926-34.

Whitefield's first novel was *Green Ice* (1930, first serialized in five parts in *Black Mask*, December 1929 to April 1930). It was a hardboiled crime story about Mal Ourney, an ex-con (actually innocent, having taken the rap for a lover) who goes on a crusade against some crime bosses and gets involved in intrigues involving emeralds and murder. The book received heady praise from critic Will Cuppy, who claimed Whitfield's writing was superior to Dashiell Hammett's. Hammett himself praised the book as "280 pages of naked action pounded into tough compactness by staccato, hammerlike writing." Since he and Whitfield were drinking buddies, though, his words need to be taken with a grain of salt, as well as a shot of rum.

Whitfield's second novel was *Death in a Bowl* (1931). Originally serialized in *Black Mask*, September-November, 1930, it began the long tradition of

Hollywood-set PI novels. In the story, private detective Ben Jardinn investigates the murder of an orchestra leader who was gunned down while conducting a concert at the Hollywood Bowl. Whitfield's last novel under his own name, *The Virgin Kills* (1932), revolves around a series of crimes committed on a yacht.

Whitfield's later life was marred by scandal and squandered talent. In 1933, he wed twice-married Emily Davies Vanderbilt Thayer, a New York socialite and former wife of wealthy magnate William H. Vanderbilt and theater producer Sigourney Thayer. In 1935, Emily shot herself to death with a .38 caliber revolver on their ranch (eerily named Deadhorse ranch) in New Mexico. She left the entirety of her substantial estate to Whitfield. Always a heavy partier, (often with fellow pulp scribes Hammett and Frederick Nebel), Whitfield continued living the high life after his wife's death, writing little and blowing his inheritance. Near the end of his life, suffering from TB, he had to borrow $500 from Hammett to pay hospital bills. He died at the age of forty-eight.

**Further Reading:**
GREEN ICE (1930; as THE GREEN ICE MURDERS, 1947)
DEATH IN A BOWL (1931)
THE VIRGIN KILLS (1932)

**As Temple Field**
FIVE (1931)
KILLER'S CARNIVAL (1932)

---

**If you like Raoul Whitfield,** you might like: Dashiell Hammett, Howard Browne

# *Harry Whittington*

(also wrote as Whit Harrison, Hallam Whitney, Ashley Carter, Robert Hart Davis, Tabor Evans, Clay Stuart, Hondo Wells, Henry White, John Dexter, J. X. Williams, Curt Colman, Kel Holland, Harriet Kathryn Myers, Suzanne Stephens, Blaine Stevens, Harry White, Henry Whittier, Howard Winslow, Steve Philips). Born in Ocala, Florida, 1915. Died in 1989.

 Harry Whittington has been rightly dubbed "The King of the Paperbacks." He wrote more than 150 novels between 1945-1965—crime fiction, westerns, "sleaze," historical fiction, "backwoods" novels and TV novelizations, along with books that perhaps can't be placed in any particular genre. It's widely regarded among paperback aficionados that the quality of Whittington's work did not suffer due to its quantity. His characters are three dimensional, believable and show psychological depth. He is noted in particular for his expertly crafted, suspense-filled plots. Mystery writer Bill Crider calls the pace of Whittington's novels "faster than a speeding bullet."

Harry Whittington grew up in Florida. After graduating high school, he worked as an advertising agency copywriter, an assistant manager and advertising manager for the Capitol Theater, and as editor of the *St. Petersburg Advocate*. He served in the United States Navy from 1945-1946.

Whittington wrote his first crime novel, *Slay Ride for a Lady*, in 1950. The books crime writers and reviewers note as being some of Whittington's best in the genre are *Fires That Destroy* (1951), *Brute in Brass* (1958), *Web of Murder* (1958), *A Ticket to Hell* (1959), *The Devil Wears Wings* (1960) and *A Night for Screaming* (1960).

Whittington rarely wrote about private detectives. In an autobiographical essay, he noted that he instead focused on everyday people, "their insides, their desires, and fears and hurts and joys of achievement and loss...If a character hurt in his guts, I wrote to make you *feel* how bad he hurt." ("I Remember It Well," by Harry Whittington, italics Whittington's.) Many of Whittington's crime novels were published by paperback publisher Gold Medal.

Whittington's first western was his first published novel, *Vengeance Valley* (1945). Notable western titles include *Saddle the Storm* (1954), *Man in the Shadow* (1958), *Trouble Rides Tall* (1958), *A Trap for Sam Dodge* (1962) and *Valley of Savage Men* (1965). As with his crime fiction, Whittington brought a personal approach to his westerns: "I never wrote westerns about 'cowboys' or Indians or 'hold-up men.' I wrote about people in a raw rugged land who loved, hated, feared and saw murder for what it was—murder....They used guns as you would in the same situation—as a last resort." (*I Remember It Well*, by Whittington.)

A number of Whittington's "backwoods" novels were written under the name Hallam Whitney. They include *Backwoods Hussy* (1952), *Shack Road* (1953), *Backwoods Shack* (1954) and *The Wild Seed* (1956).

In 1968, because of numerous hassles involving publishers and his agent, Whittington quit writing fiction. He was "too tired, too disappointed, too depleted." So from 1968-1975, he worked for the government as an editor for the U.S. Department of Agriculture.

In 1975, he returned to fiction writing. Using the name Ashley Carter, he wrote stories for the Falconhurst and Blackoaks series. These novels were set in the pre-Civil War Deep South, and revolved around plantation life and slavery. He also returned to westerns, writing novels in the *Longarm* series using the house name Tabor Evans.

Recently, nearly 40 "lost" Whittington books were discovered. They were written during the early 1960's for various softcore "sleaze" publishers under the names J. X. Williams, John Dexter and Curt Coleman. Titles include *Lust Farm* (1964, as by J. X. Williams), *Flesh Avenger* (1964, as by J. X. Williams) and *Saddle Sinners* (1964, as by John Dexter).

**Further Reading:**
VENGEANCE VALLEY (1946)
SLAY RIDE FOR A LADY (1950)
CALL ME A KILLER (1951)
FIRES THAT DESTROY (1951)
THE LADY WAS A TRAMP (1951)
MOURN THE HANGMAN (1952)
SO DEAD MY LOVE! (1953)
YOU'LL DIE NEXT! (1954)
ONE GOT AWAY (1955)
BRUTE IN BRASS (1956)
DESIRE IN THE DUST (1956)
SATURDAY NIGHT TOWN (1956))
WEB OF MURDER (1958)
BACKWOODS TRAMP (1959)
A TICKET TO HELL (1959)
THE DEVIL WEARS WINGS (1960)
A NIGHT FOR SCREAMING (1960)

**As Whit Harrison**
SWAMP KILL (1951)
BODY AND PASSION (1952)
RAPTURE ALLEY (1953)
STRIP THE TOWN NAKED (1960)
ANY WOMAN HE WANTED (1961)

**As Hallam Whitney**
BACKWOODS HUSSY (1952; as LISA, 1965)
BACKWOODS SHACK (1953)
SHACK ROAD (1953)
CITY GIRL (1954)
SHANTY ROAD (1954; as by Whit Harrison, 1956)

**As J. X. Williams**
LUST FARM (1964)
FLESH AVENGER (1964)
THE SHAME HIDERS (1964)
PASSION HANGOVER (1965)

---

**If you like Harry Whittington,** you might like: Day Keene, Gil Brewer,
Charles Williams

# Charles Willeford

(also wrote as Will Charles, W. Franklin Sanders). Born in Little Rock, Arkansas, 1919. Died in Miami, Florida, 1988.

A cult author who achieved popular success after thirty-five years of publishing novels, Charles Willeford smuggled critiques of capitalism and bits of existential philosophy between the covers of his dark and gritty paperbacks. His stories were told with a sly, sardonic narrative voice, deadpan and free from melodrama. His protagonists were bland sociopaths, with a casual attitude about the emotional and/or physical pain they inflicted on others.

Willeford started out living a hardscrabble life. Orphaned at eight years-old, he was raised by his grandmother until he was twelve, then tramped through America as a hobo for four years, and finally joined the Army at sixteen years of age (an experience he recounted in his memoir, *Something About a Soldier*, 1986). It was in the service where he encountered a number of men who would become the model for the sociopaths he wrote about. "A good half of the men you deal with in the Army are psychopaths. There's a pretty hefty overlap between the military population and the prison population, so I knew plenty of guys like Junior in *Miami Blues* and Troy in *Sideswipe*." (*Noir Fiction: Dark Highways*, by Paul Duncan, pg. 72). Willeford remained in the Army throughout WWII, where he received the Silver Star, the Bronze Star, the Purple Heart and the Luxembourg Croix de Guerre. Throughout his time in the service, Willeford exercised his writing muscles by ghost writing speeches for base commanders and penning soap opera scripts for the Armed Services radio network.

Willeford's first published work appeared in the poetry anthology, *The Outcast Poets* (1947); he then had his own book of poetry published, *Proletarian Laughter* (1948). While stationed at Hamilton Air Force Base in California, Willeford wrote his first novel. Titled *High Priest of California* (1953), Willeford published it with the low-budget, softcore adult paperback publisher, Beacon books. However, the book was hardly par-for-the course for Beacon's sleazy tales of titillation. On a surface level, Russell Haxby, an amoral used car salesman (is there any other kind?), spends the course of the book trying to get a married woman into the sack. However, during the course of the plot, Willeford is able to poke satirical jabs at the ruthlessness of the capitalist system, as well as referencing such highbrow literary authors as James Joyce and Franz Kafka. Hardly what you would expect from a book whose cover blurb reads, "No woman could resist his strange cult of lechery!"

*Pick-Up* (1955, also published by Beacon) is a bleak tale about a couple of down-on-their luck alcoholics (a man and woman) who spiral downward into despair and death; it has a surprise ending which makes you re-examine all of what has come before. *The Woman Chaser* (1960, published by Newwstand Library, another low-rent paperback publisher) is about a used car salesman who, in an effort to escape life in a mundane, mechanized capitalist system, becomes a film director and makes a cinematic opus exposing that system. *Honey Gal* (1958, reprinted by Black Lizard under Willeford's original title, *The Black Mass of Brother Springer*) has been called Willeford's funniest and most outrageous novel; the story is about a white ex-accountant/failed novelist who buys his way into becoming a minister for a small all-black church, seduces the wife of one of his congregants, and is ultimately responsible for starting a race riot.

Owing to the fact that he wasn't exactly raking in the millions by publishing with low-rung paperback publishers, Willeford sought out additional means of making a living. He decided to make up for the formal education he missed as a younger man and went to college, receiving a BA in English literature from the University of Miami in 1962, and an MA in 1964. He taught humanities at U of M from 1964-67, then moved to Miami-Dade Junior College, where he taught English and philosophy for eighteen years, from 1967-85. Willeford also wrote columns for the *Village Voice* and *Mystery Scene*, as well as reviewing crime fiction for the *Miami Herald*.

During these years he published three novels, two of which were significant. *Cockfighter* (1962), modeled on Homer's *Odyssey*, is the off-beat tale of Frank Mansfield, who is pursuing his obsession to win the title of Cockfighter of the Year. Mansfield, the first-person narrator, remains silent throughout the book, having taken a vow not to speak until he has won the title. Willeford expertly depicts the seedy world of cockpits, bars, and dusty roads of the rural South, as well as the debasing brutality of the sport of cockfighting and the men involved in it. Willeford revised *Cockfighter* in 1972 for hardcover publication, and in 1974 it was made into a movie, starring Warren Oates, directed by Monte Hellman, and produced by Roger Corman. Willeford wrote the script and played a small supporting role.

*The Burnt Orange Heresy* (1971) is considered one of Willeford's best novels. The story of Jamie Figueras, an art critic with a lust to become as famous as the artists he critiques, the book satirizes art critics, dealers and collectors, and the way they exploit the artist. Figueras is another of Willeford's classic amoral, scheming, backstabbing protagonists.

Willeford finally achieved wider critical and financial success with *Miami Blues* (1984). The story is about Miami homicide detective Hoke Moseley's clash with a brutal psychopath named Freddy "Junior" Frenger. Moseley is a crusty, put-upon older cop, just trying to do his job in the midst of much vice and corruption. The novel is filled with black humor—at one point, Frenger steals Moseley's set of false teeth. Willeford uses the novel in part to depict the seedy underbelly of South Florida. *Miami Blues* was made into a successful movie in 1990 starring Alec Baldwin, Jennifer Jason Leigh and Fred Ward.

After the success of *Miami Blues*, Willeford wrote a sequel he called *Grimhaven*, a massive departure from the previous book. Instead of acting as a conventional hero, Willeford's Moseley has retired from the police force and goes all the way to the dark side as he perpetrates unspeakable violence against his own loved ones. Willeford's agent refused to submit it to the publisher and urged Willeford to write another book instead. Fortunately Willeford took the advice and went on to pen three more Hoke Moseley novels, *New Hope For the Dead* (1985), *Sideswipe* (1987) and *The Way We Die Now* (1988). *Grimhaven* is available to be read on-site at the Willeford archive in Broward County, Florida.

Willeford died of a heart attack soon after finishing his final Moseley novel.

**Further Reading:**
*Hoke Moseley series:*
MIAMI BLUES (1984)
NEW HOPE FOR THE DEAD (1985)
SIDESWIPE (1987)
THE WAY WE DIE NOW (1988)

HIGH PRIEST OF CALIFORNIA (1953)
PICK-UP (1955)
WILD WIVES (1956)
HONEY GAL (1958; reprinted as
   THE BLACK MASS OF BROTHER SPRINGER, 1989)
LUST IS A WOMAN (1958)
THE WOMAN CHASER (1960)
THE WHIP HAND (1961, as by W. Franklin Sanders)
UNDERSTUDY FOR LOVE (1961)
COCKFIGHTER (1962, revised in 1972)
THE MACHINE IN WARD ELEVEN (1963; short stories)
THE BURNT ORANGE HERESY (1971)
THE HOMBRE FROM SONORA (1971, as by WILL CHARLES;
   reprinted as THE DIFFERENCE, 1999)
OFF THE WALL (1980, non-fiction account of Son of Sam case)
SOMETHING ABOUT A SOLDIER (1986, autobiography)

NEW FORMS OF UGLY: THE IMMOBILIZED HERO IN MODERN FICTION
(1987, non-fiction, master's thesis, literary analysis of writers including
Kafka, Dostoevsky, Samuel Beckett, Chester Himes and Saul Bellow)
I WAS LOOKING FOR A STREET (1988, autobiography)
COCKFIGHTER JOURNAL: THE STORY OF A SHOOTING (1989, non-fiction,
diary recounting the filming of the movie)
THE SHARK-INFESTED CUSTARD (1993)

---

If you like Charles Willeford, you might like: David Karp, Jim Thompson,
Charles Williams, Elliott Chaze

# Charles Williams

Born in San Angelo, Texas, 1909. Died in Van Nuys, California, 1975.

 Geoffrey O' Brien's description of the work of paper-back writer Charles Williams is apt: "Williams is at face value the epitome of the macho adventure writer. His heroes are characteristically preoccupied with hunting (*Hill Girl*), fishing (*River Girl; Go Home, Stranger; Girl Out Back*), athletics (*The Big Bite, A Touch of Death*) and above all, with sailing (*Scorpion Reef, Aground, The Sailcloth Shroud, Dead Calm*)." (*Hardboiled America: Lurid Paperbacks and the Masters of Noir*, by Geoffrey O'Brien, p.142)

Williams served as a radio operator for the United States Merchant Marine from 1929-1939. He later worked for the Radiomarine Corporation and at the Puget Sound Navy Yard.

Williams was nearly 40 years old when he wrote his first novel, *Hill Girl* (1951, Gold Medal). The book's first printing sold more than a million copies. *Hill Girl* was the first book in what became known as the "girl trilogy," along with *Big City Girl* (1951) and *River Girl* (1951). These novels are set among the backwoods swamplands of Texas and West Florida; in the stories, a man's desire for a nubile, sexually desirable woman brings about his destruction.

The novels during the middle part of Williams's writing career concern lustful, greedy men who try for a big score with money and with a woman, but who wind up losing both. *Hell Hath No Fury* (1953), *The Big Bite* (1956) and *All the Way* (1958) are notable examples. The stories are suspenseful intrigues involving classic love triangle relationships, where the male protagonists eventually realize they don't know as much about women as they had thought. *Hell Hath No Fury* was later filmed as *The Hot Spot* (1990), starring Don Johnson, Virginia Madsen and Jennifer Conelly, directed by Dennis Hopper. *All The Way* was filmed as *The 3rd Voice* in 1960, starring Edmond O'Brien, Julie London and Laraine Day.

When Williams started putting his seafaring experience to good use in his fiction, he produced what many fans and reviewers consider to be his best work. *Scorpion Reef* (1955, aka *Gulf Coast Girl*) starts off with the discovery of a mysteriously abandoned boat in the Gulf of Mexico, floating calmly, with plenty of provisions, and with no sign of violence. A logbook found on board tells the story of how the boat was abandoned— a complex plot involving sunken treasure, infidelity and two cold-blooded killers.

In *Dead Calm* (1963) John and Rae Ingram, sailing aboard the *Orpheus*, encounter a drifting boat called the *Saracen*. They become separated—John aboard the *Saracen* and under the control of a maniac, and Rae by herself on the *Orpheus*, struggling to survive with scant sailing experience. *Dead Calm* was made into a movie in 1989 starring Nicole Kidman.

Williams's wife of 33 years died of cancer in 1972, and he became increasingly depressed and despondent. In 1975, Williams's agent, Don Congdon, received a letter: "It was very strange," Congdon says. "So cold and purposeful. One morning I'm sitting in my office and I get a letter from Charlie and it says that by the time I read this, he'll have killed himself, which is exactly what he did…I couldn't tell you why, not for sure, and I would rather not speculate on it." (*Fifteen Impressions of Charles Williams*, an article by Ed Gorman in *The Big Book of Noir*, pg. 254.)

**Further Reading:**
HILL GIRL (1951)
BIG CITY GIRL (1951)
RIVER GIRL (1951)
HELL HATH NO FURY (1953)
NOTHING IN HER WAY (1953)
A TOUCH OF DEATH (1954)
GO HOME, STRANGER (1954)
SCORPION REEF (1955)
THE BIG BITE (1956)
THE DIAMOND BIKINI (1956)
GIRL OUT BACK (1958)
MAN ON THE RUN (1958)
TALK OF THE TOWN (1958)
ALL THE WAY (1958)
UNCLE SAGAMORE AND HIS GIRLS (1959)
AGROUND (1960)
THE SAILCLOTH SHROUD (1960)
NUDE ON THIN ICE (1961)
THE LONG SATURDAY NIGHT (1962)
DEAD CALM (1963)
THE WRONG VENUS (1966)
AND THE DEEP BLUE SEA (1971)
MAN ON A LEASH (1973)

---

**If you like Charles Williams,** you might like: Harry Whittington, John D. MacDonald

# Ennis Willie
Born in Louisville, Georgia, 1939.

Ennis Willie was the creator of uber tough-guy Sand, "The Man Nobody Walks On."

As a young man growing up in Louisville, Willie's literary tastes were formed by the tomes on the paperback rack at the local Rexall drug store. The stories contained within whisked him away to places more adventurous than he was likely to find in his small town:

"There was a wider world there, an education beyond the boundaries of the classroom, with alleys and avenues to explore and mean streets to travel." ("Ennis Willie Gets the Third Degree," interview by Stephen Mertz, *Paperback Parade*, #65, pg. 60)

Favorite writers included Mickey Spillane, who taught Willie that "vengeance is a better motivator than all the rest," and David Goodis, who showed that "you can find a hero even among the lowest of the low, because there can come a time when any step up, no matter how small, is a triumph."

While attending Bolen Business University in Augusta, 1961, Willie wrote his first book, a non-series book called *The Work of the Devil*. Willie's first Sand book was *Scarlet Goddess* (1963). Sand was a former member of "the Syndicate" who broke the cardinal rule that you can never quit the outfit. But of course, Sand knows the Syndicate's secrets, so he's constantly on the run from hit men.

In his *Paperback Parade* interview, Stephen Mertz writes that the hallmarks of the Sand novels are "larger than life heroes, vivid scenes of violence... and powerful last-page surprise endings." Willie wrote nine Sand novels between 1963 and 1965, notable titles including *Haven for the Damned* (1963), *And Some Were Evil* (1964) and *Warped Ambitions* (1965).

The plots in the series often revolved around Sand returning to an old town to avenge the death of a friend, or someone who'd done him a favor or kindness during his syndicate days. The settings were corrupt southern towns, many based on Phenix City, Alabama, a town where the vice and political corruption had gotten so bad during the 1940's and '50's that the state of Alabama declared martial law in order to shut it down.

Willie also wrote 11 non-series books, featuring tough guys similar to Sand with classic macho men names such as Birch Sunday, Tripp Fortune, Gard Hogan and Cruss Ballard.

Willie cranked out twenty-one books between 1961 and 1965, then burned out and stopped writing, going on to create a successful printing company. As the decades passed, his books have built a small but fervent cult following–fans include writers such as Max Allan Collins, Ed Gorman and Stephen Mertz. Recently, two collections of his Sand novels have been reissued.

**Further Reading:**
*Sand series (complete):*
SCARLET GODDESS (1963)
AURA OF SENSUALITY (1963)
HAVEN FOR THE DAMNED (1963)
GAME OF PASSION (1964)
AND SOME WERE EVIL (1964)
WARPED AMBITIONS (1964)
THE CASE OF THE LOADED GARTER HOLSTER (1964)
CODE OF VENGEANCE (1965)

THE WORK OF THE DEVIL (1961; reprinted as MODERN LOVE)
LUSCIOUS, TEASING BODY (1961; reprinted as THE SENSUALITES)
MODERN GIGOLO (1962; reprinted as EROTIC SEARCH)
VICE TOWN (1962)
CARNAL LOVE NEST (1963; reprinted as THAT KIND OF WOMAN)
CARNAL MADNESS (1963; reprinted as TO LIVE DANGEROUSLY)
TWISTED MISTRESS (1963)
POLITICIAN'S PLAYGIRL (1963)
SO NAKED! SO DEAD! (1963)
A NEW KIND OF LOVE (1964)
INCREDIBLY SEDUCTIVE (1964)
SENSUAL GAME (1964)

---

**If you like Ennis Willie,** you might like: Orrie Hitt, Mickey Spillane, Dan J. Marlowe

# Cornell Woolrich

(real name Cornell George Hopley Woolrich; also wrote as William Irish, George Hopley). Born in New York City, New York, 1903. Died in New York City, New York, 1968.

 Cornell Woolrich—poet of the dark, the vacant, the wounded, the lonely, the isolated, the alienated, the trapped and the lost.

Cornell Woolrich—who began his career by trying (but failing) to be the next F. Scott Fitzgerald, and who imbued his first five novels (starting with *Cover Charge*, 1926) with Fitzgerald's brand of youthful romanticism.

Cornell Woolrich—who learned about plotting suspense and crime fiction during the 1930's by writing for pulps such as *Black Mask*, *Dime Detective* and *Dime Mystery*, among others.

Cornell Woolrich—whose view of life was so dark that he wrote a series of books known as "the Black novels": *The Bride Wore Black* (1940), *The Black Curtain* (1941), *Black Alibi* (1942), *The Black Angel* (1943), *The Black Path of Fear* (1944) and *Rendezvous In Black* (1948).

Cornell Woolrich—who had so few close personal relationships that he dedicated *The Bride Wore Black* (1940) to his "Remington Portable [typewriter] No. NC69411" and *Phantom Lady* (1942) to "Apartment 605, Hotel M."

Cornell Woolrich—who Raymond Chandler called "the best idea man" in the suspense field, but who at times was guilty of writing sentences full of purple prose, and devising plots with incredible coincidences and obvious contrivances.

Cornell Woorich—who likely had more radio, movie and TV adaptations of his stories than any other crime writer, the highlights of which include the classic radio show *Suspense*; the movies *Phantom Lady* (1944), *Black Angel* (1946), *Night Has a Thousand Eyes* (1948), *Rear Window* (1954) and *The Bride Who Wore Black* (1968); and the TV shows *Alfred Hitchcock Presents* and *Playhouse 90*.

Cornell Woolrich—who had a brief marriage (bride and groom were separated after three months), who lived with his mother until she died at age 57 and who was an in-the-closet homosexual who wrote scathing portraits of effeminate men when they appeared in his fiction.

Cornell Woolrich—who, as young as the age of eleven, felt the spectre of death looming so keenly that he "looked up at the low hanging stars of the Valley of Anahuac, and I knew I would surely die finally, or something worse. I had that trapped feeling, like some sort of poor insect that you've put inside a downturned glass, and it tries to climb up the sides, and it can't, and it can't, and it can't." (*Blues of a Lifetime: The Autobiography of Cornell Woolrich*, Edited by Mark Bassett, pg. 16)

Cornell Woolrich—who, in 1967, developed gangrene in his leg, but who sat and sat in his hotel room—drinking, sleeping, watching TV—until it had to be amputated.

Cornell Woolrich—who, near the very end, was so lonely he invited the hotel staff (at the Sheraton-Russell in Manhattan, where he was staying at the time) to his room to drink and watch TV with him.

Cornell Woolrich—who lived and died alone.

**Further Reading:**
THE BRIDE WORE BLACK (1940; as BEWARE THE LADY, 1953)
THE BLACK CURTAIN (1941)          BLACK ALIBI (1942)
THE BLACK ANGEL (1943)          THE BLACK PATH OF FEAR (1944)
RENDEZVOUS IN BLACK (1948)          SAVAGE BRIDE (1950)
DEATH IS MY DANCING PARTNER (1959)
THE DOOM STONE (1960)

*Short story collections:*
NIGHTMARE (1956)
VIOLENCE (1958)
HOTEL ROOM (1958)
BEYOND THE NIGHT (1959)
THE TEN FACES OF CORNELL WOOLRICH (1965)
NIGHTWEBS (1971)

**As William Irish**
PHANTOM LADY (1942)
DEADLINE AT DAWN (1944)
WALKZ INTO DARKNESS (1947)
I MARRIED A DEAD MAN (1948)
YOU'LL NEVER SEE ME AGAIN (1951)
STRANGLER'S SERENADE (1951)

*Short story collections:*
I WOULDN'T BE IN YOUR SHOES (1943)
AFTER-DINNER STORY (1944; as SIX TIMES DEATH, 1948)

**As George Hopley**
NIGHT HAS A THOUSAND EYES (1945)
FRIGHT (1950)

---

**If you like Cornell Woolrich,** you might like: David Goodis, Patricia Highsmith

# Richard Wormser

(also wrote as Nick Carter, Ed Friend, Conrad Gerson). Born in New York City, New York, 1908. Died in Tumacacori, Arizona, 1977.

Richard Wormser, during a career spanning more than forty-five years, wrote pulp stories, crime novels, westerns, screenplays, movie and TV novelizations, children's books and even a non-fiction book about American Southwest cooking.

Wormser's first writing job was for pulp magazine publisher Street and Smith, in 1933. Hoping to duplicate the success of their pulp, *The Shadow*, S&S hired Wormser to write a resurrected version of dime-novel hero, Nick Carter. Wormser wrote seventeen Carter novels in ten months, nearly a million words. Some of the Nick Carter titles include *Crime Flies High* (1933), *Death Has Green Eyes* (1934) and *The Newspaper Racket* (1934).

Wormser's novels were noted for their sharp dialogue and colorful characters. *The Man with the Wax Face* (1934) and *The Communist's Corpse* (1935) feature an odd couple of detectives: police sergeant Joe Dixon and a Swedish, Amazonian left wing newspaper writer named Erika Strindberg.

Noirish non-series novels include *The Hanging Heiress* (1949, reprinted as *The Widow Wore Red*, 1958), a story about Marty Cockren, hired to guard a widow who is due to inherit a fortune in thirty days; *Perfect Pigeon* (1962), about an ex-con tempted to return to his old ways; and *Drive East On 66* (1962), about a cop hired to accompany a mentally unhinged rich kid from California to Kansas.

Besides crime novels, Wormser also wrote successful westerns. He won a WWA Spur Award for *Ride a Northbound Horse* (1964) And he received a second Spur in 1971 for his western juvenile, *The Black Mustanger.*

Wormser wrote screenplays for many fast paced B-movies, including *Rustlers On Horseback* (1950), *The Half-Breed* (1952) and the above-average film noir, *Crime Wave* (1954, starring Sterling Hayden, directed by Andre De Toth). Wormser's story, "The Road To Carmichael's," was adapted for another excellent film noir, *The Big Steal* (1949), starring Robert Mitchum and Jane Greer, written by Daniel Mainwaring/Geoffrey Homes, and directed by Don Siegel. Wormser wrote teleplays for *Cheyenne, 77 Sunset Strip, Zane Grey Theater* and *Lassie*. His movie novelizations include *McClintock* (1963, starring John Wayne), *Bedtime Story* (1964, starring Marlon Brando and David Niven), *Torn Curtain* (1966, directed by Alfred Hitchcock) and *The Scalphunters* (1968, starring Burt Lancaster). Under the name Ed Friend, he wrote TV novelizations for episodes of *The Green Hornet, High Chapparal* and *The Most Deadly Game*.

More than forty years into his career, Wormser was still capable of cranking out fine entertainments, such as the Mafia related novels *The*

*Takeover* (1971) and *The Invader* (1972), which won the Edgar award for Best Paperback.

His memoir, *How to Become a Complete Non-Entity* (2006), was published posthumously, with help from Wormser's nephew, Ira Skutch.

A curio: *Southwest Cookery; or, At Home On the Range* (1969).

**Further Reading:**
THE MAN WITH THE WAX FACE (1934)
THE COMMUNIST'S CORPSE (1935)
ALL'S FAIR…(1937)
THE HANGING HEIRESS (1949; as THE WIDOW WORE RED, 1958)
THE LONESOME QUARTER (1951)
THE BODY LOOKS FAMILIAR (1958)
SLATTERY'S RANGE (1959)
THE LATE MRS. FIVE (1960)
DRIVE EAST ON 66 (1962)
PERFECT PIGEON (1962)
A NICE GIRL LIKE YOU (1963)
RIDE A NORTHBOUND HORSE (1964, children's book)
BEDTIME STORY (1964, movie novelization)
TORN CURTAIN (1966, movie novelization)
SOUTHWEST COOKERY; OR, AT HOME ON THE RANGE (1969, non-fiction)
THE BLACK MUSTANGER (1971, children's book)
THE TAKEOVER (1972)
THE INVADER (1972)

**As Ed Friend**
THE INFERNAL LIGHT (1966, TV novelization)
THE SCALPHUNTERS (1968, movie novelization)
THE MOST DEADLY GAME (1970, TV novelization)
THE CORPSE IN THE CASTLE (1970)

------------------------------------------------------------

**If you like Richard Wormser,** you might like: Harry Whittington, Cleve F. Adams

# SOURCES

**BOOKS:**

Baker, Robert A. and Nietzel, Michael T. *Private Eyes: 101 Knights*. Bowling Green, Ohio: Bowling Green University Popular Press, 1985.

Calcutt, Andrew and Richard Shephard. *Cult Fiction: a reader's guide*. Chicago: Contemporary Books, 1999.

DeAndrea, William L.. *Encyclopedia Mysteriosa*. Prentice Hall, 1994/

Duncan, Paul. *Noir Fiction: Dark Highways*. Pocket Essentials, 2003.

Gehmen, David. *The American Private Eye: The Image in Fiction*. New York: Frederick Ungar Publishing Co, 1985.

Gorman, Ed, Bill Pronzini, and Martin H. Greenberg, eds. *American Pulp*. New York, Carroll and Graff, 1997.

Gorman, Ed, Lee Server, and Martin H. Greenberg, eds. *The Big Book of Noir*. New York: Carroll and Graf, 1998.

Goulart, Ron. *Cheap Thrills. The Amazing! Thrilling! Astonishing! History of Pulp Fiction*. Neshannock, Pennsylvania: Hermes Press, 2007.

_____. *The Dime Detectives*. New York: The Mysterious Press 1988.

Haut, Woody. *Heartbreak and Vine: The Fate of Hardboiled Writers in Hollywood*. London: Serpent's Tail, 2002.

_____. *Pulp Culture: Hardboiled Fiction and the Cold War*. London: Serpent's Tail, 1995.

Henderson, Lesley, ed. *Twentieth Century Crime and Mystery Writers, Third Edition*. Chicago and London: St. James Press, 1991.

Lupoff, Richard A. *The Great American Paperback*. Portland, Oregon: Collector's Press, 2001.

Muller, Marcia and Bill Pronzini. *1001 Midnights: The Aficionado's Guide to Mystery and Detective Fiction*. New York: Arbor House, 1986.

O'Brien, Geoffrey. *Hardboiled America: Lurid Paperbacks and the Masters of Noir*. De Capo Press, Expanded Edition, 1997.

Pronzini, Bill. *Son of Gun in Cheek: An Affectionate Guide to More of the "Worst" in Mystery Fiction*. New York: The Mysterious Press, 1987.

Pronzini, Bill and Jack Adrian, eds. *Hard-Boiled: An Anthology of American Crime Stories*. Oxford University Press, 1997.

Server, Lee. *Encyclopedia of Pulp Fiction Writers*. New York: Checkmark Books, 2002.

_____. *Over My Dead Body: The Sensational Age of the American Paperback 1945-1955*. San Francisco, Chronicle Books, 1994.

Steinbrunner, Chris and Otto Penzler, eds. Encyclopedia of Mystery &
    Detection. McGraw-Hill, 1976
Zicree, Marc Scott. *The Twilight Zone Companion, Second Edition*. Los Angeles:
    Silman-James Press, 1992.

**WEBSITES:**
Allanguthrie.co.uk
Billcrider.blogspot.com
Fantasticfiction.co.uk
Fiction Mags Index: philsp.com/homeville/fmi/a4.htm
IMDB.com
Jamesreasoner.blogspot.com
Mysteryfile.com
Newimprovedgorman.blogspot.com
Miskatonic.org/rara-avis/archives
Thrillingdetective.com
Vinpulp.blogspot.com

# PSEUDODEX
## AN INDEX OF PSEUDONYMS

This index is an attempt at compiling the known pseudonyms of the authors listed in *Paperback Confidential*. There are an enormous number of challenges in trying to build a comprehensive list of this sort; indeed, it may not even be possible. There is no single source for this information, and no easy way to get *all* of it, assuming that it's even an achievable goal. That being said, this is a solid effort aimed at providing the best list possible.

The primary name of the author appears in bold, even though in many cases this is not the author's full or real name. In some cases the primary name itself is a pseudonym, and sometimes even that pseudonym was used by other authors (e.g. Brett Halliday, Ellery Queen). Similarly, there are house names, such as "C. K. M. Scanlon" that were shared by many writers, pseudonyms that were used as by collaborators (e.g. "Franklin Charles," used by Cleve F. Adams and Robert Leslie Bellem), and even ghostwriters (e.g. Craig Rice (a nom de plume itself) writing books for George Sanders and Gypsy Rose Lee).

There are also some cases where one author wrote as or completed a book for another (e.g. Gil Brewer wrote a book published as by Day Keene). Lastly, there are cases where work originally appeared under a pseudonym but has been reprinted under a different name (e.g. Kendell Foster Crossen).

Is this list complete? Almost certainly not. Is it completely accurate? As much as we could make it at the time of this writing. Is it a useful resource and companion section to the biographies of the wonderful authors written about in the body of this book? Well, we certainly hope so.

—*Rick Ollerman*

NOTE: Primary name of an author is in **bold**. The pseudonyms, real names, house names, ghostwriter names, all appear as separate listings referring the reader to the primary name as shown in the body of the book.

Charles, Franklin (with Robert Leslie Bellem) *see* **Adams, Cleve F.; Bellem, Robert Leslie**

Charles, Will *see* **Willeford, Charles**

Chase, Adam *see* **Marlowe, Stephen**

**Chase, James Hadley** (born René Brabazon Raymond; James L. Docherty, Ambrose Grant, Raymond Marshall, R. Raymond)

**Cheyney, Peter** (real name Reginald Southouse Cheyney, Lyn Southney, Harold Brust)

Cheyney, Reginald Southouse *see* **Cheyney, Peter**

Christopher, Ben *see* **Block, Lawrence; Westlake, Donald E.**

Clark, Curt *see* **Westlake, Donald E.**

Clark, Halsey *see* **Deming, Richard**

Clarke, Anne Campbell *see* **Block, Lawrence**

Clayborne, Logan *see* **Goodis, David**

Clayford, James *see* **Gaddis, Peggy**

Coe, Tucker *see* **Westlake, Donald E.**

Collins, Hunt *see* **Hunter, Evan**

Collinson, Peter *see* **Hammett, Dashiell**

Colman, Curt *see* **Whittington, Harry**

Conroy, Al *see* **Albert, Marvin; Brewer, Gil**

Conroy, Albert *see* **Albert, Marvin**

Conway, Tom *see* **Brown, Carter**

Conway, Troy *see* **Avallone, Michael**

Corbett, John *see* **Keene, Day**

Corning, Kyle *see* **Gardner, Erle Stanley**

Costello, P. F. *see* **McGivern, William P.**

Court, Harley L. *see* **Bellem, Robert Leslie**

Courtland, Roberta *see* **Gaddis, Peggy**

**Coxe, George Harmon**

Craig, Georgia *see* **Gaddis, Peggy**

Craig, Georgiana Ann Randolph Walker *see* **Rice, Craig**

**Craig, Jonathan** (born Frank E. Smith)

Crewe, David *see* **Goodis, David**

Crossen, Ken *see* **Crossen, Kendell Foster**

**Crossen, Kendell Foster** (Richard Foster, Bennett Barlay, M. E. Chaber, Christopher Monig, Clay Richards, Kent Richards, Ken Crossen)

Crowley, Liz *see* **Block, Lawrence**

Culver, Kathryn *see* **Halliday, Brett**

Culver, Timothy J. *see* **Westlake, Donald E.**

Cunningham, J. Morgan *see* **Westlake, Donald E.**

Curtis, Richard Hale *see* **Deming, Richard**

**Cushman, Dan**

Daemer, Will *see* **Miller, Wade**

Dalton, Priscilla *see* **Avallone, Michael**
**Daly, Carroll John** (John D. Carroll)
Dane, Mark *see* **Avallone, Michael**
Dannay, Frederic *see* **Queen, Ellery**
Davis, Don *see* **Halliday, Brett**
Davis, Gordon *see* **Hunt, Howard**
Davis, Harold A. *see* **Dent, Lester**
**Davis, Jada M.** (Jada Davis)
Davis, Jada *see* **Davis, Jada M.**
**Davis, Norbert** (in collaboration with W. T. Ballard wrote as Harrison Hunt, Cedric Titus)
Davis, Robert Hart *see* **Powell, Talmage; Whittington, Harry**
Day, Evans *see* **Stout, Rex**
De Bekker, Jay *see* **Sterling, Stewart**
Dean, Spencer *see* **Sterling, Stewart**
Debrett, Hal *see* **Halliday, Brett**
Decolta, Ramon *see* **Whitfield, Raoul**
Deeming, Richard *see* **Deming, Richard**
**Deming, Richard** (Max Franklin, Ellery Queen, Halsey Clark, Nick Morino, Richard Hale Curtis, Richard Deeming, Emily Moor, Lee Davis Willoughby)
**Dent, Lester** (Harmon Cash, Tim Ryan, Kenneth Roberts, Kenneth Robeson, H. O. Cash, Harold A. Davis, Robert Wallace, C. K. M. Scanlon, George H. Wilcoxson, Johnny Wiley, Cliff Howe, Ralph Powers, Robert Lewis)
dePre, Jeanne-Anne *see* **Avallone, Michael**
Dern, Peggy *see* **Gaddis, Peggy**
**Dewey, Thomas B.** (Tom Brandt, Cord Wainer)
Dexter, John *see* **Block, Lawrence; Westlake, Donald E.; Whittington, Harry**
Dietrich, Robert *see* **Hunt, Howard**
Dillon, James *see* **Thompson, Jim**
**Dixon, H. Vernor** (real name Harry Vernor Dixon)
Dixon, Harry Vernor *see* **Dixon, H. Vernor**
Dixon, Lewis *see* **Keene, Day**
Docherty, James L. *see* **Chase, James Hadley**
**Dodge, David**
Dodge, Gil *see* **Hano, Arnold**
Donoghue, P. S. *see* **Hunt, Howard**
Douglas, Malcolm *see* **Sanderson, Douglas**
Dresser, Davis *see* **Halliday, Brett**
Drummond, John Peter *see* **McKimmey, James**
Duke, Will *see* **Gault, William Campbell**
Duncan, Lee *see* **Block, Lawrence**
Elas, Bernard *see* **Sale, Richard**

Ellson, Hal
Ellson, Hal *see* **Brewer, Gil**
Elmore, Leonard *see* **Leonard, Elmore**
Emerson, Jill *see* **Block, Lawrence**
Endicott, John S. *see* **Brown, Fredric**
Erskine, Sylvia *see* **Gaddis, Peggy**
Evans, Elaine *see* **Brewer, Gil**
Evans, John *see* **Browne, Howard**
Evans, Lesley *see* **Block, Lawrence**
Evans, Tabor *see* **Whittington, Harry**
Everett, Connie *see* **Brewer, Gil**
Fair, A. A. *see* **Gardner, Erle Stanley**
Falkner, John Wesley Thompson III *see* **Faulkner, John**
Farr, Caroline *see* **Brown, Carter**
Farr, John *see* **Webb, Jack**
Farrel, John Wade *see* **MacDonald, John D.**
**Faulkner, John** (born John Wesley Thompson Falkner III)
**Fearing, Kenneth** (Kirk Wolff, Donald F. Bedford)
Fickling, Forrest E. "Skip" *see* **Fickling, G. G.**
**Fickling, G. G.** (real names Forrest E. "Skip" Fickling and Gloria Fickling)
Fickling, Gloria *see* **Fickling, G. G.**
Field, Temple *see* **Whitfield, Raoul**
**Finney, Jack** (born Walter Braden Finney)
Finney, Walter Braden *see* **Finney, Jack**
**Fischer, Bruno** (Russell Gray, Harrison Storm, Jason K. Storm)
**Fisher, Steve** (Stephen Gould, Grant Lane)
Fiske, Tarleton *see* **Bloch, Robert**
Fitzgerald, Eric *see* **Brewer, Gil**
Flanagan, Dorothy Belle *see* **Hughes, Dorothy B.**
**Fleischman, A. S.** (Sid Fleischman, Max Brindle)
Fleischman, Sid *see* **Fleischman, A. S.**
Fleming, Guy *see* **Masur, Harold Q.**
**Flora, Fletcher** (Ellery Queen)
Flynn, J. M. *see* **Flynn, Jay**
**Flynn, Jay** (born John M. Flynn; J. M. Flynn, Jack Slade)
Flynn, John M. *see* **Flynn, Jay**
Foster, Gerald *see* **Gaddis, Peggy**
Foster, Richard *see* **Crossen, Kendell Foster**
Francis, Lee *see* **Browne, Howard**
Franklin, Max *see* **Deming, Richard**
Frazer, Andrew *see* **Marlowe, Stephen**
Freyer, Frederic *see* **Ballinger, Bill S.**
Friend, Ed *see* **Wormser, Richard**

Fuller, Roger *see* **Tracy, Don**

**Fuller, Sam** (Samuel Fuller)

Fuller, Samuel *see* **Fuller, Sam**

Gaddis, Erolie Pearl *see* **Gaddis, Peggy**

**Gaddis, Peggy** (born Erolie Pearl Gaddis; Gail Jordan, Georgia Craig, Perry Lindsay, James Clayford, Peggy Dern, Joan Tucker, John Tucker, Joan Sherman, Roberta Courtland, Sylvia Erskine, Luther Gordon, Gerald Foster, Carolina Lee)

Gant, Matthew *see* **Hano, Arnold**

**Gardner, Erle Stanley** (A. A. Fair, Carleton Kendrake, Charles J. Kenny, Charles J. Kenney, Kyle Corning, Charles M. Green, Les Tillray, Robert Parr, Robert Park, Grant Holiday)

Gargan, William *see* **Hano, Arnold**

Garrity *see* **Gerrity, David J.**

Garrity, Dave J. *see* **Gerrity, David J.**

Gault, William C. *see* **Gault, William Campbell**

**Gault, William Campbell** (Will Duke, Roney Scott, Larry Sternig, William C. Gault)

**Gerrity, David J.** (Garrity, Dave J. Garrity)

Gerson, Conrad *see* **Wormser, Richard**

Giles, Kris *see* **Nielsen, Helen**

Glenning, Raymond *see* **Brown, Carter**

**Goodis, David** (Logan Clayborne, David Crewe, Lance Kermit, Ray P. Shotwell)

Gordon, Ad *see* **Hano, Arnold**

Gordon, Anthony *see* **Bellem, Robert Leslie**

Gordon, Luther *see* **Gaddis, Peggy**

Gould, Stephen *see* **Fisher, Steve**

Graham, Felix *see* **Brown, Fredric**

Grange, John *see* **Bellem, Robert Leslie**

Granger, Darius John *see* **Jakes, John; Marlowe, Stephen**

Grant, Ambrose *see* **Chase, James Hadley**

Gray, John Lee *see* **Jakes, John**

Gray, Russell *see* **Fischer, Bruno**

Green, Charles M. *see* **Gardner, Erle Stanley**

**Gruber, Frank** (Stephen Acre, Charles K. Boston, John K. Vedder, C. K. M. Scanlon)

**Halliday, Brett** (born Davis Dresser; Asa Baker, Matthew Blood, Kathryn Culver, Don Davis, Hal Debrett, Anthony Scott, Anderson Wayne)

**Hamilton, Donald** (born Donald Bendtgsson)

**Hammett, Dashiell** (born Samuel Dashiell Hammett; Peter Collinson, Mary Jane Hammett)

Hammett, Mary Jane *see* **Hammett, Dashiell**

Hammett, Samuel Dashiell *see* **Hammett, Dashiell**

Hannon, Ezra *see* **Hunter, Evan**

**Hano, Arnold** (Gil Dodge, Matthew Gant, Ad Gordon, Mike Heller, William Gargan)

Harrison, Chip *see* **Block, Lawrence**

Harrison, Whit *see* **Whittington, Harry**

Heller, Mike *see* **Hano, Arnold**

Henry, Robert *see* **MacDonald, John D.; Powell, Talmage**

Highland, Dora *see* **Avallone, Michael**

**Highsmith, Patricia** (born Mary Patricia Plangman; Claire Morgan)

Hill, Grimes *see* **Nebel, Frederick**

Hill, Morgana *see* **Brewer, Gil**

**Himes, Chester**

**Himmel, Richard**

**Hitchens, Dolores** (D. B. Olsen, Dolan Birkley, Noel Burke)

**Hitt, Orrie** (Kay Addams, Joe Black, Roger Normandie, Charles Verne, Nicky Weaver)

Hjerstedt, Gunard *see* **Keene, Day**

Hobart, Jack *see* **Brown, Fredric**

**Holding, Elisabeth Sanxay**

Holiday, Grant *see* **Gardner, Erle Stanley**

Holland, Kel *see* **Whittington, Harry**

Holliday, Don *see* **Block, Lawrence; Westlake, Donald E.**

Holt, Samuel *see* **Westlake, Donald E.**

Homes, Geoffrey *see* **Mainwaring, Daniel**

Hopley, George *see* **Woolrich, Cornell**

Howe, Cliff *see* **Dent, Lester**

Hudson, Dean *see* **Hunter, Evan**

**Hughes, Dorothy B.** (born Dorothy Belle Flanagan)

Hunt, E. Howard *see* **Hunt, Howard**

Hunt, Everette Howard *see* **Hunt, Howard**

Hunt, Harrison **Ballard, W. T.; Davis, Norbert**

**Hunt, Howard** (born Everette Howard Hunt; E. Howard Hunt, Gordon Davis, Robert Dietrich, David St. John, P. S. Donoghue, John Baxter)

**Hunter, Evan** (born Salvatore Lombino; Ed McBain, Richard Marsten, Curt Cannon, Hunt Collins, Ezra Hannon, John Abbott, Dean Hudson)

Hunter, John *see* **Ballard, W. T.**

Irish, William *see* **Woolrich, Cornell**

**Jakes, John** (William Ard, Alan Payne, Jay Scotland, Darius John Granger, Allen Wilder, John Lee Gray)

James, Edward *see* **Masur, Harold Q.**

James, Mary *see* **Packer, Vin**

Jason, Stuart *see* **Avallone, Michael**

**Jessup, Richard** (Richard Telfair, Carey Rockwell, October Smith)

Jones, Turkel *see* **McKimmey, James**

Jordan, Gail *see* **Gaddis, Peggy**

Jorgensen, Ivar *see* **Browne, Howard**

**Kane, Frank** (Frank Boyd)

**Kane, Henry** (Kenneth R. McKay, Mario J. Sagola, Katherine Stapleton, Anthony McCall, Ellery Queen)

**Karp, David** (Wallace Ware, Adam Singer)

Kavanagh, Paul *see* **Block, Lawrence**

**Keeler, Harry Stephen**

**Keene, Day** (real name Gunard Hjerstedt; Lewis Dixon, William Richards, Daniel White, John Corbett, Donald King)

Keene, Day *see* **Brewer, Gil**

Kendrake, Carleton *see* **Gardner, Erle Stanley**

Kenney, Charles J. *see* **Gardner, Erle Stanley**

Kenny, Charles J. *see* **Gardner, Erle Stanley**

Kent, Nelson *see* **Bellem, Robert Leslie**

Kermit, Lance *see* **Goodis, David**

Kerr, Ben *see* **Ard, William**

Kerr, M. E. *see* **Packer, Vin**

Kieran, Helen *see* **Reilly, Helen**

King, Donald *see* **Keene, Day**

Kirk, Jeremy *see* **Powell, Richard**

Knight, David *see* **Prather, Richard S.**

**Lacy, Ed** (born Leonard Zinberg; Steve April)

Lamb, Milton T. *see* **Powell, Talmage**

Land, Milton *see* **Powell, Talmage**

Lane, Grant *see* **Fisher, Steve**

Lane, John *see* **MacDonald, John D.**

**Latimer, Jonathan**

Lawn, Major D. *see* **Marlowe, Dan J.**

Lawrence, B. L. *see* **Block, Lawrence**

Laye, Dee *see* **Brewer, Gil**

Lee, Carolina *see* **Gaddis, Peggy**

Lee, Gypsy Rose *see* **Rice, Craig**

Lee, Manfred B. *see* **Queen, Ellery**

Leggitt, Jeanne *see* **Tracy, Don**

**Leonard, Elmore** (Leonard Elmore, Emmett Long, Elmo Scribbles)

Lesser, Milton *see* **Marlowe, Stephen**

Lewis, Eric *see* **Nebel, Frederick**

Lewis, Robert *see* **Dent, Lester**

Lindsay, Perry *see* **Gaddis, Peggy**

Lombino, Salvatore *see* **Hunter, Evan**

Long, Emmett *see* **Leonard, Elmore**
Lord, Sheldon *see* **Block, Lawrence**
MacAlister, Ian *see* **Albert, Marvin**
MacCargo, J. T. *see* **Rabe, Peter**
**MacDonald, John D.** (also wrote short stories as John Wade Farrel, Robert Henry, John Lane, Scott O'Hara, Peter Reed, Henry Reiser)
Macdonald, John R. *see* **Macdonald, Ross**
Macdonald, John *see* **Macdonald, Ross**
**Macdonald, Ross** (real name Kenneth Millar, Ken Millar, John Macdonald, John R. Macdonald)
MacKellar, Sinclair *see* **Brown, Carter**
MacNeil, Neil *see* **Ballard, W. T.**
**Mainwaring, Daniel** (Geoffrey Homes)
Malaponte, Marco *see* **Rabe, Peter**
Malone, Ruth *see* **Rice, Craig**
Marko, Zekial *see* **Trinian, John**
Marks, Billy *see* **Brewer, Gil**
**Marlowe, Dan J.** (Dan Marlowe, Jaime Sandaval, Albert Avellano, Gar Wilson, Rod Waleman, Major D. Lawn, Mande Woljar, Alma Werdon)
Marlowe, Dan *see* **Marlowe, Dan J.**
**Marlowe, Stephen** (born Milton Lesser; Andrew Frazer, Jason Ridgeway, Adam Chase, Ellery Queen, S. M. Tenneshaw, Christopher H. Thames, C. H. Thames, Darius John Granger, Steve Wilder)
Marsh, Alan *see* **Westlake, Donald E.**
Marshall, Alan *see* **Westlake, Donald E.**
Marshall, Raymond *see* **Chase, James Hadley**
Marsten, Richard *see* **Hunter, Evan**
Mason, Tracy *see* **Tracy, Don**
Mason, Van Wyck *see* **Tracy, Don**
Masterson, Whit *see* **Miller, Wade**
Masur, Hal Q. *see* **Masur, Harold Q.**
**Masur, Harold Q.** (Hal Q. Masur, Helen Traubel, Edward James, Guy Fleming)
**Matheson, Richard** (Logan Swanson, Josh Rogan)
McBain, Ed *see* **Hunter, Evan**
McCall, Anthony *see* **Kane, Henry**
**McCoy, Horace**
McCready, Jack *see* **Powell, Talmage**
**McGivern, William P.** (Bill Peters, P. F. Costello, Gerald Vance)
McKay, Kenneth R. *see* **Kane, Henry**
**McKimmey, James** (John Peter Drummond, Turkel Jones, Benjamin Swift)
**McKnight, Bob**
McKnight, Hugh *see* **Bellem, Robert Leslie**

**McPartland, John**

Meaker, M. J. *see* **Packer, Vin**

Meaker, Marijane *see* **Packer, Vin**

Michaels, Steve *see* **Avallone, Michael**

Millar, Ken *see* **Macdonald, Ross**

Millar, Kenneth *see* **Macdonald, Ross**

**Millar, Margaret**

Miller, Bill *see* **Miller, Wade**

**Miller, Wade** (pseudonym of Robert Wade and Bill Miller; Whit Masterson, Dale Wilmer, Will Daemer)

Mixer, Marc *see* **Brewer, Gil**

Monahan, John *see* **Burnett, W. R.**

Monig, Christopher *see* **Crossen, Kendell Foster**

Moor, Emily *see* **Deming, Richard**

Moran, Mike *see* **Ard, William**

Morgan, Bailey *see* **Brewer, Gil**

Morgan, Claire *see* **Highsmith, Patricia**

Morgann, Luke *see* **Brewer, Gil**

Morino, Nick *see* **Deming, Richard**

Morse, Allen *see* **Brown, Fredric**

Morse, Benjamin *see* **Block, Lawrence**

Myers, Harriet Kathryn *see* **Whittington, Harry**

Nathan, Daniel *see* **Queen, Ellery**

**Nebel, Frederick** (Grimes Hill, Eric Lewis, Lewis Nebel)

Nebel, Lewis *see* **Nebel, Frederick**

Nelson, Kenneth A. *see* **Bellem, Robert Leslie**

**Nielsen, Helen** (Kris Giles)

Nile, Dorothea *see* **Avallone, Michael**

Noone, Edwina *see* **Avallone, Michael**

**Norman, Earl** (born Norman Thomson)

Normandie, Roger *see* **Hitt, Orrie**

O'Hara, Scott *see* **MacDonald, John D.**

Olsen, D. B. *see* **Hitchens, Dolores**

Orchards, Theodore *see* **Palmer, Stuart**

**Ozaki, Milton K.** (Robert O. Saber, Mark Shane)

**Packer, Vin** (real name Marijane Meaker; Ann Aldrich, M. E. Kerr, Mary James, M. J. Meaker, Laura Winston)

Palmer, Charles Stuart Hunter *see* **Palmer, Stuart**

**Palmer, Stuart** (real name Charles Stuart Hunter Palmer, Jay Stewart, Theodore Orchards)

Park, Robert *see* **Gardner, Erle Stanley**

Parr, Robert *see* **Gardner, Erle Stanley**

Patrick, John *see* **Avallone, Michael**

Payne, Alan *see* **Jakes, John**

Pendleton, Don *see* **Brewer, Gil**

Perry, Jerome Severs *see* **Bellem, Robert Leslie**

Peters, Bill *see* **McGivern, William P.**

Philips, Steve *see* **Whittington, Harry**

Plangman, Mary Patricia *see* **Highsmith, Patricia**

**Powell, Richard** (Jeremy Kirk)

**Powell, Talmage** (Robert Hart Davis, Robert Henry, Milton T. Lamb, Milton Land, Jack McCready, Anne Talmage, Dave Sands, Ellery Queen)

Powers, Ralph *see* **Dent, Lester**

**Prather, Richard S.** (David Knight, Douglas Ring)

Quarry, Nick *see* **Albert, Marvin**

**Queen, Ellery** (real names Manfred B. Lee, Frederic Dannay; Barnaby Ross, Daniel Nathan (Dannay only))

Queen, Ellery *see* **Brewer, Gil; Deming, Richard; Flora, Fletcher; Kane, Henry; Marlowe, Stephen; Powell, Talmage; Runyon, Charles**

**Rabe, Peter** (Marco Malaponte, J. T. MacCargo)

Raymond, R. *see* **Chase, James Hadley**

Raymond, René Brabazon *see* **Chase, James Hadley**

Reed, Peter *see* **MacDonald, John D.**

**Reilly, Helen** (born Helen Kieran; Kieran Abbey)

Reiser, Henry *see* **MacDonald, John D.**

**Rice, Craig** (pseudonym for Georgiana Ann Randolph Walker Craig; Ruth Malone, Daphne Sanders, Michael Venning, George Sanders, Gypsy Rose Lee)

Richards, Clay *see* **Crossen, Kendell Foster**

Richards, Kent *see* **Crossen, Kendell Foster**

Richards, William *see* **Keene, Day**

Ridgeway, Jason *see* **Marlowe, Stephen**

Ring, Douglas *see* **Prather, Richard S.**

Roberts, Dillon *see* **Thompson, Jim**

Roberts, Kenneth *see* **Dent, Lester**

Robeson, Kenneth *see* **Dent, Lester**

Rockwell, Carey *see* **Jessup, Richard**

Rogan, Josh *see* **Matheson, Richard**

**Rohmer, Sax** (born Arthur Henry Sarsfield Ward)

Rome, Anthony *see* **Albert, Marvin**

Ronns, Edward *see* **Aarons, Edward S.**

Roscoe, John *see* **Roscoe, Mike**

**Roscoe, Mike** (a team of two writers, John Roscoe and Mike Ruso)

Ross, Barnaby *see* **Queen, Ellery; Tracy, Don**

**Runyon, Charles** (born Charles West Runyon; Ellery Queen, Charles Runyon Jr., Charles W. Runyon, Mark West, Mark Starr)

Runyon, Charles Jr. *see* **Runyon, Charles**
Runyon, Charles W. *see* **Runyon, Charles**
Runyon, Charles West *see* **Runyon, Charles**
Ruric, Peter *see* **Cain, Paul**
Ruso, Mike *see* **Roscoe, Mike**
Ryan, Tim *see* **Dent, Lester**
Saber, Robert O. *see* **Ozaki, Milton K.**
Sagola, Mario J. *see* **Kane, Henry**
Salacious, Grace *see* **Westlake, Donald E.**
**Sale, Richard** (Bernard Elas, John St. John)
Sanborn, B. X. *see* **Ballinger, Bill S.**
Sandaval, Jaime *see* **Marlowe, Dan J.**
Sanders, Daphne *see* **Rice, Craig**
Sanders, George *see* **Brackett, Leigh; Rice, Craig**
Sanders, W. Franklin *see* **Willeford, Charles**
**Sanderson, Douglas** (born Ronald Douglas Sanderson; Martin Brett, Malcolm Douglas)
Sanderson, Ronald Douglas *see* **Sanderson, Douglas**
Sands, Dave *see* **Powell, Talmage**
Saxon, John A. *see* **Bellem, Robert Leslie**
Scanlon, C. K. M. *see* **Dent, Lester; Gruber, Frank; Tracy, Don**
Schmoker, Marvin Leroy *see* **Trinian, John**
Scotland, Jay *see* **Jakes, John**
Scott, Anthony *see* **Halliday, Brett**
Scott, Roney *see* **Gault, William Campbell**
Scribbles, Elmo *see* **Leonard, Elmore**
Sexton, Alex *see* **Brewer, Gil**
Shane, Mark *see* **Ozaki, Milton K.**
Shaw, Andrew *see* **Block, Lawrence; Westlake, Donald E.**
Shepherd, John *see* **Ballard, W. T.**
Sherman, Joan *see* **Gaddis, Peggy**
Shotwell, Ray P. *see* **Goodis, David**
Sims, George Carroll *see* **Cain, Paul**
Sinclair, Dennis *see* **Brown, Carter**
Singer, Adam *see* **Karp, David**
Slade, Jack *see* **Ballard, W. T.; Flynn, Jay**
Smith, Frank E. *see* **Craig, Jonathan**
Smith, October *see* **Jessup, Richard**
Southney, Lyn *see* **Cheyney, Peter**
Spain, John *see* **Adams, Cleve F.**
**Spicer, Bart** (Jay Barbette)
Spillane, Frank Morrison *see* **Spillane, Mickey**
**Spillane, Mickey** (real name Frank Morrison Spillane)

St. Clair, Dexter *see* **Sterling, Stewart**
St. Clare, Dexter *see* **Sterling, Stewart**
St. John, David *see* **Hunt, Howard**
St. John, John *see* **Sale, Richard**
Stanton, Vince *see* **Avallone, Michael**
Stapleton, Katherine *see* **Kane, Henry**
Stark, Richard *see* **Westlake, Donald E.**
Starr, Mark *see* **Runyon, Charles**
Stephens, Suzanne *see* **Whittington, Harry**
**Sterling, Stewart** (pseudonym of Prentice Winchell; Spencer Dean, Jay De
    Bekker, Dexter St. Clair, Dexter St. Clare)
Sternig, Larry *see* **Gault, William Campbell**
Stevens, Blaine *see* **Whittington, Harry**
Stewart, Jay *see* **Palmer, Stuart**
Storm, Harrison *see* **Fischer, Bruno**
Storm, Jason K. *see* **Fischer, Bruno**
**Stout, Rex** (Evans Day)
Stuart, Clay *see* **Whittington, Harry**
Stuart, Sidney *see* **Avallone, Michael**
Sultry, Anita *see* **Brewer, Gil**
Swanson, Logan *see* **Matheson, Richard**
Swift, Benjamin *see* **McKimmey, James**
Talmage, Anne *see* **Powell, Talmage**
Telfair, Richard *see* **Jessup, Richard**
Tenneshaw, S. M. *see* **Marlowe, Stephen**
Thames, C. H. *see* **Marlowe, Stephen**
Thames, Christopher H. *see* **Marlowe, Stephen**
Thomey, Harold John *see* **Thomey, Tedd**
**Thomey, Tedd** (real name Harold John Thomey)
Thompson, James Myers *see* **Thompson, Jim**
**Thompson, Jim** (real name James Myers Thompson; James Dillon, Dillon
    Roberts)
Thomson, Norman *see* **Norman, Earl**
Tillray, Les *see* **Gardner, Erle Stanley**
Titus, Cedric *see* **Davis, Norbert**
**Tracy, Don** (Roger Fuller, Barnaby Ross, Van Wyck Mason, Jeanne Leggitt,
    Tracy Mason, Tom Tucker, C. K. M. Scanlon)
Traubel, Helen *see* **Masur, Harold Q.**
**Trinian, John** (real name Marvin Leroy Schmoker; Zekial Marko)
Tucker, Joan *see* **Gaddis, Peggy**
Tucker, John *see* **Gaddis, Peggy**
Tucker, Tom *see* **Tracy, Don**
Turner, Clay *see* **Ballard, W. T.**

Updyke, James *see* **Burnett, W. R.**
Valdez, Paul *see* **Brown, Carter**
Vance, Gerald *see* **McGivern, William P.**
Vedder, John K. *see* **Gruber, Frank**
Venning, Michael *see* **Rice, Craig**
Verne, Charles *see* **Hitt, Orrie**
Vixen, Viola *see* **Brewer, Gil**
Wade, Robert *see* **Miller, Wade**
Wainer, Cord *see* **Dewey, Thomas B.**
Waleman, Rod *see* **Marlowe, Dan J.**
Walker, Max *see* **Avallone, Michael**
Wallace, Robert *see* **Dent, Lester**
Ward, Arthur Henry Sarsfield *see* **Rohmer, Sax**
Ward, Jonas *see* **Ard, William**
Ware, Wallace *see* **Karp, David**
Wayne, Anderson *see* **Halliday, Brett**
Weaver, Nicky *see* **Hitt, Orrie**
**Webb, Jack** (born John Alfred Webb, John Farr)
Webb, John Alfred *see* **Webb, Jack**
Weems, Harcourt *see* **Bellem, Robert Leslie**
Weldy, Ann *see* **Bannon, Ann**
Wells, Hondo *see* **Whittington, Harry**
Wells, John Warren *see* **Block, Lawrence**
Werdon, Alma *see* **Marlowe, Dan J.**
West, Edwin *see* **Westlake, Donald E.**
West, Edwina *see* **Westlake, Donald E.**
West, Mark *see* **Runyon, Charles**
**Westlake, Donald E.** (Richard Stark, Tucker Coe, Curt Clark, Samuel Holt,
    Timothy J. Culver, J. Morgan Cunningham, Judson Jack Carmichael,
    Edwin West, John B. Allan, Alan Marshall, John Dexter, Andrew Shaw,
    Barbara Wilson, P. N. Castor, Don Holliday, James Blue, Edwina West,
    Edwin Wood, Ben Christopher, Grace Salacious, Alan Marsh)
White, Daniel *see* **Keene, Day**
White, Harry *see* **Whittington, Harry**
White, Henry *see* **Whittington, Harry**
**White, Lionel** (L. W. Blanco)
**Whitfield, Raoul** (Ramon Decolta, Temple Field)
Whitney, Hallam *see* **Whittington, Harry**
Whittier, Henry *see* **Whittington, Harry**
**Whittington, Harry** (Whit Harrison, Hallam Whitney, Ashley Carter,
    Robert Hart Davis, Tabor Evans, Clay Stuart, Hondo Wells, Henry White,
    John Dexter, J. X. Williams, Curt Colman, Kel Holland, Harriet Kathryn

Myers, Suzanne Stephens, Blaine Stevens, Harry White, Henry Whittier, Howard Winslow, Steve Philips)

Wilcoxson, George H. *see* **Dent, Lester**

Wilder, Allen *see* **Jakes, John**

Wilder, Steve *see* **Marlowe, Stephen**

Wiley, Johnny *see* **Dent, Lester**

**Willeford, Charles** (Will Charles, W. Franklin Sanders)

**Williams, Charles**

Williams, J. X. *see* **Whittington, Harry**

**Willie, Ennis**

Willoughby, Lee Davis *see* **Avallone, Michael; Deming, Richard**

Wills, Thomas *see* **Ard, William**

Wilmer, Dale *see* **Miller, Wade**

Wilson, Barbara *see* **Westlake, Donald E.**

Wilson, Gar *see* **Marlowe, Dan J.**

Winchell, Prentice *see* **Sterling, Stewart**

Winslow, Howard *see* **Whittington, Harry**

Winston, Laura *see* **Packer, Vin**

Woehlke, Bob *see* **Brown, Fredric**

Wolff, Kirk *see* **Fearing, Kenneth**

Woljar, Mande *see* **Marlowe, Dan J.**

Wood, Edwin *see* **Westlake, Donald E.**

**Woolrich, Cornell** (real name Cornell George Hopley Woolrich; William Irish, George Hopley)

Woolrich, Cornell George Hopley *see* **Woolrich, Cornell**

**Wormser, Richard** (Nick Carter, Ed Friend, Conrad Gerson)

Yates, Alan Geoffrey *see* **Brown, Carter**

Young, Collier *see* **Bloch, Robert**

Zinberg, Leonard *see* **Lacy, Ed**

## *The Best in Mystery & Noir Fiction Past & Present*

1-933586-26-5 **Benjamin Appel** Sweet Money Girl / Life and Death of a Tough Guy $21.95

1-933586-03-6 **Malcolm Braly** Shake Him Till He Rattles / It's Cold Out There $19.95

1-933586-10-9 **Gil Brewer** Wild to Possess / A Taste for Sin $19.95

1-933586-20-6 **Gil Brewer** A Devil for O'Shaugnessy / The Three-Way Split $14.95

1-933586-24-9 **W. R. Burnett** It's Always Four O'Clock / Iron Man $19.95

1-933586-31-1 **Catherine Butzen** Thief of Midnight $15.95

1-933586-38-9 **James Hadley Chase** Come Easy--Go Easy / In a Vain Shadow $19.95

0-9667848-0-4 **Storm Constantine** Oracle Lips (limited hb) $45.00

1-933586-30-3 **Jada M. Davis** One for Hell $19.95

1-933586-43-5 **Bruce Elliot** One is a Lonely Number /
                 **Elliott Chaze** Black Wings Has My Angel $19.95

1-933586-34-6 **Don Elliott** Gang Girl / Sex Bum $19.95

1-933586-12-5 **A. S. Fleischman** Look Behind You Lady / The Venetian Blonde $19.95

1-933568-28-1 **A. S. Fleischman** Danger in Paradise / Malay Woman $19.95

1-933586-35-4 **Orrie Hitt** The Cheaters / Dial "M" for Man $19.95

0-9667848-7-1 **Elisabeth Sanxay Holding** Lady Killer / Miasma $19.95

0-9667848-9-8 **Elisabeth Sanxay Holding** The Death Wish / Net of Cobwebs $19.95

0-9749438-5-1 **Elisabeth Sanxay Holding** Strange Crime in Bermuda / Too Many Bottles $19.95

1-933586-16-8 **Elisabeth Sanxay Holding** The Old Battle Ax / Dark Power $19.95

1-933586-17-6 **Russell James** Underground / Collected Stories $14.95

0-9749438-8-6 **Day Keene** Framed in Guilt / My Flesh is Sweet $19.95

1-933586-33-8 **Day Keene** Dead Dolls Don't Talk / Hunt the Killer / Too Hot to Hold $23.95

1-933586-21-4 **Mercedes Lambert** Dogtown / Soultown $14.95

1-933586-14-1 **Dan Marlowe/Fletcher Flora/Charles Runyon** Trio of Gold Medals $15.95

1-933586-07-9 **Ed by McCarthy & Gorman** Invasion of the Body Snatchers: A Tribute $19.95

1-933586-09-5 **Margaret Millar** An Air That Kills / Do Evil in Return $19.95

1-933586-23-0 **Wade Miller** The Killer / Devil on Two Sticks $17.95

1-933586-27-3 **E. Phillips Oppenheim** The Amazing Judgment / Mr. Laxworthy's Adventures $19.95

0-9749438-3-5 **Vin Packer** Something in the Shadows / Intimate Victims $19.95

1-933586-05-2 **Vin Packer** Whisper His Sin / The Evil Friendship $19.95

1-933586-18-4 **Richard Powell** A Shot in the Dark / Shell Game $14.95

1-933586-19-2 **Bill Pronzini** Snowbound / Games $14.95

0-9667848-8-x **Peter Rabe** The Box / Journey Into Terror $21.95

0-9749438-4-3 **Peter Rabe** Murder Me for Nickels / Benny Muscles In $19.95

1-933586-00-1 **Peter Rabe** Blood on the Desert / A House in Naples $21.95

1-933586-11-7 **Peter Rabe** My Lovely Executioner / Agreement to Kill $19.95

1-933586-22-2 **Peter Rabe** Anatomy of a Killer / A Shroud for Jesso $14.95

1-933586-32-x **Peter Rabe** The Silent Wall / The Return of Marvin Palaver $19.95

0-9749438-2-7 **Douglas Sanderson** Pure Sweet Hell / Catch a Fallen Starlet $19.95

1-933586-06-0 **Douglas Sanderson** The Deadly Dames / A Dum-Dum for the President $19.95

1-933586-29-X **Charlie Stella** Johnny Porno $15.95

1-933586-39-7 **Charlie Stella** Rough Riders $15.95

1-933586-08-7 **Harry Whittington** A Night for Screaming / Any Woman He Wanted $19.95

1-933586-25-7 **Harry Whittington** To Find Cora / Like Mink Like Murder / Body and Passion $23.95

1-933586-36-2 **Harry Whittington** Rapture Alley / Winter Girl / Strictly for the Boys $23.95

**STARK HOUSE PRESS**
**www.StarkHousePress.com**